NON SANZ DROICT.

William Shakespeare

The Tragedy of
HAMLET
Prince of Denmark

**With New Dramatic
Criticism and an
Updated Bibliography**

Edited by Edward Hubler

The Signet Classic Shakespeare
GENERAL EDITOR: SYLVAN BARNET

A SIGNET CLASSIC

SIGNET CLASSIC
Published by the Penguin Group
Penguin Books USA Inc., 375 Hudson Street,
New York, New York 10014, U.S.A.
Penguin Books Ltd, 27 Wrights Lane,
London W8 5TZ, England
Penguin Books Australia Ltd, Ringwood,
Victoria, Australia
Penguin Books Canada Ltd, 2801 John Street,
Markham, Ontario, Canada L3R 1B4
Penguin Books (N.Z.) Ltd, 182-190 Wairau Road,
Auckland 10, New Zealand

Penguin Books Ltd, Registered Offices:
Harmondsworth, Middlesex, England

42 41 40 39 38 37 36 35

Ⓒ REGISTERED TRADEMARK—MARCA REGISTRADA

Library of Congress Catalog Card Number: 86-60159

Printed in the United States of America

Contents

Shakespeare: Prefatory Remarks

Between the record of his baptism in Stratford on 26 April 1564 and the record of his burial in Stratford on 25 April 1616, some forty documents name Shakespeare, and many others name his parents, his children, and his grandchildren. More facts are known about William Shakespeare than about any other playwright of the period except Ben Jonson. The facts should, however, be distinguished from the legends. The latter, inevitably more engaging and better known, tell us that the Stratford boy killed a calf in high style, poached deer and rabbits, and was forced to flee to London, where he held horses outside a playhouse. These traditions are only traditions; they may be true, but no evidence supports them, and it is well to stick to the facts.

Mary Arden, the dramatist's mother, was the daughter of a substantial landowner; about 1557 she married John Shakespeare, who was a glove-maker and trader in various farm commodities. In 1557 John Shakespeare was a member of the Council (the governing body of Stratford), in 1558 a constable of the borough, in 1561 one of the two town chamberlains, in 1565 an alderman (entitling him to the appellation "Mr."), in 1568 high bailiff—the town's highest political office, equivalent to mayor. After 1577, for an unknown reason he drops out of local politics. The birthday of William Shakespeare, the eldest son of this locally prominent man, is unrecorded; but the Stratford parish register records that the infant was baptized on 26 April 1564. (It is quite possible that he was born on 23 April, but this date has probably been assigned by tradition because it is the date on which, fifty-two years later, he died.) The attendance records of the Stratford grammar school of the period are not extant, but it is reasonable to assume that the son of a local official attended the school and received substantial training in Latin. The masters of the school from Shakespeare's seventh to fifteenth years held Oxford degrees; the Elizabethan curriculum excluded mathematics and the natural sciences but taught a good deal of Latin rhetoric, logic, and literature. On 27 November 1582 a marriage license was issued to Shakespeare and Anne Hathaway, eight years his senior. The couple had a child in May, 1583. Perhaps the marriage was necessary, but perhaps the couple had earlier engaged in a formal "troth plight," which would render their children legitimate even if no further ceremony were performed. In 1585 Anne Hathaway bore Shakespeare twins.

That Shakespeare was born is excellent; that he married and had children is pleasant; but that we know nothing about his departure from Stratford to London, or about the beginning of his theatrical career, is lamentable and must be admitted. We would gladly sacrifice details about his children's baptism for details about his earliest days on the stage. Perhaps the poaching episode is true (but it is first reported almost a century after Shakespeare's death), or perhaps he first left Stratford to be a schoolteacher, as another tradition holds; perhaps he was moved by

> Such wind as scatters young men through the world,
> To seek their fortunes further than at home
> Where small experience grows.

In 1592, thanks to the cantankerousness of Robert Greene, a rival playwright and a pamphleteer, we have our first reference, a snarling one, to Shakespeare as an actor and playwright. Greene warns those of his own educated friends who wrote for the theater against an actor who has presumed to turn playwright:

There is an upstart crow, beautified with our feathers,

that with his *tiger's heart wrapped in a player's hide*
supposes he is as well able to bombast out a blank
verse as the best of you, and being an absolute Johannes-
factotum is in his own conceit the only Shake-scene in
a country.

The reference to the player, as well as the allusion to
Aesop's crow (who strutted in borrowed plumage, as an
actor struts in fine words not his own), makes it clear that
by this date Shakespeare had both acted and written. That
Shakespeare is meant is indicated not only by "Shake-
scene" but by the parody of a line from one of Shakespeare's plays, *3 Henry VI*: "O, tiger's heart wrapped in a
woman's hide." If Shakespeare in 1592 was prominent
enough to be attacked by an envious dramatist, he probably
had served an apprenticeship in the theater for at least a
few years.

In any case, by 1592 Shakespeare had acted and written,
and there are a number of subsequent references to him as
an actor: documents indicate that in 1598 he is a "principal
comedian," in 1603 a "principal tragedian," in 1608 he is
one of the "men players." The profession of actor was not
for a gentleman, and it occasionally drew the scorn of university men who resented writing speeches for persons less
educated than themselves, but it was respectable enough:
players, if prosperous, were in effect members of the bour-
geoisie, and there is nothing to suggest that Stratford considered William Shakespeare less than a solid citizen. When,
in 1596, the Shakespeares were granted a coat of arms, the
grant was made to Shakespeare's father, but probably
William Shakespeare (who the next year bought the sec-
ond-largest house in town) had arranged the matter on his
own behalf. In subsequent transactions he is occasionally
styled a gentleman.

Although in 1593 and 1594 Shakespeare published two
narrative poems dedicated to the Earl of Southampton,
Venus and Adonis and *The Rape of Lucrece*, and may well
have written most or all of his sonnets in the middle
nineties, Shakespeare's literary activity seems to have been
almost entirely devoted to the theater. (It may be significant

that the two narrative poems were written in years when
the plague closed the theaters for several months.) In 1594
he was a charter member of a theatrical company called the
Chamberlain's Men (which in 1603 changed its name to
the King's Men); until he retired to Stratford (about 1611,
apparently), he was with this remarkably stable company.
From 1599 the company acted primarily at the Globe
Theatre, in which Shakespeare held a one-tenth interest.
Other Elizabethan dramatists are known to have acted, but
no other is known also to have been entitled to a share in
the profits of the playhouse.

Shakespeare's first eight published plays did not have his
name on them, but this is not remarkable; the most popular
play of the sixteenth century, Thomas Kyd's *The Spanish
Tragedy,* went through many editions without naming Kyd,
and Kyd's authorship is known only because a book on the
profession of acting happens to quote (and attribute to
Kyd) some lines on the interest of Roman emperors in the
drama. What is remarkable is that after 1598 Shakespeare's
name commonly appears on printed plays—some of which
are not his. Another indication of his popularity comes
from Francis Meres, author of *Palladis Tamia: Wit's Treas-
ury* (1598): in this anthology of snippets accompanied by
an essay on literature, many playwrights are mentioned, but
Shakespeare's name occurs more often than any other, and
Shakespeare is the only playwright whose plays are listed.

From his acting, playwriting, and share in a theater,
Shakespeare seems to have made considerable money. He
put it to work, making substantial investments in Stratford
real estate. When he made his will (less than a month
before he died), he sought to leave his property intact to
his descendants. Of small bequests to relatives and to
friends (including three actors, Richard Burbage, John
Heminges, and Henry Condell), that to his wife of the
second-best bed has provoked the most comment; perhaps
it was the bed the couple had slept in, the best being reserved for visitors. In any case, had Shakespeare not ex-
cepted it, the bed would have gone (with the rest of his
household possessions) to his daughter and her husband.
On 25 April 1616 he was buried within the chancel of the

church at Stratford. An unattractive monument to his memory, placed on a wall near the grave, says he died on 23 April. Over the grave itself are the lines, perhaps by Shakespeare, that (more than his literary fame) have kept his bones undisturbed in the crowded burial ground where old bones were often dislodged to make way for new:

> Good friend, for Jesus' sake forbear
> To dig the dust enclosèd here.
> Blessed be the man that spares these stones
> And cursed be he that moves my bones.

Thirty-seven plays, as well as some nondramatic poems, are held to constitute the Shakespeare canon. The dates of composition of most of the works are highly uncertain, but there is often evidence of a *terminus a quo* (starting point) and/or a *terminus ad quem* (terminal point) that provides a framework for intelligent guessing. For example, *Richard II* cannot be earlier than 1595, the publication date of some material to which it is indebted; *The Merchant of Venice* cannot be later than 1598, the year Francis Meres mentioned it. Sometimes arguments for a date hang on an alleged topical allusion, such as the lines about the unseasonable weather in *A Midsummer Night's Dream,* II.i.81–117, but such an allusion (if indeed it is an allusion) can be variously interpreted, and in any case there is always the possibility that a topical allusion was inserted during a revision, years after the composition of a play. Dates are often attributed on the basis of style, and although conjectures about style usually rest on other conjectures, sooner or later one must rely on one's literary sense. There is no real proof, for example, that *Othello* is not as early as *Romeo and Juliet,* but one feels *Othello* is later, and because the first record of its performance is 1604, one is glad enough to set its composition at that date and not push it back into Shakespeare's early years. The following chronology, then, is as much indebted to informed guesswork and sensitivity as it is to fact. The dates, necessarily imprecise, indicate something like a scholarly consensus.

PLAYS

1588–93	*The Comedy of Errors*
1588–94	*Love's Labor's Lost*
1590–91	*2 Henry VI*
1590–91	*3 Henry VI*
1591–92	*1 Henry VI*
1592–93	*Richard III*
1592–94	*Titus Andronicus*
1593–94	*The Taming of the Shrew*
1593–95	*The Two Gentlemen of Verona*
1594–96	*Romeo and Juliet*
1595	*Richard II*
1594–96	*A Midsummer Night's Dream*
1596–97	*King John*
1596–97	*The Merchant of Venice*
1597	*1 Henry IV*
1597–98	*2 Henry IV*
1598–1600	*Much Ado About Nothing*
1598–99	*Henry V*
1599–1600	*Julius Caesar*
1599–1600	*As You Like It*
1599–1600	*Twelfth Night*
1600–01	*Hamlet*
1597–1601	*The Merry Wives of Windsor*
1601–02	*Troilus and Cressida*
1602–04	*All's Well That Ends Well*
1603–04	*Othello*
1604–05	*Measure for Measure*
1605–06	*King Lear*
1605–06	*Macbeth*
1606–07	*Antony and Cleopatra*
1605–08	*Timon of Athens*
1607–09	*Coriolanus*
1608–09	*Pericles*
1609–10	*Cymbeline*
1610–11	*The Winter's Tale*
1611–12	*The Tempest*
1612–13	*Henry VIII*

POEMS

Shakespeare's Theater

In Shakespeare's infancy, Elizabethan actors performed wherever they could—in great halls, at court, in the courtyards of inns. The innyards must have made rather unsatisfactory theaters: on some days they were unavailable because carters bringing goods to London used them as depots; when available, they had to be rented from the innkeeper; perhaps most important, London inns were subject to the Common Council of London, which was not well disposed toward theatricals. In 1574 the Common Council required that plays and playing places in London be licensed. It asserted that

> sundry great disorders and inconveniences have been found to ensue to this city by the inordinate haunting of great multitudes of people, specially youth, to plays, interludes, and shows, namely occasion of frays and quarrels, evil practices of incontinency in great inns having chambers and secret places adjoining to their open stages and galleries,

and ordered that innkeepers who wished licenses to hold performances put on a bond and make contributions to the poor.

The requirement that plays and innyard theaters be licensed, along with the other drawbacks of playing at inns, probably drove James Burbage (a carpenter-turned-actor) to rent in 1576 a plot of land northeast of the city walls and to build here—on property outside the jurisdiction of the city—England's first permanent construction designed for plays. He called it simply the Theatre. About all that is known of its construction is that it was wood. It soon had imitators, the most famous being the Globe (1599), built across the Thames (again outside the city's jurisdiction), out of timbers of the Theatre, which had been dismantled when Burbage's lease ran out.

There are three important sources of information about the structure of Elizabethan playhouses—drawings, a contract, and stage directions in plays. Of drawings, only the so-called De Witt drawing (c. 1596) of the Swan—really a friend's copy of De Witt's drawing—is of much significance. It shows a building of three tiers, with a stage jutting from a wall into the yard or center of the building. The tiers are roofed, and part of the stage is covered by a roof that projects from the rear and is supported at its front on two posts, but the groundlings, who paid a penny to stand in front of the stage, were exposed to the sky. (Performances in such a playhouse were held only in the daytime; artificial illumination was not used.) At the rear of the stage are two doors; above the stage is a gallery. The second major source of information, the contract for the Fortune, specifies that although the Globe is to be the model, the Fortune is to be square, eighty feet outside and fifty-five inside. The stage is to be forty-three feet broad, and is to extend into the middle of the yard (i.e., it is twenty-seven and a half feet deep). For patrons willing to pay more than the general admission charged of the groundlings, there were to be three galleries provided with seats. From the third chief source, stage directions, one learns that entrance to the stage was by doors, presumably spaced widely apart at the rear ("Enter one citizen at one door, and another at the other"), and that in addition to the platform stage there was occasionally some sort of curtained booth or alcove allowing for "discovery" scenes, and some sort of playing space "aloft" or "above" to represent (for example) the top of a city's walls or a room above the street. Doubtless each theater had its own peculiarities, but perhaps we can talk about a "typical" Elizabethan theater if we realize that no theater need exactly have fit the description, just as no father is the typical father with 3.7 children. This hypothetical theater is wooden, round or polygonal (in *Henry V* Shakespeare calls it a "wooden *O*"), capable of holding some eight hundred spectators standing in the yard around the projecting elevated stage and some fifteen hundred additional spectators seated in the three roofed galleries. The stage, protected by a "shadow" or "heavens" or roof, is entered by two doors; behind the doors is the "tiring house" (attiring house, i.e., dressing room), and above the doors is some sort of gallery that may sometimes hold spectators but that can be used (for example) as the bedroom from which Romeo—according to a stage direction in one text—"goeth down." Some evidence suggests that a throne can be lowered onto the platform stage, perhaps from the "shadow"; certainly characters can descend from the stage through a trap or traps into the cellar or "hell." Sometimes this space beneath the platform accommodates a sound-effects man or musician (in *Antony and Cleopatra* "music of the hautboys is under the stage") or an actor (in *Hamlet* the "Ghost cries under the stage"). Most characters simply walk on and off, but because there is no curtain in front of the platform, corpses will have to be carried off (Hamlet must lug Polonius' guts into the neighbor room), or will have to fall at the rear, where the curtain on the alcove or booth can be drawn to conceal them.

Such may have been the so-called "public theater." Another kind of theater, called the "private theater" because its much greater admission charge limited its audience to the wealthy or the prodigal, must be briefly mentioned. The private theater was basically a large room, entirely roofed and therefore artificially illuminated, with a stage at one end. In 1576 one such theater was established in Blackfriars, a Dominican priory in London that had been suppressed in 1538 and confiscated by the Crown and thus was not under the city's jurisdiction. All the actors in the Blackfriars theater were boys about eight to thirteen years old (in the public theaters similar boys played female parts; a boy Lady Macbeth played to a man Macbeth). This private theater had a precarious existence, and ceased operations in 1584. In 1596 James Burbage, who had already made theatrical history by building the Theatre, began to construct a second Blackfriars theater. He died in 1597, and for several years this second Blackfriars theater was used by a troupe of boys, but in 1608 two of Burbage's sons and five other actors (including Shakespeare) became joint operators of the theater, using it in the winter when the open-air Globe was unsuitable. Perhaps such a smaller theater, roofed, artificially illuminated, and with a tradition of a courtly audience, exerted an influence on Shakespeare's late plays.

Performances in the private theaters may well have had intermissions during which music was played, but in the public theaters the action was probably uninterrupted, flowing from scene to scene almost without a break. Actors would enter, speak, exit, and others would immediately enter and establish (if necessary) the new locale by a few properties and by words and gestures. Here are some samples of Shakespeare's scene painting:

> This is Illyria, lady.

> Well, this is the Forest of Arden.

> This castle hath a pleasant seat; the air
> Nimbly and sweetly recommends itself
> Unto our gentle senses.

On the other hand, it is a mistake to conceive of the Elizabethan stage as bare. Although Shakespeare's Chorus in *Henry V* calls the stage an "unworthy scaffold" and urges the spectators to "eke out our performance with your mind," there was considerable spectacle. The last act of *Macbeth,* for example, has five stage directions calling for "drum and colors," and another sort of appeal to the eye is indicated by the stage direction "Enter Macduff, with Macbeth's head." Some scenery and properties may have been substantial; doubtless a throne was used, and in one play of the period we encounter this direction: "Hector takes up a great piece of rock and casts at Ajax, who tears up a young tree by the roots and assails Hector." The matter is of some importance, and will be glanced at again in the next section.

The Texts of Shakespeare

Though eighteen of his plays were published during his lifetime, Shakespeare seems never to have supervised their publication. There is nothing unusual here; when a playwright sold a play to a theatrical company he surrendered his ownership of it. Normally a company would not publish the play, because to publish it meant to allow competitors to acquire the piece. Some plays, however, did get published: apparently treacherous actors sometimes pieced together a play for a publisher, sometimes a company in need of money sold a play, and sometimes a company allowed a play to be published that no longer drew audiences. That Shakespeare did not concern himself with publication, then, is scarcely remarkable; of his contemporaries only Ben Jonson carefully supervised the publication of his own plays. In 1623, seven years after Shakespeare's death, John Heminges and Henry Condell (two senior members of Shakespeare's company, who had performed with him for about twenty years) collected his plays—published and unpublished—into a large volume, commonly called the First Folio. (A folio is a volume consisting of sheets that have been folded once, each sheet thus making two leaves, or four pages. The eighteen plays published during Shakespeare's lifetime had been issued one play per volume in small books called quartos. Each sheet in a quarto has been folded twice, making four leaves, or eight pages.) The First Folio contains thirty-six plays; a thirty-seventh, *Pericles,* though not in the Folio, is regarded as canonical. Heminges and Condell suggest in an address "To the great variety of readers" that the republished plays are presented in better form than in the quartos: "Before you were abused with diverse stolen and surreptitious copies, maimed and deformed by the frauds and stealths of injurious impostors that exposed them; even those, are now offered to your view cured and perfect of their limbs, and all the rest absolute in their numbers, as he [i.e., Shakespeare] conceived them."

Whoever was assigned to prepare the texts for publication in the First Folio seems to have taken his job seriously and yet not to have performed it with uniform care. The sources of the texts seem to have been, in general, good unpublished copies or the best published copies. The first play in the collection, *The Tempest,* is divided into acts and scenes, has unusually full stage directions and descriptions of spectacle, and concludes with a list of the characters, but the editor was not able (or willing) to present all of the succeeding texts so fully dressed. Later texts occasionally show signs of carelessness: in one scene of *Much Ado About Nothing* the names of actors, instead of characters, appear as speech prefixes, as they had in the quarto, which the Folio reprints; proofreading throughout the Folio is spotty and apparently was done without reference to the printer's copy; the pagination of *Hamlet* jumps from 156 to 257.

A modern editor of Shakespeare must first select his copy; no problem if the play exists only in the Folio, but a considerable problem if the relationship between a quarto and the Folio—or an early quarto and a later one—is unclear. When an editor has chosen what seems to him to be the most authoritative text or texts for his copy, he has not done with making decisions. First of all, he must reckon with Elizabethan spelling. If he is not producing a facsimile, he probably modernizes it, but ought he to preserve the old form of words that apparently were pronounced quite unlike their modern forms—"lanthorn," "alablaster"? If he preserves these forms, is he really preserving Shakespeare's forms or perhaps those of a compositor in the printing house? What is one to do when one finds "lanthorn" and "lantern" in adjacent lines? (The editors of this series in general, but not invariably, assume that words should be spelled in their modern form.) Elizabethan punctuation, too, presents problems. For example in the First Folio, the only text for the play, Macbeth rejects his wife's idea that he can wash the blood from his hand:

> no: this my Hand will rather
> The multitudinous Seas incarnardine,
> Making the Greene one, Red.

Obviously an editor will remove the superfluous capitals, and he will probably alter the spelling to "incarnadine," but will he leave the comma before "red," letting Macbeth speak of the sea as "the green one," or will he (like most modern editors) remove the comma and thus have Macbeth say that his hand will make the ocean *uniformly* red?

An editor will sometimes have to change more than spelling or punctuation. Macbeth says to his wife:

> I dare do all that may become a man,
> Who dares no more, is none.

For two centuries editors have agreed that the second line is unsatisfactory, and have emended "no" to "do": "Who dares do more is none." But when in the same play Ross says that fearful persons

> floate vpon a wilde and violent Sea
> Each way, and moue,

need "move" be emended to "none," as it often is, on the hunch that the compositor misread the manuscript? The editors of the Signet Classic Shakespeare have restrained themselves from making abundant emendations. In their minds they hear Dr. Johnson on the dangers of emending: "I have adopted the Roman sentiment, that it is more honorable to save a citizen than to kill an enemy." Some departures (in addition to spelling, punctuation, and lineation) from the copy text have of course been made, but the original readings are listed in a note following the play, so that the reader can evaluate them for himself.

The editors of the Signet Classic Shakespeare, following tradition, have added line numbers and in many cases act and scene divisions as well as indications of locale at the beginning of scenes. The Folio divided most of the plays into acts and some into scenes. Early eighteenth-century editors increased the divisions. These divisions, which provide a convenient way of referring to passages in the plays, have been retained, but when not in the text chosen as the basis for the Signet Classic text they are enclosed in square brackets [ ] to indicate that they are editorial additions. Similarly, although no play of Shakespeare's published during his lifetime was equipped with indications of locale at the heads of scene divisions, locales have here been added in square brackets for the convenience of the reader, who lacks the information afforded to spectators by costumes, properties, and gestures. The spectator can tell at a glance he is in the throne room, but without an editorial indication the reader may be puzzled for a while. It should be mentioned, incidentally, that there are a few authentic stage directions—perhaps Shakespeare's, perhaps a prompter's—that suggest locales: for example, "Enter Brutus in his orchard," and "They go up into the Senate house." It is hoped that the bracketed additions provide the reader with the sort of help provided in these two authentic directions, but it is equally hoped that the reader will remember that the stage was not loaded with scenery.

No editor during the course of his work can fail to recollect some words Heminges and Condell prefixed to the Folio:

> It had been a thing, we confess, worthy to have been wished, that the author himself had lived to have set forth and overseen his own writings. But since it hath been ordained otherwise, and he by death departed from that right, we pray you do not envy his friends the office of their care and pain to have collected and published them.

Nor can an editor, after he has done his best, forget Heminges and Condell's final words: "And so we leave you to other of his friends, whom if you need can be your guides. If you need them not, you can lead yourselves, and others. And such readers we wish him."

SYLVAN BARNET
Tufts University

Introduction

Tragedy of the first order is a rare phenomenon. It came into being in Greece in the fifth century B.C., where it flourished for a while, and it did not appear again until some two thousand years later when Shakespeare wrote *Hamlet* in 1600. The second incarnation of the spirit of tragedy differs greatly from the first in form and method. In Shakespeare the comic and the serious are not disassociated. His brightest moments pass quickly into shadow, and laughter often illuminates his darkest scenes. The comic and the tragic stand side by side, giving us a fuller view of the thing observed, neither canceling out the other. A hallmark of Shakespeare's mature work is its simultaneity, the presentation of things and their opposites at the same time. Coleridge called him "myriad-minded." There had been an alternation of the dark and the light in English drama almost from the beginning, but it remained for Shakespeare to make each a part of the other. He was able to do so because he knew that the difference between comedy and tragedy has nothing to do with subject matter. Each is a way of looking at life. Neither gives us a total view of life, nor does Shakespeare in his use of both; but he approaches totality more closely than any other dramatist.

In *Hamlet* we laugh at the affected and superficial Osric (this is a lightening before the storm), and we are amused by the garrulous Polonius, whose inadequate worldly wisdom stands in contrast to the deeper truths the play reveals. But the most central use of comedy is Hamlet's mordant wit. His

Thrift, thrift, Horatio. The funeral baked meats
Did coldly furnish forth the marriage tables   (I.ii.180–81)

emphasizes his revulsion at his mother's hasty remarriage.
His near-hysteria after the Ghost makes its revelation
underlines the degree to which the revelation has disturbed
him. The audience may laugh at things such as these, but
the laughter is not merry. And there will be no laughter at
all when, at the close of Hamlet's interview with his mother,
he drags the body of Polonius to the exit, remarking, "I'll
lug the guts into the neighbor room." Then he pauses at
the threshold to say, "Good night, Mother." And he says
it with all the tenderness he has, for she has looked into
her soul and repented, and in the contest with the King she
is now on Hamlet's side. Mother and son are again at one.
Bringing this about has been the essential business of the
scene, and the dragging of the body (though the body must
somehow be removed) is in no way necessary to it. Yet
this bit of grotesquerie adds to the multiplicity of the
scene's effects without in any way detracting from its deep
seriousness.

It was Aristotle's belief that a well-constructed plot
should be single in issue, and that if any one action were to
be displaced or removed, the whole would be disjointed and
disturbed. The action of *Hamlet,* however, is far from single
in issue, and the play can be judiciously cut for presentation
on the stage without serious disturbance of the whole.
Shakespeare's plays were so cut in his own theater. The
First Folio version of *Hamlet* is based upon the acting version of the play, and it omits some two hundred lines,
chiefly reflective passages, which are found in the Second
Quarto. These lines include the soliloquy beginning "How
all occasions do inform against me" (IV.iv.32–66). The
scene is richer if the soliloquy is included, but its absence
does not significantly change the play as a whole. Another
passage omitted from the acting version is Hamlet's discourse (I.iv.17–38) on the heavy drinking done in Denmark and the effect of it on the reputation of the Danes.
The speech adds little to the action, but in its movement
from the particular to the general it helps give the play

extension. This is not to suggest that Shakespeare's plays are not unified, but their unity is clearly not Aristotelian.

In a tragedy the hero normally comes to the realization of a truth of which he had been hitherto unaware. There is, as Aristotle has it, "a change from ignorance to knowledge"; but in Greek tragedy this may be little more than the clearing up of a mistaken identity. Not so with the tragedies of Shakespeare's maturity. In *Hamlet* and *King Lear*, for instance, there is a transformation in the character of the hero. Toward the close of his play Lear is the opposite of what he had been at the beginning. He has been purged of his arrogance and pride, and the pomp and circumstance of kingship, on which he had placed great store, is to him no more than an interesting spectacle. What matters now is the love of the daughter he had rejected in the first scene. When we first meet Hamlet he is in a state of depression. The world to him is "an unweeded garden" from which he would willingly depart. He has found corruption not only in the state but in existence itself. We soon learn that he had not always been so. Ophelia tells us that he had been the ideal Renaissance prince—a soldier, scholar, courtier, "the glass of fashion and the mold of form." And though we catch glimpses of his former self in his conversations with Horatio, his state of depression continues. By the final scene, however, his composure has returned. He no longer appears in slovenly dress; he apologizes to Laertes, and he treats Claudius with courtesy up to the point at which Gertrude's death discloses the King's treachery and compels him to the act of vengeance.

All this is not simply a return to Hamlet's former self. In the course of the action he has grown in stature and wisdom. He is no longer troubled by reasoning doubts, for he knows now that reason is not enough. An overreliance on reason and a belief in untrammeled free will are hallmarks of the Shakespearean villain; the heroes learn better. In the beginning of the final scene Hamlet is still beset from without and within—"thou wouldst not think how ill all's here about my heart; but it is no matter." And it does not matter, because he has now come to put his trust in providence. Earlier in the scene (V.ii.8–11) he had said,

> Our indiscretion sometime serves us well
> When our deep plots do pall, and that should learn us
> There's a divinity that shapes our ends,
> Rough-hew them how we will.

This is not, as has been said, "a fatalist's surrender of his personal responsibility." It is the realization that man is not a totally free agent. With this realization Hamlet can face the fencing match and the King's intrigues without concern for self. What matters at the end of an important tragedy is not success or failure, but what a man *is*. Tragedy of the first order moves into the realm of the human spirit, and at the close we contemplate the nature of man. In this respect Shakespeare and the Greeks are the same, but they reach the end by widely divergent paths. We may consider the path which Shakespeare took.

Early in his career Shakespeare served an apprenticeship to Christopher Marlowe, but he soon surpassed him, and he took the journey from *Romeo and Juliet* to *Hamlet* on his own. His first so-called tragedy, *Titus Andronicus*, is not a tragedy at all. It is a blood-chilling thriller, and, as a recent production at Stratford-upon-Avon demonstrated, an effective one. The management had to have attendants at the theater to minister to the patrons who fainted as the play's horrors were revealed. A like response to tragedy is impossible. Melodrama such as *Titus* uses horror and grief as entertainment, bringing them as close to the spectator as it can. Tragedy uses them as truth. These, it says, are part of our human heritage, and we must face them. And in the end, partly because they are faced, they lose their terror, and the tragedy passes beyond them. It is not surprising, then, that the greatest tragedies are those involving the greatest horrors, for facing a great horror demands greatness of spirit. This greatness of spirit is what we contemplate at the end of a Shakespearean tragedy. At the close of the tragedy we are not so much concerned with Hamlet or Othello as individuals as with the spirit of man triumphant in defeat.

Shakespeare's next attempt at tragedy brings him to the borders of the tragic realm. There is much macabre action and humor in *Richard III,* but the horrors are moral as well as physical, and there is an approach to self-recognition in the remorse Richard feels on waking from his ghost-haunted sleep. This is no longer, or at least not altogether, horror as entertainment. In this play Shakespeare mastered and improved upon Marlowe's techniques. In *Richard II* there is, no doubt, a general indebtedness to Marlowe's *Edward II*. Both kings are weak men who come to a tragic end. Toward the close of Marlowe's play we sympathize with Edward because he is the underdog and because the people who surround him are worse than he, but toward the end of *Richard II* we sympathize with the King because adversity has moved him to a kind of self-realization. There is an approach to the recognition scenes of the later tragedies. Shakespeare has brought his weak and self-willed king to a recognition, if only for a time, of his mortality and the humanity he shares with others. Later, Shakespeare was to do this profoundly with Lear. Here he shows us both power politics at work and a transformation in Richard, and in his characterization of Richard he shows us how the transfer of power to Bolingbroke was possible without Bolingbroke's being a villain. He eschews comedy and physical action, not, we may be sure, out of any disregard for them, but because other matters came first. At this stage of his career Shakespeare was not able to do at one time all the things that needed to be done. He was later to do so in *Hamlet*. In *Richard II* the primary matters are character and theme. There are impressive tableaux, but there is no action comparable to that of the earlier so-called tragedies.

There is more on-stage action in *Romeo and Juliet*, and almost all of it is integral to character and theme. The hero and heroine meet, fall in love, mature through adversity, and find that, for them, love is of more worth than life. Nor is their ordeal in vain. They have their love, and their deaths bring peace to Verona. There is laughter in the play, but it is aroused by comic characters. The principals are serious throughout. But the play's laughter and vulgarities are not by any means comic relief. They contribute to a background of lust and hatred against which the story of the young lovers stands in contrast. Besides, Shakespeare's romance is never pure; it is always rooted in reality. It is never in danger of "falling upward, as it were, into vacuity." There is a notable mingling of the comic and the serious in Mercutio's death scene. It has comedy, pathos, and irony, all at once—a promise of things to come. Shakespeare seems never to have viewed things simply, and as soon as he acquired the skill, he made contraries and varying aspects of the same thing stand side by side, nothing canceling anything else out. And so it is here. Mercutio's flippancy in no way reduces the pathos and irony of his death.

After *Romeo and Juliet* Shakespeare turned to comedy and the completion of the historical tetralogy he had begun with *Richard II*. The last of this series, *Henry V*, is a fine play of action with England as its subject and England's national hero as its hero, yet it seems to have brought Shakespeare to a dead end. He was at the height of his success and popularity, but he seems not to have been satisfied with the play. He apologizes, and directly too, for the inability of his theater to present the panoply of war. He refers to his stage as "this unworthy scaffold," and to his theater as "this cockpit," "this wooden *O*," and he begs the audience to imagine what cannot be shown them. Yet in his next serious play he uses the oldest of dramatic conventions—a few soldiers on either side of the stage representing contending armies—without apology. For with this play the essential thing is not the action itself but the idea that it embodies. In *Julius Caesar* the essential thing, the dramatic thing, is the spirit of man, and this can be portrayed without pageantry. What is needed now are words. What matters now is not so much what a man *does* but what he *is*.[1] Brutus is the precursor of tragic heroes to come. As he is brooding on the outcome of the Battle of Philippi, he says,

> O, that a man might know
> The end of this day's business ere it come!
> But it sufficeth that the day will end,
> And then the end is known.　　　　　　(V.i)

[1] In this paragraph I am indebted to "From *Henry V* to *Hamlet*," by Harley Granville-Barker, in *Aspects of Shakespeare*, Oxford, The Clarendon Press, 1933.

It might be the voice of Hamlet before the fencing match:
"If it be now, 'tis not to come. . . ." In *Richard II* there
is no comedy; now, in *Julius Caesar,* there are only a few
comic puns early in the play. First things first. But although *Julius Caesar* was Shakespeare's most important
achievement to date, it has, perhaps, too great a separation
of action and idea. What was needed was a fusion of the
two, and this he achieved in *Hamlet.*[2]

Hamlet has on-stage action in God's plenty. A ghost
walks the stage; people are killed by stabbing and
poisoning; a young woman runs mad, is drowned offstage,
and is buried on stage; two skeletons are dug up and
scattered over the stage; armies march, and there is a
fencing match that ends in a general slaughter. Yet one
scarcely thinks of *Hamlet* as a play of action. There is some
comedy, but it is most often used to intensify the serious
matters to which it is germane. There are indecencies
that were *not* put into the play to please the groundlings.

[2] *Hamlet* was first published in 1603. The play is not mentioned in
Francis Meres's *Palladis Tamia* (1598), which includes a list of Shakespeare's works. Since Meres mentions so minor a work as *Titus Andronicus,* he would have hardly omitted *Hamlet* had it existed. And we may
be sure that the *Hamlet* played by Shakespeare's company in 1594 and
1596 was not Shakespeare's, for he was not yet capable of writing the
Hamlet we now know; nor is it likely that he revised the story over
the better part of a decade, for he worked fast, writing his entire works
in the time it took James Joyce to write *Finnegans Wake.* But there is
other evidence to narrow the gap between 1598 and 1603—a definite
allusion to Shakespeare's *Hamlet* in a note written by Gabriel Harvey
in his copy of Speght's edition of Chaucer, published in 1598. Such a
note might have been written any time between the publication of the
book and Harvey's death in 1631, but in the same note he refers to
the Earl of Essex in the present tense. Since Essex was executed on
February 25, 1601, it appears that the note was written while Essex
was alive and before he made his mad attempt to seize the person of
the Queen on February 7, 1601. During the fall of 1598 and the following winter, Essex was busy preparing his ill-fated foray into Ireland. He
returned in September of 1599. Harvey's reference was therefore presumably made between the autumn of 1599 and early 1601, and it is
during that time that *Hamlet* was written. The best date is 1600, which
is confirmed by a consideration of Shakespeare's other activities. In 1599
he had rounded out his cycle of history plays with the writing of *Henry
V.* He had recently written *The Merry Wives of Windsor* (to please
Queen Elizabeth, as tradition has it), and he had completed *Julius
Caesar.* He seems to have been looking for new worlds to conquer. He
turned to comedy for a while, producing *As You Like It* and *Twelfth
Night.* Then came the most important play he had yet written, *Hamlet.*

They are the opposite of those employed at the opening of *Romeo and Juliet* to command attention. Hamlet's remarks to Ophelia early in III.ii (the scene of the play-within-the-play) reveal once more his disillusionment with women, and the indecencies of Ophelia's mad songs complete her characterization. Uninhibited in her madness, in a notable anticipation of modern psychology she sings about sex and the father who had dominated her while he lived. To be sure, the play is sometimes diffuse. Everyone is given to generalizing, even the wretched Rosencrantz and Guildenstern. It is, of couse, necessary to generalize on the action, and Shakespeare succeeds in doing so; but in the later tragedies he was to do it more compactly. In *Hamlet* Shakespeare was writing tragedy of the first order for the first time, and perhaps he could not be intellectually aware of how to do it until he had once done it, for he had no models to show him the way. (What little he knew of Greek tragedy was through Roman or other adaptations.) In any case, he knew, in 1600, the heights tragedy could achieve, and he was to achieve them again in the next great tragedies—*Othello, King Lear,* and *Macbeth.* There is a saying that Shakespeare never repeats. In most respects it is not true, but it is true that he never repeated his successes. The four great tragedies are as different from each other as plays of the same genre by the same author could be.

In each of the plays the hero is transformed into something he had not been at the beginning of the play. He recognizes that he is other than he was, but in *Hamlet* the recognition scene is not explicit. Hamlet emerges from his state of depression, and if he did not the play would be a study in pathology rather than a tragedy; but we do not see him emerging from it as we see, for instance, the change taking place in Othello's speech beginning with "Behold I have a weapon . . ." (V.ii) or in Lear's prayer for the poor:

> Poor naked wretches, wheresoe'er you are,
> That bide the pelting of this pitiless storm,
> How shall your houseless heads and unfed sides,

> Your looped and windowed raggedness, defend you
> From seasons such as these? O, I have ta'en
> Too little care of this.
>
> (III.iv)

In this speech Lear is the opposite of the arrogant, unfeel-
ing man he had been at the opening of the play, and we are
told that he is. Shakespeare liked to be explicit when he
could be. At the end of his play, Hamlet, too, is very
different from the man who had earlier longed for death
and contemplated suicide. There is no more "fighting" in
his soul; like Lear on his way to prison, he is at peace.

The movement toward Hamlet's regeneration begins
with his reflections on the Player's speech about Hecuba;
it advances further in the closet scene, and it reaches its
culmination in the gravediggers' scene. Although this
scene is crowded with action, it is essentially a meditation
on the inevitability of death. It begins lightly enough for
such a scene, but it grows steadily more serious, more
general, and more personal—more personal to Hamlet,
and through its increasing generality more personal to us—
until in the end it transcends the macabre. At the opening
of the scene it is disclosed that someone presumed a
suicide is to be buried. Her name is not mentioned, but we
know who she is. After some talk about her right to
Christian burial, there is a conundrum: "What is he that
builds stronger than either the mason, the shipwright, or
the carpenter?" And the answer: "a gravemaker. The
houses he makes lasts till doomsday." Hamlet and
Horatio enter as the digger breaks into a song about
advancing age. In the course of the song he digs up a
skull, and Hamlet comments on it: "That skull had a
tongue in it, and could sing once. How the knave jowls
it to the ground, as if 'twere Cain's jawbone, that did the
first murder!" Or it might be "the pate of a politician,"
or a courtier, or "my Lord Such-a-one. . . . And now my
Lady Worm's, chapless, and knocked about the mazzard
with a sexton's spade." While Shakespeare is thus generalizing about the fact of death, another skull is dug up. It
turns out to be the skull of Yorick, the King's jester, and
the generalization becomes personal: "I knew him,
Horatio, a fellow of infinite jest, of most excellent fancy.

He hath borne me on his back a thousand times. And now how abhorred in my imagination it is! My gorge rises at it." Here the scene passes beyond comedy, and Shakespeare tells us so: "Where be your gibes now? Your gambols, your songs? . . . Now get you to my lady's chamber, and tell her, let her paint an inch thick, to this favor she must come. Make her laugh at that." Hamlet's remarks on the bones are his last comment on the discrepancy between appearance and reality. He is coming to accept reality for what it is. Then as the generalization continues, a funeral procession enters, and Hamlet learns who is to be buried today. He has seen the body of an old friend dug up to make room for the body of the woman he loves. He has looked on death at what is for him its worst. It is after the graveyard scene that the man who had continually brooded on death is able to face it. It seems axiomatic that any horror becomes less horrible once we have looked squarely at it. When we see Hamlet again he can defy augury, for the augurs can foretell only such things as success or failure; but there is nothing, except himself, to prevent a man from facing his own private horror and rising above it. And so it is with Hamlet. When Horatio offers to cancel the fencing match "if your mind dislike anything," he is able to reply, "Not a whit, we defy augury. There is special providence in the fall of a sparrow. If it be now, 'tis not to come; if it be not to come, it will be now; if it be not now, yet it will come. The readiness is all. Since no man of aught he leaves knows, what is't to leave betimes? Let be." "Readiness" here means both submitting to providence and being in a state of preparation. It is not that death does not matter; it matters very much indeed, but readiness matters more. Shakespeare's tragic heroes do not renounce the world. The dying Hamlet is concerned about the welfare of the state and his own worldly reputation. Such values are never denied, but at the end of the tragedies they are no longer primary values. At such moments the central thing is the spirit of man achieving grandeur.

EDWARD HUBLER
Princeton University

The Tragedy of Hamlet
Prince of Denmark

[Dramatis Personae

Claudius, King of Denmark
Hamlet, son to the late, and nephew to the present, King
Polonius, Lord Chamberlain
Horatio, friend to Hamlet
Laertes, son to Polonius
Voltemand ⎫
Cornelius |
Rosencrantz |
Guildenstern ⎬ courtiers
Osric |
A Gentleman ⎭
A Priest
Marcellus ⎫
Barnardo ⎬ officers
Francisco, a soldier
Reynaldo, servant to Polonius
Players
Two Clowns, gravediggers
Fortinbras, Prince of Norway
A Norwegian Captain
English Ambassadors
Gertrude, Queen of Denmark, mother to Hamlet
Ophelia, daughter to Polonius
Ghost of Hamlet's father
Lords, Ladies, Officers, Soldiers, Sailors, Messengers, Attendants

Scene: Elsinore]

The Tragedy of Hamlet
Prince of Denmark

[ACT I

Scene I. *A guard platform of the castle.*]

Enter Barnardo and Francisco, two sentinels.

Barnardo. Who's there?

Francisco. Nay, answer me. Stand and unfold° [1] yourself.

Barnardo. Long live the King!°

Francisco. Barnardo?

Barnardo. He.   5

Francisco. You come most carefully upon your hour.

Barnardo. 'Tis now struck twelve. Get thee to bed,
Francisco.

[1] The degree sign (°) indicates a footnote, which is keyed to the
text by the line number. Text references are printed in *italic* type;
the annotation follows in roman type.
I.i.2 *unfold* disclose 3 *Long live the King* (perhaps a password,
perhaps a greeting)

Francisco. For this relief much thanks. 'Tis bitter cold,
And I am sick at heart.

Barnardo. Have you had quiet guard?

10 *Francisco.*   Not a mouse stirring.

Barnardo. Well, good night.
If you do meet Horatio and Marcellus,
The rivals° of my watch, bid them make haste.

Enter Horatio and Marcellus.

Francisco. I think I hear them. Stand, ho! Who is
there?

Horatio. Friends to this ground.

15 *Marcellus.*   And liegemen to the Dane.°

Francisco. Give you° good night.

Marcellus.   O, farewell, honest soldier.
Who hath relieved you?

Francisco.   Barnardo hath my place.
Give you good night.   *Exit Francisco.*

Marcellus.   Holla, Barnardo!

Barnardo.   Say——
What, is Horatio there?

Horatio.   A piece of him.

20 *Barnardo.* Welcome, Horatio. Welcome, good Marcellus.

Marcellus. What, has this thing appeared again tonight?

Barnardo. I have seen nothing.

Marcellus. Horatio says 'tis but our fantasy,
And will not let belief take hold of him
25   Touching this dreaded sight twice seen of us;
Therefore I have entreated him along
With us to watch the minutes of this night,
That, if again this apparition come,
He may approve° our eyes and speak to it.

13 *rivals* partners 15 *liegemen to the Dane* loyal subjects to the
King of Denmark 16 *Give you* God give you 29 *approve* confirm

Horatio. Tush, tush, 'twill not appear.

Barnardo.   Sit down awhile,   30
And let us once again assail your ears,
That are so fortified against our story,
What we have two nights seen.

Horatio.   Well, sit we down,
And let us hear Barnardo speak of this.

Barnardo. Last night of all,   35
When yond same star that's westward from the
    pole°
Had made his course t' illume that part of heaven
Where now it burns, Marcellus and myself,
The bell then beating one——

                    Enter Ghost.

Marcellus. Peace, break thee off. Look where it comes
again.   40

Barnardo. In the same figure like the king that's dead.

Marcellus. Thou art a scholar; speak to it, Horatio.

Barnardo. Looks 'a not like the king? Mark it, Horatio.

Horatio. Most like: it harrows me with fear and wonder.

Barnardo. It would be spoke to.

Marcellus.   Speak to it, Horatio.   45

Horatio. What art thou that usurp'st this time of night,
Together with that fair and warlike form
In which the majesty of buried Denmark°
Did sometimes march? By heaven I charge thee,
    speak.

Marcellus. It is offended.

Barnardo.   See, it stalks away.   50

Horatio. Stay! Speak, speak. I charge thee, speak.
                                        Exit Ghost.

36 *pole* polestar   48 *buried Denmark* the buried King of Denmark

Marcellus. 'Tis gone and will not answer.

Barnardo. How now, Horatio? You tremble and look
    pale.
    Is not this something more than fantasy?
55   What think you on't?

Horatio. Before my God, I might not this believe
    Without the sensible and true avouch°
    Of mine own eyes.

Marcellus.   Is it not like the King?

Horatio. As thou art to thyself.
60   Such was the very armor he had on
    When he the ambitious Norway° combated:
    So frowned he once, when, in an angry parle,°
    He smote the sledded Polacks° on the ice.
    'Tis strange.

Marcellus. Thus twice before, and jump° at this dead
65   hour,
    With martial stalk hath he gone by our watch.

Horatio. In what particular thought to work I know
        not;
    But, in the gross and scope° of my opinion,
    This bodes some strange eruption to our state.

Marcellus. Good now, sit down, and tell me he that
70   knows,
    Why this same strict and most observant watch
    So nightly toils the subject° of the land,
    And why such daily cast of brazen cannon
    And foreign mart° for implements of war,

57 *sensible and true avouch* sensory and true proof 61 *Norway*
King of Norway 62 *parle* parley 63 *sledded Polacks* Poles in
sledges 65 *jump* just 68 *gross and scope* general drift 72 *toils
the subject* makes the subjects toil 74 *mart* trading

Why such impress° of shipwrights, whose sore task   75
Does not divide the Sunday from the week,
What might be toward° that this sweaty haste
Doth make the night joint-laborer with the day?
Who is't that can inform me?

Horatio.   That can I.
At least the whisper goes so: our last king,   80
Whose image even but now appeared to us,
Was, as you know, by Fortinbras of Norway,
Thereto pricked on by a most emulate pride,
Dared to the combat; in which our valiant Hamlet
(For so this side of our known world esteemed him)   85
Did slay this Fortinbras, who, by a sealed compact
Well ratified by law and heraldry,°
Did forfeit, with his life, all those his lands
Which he stood seized° of, to the conqueror;
Against the which a moiety competent°   90
Was gagèd° by our King, which had returned
To the inheritance of Fortinbras,
Had he been vanquisher, as, by the same comart°
And carriage of the article designed,°
His fell to Hamlet. Now, sir, young Fortinbras,   95
Of unimprovèd° mettle hot and full,
Hath in the skirts° of Norway here and there
Sharked up° a list of lawless resolutes,°
For food and diet, to some enterprise
That hath a stomach in't;° which is no other,   100
As it doth well appear unto our state,
But to recover of us by strong hand
And terms compulsatory, those foresaid lands
So by his father lost; and this, I take it,
Is the main motive of our preparations,   105

75 *impress* forced service   77 *toward* in preparation   87 *law and
heraldry* heraldic law (governing the combat)   89 *seized* possessed
90 *moiety competent* equal portion   91 *gagèd* engaged, pledged
93 *comart* agreement   94 *carriage of the article designed* import of
the agreement drawn up   96 *unimprovèd* untried   97 *skirts* borders
98 *Sharked up* collected indiscriminately (as a shark gulps its
prey)   98 *resolutes* desperadoes   100 *hath a stomach in't* i.e.,
requires courage

The source of this our watch, and the chief head°
Of this posthaste and romage° in the land.

Barnardo. I think it be no other but e'en so;
Well may it sort° that this portentous figure
110 Comes armèd through our watch so like the King
That was and is the question of these wars.

Horatio. A mote it is to trouble the mind's eye:
In the most high and palmy state of Rome,
A little ere the mightiest Julius fell,
115 The graves stood tenantless, and the sheeted dead
Did squeak and gibber in the Roman streets;°
As stars with trains of fire and dews of blood,
Disasters° in the sun; and the moist star,°
Upon whose influence Neptune's empire stands,
120 Was sick almost to doomsday with eclipse.
And even the like precurse° of feared events,
As harbingers° preceding still° the fates
And prologue to the omen° coming on,
Have heaven and earth together demonstrated
125 Unto our climatures° and countrymen.

Enter Ghost.

But soft, behold, lo where it comes again!
I'll cross it,° though it blast me.—Stay, illusion.

> *It spreads his° arms.*

If thou hast any sound or use of voice,
Speak to me.
130 If there be any good thing to be done
That may to thee do ease and grace to me,
Speak to me.
If thou art privy to thy country's fate,
Which happily° foreknowing may avoid,

106 *head* fountainhead, origin 107 *romage* bustle 109 *sort* befit
116 *Did squeak . . . Roman streets* (the break in the sense which
follows this line suggests that a line has dropped out) 118 *Disas-
ters* threatening signs 118 *moist star* moon 121 *precurse* precursor, foreshadowing 122 *harbingers* forerunners 122 *still* always
123 *omen* calamity 125 *climatures* regions 127 *cross it* (1)
cross its path, confront it (2) make the sign of the cross in front
of it 127 s.d. *his* i.e., its, the ghost's (though possibly what is
meant is that Horatio spreads his own arms, making a cross of
himself) 134 *happily* haply, perhaps

O, speak!   *135*
Or if thou hast uphoarded in thy life
Extorted° treasure in the womb of earth,
For which, they say, you spirits oft walk in death,

                           The cock crows.

Speak of it. Stay and speak. Stop it, Marcellus.
Marcellus. Shall I strike at it with my partisan°?   *140*
Horatio. Do, if it will not stand.
Barnardo.   'Tis here.
Horatio.   'Tis here.
Marcellus. 'Tis gone.   *Exit Ghost.*
  We do it wrong, being so majestical,
  To offer it the show of violence,
  For it is as the air, invulnerable,   *145*
  And our vain blows malicious mockery.

Barnardo. It was about to speak when the cock crew.
Horatio. And then it started, like a guilty thing
  Upon a fearful summons. I have heard,
  The cock, that is the trumpet to the morn,   *150*
  Doth with his lofty and shrill-sounding throat
  Awake the god of day, and at his warning,
  Whether in sea or fire, in earth or air,
  Th' extravagant and erring° spirit hies
  To his confine; and of the truth herein   *155*
  This present object made probation.°

Marcellus. It faded on the crowing of the cock.
  Some say that ever 'gainst° that season comes
  Wherein our Savior's birth is celebrated,
  This bird of dawning singeth all night long,   *160*
  And then, they say, no spirit dare stir abroad,
  The nights are wholesome, then no planets strike,°
  No fairy takes,° nor witch hath power to charm:
  So hallowed and so gracious is that time.

Horatio. So have I heard and do in part believe it.   *165*

137 *Extorted* ill-won   140 *partisan* pike (a long-handled weapon)
154 *extravagant and erring* out of bounds and wandering   156 *probation* proof   158 *'gainst* just before   162 *strike* exert an evil influence   163 *takes* bewitches

But look, the morn in russet mantle clad
Walks o'er the dew of yon high eastward hill.
Break we our watch up, and by my advice
Let us impart what we have seen tonight
170 Unto young Hamlet, for upon my life
This spirit, dumb to us, will speak to him.
Do you consent we shall acquaint him with it,
As needful in our loves, fitting our duty?

Marcellus. Let's do't, I pray, and I this morning know
175 Where we shall find him most convenient. *Exeunt.*

[Scene II. *The castle.*]

*Flourish.° Enter Claudius, King of Denmark, Gertrude
the Queen, Councilors, Polonius and his son Laertes,
Hamlet, cum aliis° [including Voltemand and Cor-
nelius].*

King. Though yet of Hamlet our dear brother's death
The memory be green, and that it us befitted
To bear our hearts in grief, and our whole kingdom
To be contracted in one brow of woe,
5 Yet so far hath discretion fought with nature
That we with wisest sorrow think on him
Together with remembrance of ourselves.
Therefore our sometime sister,° now our Queen,
Th' imperial jointress° to this warlike state,
10 Have we, as 'twere, with a defeated joy,
With an auspicious° and a dropping eye,
With mirth in funeral, and with dirge in marriage,
In equal scale weighing delight and dole,
Taken to wife. Nor have we herein barred
15 Your better wisdoms, which have freely gone

I.ii.s.d. *Flourish* fanfare of trumpets s.d. *cum aliis* with others
(Latin) 8 *our sometime sister* my (the royal "we") former sister-
in-law 9 *jointress* joint tenant, partner 11 *auspicious* joyful

With this affair along. For all, our thanks.
Now follows that you know young Fortinbras,
Holding a weak supposal of our worth,
Or thinking by our late dear brother's death
Our state to be disjoint and out of frame,°   20
Colleaguèd with this dream of his advantage,°
He hath not failed to pester us with message,
Importing the surrender of those lands
Lost by his father, with all bands of law,
To our most valiant brother. So much for him.   25
Now for ourself and for this time of meeting.
Thus much the business is: we have here writ
To Norway, uncle of young Fortinbras—
Who, impotent and bedrid, scarcely hears
Of this his nephew's purpose—to suppress   30
His further gait° herein, in that the levies,
The lists, and full proportions° are all made
Out of his subject;° and we here dispatch
You, good Cornelius, and you, Voltemand,
For bearers of this greeting to old Norway,   35
Giving to you no further personal power
To business with the King, more than the scope
Of these delated articles° allow.
Farewell, and let your haste commend your duty.

Cornelius, Voltemand. In that, and all things, will we
show our duty.   40

King. We doubt it nothing. Heartily farewell.
                    Exit Voltemand and Cornelius.
And now, Laertes, what's the news with you?
You told us of some suit. What is't, Laertes?
You cannot speak of reason to the Dane
And lose your voice.° What wouldst thou beg,
   Laertes,   45
That shall not be my offer, not thy asking?
The head is not more native° to the heart,

20 *frame* order 21 *advantage* superiority 31 *gait* proceeding
32 *proportions* supplies for war 33 *Out of his subject* i.e., out of
old Norway's subjects and realm 38 *delated articles* detailed documents 45 *lose your voice* waste your breath 47 *native* related

The hand more instrumental to the mouth,
Than is the throne of Denmark to thy father.
What wouldst thou have, Laertes?

50 *Laertes.*   My dread lord,
Your leave and favor to return to France,
From whence, though willingly I came to Denmark
To show my duty in your coronation,
Yet now I must confess, that duty done,
55 My thoughts and wishes bend again toward France
And bow them to your gracious leave and pardon.

King. Have you your father's leave? What says
    Polonius?

Polonius. He hath, my lord, wrung from me my slow
    leave
By laborsome petition, and at last
60 Upon his will I sealed my hard consent.°
I do beseech you give him leave to go.

King. Take thy fair hour, Laertes. Time be thine,
And thy best graces spend it at thy will.
But now, my cousin° Hamlet, and my son——

Hamlet. [*Aside*] A little more than kin, and less than
65   kind!°

King. How is it that the clouds still hang on you?

Hamlet. Not so, my lord. I am too much in the sun.°

Queen. Good Hamlet, cast thy nighted color off,
And let thine eye look like a friend on Denmark.
70 Do not forever with thy vailèd° lids
Seek for thy noble father in the dust.
Thou know'st 'tis common; all that lives must die,
Passing through nature to eternity.

60 *Upon his . . . hard consent* to his desire I gave my reluctant
consent   64 *cousin* kinsman   65 *kind* (pun on the meanings
"kindly" and "natural"; though doubly related—*more than kin*—
Hamlet asserts that he neither resembles Claudius in nature or feels
kindly toward him)   67 *sun* sunshine of royal favor (with a pun
on "son")   70 *vailèd* lowered

Hamlet. Ay, madam, it is common.°

Queen.   If it be,
    Why seems it so particular with thee?   75

Hamlet. Seems, madam? Nay, it is. I know not "seems."
    'Tis not alone my inky cloak, good mother,
    Nor customary suits of solemn black,
    Nor windy suspiration° of forced breath,
    No, nor the fruitful river in the eye,   80
    Nor the dejected havior of the visage,
    Together with all forms, moods, shapes of grief,
    That can denote me truly. These indeed seem,
    For they are actions that a man might play,
    But I have that within which passes show;   85
    These but the trappings and the suits of woe.

King. 'Tis sweet and commendable in your nature,
        Hamlet,
    To give these mourning duties to your father,
    But you must know your father lost a father,
    That father lost, lost his, and the survivor bound   90
    In filial obligation for some term
    To do obsequious° sorrow. But to persever
    In obstinate condolement° is a course
    Of impious stubbornness. 'Tis unmanly grief.
    It shows a will most incorrect to heaven,   95
    A heart unfortified, a mind impatient,
    An understanding simple and unschooled.
    For what we know must be and is as common
    As any the most vulgar° thing to sense,
    Why should we in our peevish opposition   100
    Take it to heart? Fie, 'tis a fault to heaven,
    A fault against the dead, a fault to nature,
    To reason most absurd, whose common theme
    Is death of fathers, and who still hath cried,
    From the first corse° till he that died today,   105
    "This must be so." We pray you throw to earth

74 *common* (1) universal (2) vulgar   79 *windy suspiration* heavy
sighing   92 *obsequious* suitable to obsequies (funerals)   93 *con-
dolement* mourning   99 *vulgar* common   105 *corse* corpse

This unprevailing° woe, and think of us
As of a father, for let the world take note
You are the most immediate to our throne,
110   And with no less nobility of love
Than that which dearest father bears his son
Do I impart toward you. For your intent
In going back to school in Wittenberg,
It is most retrograde° to our desire,
115   And we beseech you, bend you° to remain
Here in the cheer and comfort of our eye,
Our chiefest courtier, cousin, and our son.

Queen. Let not thy mother lose her prayers, Hamlet.
I pray thee stay with us, go not to Wittenberg.

120   *Hamlet.* I shall in all my best obey you, madam.

King. Why, 'tis a loving and a fair reply.
Be as ourself in Denmark. Madam, come.
This gentle and unforced accord of Hamlet
Sits smiling to my heart, in grace whereof
125   No jocund health that Denmark drinks today,
But the great cannon to the clouds shall tell,
And the King's rouse° the heaven shall bruit° again,
Respeaking earthly thunder. Come away.
                    Flourish. Exeunt all but Hamlet.

Hamlet. O that this too too sullied° flesh would melt,
130   Thaw, and resolve itself into a dew,
Or that the Everlasting had not fixed
His canon° 'gainst self-slaughter. O God, God,
How weary, stale, flat, and unprofitable
Seem to me all the uses of this world!
135   Fie on't, ah, fie, 'tis an unweeded garden
That grows to seed. Things rank and gross in nature
Possess it merely.° That it should come to this:
But two months dead, nay, not so much, not two,

107 *unprevailing* unavailing 114 *retrograde* contrary 115 *bend
you* incline 127 *rouse* deep drink 127 *bruit* announce noisily
129 *sullied* (Q2 has *sallied,* here modernized to *sullied,* which
makes sense and is therefore given; but the Folio reading, *solid,*
which fits better with *melt,* is quite possibly correct) 132 *canon*
law 137 *merely* entirely

So excellent a king, that was to this
Hyperion° to a satyr, so loving to my mother　　　140
That he might not beteem° the winds of heaven
Visit her face too roughly. Heaven and earth,
Must I remember? Why, she would hang on him
As if increase of appetite had grown
By what it fed on; and yet within a month—　　　145
Let me not think on't; frailty, thy name is woman—
A little month, or ere those shoes were old
With which she followed my poor father's body
Like Niobe,° all tears, why she, even she—
O God, a beast that wants discourse of reason°　　　150
Would have mourned longer—married with my
　　　uncle,
My father's brother, but no more like my father
Than I to Hercules. Within a month,
Ere yet the salt of most unrighteous tears
Had left the flushing° in her gallèd eyes,　　　155
She married. O, most wicked speed, to post°
With such dexterity to incestuous° sheets!
It is not, nor it cannot come to good.
But break my heart, for I must hold my tongue.

Enter Horatio, Marcellus, and Barnardo.

Horatio. Hail to your lordship!

Hamlet.　　　　　　　　　　I am glad to see you well.　160
　Horatio—or I do forget myself.

Horatio. The same, my lord, and your poor servant
　ever.

Hamlet. Sir, my good friend, I'll change° that name
　with you.
　And what make you from Wittenberg, Horatio?
　Marcellus.　　　　　　　　　　　　　　　　165

140 *Hyperion* the sun god, a model of beauty　141 *beteem* allow
149 *Niobe* (a mother who wept profusely at the death of her
children)　150 *wants discourse of reason* lacks reasoning power
155 *left the flushing* stopped reddening　156 *post* hasten　157 *incestuous* (canon law considered marriage with a deceased brother's
widow to be incestuous)　163 *change* exchange

Marcellus. My good lord!

Hamlet. I am very glad to see you. [*To Barnardo*]
    Good even, sir.
But what, in faith, make you from Wittenberg?

Horatio. A truant disposition, good my lord.

170 *Hamlet.* I would not hear your enemy say so,
    Nor shall you do my ear that violence
    To make it truster° of your own report
    Against yourself. I know you are no truant.
    But what is your affair in Elsinore?
175   We'll teach you to drink deep ere you depart.

Horatio. My lord, I came to see your father's funeral.

Hamlet. I prithee do not mock me, fellow student.
    I think it was to see my mother's wedding.

Horatio. Indeed, my lord, it followed hard upon.

180 *Hamlet.* Thrift, thrift, Horatio. The funeral baked
    meats
    Did coldly furnish forth the marriage tables.
    Would I had met my dearest° foe in heaven
    Or ever I had seen that day, Horatio!
    My father, methinks I see my father.

Horatio. Where, my lord?

185 *Hamlet.*   In my mind's eye, Horatio.

Horatio. I saw him once. 'A° was a goodly king.

Hamlet. 'A was a man, take him for all in all,
    I shall not look upon his like again.

Horatio. My lord, I think I saw him yesternight.

190 *Hamlet.* Saw? Who?

Horatio. My lord, the King your father.

Hamlet.   The King my father?

Horatio. Season your admiration° for a while
    With an attent ear till I may deliver
    Upon the witness of these gentlemen

172 *truster* believer   182 *dearest* most intensely felt   186 *'A* he
192 *Season your admiration* control your wonder

This marvel to you.

Hamlet.   For God's love let me hear!   *195*

Horatio. Two nights together had these gentlemen,
    Marcellus and Barnardo, on their watch
    In the dead waste and middle of the night
    Been thus encountered. A figure like your father,
    Armèd at point exactly, cap-a-pe,°   *200*
    Appears before them, and with solemn march
    Goes slow and stately by them. Thrice he walked
    By their oppressed and fear-surprisèd eyes,
    Within his truncheon's length,° whilst they, distilled°
    Almost to jelly with the act° of fear,   *205*
    Stand dumb and speak not to him. This to me
    In dreadful° secrecy impart they did,
    And I with them the third night kept the watch,
    Where, as they had delivered, both in time,
    Form of the thing, each word made true and good,   *210*
    The apparition comes. I knew your father.
    These hands are not more like.

Hamlet.   But where was this?

Marcellus. My lord, upon the platform where we
    watched.

Hamlet. Did you not speak to it?

Horatio.   My lord, I did;
    But answer made it none. Yet once methought   *215*
    It lifted up it° head and did address
    Itself to motion like as it would speak:
    But even then the morning cock crew loud,
    And at the sound it shrunk in haste away
    And vanished from our sight.

Hamlet.   'Tis very strange.   *220*

Horatio. As I do live, my honored lord, 'tis true,
    And we did think it writ down in our duty
    To let you know of it.

---

200 *cap-a-pe* head to foot   204 *truncheon's length* space of a short
staff   204 *distilled* reduced   205 *act* action   207 *dreadful* terrified
216 *it* its

Hamlet. Indeed, indeed, sirs, but this troubles me.
　　Hold you the watch tonight?

225 *All.*   We do, my lord.

Hamlet. Armed, say you?

All. Armed, my lord.

Hamlet. From top to toe?

All.   My lord, from head to foot.

Hamlet. Then saw you not his face.

230 *Horatio.* O, yes, my lord. He wore his beaver° up.

Hamlet. What, looked he frowningly?

Horatio. A countenance more in sorrow than in anger.

Hamlet. Pale or red?

Horatio. Nay, very pale.

Hamlet.   And fixed his eyes upon you?

Horatio. Most constantly.

235 *Hamlet.*   I would I had been there.

Horatio. It would have much amazed you.

Hamlet. Very like, very like. Stayed it long?

Horatio. While one with moderate haste might tell° a
　　hundred.

Both. Longer, longer.

Horatio. Not when I saw't.

240 *Hamlet.*   His beard was grizzled,° no?

Horatio. It was as I have seen it in his life,
　　A sable silvered.°

Hamlet.   I will watch tonight.
　　Perchance 'twill walk again.

Horatio.   I warr'nt it will.

Hamlet. If it assume my noble father's person,

230 *beaver* visor, face guard 238 *tell* count 240 *grizzled* gray
242 *sable silvered* black mingled with white

I'll speak to it though hell itself should gape   245
And bid me hold my peace. I pray you all,
If you have hitherto concealed this sight,
Let it be tenable° in your silence still,
And whatsomever else shall hap tonight,
Give it an understanding but no tongue;   250
I will requite your loves. So fare you well.
Upon the platform 'twixt eleven and twelve
I'll visit you.

All.   Our duty to your honor.

Hamlet. Your loves, as mine to you. Farewell.
                              Exeunt [all but Hamlet].
My father's spirit—in arms? All is not well.   255
I doubt° some foul play. Would the night were come!
Till then sit still, my soul. Foul deeds will rise,
Though all the earth o'erwhelm them, to men's eyes.
                                                Exit.

[Scene III. *A room.*]

Enter Laertes and Ophelia, his sister.

Laertes. My necessaries are embarked. Farewell.
  And, sister, as the winds give benefit
  And convoy° is assistant, do not sleep,
  But let me hear from you.

Ophelia.   Do you doubt that?

Laertes. For Hamlet, and the trifling of his favor,   5
  Hold it a fashion and a toy° in blood,
  A violet in the youth of primy° nature,
  Forward,° not permanent, sweet, not lasting,
  The perfume and suppliance° of a minute,

248 *tenable* held   256 *doubt* suspect   I.iii.3 *convoy* conveyance
6 *toy* idle fancy   7 *primy* springlike   8 *Forward* premature   9 *suppliance* diversion

No more.

Ophelia.   No more but so?

10   *Laertes.*   Think it no more.
For nature crescent° does not grow alone
In thews° and bulk, but as this temple° waxes,
The inward service of the mind and soul
Grows wide withal. Perhaps he loves you now,
15   And now no soil nor cautel° doth besmirch
The virtue of his will; but you must fear,
His greatness weighed,° his will is not his own.
For he himself is subject to his birth.
He may not, as unvalued° persons do,
20   Carve for himself; for on his choice depends
The safety and health of this whole state;
And therefore must his choice be circumscribed
Unto the voice and yielding of that body
Whereof he is the head. Then if he says he loves you,
25   It fits your wisdom so far to believe it
As he in his particular act and place
May give his saying deed, which is no further
Than the main voice of Denmark goes withal.
Then weigh what loss your honor may sustain
30   If with too credent° ear you list his songs,
Or lose your heart, or your chaste treasure open
To his unmastered importunity.
Fear it, Ophelia, fear it, my dear sister,
And keep you in the rear of your affection,
35   Out of the shot and danger of desire.
The chariest maid is prodigal enough
If she unmask her beauty to the moon.
Virtue itself scapes not calumnious strokes.
The canker° galls the infants of the spring
40   Too oft before their buttons° be disclosed,
And in the morn and liquid dew of youth
Contagious blastments are most imminent.

11 *crescent* growing   12 *thews* muscles and sinews   12 *temple* i.e.,
the body   15 *cautel* deceit   17 *greatness weighed* high rank considered   19 *unvalued* of low rank   30 *credent* credulous   39 *canker* cankerworm   40 *buttons* buds

Be wary then; best safety lies in fear;
Youth to itself rebels, though none else near.

Ophelia. I shall the effect of this good lesson keep　　　45
As watchman to my heart, but, good my brother,
Do not, as some ungracious° pastors do,
Show me the steep and thorny way to heaven,
Whiles, like a puffed and reckless libertine,
Himself the primrose path of dalliance treads　　　50
And recks not his own rede.°

Enter Polonius.

Laertes.　　　　　　　　　O, fear me not.
I stay too long. But here my father comes.
A double blessing is a double grace;
Occasion smiles upon a second leave.

Polonius. Yet here, Laertes? Aboard, aboard, for
shame!　　　55
The wind sits in the shoulder of your sail,
And you are stayed for. There—my blessing with
thee,
And these few precepts in thy memory
Look thou character.° Give thy thoughts no tongue,
Nor any unproportioned° thought his act.　　　60
Be thou familiar, but by no means vulgar.
Those friends thou hast, and their adoption tried,
Grapple them unto thy soul with hoops of steel,
But do not dull thy palm with entertainment
Of each new-hatched, unfledged courage.° Beware　　　65
Of entrance to a quarrel; but being in,
Bear't that th' opposèd may beware of thee.
Give every man thine ear, but few thy voice;
Take each man's censure,° but reserve thy judgment.
Costly thy habit as thy purse can buy,　　　70
But not expressed in fancy; rich, not gaudy,
For the apparel oft proclaims the man,
And they in France of the best rank and station

---

47 *ungracious* lacking grace　51 *recks not his own rede* does not
heed his own advice　59 *character* inscribe　60 *unproportioned*
unbalanced　65 *courage* gallant youth　69 *censure* opinion

Are of a most select and generous, chief in that.°
75 Neither a borrower nor a lender be,
For loan oft loses both itself and friend,
And borrowing dulleth edge of husbandry.°
This above all, to thine own self be true,
And it must follow, as the night the day,
80 Thou canst not then be false to any man.
Farewell. My blessing season this° in thee!

Laertes. Most humbly do I take my leave, my lord.

Polonius. The time invites you. Go, your servants
    tend.°

Laertes. Farewell, Ophelia, and remember well
    What I have said to you.

85 *Ophelia.*   'Tis in my memory locked,
    And you yourself shall keep the key of it.

Laertes. Farewell.   *Exit Laertes.*

Polonius. What is't, Ophelia, he hath said to you?

Ophelia. So please you, something touching the Lord
    Hamlet.

90 *Polonius.* Marry,° well bethought.
    'Tis told me he hath very oft of late
    Given private time to you, and you yourself
    Have of your audience been most free and bounte-
      ous.
    If it be so—as so 'tis put on me,
95 And that in way of caution—I must tell you
    You do not understand yourself so clearly
    As it behooves my daughter and your honor.
    What is between you? Give me up the truth.

Ophelia. He hath, my lord, of late made many tenders°
100 Of his affection to me.

74 *Are of . . . in that* show their fine taste and their gentlemanly
instincts more in that than in any other point of manners (Kitt-
redge) 77 *husbandry* thrift 81 *season this* make fruitful this (advice) 83 *tend* attend 90 *Marry* (a light oath, from "By the Virgin
Mary") 99 *tenders* offers (in line 103 it has the same meaning,
but in line 106 Polonius speaks of *tenders* in the sense of counters
or chips; in line 109 *Tend'ring* means "holding," and *tender* means
"give," "present")

Polonius. Affection pooh! You speak like a green girl,
  Unsifted° in such perilous circumstance.
  Do you believe his tenders, as you call them?

Ophelia. I do not know, my lord, what I should think.

Polonius. Marry, I will teach you. Think yourself a
    baby   *105*
  That you have ta'en these tenders for true pay
  Which are not sterling. Tender yourself more dearly,
  Or (not to crack the wind of the poor phrase)
  Tend'ring it thus you'll tender me a fool.°

Ophelia. My lord, he hath importuned me with love   *110*
  In honorable fashion.

Polonius. Ay, fashion you may call it. Go to, go to.

Ophelia. And hath given countenance to his speech, my
    lord,
  With almost all the holy vows of heaven.

Polonius. Ay, springes to catch woodcocks.° I do know,   *115*
  When the blood burns, how prodigal the soul
  Lends the tongue vows. These blazes, daughter,
  Giving more light than heat, extinct in both,
  Even in their promise, as it is a-making,
  You must not take for fire. From this time   *120*
  Be something scanter of your maiden presence.
  Set your entreatments° at a higher rate
  Than a command to parley. For Lord Hamlet,
  Believe so much in him that he is young,
  And with a larger tether may he walk   *125*
  Than may be given you. In few, Ophelia,
  Do not believe his vows, for they are brokers,°
  Not of that dye° which their investments° show,
  But mere implorators° of unholy suits,
  Breathing like sanctified and pious bonds,°   *130*
  The better to beguile. This is for all:

102 *Unsifted* untried   109 *tender me a fool* (1) present me with a
fool (2) present me with a baby   115 *springes to catch woodcocks* snares to catch stupid birds   122 *entreatments* interviews
127 *brokers* procurers   128 *dye* i.e., kind   128 *investments* garments   129 *implorators* solicitors   130 *bonds* pledges

Don't see Hamlet!

I would not, in plain terms, from this time forth
Have you so slander° any moment leisure
As to give words or talk with the Lord Hamlet.
135   Look to't, I charge you. Come your ways.

Ophelia. I shall obey, my lord.   *Exeunt.*

[Scene IV. *A guard platform.*]

Enter Hamlet, Horatio, and Marcellus.

Hamlet. The air bites shrewdly;° it is very cold.

Horatio. It is a nipping and an eager° air.

Hamlet. What hour now?

Horatio.   I think it lacks of twelve.

Marcellus. No, it is struck.

Horatio. Indeed? I heard it not. It then draws near the
5   season
Wherein the spirit held his wont to walk.
        A flourish of trumpets, and two pieces go off.
What does this mean, my lord?

Hamlet. The King doth wake° tonight and takes his
     rouse,°
Keeps wassail, and the swagg'ring upspring° reels,
10   And as he drains his draughts of Rhenish° down
The kettledrum and trumpet thus bray out
The triumph of his pledge.°

Horatio.   Is it a custom?

133 *slander* disgrace I.iv.1 *shrewdly* bitterly   2 *eager* sharp   8 *wake*
hold a revel by night   8 *takes his rouse* carouses   9 *upspring* (a
dance)   10 *Rhenish* Rhine wine   12 *The triumph of his pledge*
the achievement (of drinking a wine cup in one draught) of his
toast

Hamlet. Ay, marry, is't,
   But to my mind, though I am native here
   And to the manner born, it is a custom   15
   More honored in the breach than the observance.
   This heavy-headed revel east and west
   Makes us traduced and taxed of° other nations.
   They clepe° us drunkards and with swinish phrase
   Soil our addition,° and indeed it takes   20
   From our achievements, though performed at height,
   The pith and marrow of our attribute.°
   So oft it chances in particular men
   That for some vicious mole° of nature in them,
   As in their birth, wherein they are not guilty,   25
   (Since nature cannot choose his origin)
   By the o'ergrowth of some complexion,°
   Oft breaking down the pales° and forts of reason,
   Or by some habit that too much o'erleavens°
   The form of plausive° manners, that (these men,   30
   Carrying, I say, the stamp of one defect,
   Being nature's livery, or fortune's star°)
   Their virtues else, be they as pure as grace,
   As infinite as man may undergo,
   Shall in the general censure° take corruption   35
   From that particular fault. The dram of evil
   Doth all the noble substance of a doubt,
   To his own scandal.°

Enter Ghost.

Horatio.   Look, my lord, it comes.

Hamlet. Angels and ministers of grace defend us!
   Be thou a spirit of health° or goblin damned,   40
   Bring with thee airs from heaven or blasts from hell,
   Be thy intents wicked or charitable,

18 *taxed of* blamed by   19 *clepe* call   20 *addition* reputation (literally, "title of honor")   22 *attribute* reputation   24 *mole* blemish   27 *complexion* natural disposition   28 *pales* enclosures   29 *o'erleavens* mixes with, corrupts   30 *plausive* pleasing   32 *nature's livery, or fortune's star* nature's equipment (i.e., "innate"), or a person's destiny determined by the stars   35 *general censure* popular judgment   36–38 *The dram . . . own scandal* (though the drift is clear, there is no agreement as to the exact meaning of these lines)   40 *spirit of health* good spirit

Thou com'st in such a questionable° shape
That I will speak to thee. I'll call thee Hamlet,
45   King, father, royal Dane. O, answer me!
Let me not burst in ignorance, but tell
Why thy canonized° bones, hearsèd in death,
Have burst their cerements,° why the sepulcher
Wherein we saw thee quietly interred
50   Hath oped his ponderous and marble jaws
To cast thee up again. What may this mean
That thou, dead corse, again in complete steel,
Revisits thus the glimpses of the moon,
Making night hideous, and we fools of nature
55   So horridly to shake our disposition°
With thoughts beyond the reaches of our souls?
Say, why is this? Wherefore? What should we do?
                                   Ghost beckons Hamlet.

Horatio. It beckons you to go away with it,
As if it some impartment° did desire
To you alone.

60   *Marcellus.*   Look with what courteous action
It waves you to a more removèd ground.
But do not go with it.

Horatio.   No, by no means.

Hamlet. It will not speak. Then I will follow it.

Horatio. Do not, my lord.

Hamlet.   Why, what should be the fear?
65   I do not set my life at a pin's fee,
And for my soul, what can it do to that,
Being a thing immortal as itself?
It waves me forth again. I'll follow it.

Horatio. What if it tempt you toward the flood, my
          lord,
70   Or to the dreadful summit of the cliff

43 *questionable* (1) capable of discourse (2) dubious 47 *canon-
ized* buried according to the canon or ordinance of the church
48 *cerements* waxed linen shroud 55 *shake our disposition* disturb
us 59 *impartment* communication

That beetles° o'er his base into the sea,
And there assume some other horrible form,
Which might deprive your sovereignty of reason°
And draw you into madness? Think of it.
The very place puts toys° of desperation,　　　　　　　75
Without more motive, into every brain
That looks so many fathoms to the sea
And hears it roar beneath.

Hamlet.　　　　　　　　　　　　It waves me still.
　Go on; I'll follow thee.

Marcellus. You shall not go, my lord.

Hamlet.　　　　　　　　　　　Hold off your hands.　80

Horatio. Be ruled. You shall not go.

Hamlet.　　　　　　　　　　　My fate cries out
　And makes each petty artere° in this body
　As hardy as the Nemean lion's nerve.°
　Still am I called! Unhand me, gentlemen.
　By heaven, I'll make a ghost of him that lets° me!　85
　I say, away! Go on. I'll follow thee.

　　　　　　　　　　　　　Exit Ghost, and Hamlet.

Horatio. He waxes desperate with imagination.

Marcellus. Let's follow. 'Tis not fit thus to obey him.

Horatio. Have after! To what issue will this come?

Marcellus. Something is rotten in the state of Denmark.　90

Horatio. Heaven will direct it.

Marcellus.　　　　　　Nay, let's follow him.　*Exeunt.*

---

71 *beetles* juts out　73 *deprive your sovereignty of reason* destroy
the sovereignty of your reason　75 *toys* whims, fancies　82 *artere*
artery　83 *Nemean lion's nerve* sinews of the mythical lion slain
by Hercules　85 *lets* hinders

[Scene V. *The battlements.*]

Enter Ghost and Hamlet.

Hamlet. Whither wilt thou lead me? Speak; I'll go no
    further.

Ghost. Mark me.

Hamlet.   I will.

Ghost.   My hour is almost come,
    When I to sulf'rous and tormenting flames
    Must render up myself.

Hamlet.   Alas, poor ghost.

5 *Ghost.* Pity me not, but lend thy serious hearing
    To what I shall unfold.

Hamlet.   Speak. I am bound to hear.

Ghost. So art thou to revenge, when thou shalt hear.

Hamlet. What?

Ghost. I am thy father's spirit,
10   Doomed for a certain term to walk the night,
    And for the day confined to fast in fires,
    Till the foul crimes° done in my days of nature
    Are burnt and purged away. But that I am forbid
    To tell the secrets of my prison house,
15   I could a tale unfold whose lightest word
    Would harrow up thy soul, freeze thy young blood,
    Make thy two eyes like stars start from their
        spheres,°
    Thy knotted and combinèd locks to part,
    And each particular hair to stand an end

I.v.12 *crimes* sins 17 *spheres* (in Ptolemaic astronomy, each planet
was fixed in a hollow transparent shell concentric with the earth)

　　Like quills upon the fearful porpentine.°　　　　20
　　But this eternal blazon° must not be
　　To ears of flesh and blood. List, list, O, list!
　　If thou didst ever thy dear father love——

Hamlet. O God!

Ghost. Revenge his foul and most unnatural murder.　　25

Hamlet. Murder?

Ghost. Murder most foul, as in the best it is,
　　But this most foul, strange, and unnatural.

Hamlet. Haste me to know't, that I, with wings as swift
　　As meditation° or the thoughts of love,　　　　30
　　May sweep to my revenge.

Ghost.　　　　　　　　I find thee apt,
　　And duller shouldst thou be than the fat weed
　　That roots itself in ease on Lethe wharf,°
　　Wouldst thou not stir in this. Now, Hamlet, hear.
　　'Tis given out that, sleeping in my orchard,　　35
　　A serpent stung me. So the whole ear of Denmark
　　Is by a forgèd process° of my death
　　Rankly abused. But know, thou noble youth,
　　The serpent that did sting thy father's life
　　Now wears his crown.

Hamlet.　　　　　　　O my prophetic soul!　　40
　　My uncle?

Ghost. Ay, that incestuous, that adulterate° beast,
　　With witchcraft of his wits, with traitorous gifts—
　　O wicked wit and gifts, that have the power
　　So to seduce!—won to his shameful lust　　45
　　The will of my most seeming-virtuous queen.
　　O Hamlet, what a falling-off was there,
　　From me, whose love was of that dignity
　　That it went hand in hand even with the vow
　　I made to her in marriage, and to decline　　50

20 *fearful porpentine* timid porcupine　21 *eternal blazon* revelation
of eternity　30 *meditation* thought　33 *Lethe wharf* bank of the
river of forgetfulness in Hades　37 *forgèd process* false account
42 *adulterate* adulterous

Upon a wretch whose natural gifts were poor
To those of mine.
But virtue, as it never will be moved,
Though lewdness° court it in a shape of heaven,
55   So lust, though to a radiant angel linked,
Will sate itself in a celestial bed
And prey on garbage.
But soft, methinks I scent the morning air;
Brief let me be. Sleeping within my orchard,
60   My custom always of the afternoon,
Upon my secure° hour thy uncle stole
With juice of cursed hebona° in a vial,
And in the porches of my ears did pour
The leperous distillment, whose effect
65   Holds such an enmity with blood of man
That swift as quicksilver it courses through
The natural gates and alleys of the body,
And with a sudden vigor it doth posset°
And curd, like eager° droppings into milk,
70   The thin and wholesome blood. So did it mine,
And a most instant tetter° barked about
Most lazarlike° with vile and loathsome crust
All my smooth body.
Thus was I, sleeping, by a brother's hand
75   Of life, of crown, of queen at once dispatched,
Cut off even in the blossoms of my sin,
Unhouseled, disappointed, unaneled,°
No reck'ning made, but sent to my account
With all my imperfections on my head.
80   O, horrible! O, horrible! Most horrible!
If thou hast nature in thee, bear it not.
Let not the royal bed of Denmark be
A couch for luxury° and damnèd incest.
But howsomever thou pursues this act,
85   Taint not thy mind, nor let thy soul contrive

54 *lewdness* lust 61 *secure* unsuspecting 62 *hebona* a poisonous
plant 68 *posset* curdle 69 *eager* acid 71 *tetter* scab 72 *lazar-
like* leperlike 77 *Unhouseled, disappointed, unaneled* without the
sacrament of communion, unabsolved, without extreme unction
83 *luxury* lust

Against thy mother aught. Leave her to heaven
And to those thorns that in her bosom lodge
To prick and sting her. Fare thee well at once.
The glowworm shows the matin° to be near
And 'gins to pale his uneffectual fire.   90
Adieu, adieu, adieu. Remember me.   *Exit.*

Hamlet. O all you host of heaven! O earth! What else?
And shall I couple hell? O fie! Hold, hold, my heart,
And you, my sinews, grow not instant old,
But bear me stiffly up. Remember thee?   95
Ay, thou poor ghost, whiles memory holds a seat
In this distracted globe.° Remember thee?
Yea, from the table° of my memory
I'll wipe away all trivial fond° records,
All saws° of books, all forms, all pressures° past   100
That youth and observation copied there,
And thy commandment all alone shall live
Within the book and volume of my brain,
Unmixed with baser matter. Yes, by heaven!
O most pernicious woman!   105
O villain, villain, smiling, damnèd villain!
My tables—meet it is I set it down
That one may smile, and smile, and be a villain.
At least I am sure it may be so in Denmark. [*Writes.*]
So, uncle, there you are. Now to my word: 110
It is "Adieu, adieu, remember me."
I have sworn't.

Horatio and Marcellus. (*Within*) My lord, my lord!

Enter Horatio and Marcellus.

Marcellus.   Lord Hamlet!

Horatio.   Heavens secure him!

Hamlet. So be it!

Marcellus. Illo, ho, ho,° my lord!   115

Hamlet. Hillo, ho, ho, boy! Come, bird, come.

89 *matin* morning   97 *globe* i.e., his head   98 *table* tablet, note-
book   99 *fond* foolish   100 *saws* maxims   100 *pressures* impres-
sions   115 *Illo, ho, ho* (falconer's call to his hawk)

Marcellus. How is't, my noble lord?

Horatio.   What news, my lord?

Hamlet. O, wonderful!

Horatio. Good my lord, tell it.

Hamlet.   No, you will reveal it.

Horatio. Not I, my lord, by heaven.

120 *Marcellus.*   Nor I, my lord.

Hamlet. How say you then? Would heart of man once
    think it?
  But you'll be secret?

Both.   Ay, by heaven, my lord.

Hamlet. There's never a villain dwelling in all Denmark
  But he's an arrant knave.

Horatio. There needs no ghost, my lord, come from the
125   grave
  To tell us this.

Hamlet.   Why, right, you are in the right;
  And so, without more circumstance° at all,
  I hold it fit that we shake hands and part:
  You, as your business and desire shall point you,
130 For every man hath business and desire
  Such as it is, and for my own poor part,
  Look you, I'll go pray.

Horatio. These are but wild and whirling words, my
    lord.

Hamlet. I am sorry they offend you, heartily;
  Yes, faith, heartily.

135 *Horatio.*   There's no offense, my lord.

Hamlet. Yes, by Saint Patrick, but there is, Horatio,
  And much offense too. Touching this vision here,
  It is an honest ghost,° that let me tell you.
  For your desire to know what is between us,
140 O'ermaster't as you may. And now, good friends,

127 *circumstance* details 138 *honest ghost* i.e., not a demon in
his father's shape

Secret

　　As you are friends, scholars, and soldiers,
　　Give me one poor request.

Horatio. What is't, my lord? We will.

Hamlet. Never make known what you have seen to-
　　night.

Both. My lord, we will not.

Hamlet.　　　　　　　　Nay, but swear't.

Horatio.　　　　　　　　　　　　In faith,　　*145*
　　My lord, not I.

Marcellus.　　　Nor I, my lord—in faith.

Hamlet. Upon my sword.

Marcellus.　　　　We have sworn, my lord, already.

Hamlet. Indeed, upon my sword, indeed.
　　　　　　　　　　Ghost cries under the stage.

Ghost. Swear.

Hamlet. Ha, ha, boy, say'st thou so? Art thou there,
　　truepenny?°　　　　　　　　　　　　*150*
　　Come on. You hear this fellow in the cellarage.
　　Consent to swear.

Horatio.　　　　　Propose the oath, my lord.

Hamlet. Never to speak of this that you have seen.
　　Swear by my sword.

Ghost. [*Beneath*] Swear.　　　　　　*155*

Hamlet. Hic et ubique?° Then we'll shift our ground;
　　Come hither, gentlemen,
　　And lay your hands again upon my sword.
　　Swear by my sword
　　Never to speak of this that you have heard.　　*160*

Ghost. [*Beneath*] Swear by his sword.

Hamlet. Well said, old mole! Canst work i' th' earth so
　　fast?
　　A worthy pioner!° Once more remove, good friends.

150 *truepenny* honest fellow　156 *Hic et ubique* here and everywhere (Latin)　163 *pioner* digger of mines

Horatio. O day and night, but this is wondrous strange!

165 *Hamlet.* And therefore as a stranger give it welcome.
There are more things in heaven and earth, Horatio,
Than are dreamt of in your philosophy.
But come:
Here as before, never, so help you mercy,
170 How strange or odd some'er I bear myself
(As I perchance hereafter shall think meet
To put an antic disposition° on),
That you, at such times seeing me, never shall
With arms encumb'red° thus, or this headshake,
175 Or by pronouncing of some doubtful phrase,
As "Well, well, we know," or "We could, an if we
would,"
Or "If we list to speak," or "There be, an if they
might,"
Or such ambiguous giving out, to note
That you know aught of me—this do swear,
180 So grace and mercy at your most need help you.

Ghost. [*Beneath*] Swear.   [*They swear.*]

Hamlet. Rest, rest, perturbèd spirit. So, gentlemen,
With all my love I do commend me° to you,
And what so poor a man as Hamlet is
185 May do t' express his love and friending to you,
God willing, shall not lack. Let us go in together,
And still your fingers on your lips, I pray.
The time is out of joint. O cursèd spite,
That ever I was born to set it right!
190 Nay, come, let's go together.   *Exeunt.*

172 *antic disposition* fantastic behavior   174 *encumb'red* folded
183 *commend me* entrust myself

[ACT II

Scene I. *A room.*]

Enter old Polonius, with his man Reynaldo.

Polonius. Give him this money and these notes, Reynaldo.

Reynaldo. I will, my lord.

Polonius. You shall do marvell's° wisely, good Reynaldo,
　Before you visit him, to make inquire
　Of his behavior.

Reynaldo.　　　My lord, I did intend it.　　　　　*5*

Polonius. Marry, well said, very well said. Look you sir,
　Inquire me first what Danskers° are in Paris,
　And how, and who, what means, and where they keep,°
　What company, at what expense; and finding
　By this encompassment° and drift of question　　*10*
　That they do know my son, come you more nearer
　Than your particular demands° will touch it.
　Take you as 'twere some distant knowledge of him,
　As thus, "I know his father and his friends,
　And in part him." Do you mark this, Reynaldo?　　*15*

Reynaldo. Ay, very well, my lord.

II.i.3 *marvell's* marvelous(ly)　**7** *Danskers* Danes　**8** *keep* dwell
10 *encompassment* circling　**12** *demands* questions

Polonius. "And in part him, but," you may say, "not well,
 But if't be he I mean, he's very wild,
 Addicted so and so." And there put on him
20 What forgeries° you please; marry, none so rank
 As may dishonor him—take heed of that—
 But, sir, such wanton, wild, and usual slips
 As are companions noted and most known
 To youth and liberty.

Reynaldo.   As gaming, my lord.

Polonius. Ay, or drinking, fencing, swearing, quarreling,
25 Drabbing.° You may go so far.

Reynaldo. My lord, that would dishonor him.

Polonius. Faith, no, as you may season it in the charge.
 You must not put another scandal on him,
30 That he is open to incontinency.°
 That's not my meaning. But breathe his faults so quaintly°
 That they may seem the taints of liberty,
 The flash and outbreak of a fiery mind,
 A savageness in unreclaimèd blood,
 Of general assault.°

35 *Reynaldo.*   But, my good lord——

Polonius. Wherefore should you do this?

Reynaldo.   Ay, my lord,
 I would know that.

Polonius.   Marry, sir, here's my drift,
 And I believe it is a fetch of warrant.°
 You laying these slight sullies on my son
40 As 'twere a thing a little soiled i' th' working,
 Mark you,
 Your party in converse, him you would sound,

20 *forgeries* inventions 26 *Drabbing* wenching 30 *incontinency* habitual licentiousness 31 *quaintly* ingeniously, delicately 35 *Of general assault* common to all men 38 *fetch of warrant* justifiable device

Having ever seen in the prenominate crimes°
The youth you breathe of guilty, be assured
He closes with you in this consequence:°   45
"Good sir," or so, or "friend," or "gentleman"—
According to the phrase or the addition°
Of man and country—

Reynaldo.   Very good, my lord.

Polonius. And then, sir, does 'a° this—'a does—
What was I about to say? By the mass, I was about   50
to say something! Where did I leave?

Reynaldo. At "closes in the consequence," at "friend
or so," and "gentleman."

Polonius. At "closes in the consequence"—Ay, marry!
He closes thus: "I know the gentleman;   55
I saw him yesterday, or t'other day,
Or then, or then, with such or such, and, as you say,
There was 'a gaming, there o'ertook in's rouse,
There falling out at tennis"; or perchance,
"I saw him enter such a house of sale,"   60
Videlicet,° a brothel, or so forth.
See you now—
Your bait of falsehood take this carp of truth,
And thus do we of wisdom and of reach,°
With windlasses° and with assays of bias,°   65
By indirections find directions out.
So, by my former lecture and advice,
Shall you my son. You have me, have you not?

Reynaldo. My lord, I have.

Polonius.   God bye ye, fare ye well.

Reynaldo. Good my lord.   70

Polonius. Observe his inclination in yourself.°

43 *Having . . . crimes* if he has ever seen in the aforementioned
crimes 45 *He closes . . . this consequence* he falls in with you in
this conclusion 47 *addition* title 49 *'a* he 61 *Videlicet* namely
64 *reach* far-reaching awareness(?) 65 *windlasses* circuitous
courses 65 *assays of bias* indirect attempts (metaphor from bowl-
ing; *bias* = curved course) 71 *in yourself* for yourself

Reynaldo. I shall, my lord.

Polonius. And let him ply his music.

Reynaldo. Well, my lord.

Polonius. Farewell. *Exit Reynaldo.*

Enter Ophelia.

How now, Ophelia, what's the matter?

75 *Ophelia.* O my lord, my lord, I have been so affrighted!

Polonius. With what, i' th' name of God?

Ophelia. My lord, as I was sewing in my closet,°
Lord Hamlet, with his doublet all unbraced,°
No hat upon his head, his stockings fouled,
80 Ungartered, and down-gyvèd° to his ankle,
Pale as his shirt, his knees knocking each other,
And with a look so piteous in purport,°
As if he had been loosèd out of hell
To speak of horrors—he comes before me.

Polonius. Mad for thy love?

85 *Ophelia.* My lord, I do not know,
But truly I do fear it.

Polonius. What said he?

Ophelia. He took me by the wrist and held me hard;
Then goes he to the length of all his arm,
And with his other hand thus o'er his brow
90 He falls to such perusal of my face
As 'a would draw it. Long stayed he so.
At last, a little shaking of mine arm,
And thrice his head thus waving up and down,
He raised a sigh so piteous and profound
95 As it did seem to shatter all his bulk
And end his being. That done, he lets me go,
And, with his head over his shoulder turned,
He seemed to find his way without his eyes,

---

77 *closet* private room **78** *doublet all unbraced* jacket entirely
unlaced **80** *down-gyvèd* hanging down like fetters **82** *purport*
expression

For out o' doors he went without their helps,
And to the last bended their light on me.　　　　*100*

Polonius. Come, go with me. I will go seek the King.
This is the very ecstasy° of love,
Whose violent property fordoes° itself
And leads the will to desperate undertakings
As oft as any passions under heaven　　　　*105*
That does afflict our natures. I am sorry.
What, have you given him any hard words of late?

Ophelia. No, my good lord; but as you did command,
I did repel his letters and denied
His access to me.

Polonius.　　　　That hath made him made.　　　　*110*
I am sorry that with better heed and judgment
I had not quoted° him. I feared he did but trifle
And meant to wrack thee; but beshrew my jealousy.°
By heaven, it is as proper° to our age
To cast beyond ourselves° in our opinions　　　　*115*
As it is common for the younger sort
To lack discretion. Come, go we to the King.
This must be known, which, being kept close, might move
More grief to hide than hate to utter love.°
Come.　　　　　　　　　　　　　*Exeunt.*　*120*

Polonius regrets!

---

102 *ecstasy* madness　103 *property fordoes* quality destroys
112 *quoted* noted　113 *beshrew my jealousy* curse on my suspicions
114 *proper* natural　115 *To cast beyond ourselves* to be over-
calculating　117–19 *Come, go . . . utter love* (the general meaning is that while telling the King of Hamlet's love may anger the
King, more grief would come from keeping it secret)

[Scene II. *The castle.*]

*Flourish. Enter King and Queen, Rosencrantz, and
Guildenstern [with others].*

King. Welcome, dear Rosencrantz and Guildenstern.
　　　Moreover that° we much did long to see you,
　　　The need we have to use you did provoke
　　　Our hasty sending. Something have you heard
5　　Of Hamlet's transformation: so call it,
　　　Sith° nor th' exterior nor the inward man
　　　Resembles that it was. What it should be,
　　　More than his father's death, that thus hath put him
　　　So much from th' understanding of himself,
10　　I cannot dream of. I entreat you both
　　　That, being of so° young days brought up with him,
　　　And sith so neighbored to his youth and havior,°
　　　That you vouchsafe your rest° here in our court
　　　Some little time, so by your companies
15　　To draw him on to pleasures, and to gather
　　　So much as from occasion you may glean,
　　　Whether aught to us unknown afflicts him thus,
　　　That opened° lies within our remedy.

Queen. Good gentlemen, he hath much talked of you,
20　　And sure I am, two men there is not living
　　　To whom he more adheres. If it will please you
　　　To show us so much gentry° and good will
　　　As to expend your time with us awhile
　　　For the supply and profit of our hope,
25　　Your visitation shall receive such thanks
　　　As fits a king's remembrance.

Rosencrantz.　　　　　　　　Both your Majesties

II.ii.2 *Moreover that* beside the fact that　6 *Sith* since　11 *of so*
from such　12 *youth and havior* behavior in his youth　13 *vouchsafe your rest* consent to remain　18 *opened* revealed　22 *gentry*
courtesy

 Might, by the sovereign power you have of us,
 Put your dread pleasures more into command
 Than to entreaty.

Guildenstern.   But we both obey,
 And here give up ourselves in the full bent°   *80*
 To lay our service freely at your feet,
 To be commanded.

King. Thanks, Rosencrantz and gentle Guildenstern.

Queen. Thanks, Guildenstern and gentle Rosencrantz.
 And I beseech you instantly to visit   *35*
 My too much changèd son. Go, some of you,
 And bring these gentlemen where Hamlet is.

Guildenstern. Heavens make our presence and our
   practices
 Pleasant and helpful to him!

Queen.   Ay, amen!
  Exeunt Rosencrantz and Guildenstern [with some
           Attendants].

     Enter Polonius.

Polonius. Th' ambassadors from Norway, my good
   lord,
 Are joyfully returned.   *40*

King. Thou still° hast been the father of good news.

Polonius. Have I, my lord? Assure you, my good liege,
 I hold my duty, as I hold my soul,
 Both to my God and to my gracious king;   *45*
 And I do think, or else this brain of mine
 Hunts not the trail of policy so sure°
 As it hath used to do, that I have found
 The very cause of Hamlet's lunacy.

King. O, speak of that! That do I long to hear.   *50*

Polonius. Give first admittance to th' ambassadors.
 My news shall be the fruit to that great feast.

30 *in the full bent* entirely (the figure is of a bow bent to its
capacity) 42 *still* always 47 *Hunts not . . . so sure* does not
follow clues of political doings with such sureness

King. Thyself do grace to them and bring them in.
[*Exit Polonius.*]
He tells me, my dear Gertrude, he hath found
55 The head and source of all your son's distemper.

Queen. I doubt° it is no other but the main,°
His father's death and our o'erhasty marriage.

King. Well, we shall sift him.

Enter Polonius, Voltemand, and Cornelius.

Welcome, my good friends.
Say, Voltemand, what from our brother Norway?

60 *Voltemand.* Most fair return of greetings and desires.
Upon our first,° he sent out to suppress
His nephew's levies, which to him appeared
To be a preparation 'gainst the Polack;
But better looked into, he truly found
65 It was against your Highness, whereat grieved,
That so his sickness, age, and impotence
Was falsely borne in hand,° sends out arrests
On Fortinbras; which he, in brief, obeys,
Receives rebuke from Norway, and in fine,°
70 Makes vow before his uncle never more
To give th' assay° of arms against your Majesty.
Whereon old Norway, overcome with joy,
Gives him threescore thousand crowns in annual fee
And his commission to employ those soldiers,
75 So levied as before, against the Polack,
With an entreaty, herein further shown,
[*Gives a paper.*]
That it might please you to give quiet pass
Through your dominions for this enterprise,
On such regards of safety and allowance°
As therein are set down.

80 *King.*   It likes us well;
And at our more considered time° we'll read,
Answer, and think upon this business.

56 *doubt* suspect 56 *main* principal point 61 *first* first audience
67 *borne in hand* deceived 69 *in fine* finally 71 *assay* trial 79 *regards of safety and allowance* i.e., conditions 81 *considered time*
time proper for considering

Meantime, we thank you for your well-took labor.
Go to your rest; at night we'll feast together.
Most welcome home!　　　　*Exeunt Ambassadors.*

Polonius.　　　　This business is well ended.　　85
My liege and madam, to expostulate°
What majesty should be, what duty is,
Why day is day, night night, and time is time,
Were nothing but to waste night, day, and time.
Therefore, since brevity is the soul of wit,°　　90
And tediousness the limbs and outward flourishes,
I will be brief. Your noble son is mad.
Mad call I it, for, to define true madness,
What is't but to be nothing else but mad?
But let that go.

Queen.　　　　More matter, with less art.　　95

Polonius. Madam, I swear I use no art at all.
That he's mad, 'tis true: 'tis true 'tis pity,
And pity 'tis 'tis true—a foolish figure.°
But farewell it, for I will use no art.
Mad let us grant him then; and now remains　　100
That we find out the cause of this effect,
Or rather say, the cause of this defect,
For this effect defective comes by cause.
Thus it remains, and the remainder thus.
Perpend.°　　　　105
I have a daughter: have, while she is mine,
Who in her duty and obedience, mark,
Hath given me this. Now gather, and surmise.
　　　　　　　　[Reads] the letter.
"To the celestial, and my soul's idol, the most
beautified Ophelia"—　　110
That's an ill phrase, a vile phrase; "beautified" is a
vile phrase. But you shall hear. Thus:
"In her excellent white bosom, these, &c."

Queen. Came this from Hamlet to her?

Polonius. Good madam, stay awhile. I will be faithful.　　115
　　"Doubt thou the stars are fire,

<hr>

86 *expostulate* discuss　90 *wit* wisdom, understanding　98 *figure*
figure of rhetoric　105 *Perpend* consider carefully

Doubt that the sun doth move;
Doubt° truth to be a liar,
But never doubt I love.

120 O dear Ophelia, I am ill at these numbers.° I have
not art to reckon my groans; but that I love thee
best, O most best, believe it. Adieu.
Thine evermore, most dear lady, whilst this
machine° is to him, HAMLET."

125 This in obedience hath my daughter shown me,
And more above° hath his solicitings,
As they fell out by time, by means, and place,
All given to mine ear.

King.   But how hath she
Received his love?

Polonius.   What do you think of me?

130 *King.* As of a man faithful and honorable.

Polonius. I would fain prove so. But what might you
think,
When I had seen this hot love on the wing
(As I perceived it, I must tell you that,
Before my daughter told me), what might you,
135 Or my dear Majesty your Queen here, think,
If I had played the desk or table book,°
Or given my heart a winking,° mute and dumb,
Or looked upon this love with idle sight?
What might you think? No, I went round to work
140 And my young mistress thus I did bespeak:
"Lord Hamlet is a prince, out of thy star.°
This must not be." And then I prescripts gave her,
That she should lock herself from his resort,
Admit no messengers, receive no tokens.
145 Which done, she took the fruits of my advice,
And he, repellèd, a short tale to make,

118 *Doubt* suspect 120 *ill at these numbers* unskilled in verses
124 *machine* complex device (here, his body) 126 *more above* in
addition 136 *played the desk or table book* i.e., been a passive
recipient of secrets 137 *winking* closing of the eyes 141 *star*
sphere

Fell into a sadness, then into a fast,
Thence to a watch,° thence into a weakness,
Thence to a lightness,° and, by this declension,
Into the madness wherein now he raves,   150
And all we mourn for.

King.   Do you think 'tis this?

Queen. It may be, very like.

Polonius. Hath there been such a time, I would fain
  know that,
That I have positively said " 'Tis so,"
When it proved otherwise?

King.   Not that I know.   155

Polonius. [*Pointing to his head and shoulder*] Take
  this from this, if this be otherwise.
If circumstances lead me, I will find
Where truth is hid, though it were hid indeed
Within the center.°

King.   How may we try it further?

Polonius. You know sometimes he walks four hours
  together
Here in the lobby.   160

Queen.   So he does indeed.

Polonius. At such a time I'll loose my daughter to him.
Be you and I behind an arras° then.
Mark the encounter. If he love her not,
And be not from his reason fall'n thereon,   165
Let me be no assistant for a state
But keep a farm and carters.

King.   We will try it.

Enter Hamlet reading on a book.

Queen. But look where sadly the poor wretch comes
  reading.

Polonius. Away, I do beseech you both, away.

                    Exit King and Queen.

148 *watch* wakefulness   149 *lightness* mental derangement
159 *center* center of the earth   163 *arras* tapestry hanging in front
of a wall

170   I'll board him presently.° O, give me leave.
        How does my good Lord Hamlet?

Hamlet. Well, God-a-mercy.

Polonius. Do you know me, my lord?

Hamlet. Excellent well. You are a fishmonger.°

175 *Polonius.* Not I, my lord.

Hamlet. Then I would you were so honest a man.

Polonius. Honest, my lord?

Hamlet. Ay, sir. To be honest, as this world goes, is to
        be one man picked out of ten thousand.

180 *Polonius.* That's very true, my lord.

Hamlet. For if the sun breed maggots in a dead dog,
        being a good kissing carrion°—— Have you a
        daughter?

Polonius. I have, my lord.

185 *Hamlet.* Let her not walk i' th' sun. Conception° is a
        blessing, but as your daughter may conceive, friend,
        look to't.

Polonius. [*Aside*] How say you by that? Still harping
        on my daughter. Yet he knew me not at first. 'A said
190   I was a fishmonger. 'A is far gone, far gone. And
        truly in my youth I suffered much extremity for
        love, very near this. I'll speak to him again.—What
        do you read, my lord?

Hamlet. Words, words, words.

195 *Polonius.* What is the matter, my lord?

Hamlet. Between who?

Polonius. I mean the matter° that you read, my lord.

170 *board him presently* accost him at once   174 *fishmonger* dealer
in fish (slang for a procurer)   182 *a good kissing carrion* (perhaps
the meaning is "a good piece of flesh to kiss," but many editors
emend *good* to *god*, taking the word to refer to the sun)   185 *Conception* (1) understanding (2) becoming pregnant   197 *matter*
(Polonius means "subject matter," but Hamlet pretends to take
the word in the sense of "quarrel")

Hamlet. Slanders, sir; for the satirical rogue says here
　　that old men have gray beards, that their faces are
　　wrinkled, their eyes purging thick amber and plum- 200
　　tree gum, and that they have a plentiful lack of wit,
　　together with most weak hams. All which, sir,
　　though I most powerfully and potently believe, yet
　　I hold it not honesty° to have it thus set down; for
　　you yourself, sir, should be old as I am if, like a 205
　　crab, you could go backward.

Polonius. [*Aside*] Though this be madness, yet there
　　is method in't. Will you walk out of the air, my lord?

Hamlet. Into my grave.

Polonius. Indeed, that's out of the air. [*Aside*] How 210
　　pregnant° sometimes his replies are! A happiness°
　　that often madness hits on, which reason and sanity
　　could not so prosperously be delivered of. I will
　　leave him and suddenly contrive the means of
　　meeting between him and my daughter.—My lord, 215
　　I will take my leave of you.

Hamlet. You cannot take from me anything that I will
　　more willingly part withal—except my life, except
　　my life, except my life.

　　　　　Enter Guildenstern and Rosencrantz.

Polonius. Fare you well, my lord.   220

Hamlet. These tedious old fools!

Polonius. You go to seek the Lord Hamlet? There he
　　is.

Rosencrantz. [*To Polonius*] God save you, sir!
　　　　　　　　　　　　　　[*Exit Polonius.*]

Guildenstern. My honored lord!   225

Rosencrantz. My most dear lord!

Hamlet. My excellent good friends! How dost thou,
　　Guildenstern? Ah, Rosencrantz! Good lads, how do
　　you both?

204 *honesty* decency   211 *pregnant* meaningful   211 *happiness* apt
turn of phrase

230 *Rosencrantz.* As the indifferent° children of the earth.

Guildenstern. Happy in that we are not overhappy.
On Fortune's cap we are not the very button.

Hamlet. Nor the soles of her shoe?

Rosencrantz. Neither, my lord.

235 *Hamlet.* Then you live about her waist, or in the middle
of her favors?

Guildenstern. Faith, her privates° we.

Hamlet. In the secret parts of Fortune? O, most true!
She is a strumpet. What news?

240 *Rosencrantz.* None, my lord, but that the world's
grown honest.

Hamlet. Then is doomsday near. But your news is not
true. Let me question more in particular. What
have you, my good friends, deserved at the hands of
245 Fortune that she sends you to prison hither?

Guildenstern. Prison, my lord?

Hamlet. Denmark's a prison.

Rosencrantz. Then is the world one.

Hamlet. A goodly one, in which there are many
250 confines, wards,° and dungeons, Denmark being
one o' th' worst.

Rosencrantz. We think not so, my lord.

Hamlet. Why, then 'tis none to you, for there is nothing
either good or bad but thinking makes it so. To me
255 it is a prison.

Rosencrantz. Why then your ambition makes it one.
'Tis too narrow for your mind.

Hamlet. O God, I could be bounded in a nutshell and
count myself a king of infinite space, were it not
260 that I have bad dreams.

Guildenstern. Which dreams indeed are ambition, for

230 *indifferent* ordinary   237 *privates* ordinary men (with a pun
on "private parts")   250 *wards* cells

the very substance of the ambitious is merely the shadow of a dream.

Hamlet. A dream itself is but a shadow.

Rosencrantz. Truly, and I hold ambition of so airy and 265 light a quality that it is but a shadow's shadow.

Hamlet. Then are our beggars bodies, and our monarchs and outstretched heroes the beggars' shadows.° Shall we to th' court? For, by my fay,° I cannot reason.　　　　　270

Both. We'll wait upon you.

Hamlet. No such matter. I will not sort you with the rest of my servants, for, to speak to you like an honest man, I am most dreadfully attended. But in the beaten way of friendship, what make you at 275 Elsinore?

Rosencrantz. To visit you, my lord; no other occasion.

Hamlet. Beggar that I am, I am even poor in thanks, but I thank you; and sure, dear friends, my thanks are too dear a halfpenny.° Were you not sent for? 280 Is it your own inclining? Is it a free visitation? Come, come, deal justly with me. Come, come; nay, speak.

Guildenstern. What should we say, my lord?

Hamlet. Why anything—but to th' purpose. You were 285 sent for, and there is a kind of confession in your looks, which your modesties have not craft enough to color. I know the good King and Queen have sent for you.

Rosencrantz. To what end, my lord?　　　　　290

Hamlet. That you must teach me. But let me conjure you by the rights of our fellowship, by the consonancy of our youth, by the obligation of our ever-

---

267—69 *Then are . . . beggars' shadows* i.e., by your logic, beggars (lacking ambition) are substantial, and great men are elongated shadows　269 *fay* faith　280 *too dear a halfpenny* i.e., not worth a halfpenny

preserved love, and by what more dear a better
295 proposer can charge you withal, be even and direct
with me, whether you were sent for or no.

Rosencrantz. [*Aside to Guildenstern*] What say you?

Hamlet. [*Aside*] Nay then, I have an eye of you.—If
you love me, hold not off.

300 *Guildenstern.* My lord, we were sent for.

Hamlet. I will tell you why; so shall my anticipation
prevent your discovery,° and your secrecy to the
King and Queen molt no feather. I have of late, but
wherefore I know not, lost all my mirth, forgone all
305 custom of exercises; and indeed, it goes so heavily
with my disposition that this goodly frame, the
earth, seems to me a sterile promontory; this most
excellent canopy, the air, look you, this brave
o'erhanging firmament, this majestical roof fretted°
310 with golden fire: why, it appeareth nothing to me
but a foul and pestilent congregation of vapors.
What a piece of work is a man, how noble in reason,
how infinite in faculties, in form and moving how
express° and admirable, in action how like an angel,
315 in apprehension how like a god: the beauty of the
world, the paragon of animals; and yet to me, what
is this quintessence of dust? Man delights not me;
nor woman neither, though by your smiling you
seem to say so.

320 *Rosencrantz.* My lord, there was no such stuff in my
thoughts.

Hamlet. Why did ye laugh then, when I said "Man
delights not me"?

Rosencrantz. To think, my lord, if you delight not in
325 man, what lenten° entertainment the players shall
receive from you. We coted° them on the way, and
hither are they coming to offer you service.

302 *prevent your discovery* forestall your disclosure 309 *fretted*
adorned 314 *express* exact 325 *lenten* meager 326 *coted* overtook

Hamlet. He that plays the king shall be welcome; his
Majesty shall have tribute of me; the adventurous
knight shall use his foil and target;° the lover shall 330
not sigh gratis; the humorous man° shall end his
part in peace; the clown shall make those laugh
whose lungs are tickle o' th' sere;° and the lady shall
say her mind freely, or° the blank verse shall halt°
for't. What players are they? 335

Rosencrantz. Even those you were wont to take such
delight in, the tragedians of the city.

Hamlet. How chances it they travel? Their residence,
both in reputation and profit, was better both ways.

Rosencrantz. I think their inhibition° comes by the 340
means of the late innovation.°

Hamlet. Do they hold the same estimation they did
when I was in the city? Are they so followed?

Rosencrantz. No indeed, are they not.

Hamlet. How comes it? Do they grow rusty? 345

Rosencrantz. Nay, their endeavor keeps in the wonted
pace, but there is, sir, an eyrie° of children, little
eyases, that cry out on the top of question° and are
most tyrannically° clapped for't. These are now
the fashion, and so berattle the common stages° (so 350
they call them) that many wearing rapiers are afraid
of goosequills° and dare scarce come thither.

Hamlet. What, are they children? Who maintains 'em?
How are they escoted?° Will they pursue the

330 *target* shield 331 *humorous man* i.e., eccentric man (among
stock characters in dramas were men dominated by a "humor" or
odd trait) 333 *tickle o' th' sere* on hair trigger (*sere* = part of the
gunlock) 334 *or* else 334 *halt* limp 340 *inhibition* hindrance
341 *innovation* (probably an allusion to the companies of child
actors that had become popular and were offering serious compe-
tition to the adult actors) 347 *eyrie* nest 348 *eyases, that . . .
of question* unfledged hawks that cry shrilly above others in matters of debate 349 *tyrannically* violently 350 *berattle the common stages* cry down the public theaters (with the adult acting
companies) 352 *goosequills* pens (of satirists who ridicule the
public theaters and their audiences) 354 *escoted* financially supported

355   quality° no longer than they can sing? Will they not
      say afterwards, if they should grow themselves to
      common players (as it is most like, if their means
      are no better), their writers do them wrong to make
      them exclaim against their own succession?°

360 *Rosencrantz.* Faith, there has been much to-do on
      both sides, and the nation holds it no sin to tarre°
      them to controversy. There was, for a while, no
      money bid for argument° unless the poet and the
      player went to cuffs in the question.

365 *Hamlet.* Is't possible?

Guildenstern. O, there has been much throwing about
      of brains.

Hamlet. Do the boys carry it away?

Rosencrantz. Ay, that they do, my lord—Hercules and
370   his load° too.

Hamlet. It is not very strange, for my uncle is King of
      Denmark, and those that would make mouths at
      him while my father lived give twenty, forty, fifty,
      a hundred ducats apiece for his picture in little.
375   'Sblood,° there is something in this more than
      natural, if philosophy could find it out.

                                           A flourish.

Guildenstern. There are the players.

Hamlet. Gentlemen, you are welcome to Elsinore.
      Your hands, come then. Th' appurtenance of wel-
380   come is fashion and ceremony. Let me comply°
      with you in this garb,° lest my extent° to the players
      (which I tell you must show fairly outwards) should
      more appear like entertainment than yours. You are
      welcome. But my uncle-father and aunt-mother are
385   deceived.

355 *quality* profession of acting   359 *succession* future   361 *tarre*
incite   363 *argument* plot of a play   369–70 *Hercules and his load*
i.e., the whole world (with a reference to the Globe Theatre, which
had a sign that represented Hercules bearing the globe)   375
'*Sblood* by God's blood   380 *comply* be courteous   381 *garb* outward show   381 *extent* behavior

Guildenstern. In what, my dear lord?

Hamlet. I am but mad north-northwest:° when the
wind is southerly I know a hawk from a handsaw.°

Enter Polonius.

Polonius. Well be with you, gentlemen.

Hamlet. Hark you, Guildenstern, and you too; at each   390
ear a hearer. That great baby you see there is not
yet out of his swaddling clouts.

Rosencrantz. Happily° he is the second time come to
them, for they say an old man is twice a child.

Hamlet. I will prophesy he comes to tell me of the   395
players. Mark it.—You say right, sir; a Monday
morning, 'twas then indeed.

Polonius. My lord, I have news to tell you.

Hamlet. My lord, I have news to tell you. When
Roscius° was an actor in Rome——   400

Polonius. The actors are come hither, my lord.

Hamlet. Buzz, buzz.°

Polonius. Upon my honor——

Hamlet. Then came each actor on his ass——

Polonius. The best actors in the world, either for   405
tragedy, comedy, history, pastoral, pastoral-comical,
historical-pastoral, tragical-historical, tragical-comical-historical-pastoral; scene individable,° or poem
unlimited.° Seneca° cannot be too heavy, nor
Plautus° too light. For the law of writ and the   410
liberty,° these are the only men.

387 *north-northwest* i.e., on one point of the compass only
388 *hawk from a handsaw* (*hawk* can refer not only to a bird
but to a kind of pickax; *handsaw*—a carpenter's tool—may involve a similar pun on "hernshaw," a heron)   393 *Happily* perhaps
400 *Roscius* (a famous Roman comic actor)   402 *Buzz, buzz* (an
interjection, perhaps indicating that the news is old)   408 *scene
individable* plays observing the unities of time, place, and action
408–09 *poem unlimited* plays not restricted by the tenets of criticism   409 *Seneca* (Roman tragic dramatist)   410 *Plautus* (Roman
comic dramatist)   410–11 *For the law of writ and the liberty*
(perhaps "for sticking to the text and for improvising"; perhaps
"for classical plays and for modern loosely written plays")

Hamlet. O Jeptha, judge of Israel,° what a treasure
hadst thou!

Polonius. What a treasure had he, my lord?

415 *Hamlet.* Why,
                    "One fair daughter, and no more,
                        The which he lovèd passing well."

Polonius. [*Aside*] Still on my daughter.

Hamlet. Am I not i' th' right, old Jeptha?

420 *Polonius.* If you call me Jeptha, my lord, I have a
daughter that I love passing well.

Hamlet. Nay, that follows not.

Polonius. What follows then, my lord?

Hamlet. Why,
425   "As by lot, God wot,"
and then, you know,
                    "It came to pass, as most like it was."
The first row of the pious chanson° will show you
more, for look where my abridgment° comes.

Enter the Players.

430 You are welcome, masters, welcome, all. I am glad
to see thee well. Welcome, good friends. O, old
friend, why, thy face is valanced° since I saw thee
last. Com'st thou to beard me in Denmark? What,
my young lady° and mistress? By'r Lady, your
435 ladyship is nearer to heaven than when I saw you
last by the altitude of a chopine.° Pray God your
voice, like a piece of uncurrent gold, be not cracked
within the ring.°—Masters, you are all welcome.
We'll e'en to't like French falconers, fly at any-

412 *Jeptha, judge of Israel* (the title of a ballad on the Hebrew
judge who sacrificed his daughter; see Judges 11)   428 *row of
the pious chanson* stanza of the scriptural song   429 *abridgment*
(1) i.e., entertainers, who abridge the time (2) interrupters
432 *valanced* fringed (with a beard)   434 *young lady* i.e., boy
for female roles   436 *chopine* thick-soled shoe   437–38 *like a
piece . . . the ring* (a coin was unfit for legal tender if a crack
extended from the edge through the ring enclosing the monarch's
head. Hamlet, punning on *ring*, refers to the change of voice that
the boy actor will undergo)

thing we see. We'll have a speech straight. Come, *440*
give us a taste of your quality. Come, a passionate
speech.

Player. What speech, my good lord?

Hamlet. I heard thee speak me a speech once, but it
was never acted, or if it was, not above once, for *445*
the play, I remember, pleased not the million; 'twas
caviary to the general,° but it was (as I received it,
and others, whose judgments in such matters cried
in the top of° mine) an excellent play, well digested
in the scenes, set down with as much modesty as *450*
cunning.° I remember one said there were no
sallets° in the lines to make the matter savory;
nor no matter in the phrase that might indict the
author of affectation, but called it an honest method,
as wholesome as sweet, and by very much more *455*
handsome than fine.° One speech in't I chiefly loved.
'Twas Aeneas' tale to Dido, and thereabout of it
especially when he speaks of Priam's slaughter. If
it live in your memory, begin at this line—let me
see, let me see: *460*
        "The rugged Pyrrhus, like th' Hyrcanian
                beast°——"
'Tis not so; it begins with Pyrrhus:
        "The rugged Pyrrhus, he whose sable° arms,
        Black as his purpose, did the night resemble
        When he lay couchèd in th' ominous horse,° *465*
        Hath now this dread and black complexion
                smeared
        With heraldry more dismal.° Head to foot
        Now is he total gules, horridly tricked°
        With blood of fathers, mothers, daughters, sons,
        Baked and impasted° with the parching streets, *470*

447 *caviary to the general* i.e., too choice for the multitude 449 *in the top of* overtopping 450–51 *modesty as cunning* restraint as art 452 *sallets* salads, spicy jests 455–56 *more handsome than fine* well-proportioned rather than ornamented 461 *Hyrcanian beast* i.e., tiger (Hyrcania was in Asia) 463 *sable* black 465 *ominous horse* i.e., wooden horse at the siege of Troy 467 *dismal* ill-omened 468 *total gules, horridly tricked* all red, horridly adorned 470 *impasted* encrusted

That lend a tyrannous and a damnèd light
To their lord's murder. Roasted in wrath and fire,
And thus o'ersizèd° with coagulate gore,
With eyes like carbuncles, the hellish Pyrrhus
475   Old grandsire Priam seeks."
So, proceed you.

Polonius. Fore God, my lord, well spoken, with good
    accent and good discretion.

Player.   "Anon he finds him,
480   Striking too short at Greeks. His antique sword,
Rebellious to his arm, lies where it falls,
Repugnant to command.° Unequal matched,
Pyrrhus at Priam drives, in rage strikes wide,
But with the whiff and wind of his fell sword
485   Th' unnervèd father falls. Then senseless Ilium,°
Seeming to feel this blow, with flaming top
Stoops to his base,° and with a hideous crash
Takes prisoner Pyrrhus' ear. For lo, his sword,
Which was declining on the milky head
490   Of reverend Priam, seemed i' th' air to stick.
So as a painted tyrant° Pyrrhus stood,
And like a neutral to his will and matter°
Did nothing.
But as we often see, against° some storm,
495   A silence in the heavens, the rack° stand still,
The bold winds speechless, and the orb below
As hush as death, anon the dreadful thunder
Doth rend the region, so after Pyrrhus' pause,
A rousèd vengeance sets him new awork,
500   And never did the Cyclops' hammers fall
On Mars's armor, forged for proof eterne,°
With less remorse than Pyrrhus' bleeding sword
Now falls on Priam.
Out, out, thou strumpet Fortune! All you gods,
505   In general synod° take away her power,

473 *o'ersizèd* smeared over   482 *Repugnant to command* diso-
bedient   485 *senseless Ilium* insensate Troy   487 *Stoops to his
base* collapses (*his* = its)   491 *painted tyrant* tyrant in a picture
492 *matter* task   494 *against* just before   495 *rack* clouds
501 *proof eterne* eternal endurance   505 *synod* council

Break all the spokes and fellies° from her wheel,
And bowl the round nave° down the hill of
  heaven,
As low as to the fiends."

Polonius. This is too long.

Hamlet. It shall to the barber's, with your beard.— 510
Prithee say on. He's for a jig or a tale of bawdry,
or he sleeps. Say on; come to Hecuba.

Player. "But who (ah woe!) had seen the mobled°
  queen——"

Hamlet. "The mobled queen"?

Polonius. That's good. "Mobled queen" is good.   515

Player. "Run barefoot up and down, threat'ning the
  flames
With bisson rheum;° a clout° upon that head
Where late the diadem stood, and for a robe,
About her lank and all o'erteemèd° loins,
A blanket in the alarm of fear caught up—   520
Who this had seen, with tongue in venom steeped
'Gainst Fortune's state would treason have pro-
  nounced.
But if the gods themselves did see her then,
When she saw Pyrrhus make malicious sport
In mincing with his sword her husband's limbs,   525
The instant burst of clamor that she made
(Unless things mortal move them not at all)
Would have made milch° the burning eyes of
  heaven
And passion in the gods."

Polonius. Look, whe'r° he has not turned his color, 530
and has tears in's eyes. Prithee no more.

Hamlet. 'Tis well. I'll have thee speak out the rest of
this soon. Good my lord, will you see the players
well bestowed?° Do you hear? Let them be well

506 *fellies* rims 507 *nave* hub 513 *mobled* muffled 517 *bisson
rheum* blinding tears 517 *clout* rag 519 *o'erteemèd* exhausted
with childbearing 528 *milch* moist (literally, "milk-giving")
530 *whe'r* whether 534 *bestowed* housed

535   used, for they are the abstract and brief chronicles
of the time. After your death you were better have
a bad epitaph than their ill report while you live.

Polonius. My lord, I will use them according to their
desert.

540 *Hamlet.* God's bodkin,° man, much better! Use every
man after his desert, and who shall scape whipping?
Use them after your own honor and dignity. The
less they deserve, the more merit is in your bounty.
Take them in.

545 *Polonius.* Come, sirs.

Hamlet. Follow him, friends. We'll hear a play tomorrow. [*Aside to Player*] Dost thou hear me, old
friend? Can you play *The Murder of Gonzago*?

Player. Ay, my lord.

550 *Hamlet.* We'll ha't tomorrow night. You could for a
need study a speech of some dozen or sixteen lines
which I would set down and insert in't, could you
not?

Player. Ay, my lord.

555 *Hamlet.* Very well. Follow that lord, and look you
mock him not. My good friends, I'll leave you till
night. You are welcome to Elsinore.

                    Exeunt Polonius and Players.

Rosencrantz. Good my lord.
                    Exeunt [Rosencrantz and Guildenstern].

Hamlet. Ay, so, God bye to you.—Now I am alone.
560   O, what a rogue and peasant slave am I!
Is it not monstrous that this player here,
But in a fiction, in a dream of passion,°
Could force his soul so to his own conceit°
That from her working all his visage wanned,
565   Tears in his eyes, distraction in his aspect,
A broken voice, and his whole function° suiting

540 *God's bodkin* by God's little body   562 *dream of passion*
imaginary emotion   563 *conceit* imagination   566 *function* action

With forms° to his conceit? And all for nothing!
For Hecuba!
What's Hecuba to him, or he to Hecuba,
That he should weep for her? What would he do   570
Had he the motive and the cue for passion
That I have? He would drown the stage with tears
And cleave the general ear with horrid speech,
Make mad the guilty and appall the free,°
Confound the ignorant, and amaze indeed   575
The very faculties of eyes and ears.
Yet I,
A dull and muddy-mettled° rascal, peak
Like John-a-dreams,° unpregnant of° my cause,
And can say nothing. No, not for a king,   580
Upon whose property and most dear life
A damned defeat was made. Am I a coward?
Who calls me villain? Breaks my pate across?
Plucks off my beard and blows it in my face?
Tweaks me by the nose? Gives me the lie i' th' throat 585
As deep as to the lungs? Who does me this?
Ha, 'swounds,° I should take it, for it cannot be
But I am pigeon-livered° and lack gall
To make oppression bitter, or ere this
I should ha' fatted all the region kites°   590
With this slave's offal. Bloody, bawdy villain!
Remorseless, treacherous, lecherous, kindless° vil-
    lain!
O, vengeance!
Why, what an ass am I! This is most brave,°
That I, the son of a dear father murdered,   595
Prompted to my revenge by heaven and hell,
Must, like a whore, unpack my heart with words
And fall a-cursing like a very drab,°

567 *forms* bodily expressions   574 *appall the free* terrify
(make pale?) the guiltless   578 *muddy-mettled* weak-spirited
578–79 *peak/Like John-a-dreams* mope like a dreamer   579 *unpregnant of* unquickened by   587 *'swounds* by God's wounds
588 *pigeon-livered* gentle as a dove   590 *region kites* kites (scav-
enger birds) of the sky   592 *kindless* unnatural   594 *brave* fine
598 *drab* prostitute

A stallion!° Fie upon't, foh! About,° my brains.
600 Hum——
I have heard that guilty creatures sitting at a play
Have by the very cunning of the scene
Been struck so to the soul that presently°
They have proclaimed their malefactions.
605 For murder, though it have no tongue, will speak
With most miraculous organ. I'll have these players
Play something like the murder of my father
Before mine uncle. I'll observe his looks,
I'll tent° him to the quick. If 'a do blench,°
610 I know my course. The spirit that I have seen
May be a devil, and the devil hath power
T' assume a pleasing shape, yea, and perhaps
Out of my weakness and my melancholy,
As he is very potent with such spirits,
615 Abuses me to damn me. I'll have grounds
More relative° than this. The play's the thing
Wherein I'll catch the conscience of the King. *Exit.*

599 *stallion* male prostitute (perhaps one should adopt the Folio reading, *scullion* = kitchen wench) 599 *About* to work 603 *presently* immediately 609 *tent* probe 609 *blench* flinch 616 *relative* (probably "pertinent," but possibly "able to be related plausibly")

[ACT III

Scene I. *The castle.*]

Enter King, Queen, Polonius, Ophelia, Rosencrantz,
Guildenstern, Lords.

King. And can you by no drift of conference°
    Get from him why he puts on this confusion,
    Grating so harshly all his days of quiet
    With turbulent and dangerous lunacy?

Rosencrantz. He does confess he feels himself dis-
    tracted,   5
    But from what cause 'a will by no means speak.

Guildenstern. Nor do we find him forward to be
    sounded,°
    But with a crafty madness keeps aloof
    When we would bring him on to some confession
    Of his true state.

Queen.   Did he receive you well?   10

Rosencrantz. Most like a gentleman.

Guildenstern. But with much forcing of his disposi-
    tion.°

Rosencrantz. Niggard of question,° but of our demands
    Most free in his reply.

III.i.1 *drift of conference* management of conversation 7 *forward
to be sounded* willing to be questioned 12 *forcing of his disposition* effort 13 *Niggard of question* uninclined to talk

Queen.   Did you assay° him
15   To any pastime?

Rosencrantz. Madam, it so fell out that certain players
        We o'erraught° on the way; of these we told him,
        And there did seem in him a kind of joy
        To hear of it. They are here about the court,
20   And, as I think, they have already order
        This night to play before him.

Polonius.   'Tis most true,
        And he beseeched me to entreat your Majesties
        To hear and see the matter.

King. With all my heart, and it doth much content me
25   To hear him so inclined.
        Good gentlemen, give him a further edge
        And drive his purpose into these delights.

Rosencrantz. We shall, my lord.
                    Exeunt Rosencrantz and Guildenstern.

King.   Sweet Gertrude, leave us too,
        For we have closely° sent for Hamlet hither,
30   That he, as 'twere by accident, may here
        Affront° Ophelia.
        Her father and myself (lawful espials°)
        Will so bestow ourselves that, seeing unseen,
        We may of their encounter frankly judge
35   And gather by him, as he is behaved,
        If't be th' affliction of his love or no
        That thus he suffers for.

Queen.   I shall obey you.
        And for your part, Ophelia, I do wish
        That your good beauties be the happy cause
40   Of Hamlet's wildness. So shall I hope your virtues
        Will bring him to his wonted way again,
        To both your honors.

Ophelia.   Madam, I wish it may.
                                        [*Exit Queen.*]

14 *assay* tempt   17 *o'erraught* overtook   29 *closely* secretly
31 *Affront* meet face to face   32 *espials* spies

Polonius. Ophelia, walk you here.—Gracious, so please
　　you,
　　We will bestow ourselves. [*To Ophelia*] Read on this
　　　book,
　　That show of such an exercise may color°　　　　　45
　　Your loneliness. We are oft to blame in this,
　　'Tis too much proved, that with devotion's visage
　　And pious action we do sugar o'er
　　The devil himself.

King.　　　　　　　[*Aside*] O, 'tis too true.
　　How smart a lash that speech doth give my con-
　　　science!　　　　　　　　　　　　　　　　50
　　The harlot's cheek, beautied with plast'ring art,
　　Is not more ugly to the thing that helps it
　　Than is my deed to my most painted word.
　　O heavy burden!

Polonius. I hear him coming. Let's withdraw, my lord.　55
　　　　　　　[*Exeunt King and Polonius.*]

　　　　　　　Enter Hamlet.

Hamlet. To be, or not to be: that is the question:
　　Whether 'tis nobler in the mind to suffer
　　The slings and arrows of outrageous fortune,
　　Or to take arms against a sea of troubles,
　　And by opposing end them. To die, to sleep—　　60
　　No more—and by a sleep to say we end
　　The heartache, and the thousand natural shocks
　　That flesh is heir to! 'Tis a consummation
　　Devoutly to be wished. To die, to sleep—
　　To sleep—perchance to dream: ay, there's the rub,°　65
　　For in that sleep of death what dreams may come
　　When we have shuffled off this mortal coil,°
　　Must give us pause. There's the respect°
　　That makes calamity of so long life:°
　　For who would bear the whips and scorns of time,　70

45 *exercise may color* act of devotion may give a plausible hue to
(the book is one of devotion)　65 *rub* impediment (obstruction
to a bowler's ball)　67 *coil* (1) turmoil (2) a ring of rope (here
the flesh encircling the soul)　68 *respect* consideration　69 *makes
calamity of so long life* (1) makes calamity so long-lived (2)
makes living so long a calamity

Th' oppressor's wrong, the proud man's contumely,
The pangs of despised love, the law's delay,
The insolence of office, and the spurns
That patient merit of th' unworthy takes,
75   When he himself might his quietus° make
With a bare bodkin?° Who would fardels° bear,
To grunt and sweat under a weary life,
But that the dread of something after death,
The undiscovered country, from whose bourn°
80   No traveler returns, puzzles the will,
And makes us rather bear those ills we have,
Than fly to others that we know not of?
Thus conscience° does make cowards of us all,
And thus the native hue of resolution
85   Is sicklied o'er with the pale cast° of thought,
And enterprises of great pitch° and moment,
With this regard° their currents turn awry,
And lose the name of action.—Soft you now,
The fair Ophelia!—Nymph, in thy orisons°
Be all my sins remembered.

90   *Ophelia.*   Good my lord,
How does your honor for this many a day?

Hamlet. I humbly thank you; well, well, well.

Ophelia. My lord, I have remembrances of yours
That I have longèd long to redeliver.
I pray you now, receive them.

95   *Hamlet.*   No, not I,
I never gave you aught.

Ophelia. My honored lord, you know right well you
        did,
And with them words of so sweet breath composed
As made these things more rich. Their perfume lost,
100   Take these again, for to the noble mind

75 *quietus* full discharge (a legal term) 76 *bodkin* dagger 76 *fardels* burdens 79 *bourn* region 83 *conscience* self-consciousness, introspection 85 *cast* color 86 *pitch* height (a term from falconry) 87 *regard* consideration 89 *orisons* prayers

Rich gifts wax poor when givers prove unkind.
There, my lord.

Hamlet. Ha, ha! Are you honest?°

Ophelia. My lord?

Hamlet. Are you fair?   *105*

Ophelia. What means your lordship?

Hamlet. That if you be honest and fair, your honesty
should admit no discourse to your beauty.°

Ophelia. Could beauty, my lord, have better commerce
than with honesty?   *110*

Hamlet. Ay, truly; for the power of beauty will sooner
transform honesty from what it is to a bawd° than
the force of honesty can translate beauty into his
likeness. This was sometime a paradox, but now
the time gives it proof. I did love you once.   *115*

Ophelia. Indeed, my lord, you made me believe so.

Hamlet. You should not have believed me, for virtue
cannot so inoculate° our old stock but we shall relish
of it.° I loved you not.

Ophelia. I was the more deceived.   *120*

Hamlet. Get thee to a nunnery. Why wouldst thou be
a breeder of sinners? I am myself indifferent honest,°
but yet I could accuse me of such things that it were
better my mother had not borne me: I am very
proud, revengeful, ambitious, with more offenses at   *125*
my beck° than I have thoughts to put them in,
imagination to give them shape, or time to act them
in. What should such fellows as I do crawling between earth and heaven? We are arrant knaves all;
believe none of us. Go thy ways to a nunnery.   *130*
Where's your father?

103 *Are you honest* (1) are you modest (2) are you chaste (3)
have you integrity   107–08 *your honesty . . . to your beauty*
your modesty should permit no approach to your beauty
112 *bawd* procurer   118 *inoculate* graft   118–19 *relish of it* smack
of it (our old sinful nature)   122 *indifferent honest* moderately
virtuous   126 *beck* call

Ophelia. At home, my lord.

Hamlet. Let the doors be shut upon him, that he may
    play the fool nowhere but in's own house. Farewell.

135 *Ophelia.* O help him, you sweet heavens!

Hamlet. If thou dost marry, I'll give thee this plague
    for thy dowry: be thou as chaste as ice, as pure as
    snow, thou shalt not escape calumny. Get thee to a
    nunnery. Go, farewell. Or if thou wilt needs marry,
140   marry a fool, for wise men know well enough what
    monsters° you make of them. To a nunnery, go,
    and quickly too. Farewell.

Ophelia. Heavenly powers, restore him!

Hamlet. I have heard of your paintings, well enough.
145   God hath given you one face, and you make your-
    selves another. You jig and amble, and you lisp;
    you nickname God's creatures and make your
    wantonness your ignorance.° Go to, I'll no more
    on't; it hath made me mad. I say we will have no
150   moe° marriage. Those that are married already—all
    but one—shall live. The rest shall keep as they are.
    To a nunnery, go.   *Exit.*

Ophelia. O what a noble mind is here o'erthrown!
    The courtier's, soldier's, scholar's, eye, tongue, sword,
155   Th' expectancy and rose° of the fair state,
    The glass of fashion, and the mold of form,°
    Th' observed of all observers, quite, quite down!
    And I, of ladies most deject and wretched,
    That sucked the honey of his musicked vows,
160   Now see that noble and most sovereign reason
    Like sweet bells jangled, out of time and harsh,
    That unmatched form and feature of blown° youth
    Blasted with ecstasy.° O, woe is me
    T' have seen what I have seen, see what I see!

          Enter King and Polonius.

141 *monsters* horned beasts, cuckolds 147–48 *make your wan-
tonness your ignorance* excuse your wanton speech by pretending
ignorance 150 *moe* more 155 *expectancy and rose* i.e., fair hope
156 *The glass . . . of form* the mirror of fashion, and the pattern
of excellent behavior 162 *blown* blooming 163 *ecstasy* madness

King. Love? His affections° do not that way tend,   165
   Nor what he spake, though it lacked form a little,
   Was not like madness. There's something in his soul
   O'er which his melancholy sits on brood,
   And I do doubt° the hatch and the disclose
   Will be some danger; which for to prevent,   170
   I have in quick determination
   Thus set it down: he shall with speed to England
   For the demand of our neglected tribute.
   Haply the seas, and countries different,
   With variable objects, shall expel   175
   This something-settled° matter in his heart,
   Whereon his brains still beating puts him thus
   From fashion of himself. What think you on't?

Polonius. It shall do well. But yet do I believe
   The origin and commencement of his grief   180
   Sprung from neglected love. How now, Ophelia?
   You need not tell us what Lord Hamlet said;
   We heard it all. My lord, do as you please,
   But if you hold it fit, after the play,
   Let his queen mother all alone entreat him   185
   To show his grief. Let her be round° with him,
   And I'll be placed, so please you, in the ear
   Of all their conference. If she find him not,°
   To England send him, or confine him where
   Your wisdom best shall think.

King.   It shall be so.   190
   Madness in great ones must not unwatched go.
                                        Exeunt.

165 *affections* inclinations 169 *doubt* fear 176 *something-settled* somewhat settled 186 *round* blunt 188 *find him not* does not find him out

[Scene II. *The castle.*]

Enter Hamlet and three of the Players.

Hamlet. Speak the speech, I pray you, as I pronounced
it to you, trippingly on the tongue. But if you mouth
it, as many of our players do, I had as lief the town
crier spoke my lines. Nor do not saw the air too much
5   with your hand, thus, but use all gently, for in the
very torrent, tempest, and (as I may say) whirlwind
of your passion, you must acquire and beget a temperance that may give it smoothness. O, it offends
me to the soul to hear a robustious periwig-pated°
10 fellow tear a passion to tatters, to very rags, to split
the ears of the groundlings,° who for the most part
are capable of° nothing but inexplicable dumb
shows° and noise. I would have such a fellow
whipped for o'erdoing Termagant. It out-herods
15 Herod.° Pray you avoid it.

Player. I warrant your honor.

Hamlet. Be not too tame neither, but let your own discretion be your tutor. Suit the action to the word, the
word to the action, with this special observance, that
20 you o'erstep not the modesty of nature. For anything
so o'erdone is from° the purpose of playing, whose
end, both at the first and now, was and is, to hold,
as 'twere, the mirror up to nature; to show virtue
her own feature, scorn her own image, and the very
25 age and body of the time his form and pressure.°

III.ii.9 *robustious periwig-pated* boisterous wig-headed 11 *groundlings* those who stood in the pit of the theater (the poorest and
presumably most ignorant of the audience) 12 *are capable of*
are able to understand 12–13 *dumb shows* (it had been the
fashion for actors to preface plays or parts of plays with silent
mime) 14–15 *Termagant . . . Herod* (boisterous characters in
the old mystery plays) 21 *from* contrary to 25 *pressure* image,
impress

Now, this overdone, or come tardy off, though it
makes the unskillful laugh, cannot but make the
judicious grieve, the censure of the which one must
in your allowance o'erweigh a whole theater of
others. O, there be players that I have seen play,   30
and heard others praise, and that highly (not to
speak it profanely), that neither having th' accent of
Christians, nor the gait of Christian, pagan, nor
man, have so strutted and bellowed that I have
thought some of Nature's journeymen° had made   35
men, and not made them well, they imitated humanity so abominably.

Player. I hope we have reformed that indifferently°
with us, sir.

Hamlet. O, reform it altogether! And let those that   40
play your clowns speak no more than is set down
for them, for there be of them that will themselves
laugh, to set on some quantity of barren spectators to
laugh too, though in the meantime some necessary
question of the play be then to be considered. That's   45
villainous and shows a most pitiful ambition in the
fool that uses it. Go make you ready.

Exit Players.

Enter Polonius, Guildenstern, and Rosencrantz.

How now, my lord? Will the King hear this piece of
work?

Polonius. And the Queen too, and that presently.   50

Hamlet. Bid the players make haste.   *Exit Polonius.*
Will you two help to hasten them?

Rosencrantz. Ay, my lord.   *Exeunt they two.*

Hamlet. What, ho, Horatio!

Enter Horatio.

Horatio. Here, sweet lord, at your service.   55

Hamlet. Horatio, thou art e'en as just a man

35 *journeymen* workers not yet masters of their craft   38 *indif-
ferently* tolerably

As e'er my conversation coped withal.°

Horatio. O, my dear lord——

Hamlet.   Nay, do not think I flatter.
For what advancement° may I hope from thee,
60   That no revenue hast but thy good spirits
To feed and clothe thee? Why should the poor be
     flattered?
No, let the candied° tongue lick absurd pomp,
And crook the pregnant° hinges of the knee
Where thrift° may follow fawning. Dost thou hear?
65   Since my dear soul was mistress of her choice
And could of men distinguish her election,
S' hath sealed thee° for herself, for thou hast been
As one, in suff'ring all, that suffers nothing,
A man that Fortune's buffets and rewards
70   Hast ta'en with equal thanks; and blest are those
Whose blood° and judgment are so well com-
     meddled°
That they are not a pipe for Fortune's finger
To sound what stop she please. Give me that man
That is not passion's slave, and I will wear him
75   In my heart's core, ay, in my heart of heart,
As I do thee. Something too much of this—
There is a play tonight before the King.
One scene of it comes near the circumstance
Which I have told thee, of my father's death.
80   I prithee, when thou seest that act afoot,
Even with the very comment° of thy soul
Observe my uncle. If his occulted° guilt
Do not itself unkennel in one speech,
It is a damnèd ghost that we have seen,
85   And my imaginations are as foul
As Vulcan's stithy.° Give him heedful note,
For I mine eyes will rivet to his face,

---

57 *coped withal* met with   59 *advancement* promotion   62 *candied*
sugared, flattering   63 *pregnant* (1) pliant (2) full of promise of
good fortune   64 *thrift* profit   67 *S' hath sealed thee* she (the
soul) has set a mark on you   71 *blood* passion   71 *commeddled*
blended   81 *very comment* deepest wisdom   82 *occulted* hidden
86 *stithy* forge, smithy

And after we will both our judgments join
In censure of his seeming.°

Horatio.   Well, my lord.
If 'a steal aught the whilst this play is playing,   90
And scape detecting, I will pay the theft.

*Enter Trumpets and Kettledrums, King, Queen,
Polonius, Ophelia, Rosencrantz, Guildenstern,
and other Lords attendant with his Guard carrying
torches. Danish March. Sound a Flourish.*

Hamlet. They are coming to the play: I must be idle;°
Get you a place.

King. How fares our cousin Hamlet?

Hamlet. Excellent, i' faith, of the chameleon's dish;°   95
I eat the air, promise-crammed; you cannot feed
capons so.

King. I have nothing with this answer, Hamlet; these
words are not mine.

Hamlet. No, nor mine now. [*To Polonius*] My lord, you   101
played once i' th' university, you say?

Polonius. That did I, my lord, and was accounted a good
actor.

Hamlet. What did you enact?

Polonius. I did enact Julius Caesar. I was killed i' th'   105
Capitol; Brutus killed me.

Hamlet. It was a brute part of him to kill so capital a
calf there. Be the players ready?

Rosencrantz. Ay, my lord. They stay upon your
patience.   110

Queen. Come hither, my dear Hamlet, sit by me.

Hamlet. No, good mother. Here's metal more attractive.°

89 *censure of his seeming* judgement on his looks   92 *be idle* play
the fool   95 *the chameleon's dish* air (on which chameleons were
thought to live)   112–13 *attractive* magnetic

Polonius. [*To the King*] O ho! Do you mark that?

115 *Hamlet.* Lady, shall I lie in your lap?

                         [*He lies at Ophelia's feet.*]

Ophelia. No, my lord.

Hamlet. I mean, my head upon your lap?

Ophelia. Ay, my lord.

Hamlet. Do you think I meant country matters?°

120 *Ophelia.* I think nothing, my lord.

Hamlet. That's a fair thought to lie between maids'
legs.

Ophelia. What is, my lord?

Hamlet. Nothing.

125 *Ophelia.* You are merry, my lord.

Hamlet. Who, I?

Ophelia. Ay, my lord.

Hamlet. O God, your only jig-maker!° What should a
man do but be merry? For look you how cheerfully
130 my mother looks, and my father died within's two
hours.

Ophelia. Nay, 'tis twice two months, my lord.

Hamlet. So long? Nay then, let the devil wear black,
for I'll have a suit of sables.° O heavens! Die two
135 months ago, and not forgotten yet? Then there's
hope a great man's memory may outlive his life half
a year. But, by'r Lady, 'a must build churches then,
or else shall 'a suffer not thinking on, with the hobbyhorse,° whose epitaph is "For O, for O, the hobby-
140 horse is forgot!"

The trumpets sound. Dumb show follows:

119 *country matters* rustic doings (with a pun on the vulgar word
for the pudendum)   128 *jig-maker* composer of songs and dances
(often a Fool, who performed them)   134 *sables* (pun on "black"
and "luxurious furs")   138–39 *hobbyhorse* mock horse worn by a
performer in the morris dance

Enter a King and a Queen very lovingly, the Queen em-
bracing him, and he her. She kneels; and makes show
of protestation unto him. He takes her up, and declines
his head upon her neck. He lies him down upon a bank
of flowers. She, seeing him asleep, leaves him. Anon
come in another man: takes off his crown, kisses it,
pours poison in the sleeper's ears, and leaves him. The
Queen returns, finds the King dead, makes passionate
action. The poisoner, with some three or four, come in
again, seem to condole with her. The dead body is car-
ried away. The poisoner woos the Queen with gifts; she
seems harsh awhile, but in the end accepts love.

                                             Exeunt.

Ophelia. What means this, my lord?

Hamlet. Marry, this is miching mallecho;° it means
     mischief.

Ophelia. Belike this show imports the argument° of
     the play.   *145*

                    Enter Prologue.

Hamlet. We shall know by this fellow. The players
     cannot keep counsel; they'll tell all.

Ophelia. Will 'a tell us what this show meant?

Hamlet. Ay, or any show that you will show him. Be
     not you ashamed to show, he'll not shame to tell you *150*
     what it means.

Ophelia. You are naught,° you are naught; I'll mark the
     play.

Prologue. For us, and for our tragedy,
          Here stooping to your clemency,   *155*
          We beg your hearing patiently.   [*Exit.*]

Hamlet. Is this a prologue, or the posy of a ring?°

Ophelia. 'Tis brief, my lord.

Hamlet. As woman's love.

142 *miching   mallecho* sneaking mischief 144 *argument* plot
152 *naught* wicked, improper 157 *posy of a ring* motto inscribed
in a ring

Enter [two Players as] King and Queen.

Player King. Full thirty times hath Phoebus' cart° gone
160   round
      Neptune's salt wash° and Tellus'° orbèd ground,
      And thirty dozen moons with borrowed sheen
      About the world have times twelve thirties been,
      Since love our hearts, and Hymen did our hands,
165   Unite commutual in most sacred bands.

Player Queen. So many journeys may the sun and
      moon
      Make us again count o'er ere love be done!
      But woe is me, you are so sick of late,
      So far from cheer and from your former state,
170   That I distrust° you. Yet, though I distrust,
      Discomfort you, my lord, it nothing must.
      For women fear too much, even as they love,
      And women's fear and love hold quantity,
      In neither aught, or in extremity.°
175   Now what my love is, proof° hath made you know,
      And as my love is sized, my fear is so.
      Where love is great, the littlest doubts are fear;
      Where little fears grow great, great love grows there.

Player King. Faith, I must leave thee, love, and shortly
      too;
180   My operant° powers their functions leave to do:
      And thou shalt live in this fair world behind,
      Honored, beloved, and haply one as kind
      For husband shalt thou——

Player Queen.   O, confound the rest!
      Such love must needs be treason in my breast.
185   In second husband let me be accurst!
      None wed the second but who killed the first.

---

160 *Phoebus' cart* the sun's chariot 161 *Neptune's salt wash* the
sea 161 *Tellus* Roman goddess of the earth 170 *distrust* am
anxious about 173–74 *And women's . . . in extremity* (perhaps
the idea is that women's anxiety is great or little in proportion
to their love. The previous line, unrhymed, may be a false start
that Shakespeare neglected to delete) 175 *proof* experience
180 *operant* active

Hamlet. [*Aside*] That's wormwood.°

Player Queen. The instances° that second marriage
  move°
  Are base respects of thrift,° but none of love.
  A second time I kill my husband dead   *190*
  When second husband kisses me in bed.

Player King. I do believe you think what now you
  speak,
  But what we do determine oft we break.
  Purpose is but the slave to memory,
  Of violent birth, but poor validity,°   *195*
  Which now like fruit unripe sticks on the tree,
  But fall unshaken when they mellow be.
  Most necessary 'tis that we forget
  To pay ourselves what to ourselves is debt.
  What to ourselves in passion we propose,   *200*
  The passion ending, doth the purpose lose.
  The violence of either grief or joy
  Their own enactures° with themselves destroy:
  Where joy most revels, grief doth most lament;
  Grief joys, joy grieves, on slender accident.   *205*
  This world is not for aye, nor 'tis not strange
  That even our loves should with our fortunes
    change,
  For 'tis a question left us yet to prove,
  Whether love lead fortune, or else fortune love.
  The great man down, you mark his favorite flies;   *210*
  The poor advanced makes friends of enemies;
  And hitherto doth love on fortune tend,
  For who not needs shall never lack a friend;
  And who in want a hollow friend doth try,
  Directly seasons him° his enemy.   *215*
  But, orderly to end where I begun,
  Our wills and fates do so contrary run
  That our devices still are overthrown;
  Our thoughts are ours, their ends none of our own.

---

187 *wormwood* a bitter herb 188 *instances* motives 188 *move*
induce 189 *respects of thrift* considerations of profit 195 *validity*
strength 203 *enactures* acts 215 *seasons him* ripens him into

220 So think thou wilt no second husband wed,
But die thy thoughts when thy first lord is dead.

Player Queen. Nor earth to me give food, nor heaven
light,
Sport and repose lock from me day and night,
To desperation turn my trust and hope,
225 An anchor's° cheer in prison be my scope,
Each opposite that blanks° the face of joy
Meet what I would have well, and it destroy:
Both here and hence pursue me lasting strife,
If, once a widow, ever I be wife!

230 *Hamlet.* If she should break it now!

Player King. 'Tis deeply sworn. Sweet, leave me here
awhile;
My spirits grow dull, and fain I would beguile
The tedious day with sleep.

Player Queen.   Sleep rock thy brain,
                                   [*He*] *sleeps.*
And never come mischance between us twain! *Exit.*

235 *Hamlet.* Madam, how like you this play?

Queen. The lady doth protest too much, methinks.

Hamlet. O, but she'll keep her word.

King. Have you heard the argument?° Is there no
offense in't?

240 *Hamlet.* No, no, they do but jest, poison in jest; no
offense i' th' world.

King. What do you call the play?

Hamlet. *The Mousetrap.* Marry, how? Tropically.°
This play is the image of a murder done in Vienna:
245 Gonzago is the Duke's name; his wife, Baptista. You
shall see anon. 'Tis a knavish piece of work, but
what of that? Your Majesty, and we that have free°

---

225 *anchor's* anchorite's, hermit's 226 *opposite that blanks* adverse thing that blanches 238 *argument* plot 243 *Tropically* figuratively (with a pun on "trap") 247 *free* innocent

souls, it touches us not. Let the galled jade winch;° our withers are unwrung.

Enter Lucianus.

This is one Lucianus, nephew to the King.   250

Ophelia. You are as good as a chorus, my lord.

Hamlet. I could interpret° between you and your love, if I could see the puppets dallying.

Ophelia. You are keen,° my lord, you are keen.

Hamlet. It would cost you a groaning to take off mine 255 edge.

Ophelia. Still better, and worse.

Hamlet. So you mistake° your husbands.—Begin, murderer. Leave thy damnable faces and begin. Come, the croaking raven doth bellow for revenge. 260

Lucianus. Thoughts black, hands apt, drugs fit, and time agreeing,
Confederate season,° else no creature seeing,
Thou mixture rank, of midnight weeds collected,
With Hecate's ban° thrice blasted, thrice infected,
Thy natural magic and dire property°   265
On wholesome life usurps immediately.
                    Pours the poison in his ears.

Hamlet. 'A poisons him i' th' garden for his estate. His name's Gonzago. The story is extant, and written in very choice Italian. You shall see anon how the murderer gets the love of Gonzago's wife.   270

Ophelia. The King rises.

Hamlet. What, frighted with false fire?°

Queen. How fares my lord?

Polonius. Give o'er the play.

248 *galled jade winch* chafed horse wince 252 *interpret* (like a showman explaining the action of puppets) 254 *keen* (1) sharp (2) sexually aroused 258 *mistake* err in taking 262 *Confederate season* the opportunity allied with me 264 *Hecate's ban* the curse of the goddess of sorcery 265 *property* nature 272 *false fire* blank discharge of firearms

275 *King.* Give me some light. Away!

Polonius. Lights, lights, lights!

> *Exeunt all but Hamlet and Horatio.*

Hamlet. Why, let the strucken deer go weep,
>> The hart ungallèd play:
>>> For some must watch, while some must sleep;
280 >>> Thus runs the world away.
> Would not this, sir, and a forest of feathers°—if the
> rest of my fortunes turn Turk° with me—with two
> Provincial roses° on my razed° shoes, get me a
> fellowship in a cry° of players?

285 *Horatio.* Half a share.

Hamlet. A whole one, I.
>> For thou dost know, O Damon dear,
>>> This realm dismantled was
>> Of Jove himself; and now reigns here
290 >>> A very, very—pajock.°

Horatio. You might have rhymed.°

Hamlet. O good Horatio, I'll take the ghost's word for
a thousand pound. Didst perceive?

Horatio. Very well, my lord.

295 *Hamlet.* Upon the talk of poisoning?

Horatio. I did very well note him.

Hamlet. Ah ha! Come, some music! Come, the recorders!°
>> For if the King like not the comedy,
300 >>> Why then, belike he likes it not, perdy.°
Come, some music!

> *Enter Rosencrantz and Guildenstern.*

Guildenstern. Good my lord, vouchsafe me a word
with you.

---

281 *feathers* (plumes were sometimes part of a costume)   282 *turn Turk* i.e., go bad, treat me badly   283 *Provincial roses* rosettes like the roses of Provence (?)   283 *razed* ornamented with slashes   284 *cry* pack, company   290 *pajock* peacock   291 *You might have rhymed* i.e., rhymed "was" with "ass"   297–98 *recorders* flutelike instruments   300 *perdy* by God (French : *par dieu*)

Hamlet. Sir, a whole history.

Guildenstern. The King, sir——   305

Hamlet. Ay, sir, what of him?

Guildenstern. Is in his retirement marvelous distemp'red.

Hamlet. With drink, sir?

Guildenstern. No, my lord, with choler.°   310

Hamlet. Your wisdom should show itself more richer to signify this to the doctor, for for me to put him to his purgation would perhaps plunge him into more choler.

Guildenstern. Good my lord, put your discourse into   315 some frame,° and start not so wildly from my affair.

Hamlet. I am tame, sir; pronounce.

Guildenstern. The Queen, your mother, in most great affliction of spirit hath sent me to you.

Hamlet. You are welcome.   320

Guildenstern. Nay, good my lord, this courtesy is not of the right breed. If it shall please you to make me a wholesome answer, I will do your mother's commandment: if not, your pardon and my return shall be the end of my business.   325

Hamlet. Sir, I cannot.

Rosencrantz. What, my lord?

Hamlet. Make you a wholesome° answer; my wit's diseased. But, sir, such answer as I can make, you shall command, or rather, as you say, my mother.   330 Therefore no more, but to the matter. My mother, you say——

Rosencrantz. Then thus she says: your behavior hath struck her into amazement and admiration.°

310 *choler* anger (but Hamlet pretends to take the word in its sense of "biliousness")   316 *frame* order, control   328 *wholesome* sane   334 *admiration* wonder

835 *Hamlet.* O wonderful son, that can so stonish a mother! But is there no sequel at the heels of this mother's admiration? Impart.

Rosencrantz. She desires to speak with you in her closet ere you go to bed.

840 *Hamlet.* We shall obey, were she ten times our mother. Have you any further trade with us?

Rosencrantz. My lord, you once did love me.

Hamlet. And do still, by these pickers and stealers.°

Rosencrantz. Good my lord, what is your cause of dis-
845 temper? You do surely bar the door upon your own liberty, if you deny your griefs to your friend.

Hamlet. Sir, I lack advancement.°

Rosencrantz. How can that be, when you have the voice of the King himself for your succession in
850 Denmark?

Enter the Players with recorders.

Hamlet. Ay, sir, but "while the grass grows"—the proverb° is something musty. O, the recorders. Let me see one. To withdraw° with you—why do you go about to recover the wind° of me as if you would
855 drive me into a toil?°

Guildenstern. O my lord, if my duty be too bold, my love is too unmannerly.°

Hamlet. I do not well understand that. Will you play upon this pipe?

860 *Guildenstern.* My lord, I cannot.

Hamlet. I pray you.

Guildenstern. Believe me, I cannot.

Hamlet. I pray you.

Guildenstern. Believe me, I cannot.

343 *pickers and stealers* i.e., hands (with reference to the prayer; "Keep my hands from picking and stealing") 347 *advancement* promotion 352 *proverb* ("While the grass groweth, the horse starveth") 353 *withdraw* speak in private 354 *recover the wind* get on the windward side (as in hunting) 355 *toil* snare 356–57 *if my duty . . . too unmannerly* i.e., if these questions seem rude, it is because my love for you leads me beyond good manners.

Hamlet. I do beseech you.

Guildenstern. I know no touch of it, my lord.

Hamlet. It is as easy as lying. Govern these ventages° 365
    with your fingers and thumb, give it breath with your
    mouth, and it will discourse most eloquent music.
    Look you, these are the stops.

Guildenstern. But these cannot I command to any
    utt'rance of harmony; I have not the skill.   370

Hamlet. Why, look you now, how unworthy a thing
    you make of me! You would play upon me; you
    would seem to know my stops; you would pluck
    out the heart of my mystery; you would sound me
    from my lowest note to the top of my compass;° 375
    and there is much music, excellent voice, in this little
    organ,° yet cannot you make it speak. 'Sblood, do
    you think I am easier to be played on than a pipe?
    Call me what instrument you will, though you can
    fret° me, you cannot play upon me.   380

Enter Polonius.

God bless you, sir!

Polonius. My lord, the Queen would speak with you,
    and presently.

Hamlet. Do you see yonder cloud that's almost in
    shape of a camel?   385

Polonius. By th' mass and 'tis, like a camel indeed.

Hamlet. Methinks it is like a weasel.

Polonius. It is backed like a weasel.

Hamlet. Or like a whale.

Polonius. Very like a whale.   390

Hamlet. Then I will come to my mother by and by.

---

365 *ventages* vents, stops on a recorder   375 *compass* range of
voice   377 *organ* i.e., the recorder   380 *fret* vex (with a pun
alluding to the frets, or ridges, that guide the fingering on some
instruments)

[*Aside*] They fool me to the top of my bent.°—I
will come by and by.°

Polonius. I will say so.   *Exit.*

395 *Hamlet.* "By and by" is easily said. Leave me, friends.
                              [*Exeunt all but Hamlet.*]

'Tis now the very witching time of night,
When churchyards yawn, and hell itself breathes out
Contagion to this world. Now could I drink hot
    blood
And do such bitter business as the day
400 Would quake to look on. Soft, now to my mother.
O heart, lose not thy nature; let not ever
The soul of Nero° enter this firm bosom.
Let me be cruel, not unnatural;
I will speak daggers to her, but use none.
405 My tongue and soul in this be hypocrites:
How in my words somever she be shent,°
To give them seals° never, my soul, consent!   *Exit.*

[Scene III. *The castle.*]

Enter King, Rosencrantz, and Guildenstern.

King. I like him not, nor stands it safe with us
To let his madness range. Therefore prepare you.
I your commission will forthwith dispatch,
And he to England shall along with you.
5 The terms° of our estate may not endure
Hazard so near's° as doth hourly grow
Out of his brows.

Guildenstern.   We will ourselves provide.

392 *They fool . . . my bent* they compel me to play the fool to
the limit of my capacity   393 *by and by* very soon   402 *Nero*
(Roman emperor who had his mother murdered)   406 *shent*
rebuked   407 *give them seals* confirm them with deeds
III.iii.5 *terms* conditions   6 *near's* near us

Most holy and religious fear it is
To keep those many many bodies safe
That live and feed upon your Majesty.   *10*

Rosencrantz. The single and peculiar° life is bound
With all the strength and armor of the mind
To keep itself from noyance,° but much more
That spirit upon whose weal depends and rests
The lives of many. The cess of majesty°   *15*
Dies not alone, but like a gulf° doth draw
What's near it with it; or it is a massy wheel
Fixed on the summit of the highest mount,
To whose huge spokes ten thousand lesser things
Are mortised and adjoined, which when it falls,   *20*
Each small annexment, petty consequence,
Attends° the boist'rous ruin. Never alone
Did the King sigh, but with a general groan.

King. Arm° you, I pray you, to this speedy voyage,
For we will fetters put about this fear,   *25*
Which now goes too free-footed.

Rosencrantz.   We will haste us.
                                 Exeunt Gentlemen.

                        Enter Polonius.

Polonius. My lord, he's going to his mother's closet.°
Behind the arras I'll convey myself
To hear the process.° I'll warrant she'll tax him
    home,°
And, as you said, and wisely was it said,   *30*
'Tis meet that some more audience than a mother,
Since nature makes them partial, should o'erhear
The speech of vantage.° Fare you well, my liege.
I'll call upon you ere you go to bed
And tell you what I know.

King.   Thanks, dear my lord.   *35*
                                 Exit [Polonius].

---

11 *peculiar* individual, private   13 *noyance* injury   15 *cess of
majesty* cessation (death) of a king   16 *gulf* whirlpool   22 *Attends*
waits on, participates in   24 *Arm* prepare   27 *closet* private room
29 *process* proceedings   29 *tax him home* censure him sharply
33 *of vantage* from an advantageous place

Claudius
Soliloquy

O, my offense is rank, it smells to heaven;
It hath the primal eldest curse° upon't,
A brother's murder. Pray can I not,
Though inclination be as sharp as will.

40   My stronger guilt defeats my strong intent,
And like a man to double business bound
I stand in pause where I shall first begin,
And both neglect. What if this cursèd hand
Were thicker than itself with brother's blood,

45   Is there not rain enough in the sweet heavens
To wash it white as snow? Whereto serves mercy   *mercy*
But to confront° the visage of offense?
And what's in prayer but this twofold force,
To be forestallèd ere we come to fall,

50   Or pardoned being down? Then I'll look up.
My fault is past. But, O, what form of prayer
Can serve my turn? "Forgive me my foul murder"?
That cannot be, since I am still possessed
Of those effects° for which I did the murder,

55   My crown, mine own ambition, and my queen.   *reason*
May one be pardoned and retain th' offense?
In the corrupted currents of this world
Offense's gilded hand may shove by justice,
And oft 'tis seen the wicked prize itself

60   Buys out the law. But 'tis not so above.
There is no shuffling;° there the action lies
In his true nature, and we ourselves compelled,
Even to the teeth and forehead of our faults,
To give in evidence. What then? What rests?°

65   Try what repentance can. What can it not?
Yet what can it when one cannot repent?
O wretched state! O bosom black as death!
O limèd° soul, that struggling to be free
Art more engaged!° Help, angels! Make assay.°

70   Bow, stubborn knees, and, heart with strings of steel,

---

37 *primal eldest curse* (curse of Cain, who killed Abel)   47 *confront* oppose   54 *effects* things gained   61 *shuffling* trickery
64 *rests* remains   68 *limèd* caught (as with birdlime, a sticky
substance spread on boughs to snare birds)   69 *engaged* en-
snared   69 *assay* an attempt

Be soft as sinews of the newborn babe.
All may be well.   [*He kneels.*]

Enter Hamlet.

Hamlet. Now might I do it pat, now 'a is a-praying,
And now I'll do't. And so 'a goes to heaven,
And so am I revenged. That would be scanned.°   75
A villain kills my father, and for that
I, his sole son, do this same villain send
To heaven.
Why, this is hire and salary, not revenge.
'A took my father grossly, full of bread,°   80
With all his crimes broad blown,° as flush° as May;
And how his audit° stands, who knows save heaven?
But in our circumstance and course of thought,
'Tis heavy with him; and am I then revenged,
To take him in the purging of his soul,   85
When he is fit and seasoned for his passage?
No.
Up, sword, and know thou a more horrid hent.°
When he is drunk asleep, or in his rage,
Or in th' incestuous pleasure of his bed,   90
At game a-swearing, or about some act
That has no relish° of salvation in't—
Then trip him, that his heels may kick at heaven,
And that his soul may be as damned and black
As hell, whereto it goes. My mother stays.   95
This physic° but prolongs thy sickly days.   *Exit.*

King. [*Rises*] My words fly up, my thoughts remain
     below.
Words without thoughts never to heaven go.   *Exit.*

---

75 *would be scanned* ought to be looked into   80 *bread* i.e.,
worldly gratification   81 *crimes broad blown* sins in full bloom
81 *flush* vigorous   82 *audit* account   88 *hent* grasp (here, occasion
for seizing)   92 *relish* flavor   96 *physic* (Claudius' purgation by
prayer, as Hamlet thinks in line 85)

[Scene IV. *The Queen's closet.*]

Enter [*Queen*] *Gertrude and Polonius.*

Polonius. 'A will come straight. Look you lay home°
to him.
Tell him his pranks have been too broad° to bear
with,
And that your Grace hath screened and stood between
Much heat and him. I'll silence me even here.
5 Pray you be round with him.

Hamlet. (*Within*) Mother, Mother, Mother!

Queen. I'll warrant you; fear me not. Withdraw; I hear
him coming.   [*Polonius hides behind the arras.*]

Enter Hamlet.

Hamlet. Now, Mother, what's the matter?

10 *Queen.* Hamlet, thou hast thy father much offended.

Hamlet. Mother, you have my father much offended.

Queen. Come, come, you answer with an idle° tongue.

Hamlet. Go, go, you question with a wicked tongue.

Queen. Why, how now, Hamlet?

Hamlet.   What's the matter now?

Queen. Have you forgot me?

15 *Hamlet.*   No, by the rood,° not so!
You are the Queen, your husband's brother's wife,
And, would it were not so, you are my mother.

Queen. Nay, then I'll set those to you that can speak.

Hamlet. Come, come, and sit you down. You shall not
budge.

III.iv.1 *lay home* thrust (rebuke) him sharply 2 *broad* unre-
strained 12 *idle* foolish 15 *rood* cross

You go not till I set you up a glass°   20
Where you may see the inmost part of you!

Queen. What wilt thou do? Thou wilt not murder me?
  Help, ho!

Polonius. [*Behind*] What, ho! Help!

Hamlet. [*Draws*] How now? A rat? Dead for a ducat,
  dead!   25
  [*Makes a pass through the arras and*] *kills Polonius.*

Polonius. [*Behind*] O, I am slain!

Queen.   O me, what hast thou done?

Hamlet. Nay, I know not. Is it the King?

Queen. O, what a rash and bloody deed is this!

Hamlet. A bloody deed—almost as bad, good Mother,
  As kill a king, and marry with his brother.   30

Queen. As kill a king?

Hamlet.   Ay, lady, it was my word.
          [*Lifts up the arras and sees Polonius.*]
Thou wretched, rash, intruding fool, farewell!
I took thee for thy better. Take thy fortune.
Thou find'st to be too busy is some danger.—
Leave wringing of your hands. Peace, sit you down   35
And let me wring your heart, for so I shall
If it be made of penetrable stuff,
If damnèd custom have not brazed° it so
That it be proof° and bulwark against sense.°

Queen. What have I done that thou dar'st wag thy
  tongue   40
In noise so rude against me?

Hamlet.   Such an act
That blurs the grace and blush of modesty,
Calls virtue hypocrite, takes off the rose
From the fair forehead of an innocent love,
And sets a blister° there, makes marriage vows   45

---

20 *glass* mirror 38 *brazed* hardened like brass 39 *proof* armor
39 *sense* feeling 45 *sets a blister* brands (as a harlot)

As false as dicers' oaths. O, such a deed
As from the body of contraction° plucks
The very soul, and sweet religion makes
A rhapsody° of words! Heaven's face does glow
50 O'er this solidity and compound mass
With heated visage, as against the doom
Is thoughtsick at the act.°

Queen.   Ay me, what act,
That roars so loud and thunders in the index?°

Hamlet. Look here upon this picture, and on this,
55 The counterfeit presentment° of two brothers.
See what a grace was seated on this brow:
Hyperion's curls, the front° of Jove himself,
An eye like Mars, to threaten and command,
A station° like the herald Mercury
60 New lighted on a heaven-kissing hill—
A combination and a form indeed
Where every god did seem to set his seal
To give the world assurance of a man.
This was your husband. Look you now what follows.
65 Here is your husband, like a mildewed ear
Blasting his wholesome brother. Have you eyes?
Could you on this fair mountain leave to feed,
And batten° on this moor? Ha! Have you eyes?
You cannot call it love, for at your age
70 The heyday° in the blood is tame, it's humble,
And waits upon the judgment, and what judgment
Would step from this to this? Sense° sure you have,
Else could you not have motion, but sure that sense
Is apoplexed,° for madness would not err,
75 Nor sense to ecstasy° was ne'er so thralled
But it reserved some quantity of choice

---

47 *contraction* marriage contract 49 *rhapsody* senseless string
49–52 *Heaven's face . . . the act* i.e., the face of heaven blushes
over this earth (compounded of four elements), the face hot, as
if Judgment Day were near, and it is thoughtsick at the act
53 *index* prologue 55 *counterfeit presentment* represented image
57 *front* forehead 59 *station* bearing 68 *batten* feed gluttonously
70 *heyday* excitement 72 *Sense* feeling 74 *apoplexed* paralyzed
75 *ecstasy* madness

To serve in such a difference. What devil was't
That thus hath cozened you at hoodman-blind?°
Eyes without feeling, feeling without sight,
Ears without hands or eyes, smelling sans° all,   80
Or but a sickly part of one true sense
Could not so mope.°
O shame, where is thy blush? Rebellious hell,
If thou canst mutine in a matron's bones,
To flaming youth let virtue be as wax   85
And melt in her own fire. Proclaim no shame
When the compulsive ardor° gives the charge,
Since frost itself as actively doth burn,
And reason panders will.°

Queen.   O Hamlet, speak no more.
Thou turn'st mine eyes into my very soul,   90
And there I see such black and grainèd° spots
As will not leave their tinct.°

Hamlet.   Nay, but to live
In the rank sweat of an enseamèd° bed,
Stewed in corruption, honeying and making love
Over the nasty sty——

Queen.   O, speak to me no more.   95
These words like daggers enter in my ears.
No more, sweet Hamlet.

Hamlet.   A murderer and a villain,
A slave that is not twentieth part the tithe°
Of your precedent lord, a vice° of kings,
A cutpurse of the empire and the rule,   100
That from a shelf the precious diadem stole
And put it in his pocket——

Queen.   No more.

---

78 *cozened you at hoodman-blind* cheated you at blindman's buff
80 *sans* without 82 *mope* be stupid 87 *compulsive ardor* com-
pelling passion 89 *reason panders will* reason acts as a procurer
for desire 91 *grainèd* dyed in grain (fast dyed) 92 *tinct* color
93 *enseamèd* (perhaps "soaked in grease," i.e., sweaty; perhaps
"much wrinkled") 98 *tithe* tenth part 99 *vice* (like the Vice, a
fool and mischief-maker in the old morality plays)

Enter Ghost.

Hamlet. A king of shreds and patches—
 Save me and hover o'er me with your wings,
 You heavenly guards! What would your gracious
105 figure?

Queen. Alas, he's mad.

Hamlet. Do you not come your tardy son to chide,
 That, lapsed in time and passion, lets go by
 Th' important acting of your dread command?
110 O, say!

Ghost. Do not forget. This visitation
 Is but to whet thy almost blunted purpose.
 But look, amazement on thy mother sits.
 O, step between her and her fighting soul!
115 Conceit° in weakest bodies strongest works.
 Speak to her, Hamlet.

Hamlet.   How is it with you, lady?

Queen. Alas, how is't with you,
 That you do bend your eye on vacancy,
 And with th' incorporal° air do hold discourse?
120 Forth at your eyes your spirits wildly peep,
 And as the sleeping soldiers in th' alarm
 Your bedded hair° like life in excrements°
 Start up and stand an end.° O gentle son,
 Upon the heat and flame of thy distemper
125 Sprinkle cool patience. Whereon do you look?

Hamlet. On him, on him! Look you, how pale he
  glares!
 His form and cause conjoined, preaching to stones,
 Would make them capable.°—Do not look upon
  me,
 Lest with this piteous action you convert
130 My stern effects.° Then what I have to do
 Will want true color; tears perchance for blood.

Queen. To whom do you speak this?

115 *Conceit* imagination 119 *incorporal* bodiless 122 *bedded hair* hairs laid flat 122 *excrements* outgrowths (here, the hair) 123 *an end* on end 128 *capable* receptive 129–30 *convert/My stern effects* divert my stern deeds

Hamlet.　　　　　　　　Do you see nothing there?

Queen. Nothing at all; yet all that is I see.

Hamlet. Nor did you nothing hear?

Queen.　　　　　　　　No, nothing but ourselves.

Hamlet. Why, look you there! Look how it steals away! 135
　　My father, in his habit° as he lived!
　　Look where he goes even now out at the portal!
　　　　　　　　　　　　　　　　Exit Ghost.

Queen. This is the very coinage of your brain.
　　This bodiless creation ecstasy
　　Is very cunning in.

Hamlet.　　　　Ecstasy?　　　　　　　　140
　　My pulse as yours doth temperately keep time
　　And makes as healthful music. It is not madness
　　That I have uttered. Bring me to the test,
　　And I the matter will reword, which madness
　　Would gambol° from. Mother, for love of grace, 145
　　Lay not that flattering unction° to your soul,
　　That not your trespass but my madness speaks.
　　It will but skin and film the ulcerous place
　　Whiles rank corruption, mining° all within,
　　Infects unseen. Confess yourself to heaven, 150
　　Repent what's past, avoid what is to come,
　　And do not spread the compost° on the weeds
　　To make them ranker. Forgive me this my virtue.
　　For in the fatness of these pursy° times
　　Virtue itself of vice must pardon beg, 155
　　Yea, curb° and woo for leave to do him good.

Queen. O Hamlet, thou hast cleft my heart in twain.

Hamlet. O, throw away the worser part of it,
　　And live the purer with the other half.
　　Good night—but go not to my uncle's bed. 160
　　Assume a virtue, if you have it not.

136 *habit* garment (Q1, though a "bad" quarto, is probably correct in saying that at line 102 the ghost enters "in his nightgown," i.e., dressing gown) 145 *gambol* start away 146 *unction* ointment 149 *mining* undermining 152 *compost* fertilizing substance 154 *pursy* bloated 156 *curb* bow low

That monster custom, who all sense doth eat,
Of habits devil, is angel yet in this,
That to the use°of actions fair and good
165 He likewise gives a frock or livery°
That aptly is put on. Refrain tonight,
And that shall lend a kind of easiness
To the next abstinence; the next more easy;
For use almost can change the stamp of nature,
170 And either° the devil, or throw him out
With wondrous potency. Once more, good night,
And when you are desirous to be blest,
I'll blessing beg of you.——For this same lord,
I do repent; but heaven hath pleased it so,
175 To punish me with this, and this with me,
That I must be their° scourge and minister.
I will bestow° him and will answer well
The death I gave him. So again, good night.
I must be cruel only to be kind.
180 Thus bad begins, and worse remains behind.
One word more, good lady.

Queen.   What shall I do?

Hamlet. Not this, by no means, that I bid you do:
Let the bloat King tempt you again to bed,
185 Pinch wanton on your cheek, call you his mouse,
And let him, for a pair of reechy° kisses,
Or paddling in your neck with his damned fingers,
Make you to ravel° all this matter out,
That I essentially am not in madness,
But mad in craft. 'Twere good you let him know,
190 For who that's but a queen, fair, sober, wise,
Would from a paddock,° from a bat, a gib,°
Such dear concernings hide? Who would do so?
No, in despite of sense and secrecy,

---

164 *use* practice   165 *livery* characteristic garment (punning on
"habits" in line 163)   170 *either* (probably a word is missing after
either; among suggestions are "master," "curb," and "house"; but
possibly *either* is a verb meaning "make easier")   176 *their* i.e.,
the heavens'   177 *bestow* stow, lodge   185 *reechy* foul (literally
"smoky")   187 *ravel* unravel, reveal   191 *paddock* toad   191 *gib*
tomcat

　　Unpeg the basket on the house's top,
　　Let the birds fly, and like the famous ape,　　　　　195
　　To try conclusions,° in the basket creep
　　And break your own neck down.

Queen. Be thou assured, if words be made of breath,
　　And breath of life, I have no life to breathe
　　What thou hast said to me.　　　　　　　　　　　200

Hamlet. I must to England; you know that?

Queen.　　　　　　　　　　　　　　　　Alack,
　　I had forgot. 'Tis so concluded on.

Hamlet. There's letters sealed, and my two school-
　　fellows,
　　Whom I will trust as I will adders fanged,
　　They bear the mandate;° they must sweep my way　　205
　　And marshal me to knavery. Let it work;
　　For 'tis the sport to have the enginer
　　Hoist with his own petar,° and 't shall go hard
　　But I will delve one yard below their mines
　　And blow them at the moon. O, 'tis most sweet　　210
　　When in one line two crafts° directly meet.
　　This man shall set me packing:
　　I'll lug the guts into the neighbor room.
　　Mother, good night. Indeed, this counselor
　　Is now most still, most secret, and most grave,　　215
　　Who was in life a foolish prating knave.
　　Come, sir, to draw toward an end with you.
　　Good night, Mother.
　　　　　[Exit the Queen. Then] exit Hamlet, tugging in
　　　　　　　　　　　　　　　　　　　　　Polonius.

196 *To try conclusions* to make experiments　205 *mandate* command　208 *petar* bomb　211 *crafts* (1) boats (2) acts of guile,
crafty schemes

[ACT IV

Scene I. *The castle.*]

*Enter King and Queen, with Rosencrantz and
Guildenstern.*

King. There's matter in these sighs. These profound
heaves
You must translate; 'tis fit we understand them.
Where is your son?

Queen. Bestow this place on us a little while.
                  [*Exeunt Rosencrantz and Guildenstern.*]
5   Ah, mine own lord, what have I seen tonight!

King. What, Gertrude? How does Hamlet?

Queen. Mad as the sea and wind when both contend
Which is the mightier. In his lawless fit,
Behind the arras hearing something stir,
10   Whips out his rapier, cries, "A rat, a rat!"
And in this brainish apprehension° kills
The unseen good old man.

King.   O heavy deed!
It had been so with us, had we been there.
His liberty is full of threats to all,
15   To you yourself, to us, to every one.
Alas, how shall this bloody deed be answered?
It will be laid to us, whose providence°

IV.i.11 *brainish apprehension* mad imagination 17 *providence*
foresight

124

Should have kept short, restrained, and out of haunt°
This mad young man. But so much was our love
We would not understand what was most fit,   20
But, like the owner of a foul disease,
To keep it from divulging, let it feed
Even on the pith of life. Where is he gone?

Queen. To draw apart the body he hath killed;
O'er whom his very madness, like some ore   25
Among a mineral° of metals base,
Shows itself pure. 'A weeps for what is done.

King. O Gertrude, come away!
The sun no sooner shall the mountains touch
But we will ship him hence, and this vile deed   30
We must with all our majesty and skill
Both countenance and excuse. Ho, Guildenstern!

Enter Rosencrantz and Guildenstern.

Friends both, go join you with some further aid:
Hamlet in madness hath Polonius slain,
And from his mother's closet hath he dragged him.   35
Go seek him out; speak fair, and bring the body
Into the chapel. I pray you haste in this.
          [*Exeunt Rosencrantz and Guildenstern.*]
Come, Gertrude, we'll call up our wisest friends
And let them know both what we mean to do
And what's untimely done . . .°   40
Whose whisper o'er the world's diameter,
As level as the cannon to his blank°
Transports his poisoned shot, may miss our name
And hit the woundless° air. O, come away!
My soul is full of discord and dismay.   *Exeunt.*   45

18 *out of haunt* away from association with others   25–26 *ore/
Among a mineral* vein of gold in a mine   40 *done* . . . (evidently
something has dropped out of the text. Capell's conjecture, "So,
haply slander," is usually printed)   42 *blank* white center of a
target   44 *woundless* invulnerable

[Scene II. *The castle.*]

Enter Hamlet.

Hamlet. Safely stowed.

Gentlemen. (*Within*) Hamlet! Lord Hamlet!

Hamlet. But soft, what noise? Who calls on Hamlet?
O, here they come.

Enter Rosencrantz and Guildenstern.

Rosencrantz. What have you done, my lord, with the
5   dead body?

Hamlet. Compounded it with dust, whereto 'tis kin.

Rosencrantz. Tell us where 'tis, that we may take it
    thence
And bear it to the chapel.

Hamlet. Do not believe it.

10 *Rosencrantz.* Believe what?

Hamlet. That I can keep your counsel and not mine
    own. Besides, to be demanded of° a sponge, what
    replication° should be made by the son of a king?

Rosencrantz. Take you me for a sponge, my lord?

15 *Hamlet.* Ay, sir, that soaks up the King's countenance,°
    his rewards, his authorities. But such officers do the
    King best service in the end. He keeps them, like an
    ape, in the corner of his jaw, first mouthed, to be
    last swallowed. When he needs what you have
20   gleaned, it is but squeezing you and, sponge, you
    shall be dry again.

Rosencrantz. I understand you not, my lord.

Hamlet. I am glad of it: a knavish speech sleeps in a
    foolish ear.

IV.ii.12 *demanded of* questioned by   13 *replication* reply   15 *countenance* favor

Rosencrantz. My lord, you must tell us where the body　25
　is and go with us to the King.

Hamlet. The body is with the King, but the King is not
　with the body. The King is a thing——

Guildenstern. A thing, my lord?

Hamlet. Of nothing. Bring me to him. Hide fox, and　30
　all after.°　　　　　　　　　　　　　　　　*Exeunt.*

[Scene III. *The castle.*]

Enter King, and two or three.

King. I have sent to seek him and to find the body:
　How dangerous is it that this man goes loose!
　Yet must not we put the strong law on him:
　He's loved of the distracted° multitude,
　Who like not in their judgment, but their eyes,　　　5
　And where 'tis so, th' offender's scourge is weighed,
　But never the offense. To bear° all smooth and even,
　This sudden sending him away must seem
　Deliberate pause.° Diseases desperate grown
　By desperate appliance are relieved,　　　　　　10
　Or not at all.

　　Enter Rosencrantz, [Guildenstern,] and all the rest.

　　　　How now? What hath befall'n?

Rosencrantz. Where the dead body is bestowed, my
　　lord,
　We cannot get from him.

King.　　　　　　　　But where is he?

Rosencrantz. Without, my lord; guarded, to know your
　　pleasure.

30–31 *Hide fox, and all after* (a cry in a game such as hide-and-
seek; Hamlet runs from the stage)　IV.iii.4 *distracted* bewildered,
senseless　7 *bear* carry out　9 *pause* planning

King. Bring him before us.

15 *Rosencrantz.*   Ho! Bring in the lord.

                         They enter.

King. Now, Hamlet, where's Polonius?

Hamlet. At supper.

King. At supper? Where?

Hamlet. Not where he eats, but where 'a is eaten. A
20   certain convocation of politic° worms are e'en at
     him. Your worm is your only emperor for diet. We
     fat all creatures else to fat us, and we fat ourselves
     for maggots. Your fat king and your lean beggar is
     but variable service°—two dishes, but to one table.
25   That's the end.

King. Alas, alas!

Hamlet. A man may fish with the worm that hath eat of
     a king, and eat of the fish that hath fed of that worm.

King. What dost thou mean by this?

30 *Hamlet.* Nothing but to show you how a king may
     go a progress° through the guts of a beggar.

King. Where is Polonius?

Hamlet. In heaven. Send thither to see. If your mes-
     senger find him not there, seek him i' th' other
35   place yourself. But if indeed you find him not
     within this month, you shall nose him as you go
     up the stairs into the lobby.

King. [*To Attendants*] Go seek him there.

Hamlet. 'A will stay till you come.

                         [*Exeunt Attendants.*]

40 *King.* Hamlet, this deed, for thine especial safety,
     Which we do tender° as we dearly grieve
     For that which thou hast done, must send thee hence
     With fiery quickness. Therefore prepare thyself.

---

20 *politic* statesmanlike, shrewd   24 *variable service* different courses
31 *progress* royal journey   41 *tender* hold dear

The bark is ready and the wind at help,
Th' associates tend,° and everything is bent   45
For England.

Hamlet.   For England?

King.   Ay, Hamlet.

Hamlet.   Good.

King. So is it, if thou knew'st our purposes.

Hamlet. I see a cherub° that sees them. But come, for
England! Farewell, dear Mother.

King. Thy loving father, Hamlet.   50

Hamlet. My mother—father and mother is man and
wife, man and wife is one flesh, and so, my mother.
Come, for England!   *Exit.*

King. Follow him at foot;° tempt him with speed
aboard.
Delay it not; I'll have him hence tonight.   55
Away! For everything is sealed and done
That else leans° on th' affair. Pray you make haste.
                    [*Exeunt all but the King.*]
And, England, if my love thou hold'st at aught—
As my great power thereof may give thee sense,
Since yet thy cicatrice° looks raw and red   60
After the Danish sword, and thy free awe°
Pays homage to us—thou mayst not coldly set
Our sovereign process,° which imports at full
By letters congruing to that effect
The present° death of Hamlet. Do it, England,   65
For like the hectic° in my blood he rages,
And thou must cure me. Till I know 'tis done,
Howe'er my haps,° my joys were ne'er begun.
                              Exit.

45 *tend* wait   48 *cherub* angel of knowledge   54 *at foot* closely
57 *leans* depends   60 *cicatrice* scar   61 *free awe* uncompelled sub-
mission   62–63 *coldly set/Our sovereign process* regard slightly
our royal command   65 *present* instant   66 *hectic* fever   68 *haps*
chances, fortunes

[Scene IV. *A plain in Denmark.*]

Enter Fortinbras with his Army over the stage.

Fortinbras. Go, Captain, from me greet the Danish
    king.
    Tell him that by his license Fortinbras
    Craves the conveyance of° a promised march
    Over his kingdom. You know the rendezvous.
5   If that his Majesty would aught with us,
    We shall express our duty in his eye;°
    And let him know so.

Captain.   I will do't, my lord.

Fortinbras. Go softly° on.
                    [*Exeunt all but the Captain.*]
        Enter Hamlet, Rosencrantz, &c.

Hamlet. Good sir, whose powers° are these?

10 *Captain.* They are of Norway, sir.

Hamlet. How purposed, sir, I pray you?

Captain. Against some part of Poland.

Hamlet. Who commands them, sir?

Captain. The nephew to old Norway, Fortinbras.

15 *Hamlet.* Goes it against the main° of Poland, sir,
    Or for some frontier?

Captain. Truly to speak, and with no addition,°
    We go to gain a little patch of ground
    That hath in it no profit but the name.
20   To pay five ducats, five, I would not farm it,
    Nor will it yield to Norway or the Pole
    A ranker° rate, should it be sold in fee.°

IV.iv.3 *conveyance of* escort for 6 *in his eye* before his eyes (i.e.,
in his presence) 8 *softly* slowly 9 *powers* forces 15 *main* main
part 17 *with no addition* plainly 22 *ranker* higher 22 *in fee*
outright

Hamlet. Why, then the Polack never will defend it.

Captain. Yes, it is already garrisoned.

Hamlet. Two thousand souls and twenty thousand
    ducats   25
  Will not debate° the question of this straw.
  This is th' imposthume° of much wealth and peace,
  That inward breaks, and shows no cause without
  Why the man dies. I humbly thank you, sir.

Captain. God bye you, sir.   [*Exit.*]

Rosencrantz.   Will't please you go, my lord?   30

Hamlet. I'll be with you straight. Go a little before.
                      [*Exeunt all but Hamlet.*]
  How all occasions do inform against me
  And spur my dull revenge! What is a man,
  If his chief good and market° of his time
  Be but to sleep and feed? A beast, no more.   35
  Sure he that made us with such large discourse,°
  Looking before and after, gave us not
  That capability and godlike reason
  To fust° in us unused. Now, whether it be
  Bestial oblivion,° or some craven scruple   40
  Of thinking too precisely on th' event°—
  A thought which, quartered, hath but one part
    wisdom
  And ever three parts coward—I do not know
  Why yet I live to say, "This thing's to do,"
  Sith I have cause, and will, and strength, and means)   45
  To do't. Examples gross° as earth exhort me.
  Witness this army of such mass and charge,°
  Led by a delicate and tender prince,
  Whose spirit, with divine ambition puffed,
  Makes mouths at the invisible event,°   50
  Exposing what is mortal and unsure
  To all that fortune, death, and danger dare,

26 *debate* settle   27 *imposthume* abscess, ulcer   34 *market* profit
36 *discourse* understanding   39 *fust* grow moldy   40 *oblivion* forgetfulness   41 *event* outcome   46 *gross* large, obvious   47 *charge*
expense   50 *Makes mouths at the invisible event* makes scornful
faces (is contemptuous of) the unseen outcome

Even for an eggshell. Rightly to be great
Is not° to stir without great argument,°
55 But greatly° to find quarrel in a straw
When honor's at the stake. How stand I then,
That have a father killed, a mother stained,
Excitements° of my reason and my blood,
And let all sleep, while to my shame I see
60 The imminent death of twenty thousand men
That for a fantasy and trick of fame°
Go to their graves like beds, fight for a plot
Whereon the numbers cannot try the cause,
Which is not tomb enough and continent°
65 To hide the slain? O, from this time forth,
My thoughts be bloody, or be nothing worth! *Exit.*

[Scene V. *The castle.*]

Enter Horatio, [Queen] Gertrude, and a Gentleman.

Queen. I will not speak with her.

Gentleman. She is importunate, indeed distract.
Her mood will needs be pitied.

Queen.   What would she have?

Gentleman. She speaks much of her father, says she hears
There's tricks i' th' world, and hems, and beats her
5   heart,
Spurns enviously at straws,° speaks things in doubt°
That carry but half sense. Her speech is nothing,
Yet the unshapèd use of it doth move

54 *not* (the sense seems to require "not not") 54 *argument*
reason 55 *greatly* i.e., nobly 58 *Excitements* incentives 61 *fan-*
tasy and trick of fame illusion and trifle of reputation 64 *conti-*
nent receptacle, container IV.v.6 *Spurns enviously at straws*
objects spitefully to insignificant matters 6 *in doubt* uncertainly

The hearers to collection;° they yawn° at it,
And botch the words up fit to their own thoughts,　　10
Which, as her winks and nods and gestures yield them,
Indeed would make one think there might be thought,
Though nothing sure, yet much unhappily.

Horatio. 'Twere good she were spoken with, for she may strew
Dangerous conjectures in ill-breeding minds.　　15

Queen. Let her come in.　　　　　[*Exit Gentleman.*]
　[*Aside*] To my sick soul (as sin's true nature is)
Each toy seems prologue to some great amiss;°
So full of artless jealousy° is guilt
It spills° itself in fearing to be spilt.　　20

　　　　Enter Ophelia [*distracted.*]

Ophelia. Where is the beauteous majesty of Denmark?

Queen. How now, Ophelia?

Ophelia. (*She sings.*) How should I your truelove know
　　　　　From another one?
　　　　By his cockle hat° and staff　　25
　　　　　And his sandal shoon.°

Queen. Alas, sweet lady, what imports this song?

Ophelia. Say you? Nay, pray you mark.
　　　　He is dead and gone, lady,　　　　(*Song*)
　　　　　He is dead and gone;　　30
　　　　At his head a grass-green turf,
　　　　　At his heels a stone.
　O, ho!

Queen. Nay, but Ophelia——

Ophelia. Pray you mark.　　35

8–9 *Yet the . . . to collection* i.e., yet the formless manner of it
moves her listeners to gather up some sort of meaning 9 *yawn*
gape (?) 18 *amiss* misfortune 19 *artless jealousy* crude suspicion
20 *spills* destroys 25 *cockle hat* (a cockleshell on the hat was the
sign of a pilgrim who had journeyed to shrines overseas. The
association of lovers and pilgrims was a common one) 26 *shoon*
shoes

[*Sings.*] White his shroud as the mountain snow——

Enter King.

Queen. Alas, look here, my lord.

Ophelia. Larded°all with sweet flowers (*Song*)
Which bewept to the grave did not go
40 With truelove showers.

King. How do you, pretty lady?

Ophelia. Well, God dild° you! They say the owl was a
baker's daughter.° Lord, we know what we are, but
know not what we may be. God be at your table!

45 *King.* Conceit° upon her father.

Ophelia. Pray let's have no words of this, but when
they ask you what it means, say you this:
Tomorrow is Saint Valentine's day.° (*Song*)
All in the morning betime,
50 And I a maid at your window,
To be your Valentine.

Then up he rose and donned his clothes
And dupped° the chamber door,
Let in the maid, that out a maid
55 Never departed more.

King. Pretty Ophelia.

Ophelia. Indeed, la, without an oath, I'll make an end
on't:
[*Sings.*] By Gis° and by Saint Charity,
Alack, and fie for shame!
60 Young men will do't if they come to't,
By Cock,° they are to blame.
Quoth she, "Before you tumbled me,
You promised me to wed."

38 *Larded* decorated 42 *dild* yield, i.e., reward 43 *baker's daughter* (an allusion to a tale of a baker's daughter who begrudged
bread to Christ and was turned into an owl) 45 *Conceit* brooding
48 *Saint Valentine's day* Feb. 14 (the notion was that a bachelor
would become the truelove of the first girl he saw on this day)
53 *dupped* opened (did up) 58 *Gis* (contraction of "Jesus")
61 *Cock* (1) God (2) phallus

He answers:

> "So would I 'a' done, by yonder sun,   65
> An thou hadst not come to my bed."

King. How long hath she been thus?

Ophelia. I hope all will be well. We must be patient,
but I cannot choose but weep to think they would
lay him i' th' cold ground. My brother shall know   70
of it; and so I thank you for your good counsel.
Come, my coach! Good night, ladies, good night.
Sweet ladies, good night, good night.   *Exit.*

King. Follow her close; give her good watch, I pray
you.   [*Exit Horatio.*]
O, this is the poison of deep grief; it springs   75
All from her father's death—and now behold!
O Gertrude, Gertrude,
When sorrows come, they come not single spies,
But in battalions: first, her father slain;
Next, your son gone, and he most violent author   80
Of his own just remove; the people muddied,°
Thick and unwholesome in their thoughts and
    whispers
For good Polonius' death, and we have done but
    greenly°
In huggermugger° to inter him; poor Ophelia
Divided from herself and her fair judgment,
Without the which we are pictures or mere beasts;   85
Last, and as much containing as all these,
Her brother is in secret come from France,
Feeds on his wonder,° keeps himself in clouds,
And wants not buzzers° to infect his ear   90
With pestilent speeches of his father's death,
Wherein necessity, of matter beggared,°
Will nothing stick° our person to arraign
In ear and ear. O my dear Gertrude, this,

---

81 *muddied*   muddled   83 *greenly*   foolishly   84 *huggermugger*
secret haste   89 *wonder* suspicion   90 *wants not buzzers* does not
lack talebearers   92 *of matter beggared* unprovided with facts
93 *Will nothing stick* will not hesitate

95   Like to a murd'ring piece,° in many places
        Gives me superfluous death.   *A noise within.*

                    Enter a Messenger.

Queen.   Alack, what noise is this?

King. Attend, where are my Switzers?° Let them
    guard the door.
    What is the matter?

Messenger.   Save yourself, my lord.
        The ocean, overpeering of his list,°
100   Eats not the flats with more impiteous haste
        Than young Laertes, in a riotous head,°
        O'erbears your officers. The rabble call him lord,
        And, as the world were now but to begin,
        Antiquity forgot, custom not known,
105   The ratifiers and props of every word,
        They cry, "Choose we! Laertes shall be king!"
        Caps, hands, and tongues applaud it to the clouds,
        "Laertes shall be king! Laertes king!" *A noise within.*

Queen. How cheerfully on the false trail they cry!
110   O, this is counter,° you false Danish dogs!

                Enter Laertes with others.

King. The doors are broke.

Laertes. Where is this king?—Sirs, stand you all
    without.

All. No, let's come in.

Laertes.   I pray you give me leave.

All. We will, we will.

Laertes. I thank you. Keep the door. [*Exeunt his*
115   *Followers.*] O thou vile King,
        Give me my father.

Queen.   Calmly, good Laertes.

95 *murd'ring piece* (a cannon that shot a kind of shrapnel)
97 *Switzers* Swiss guards 99 *list*   shore 101 *in a riotous head*
with a rebellious force 110 *counter* (a hound runs counter when
he follows the scent backward from the prey)

Laertes. That drop of blood that's calm proclaims me
    bastard,
    Cries cuckold° to my father, brands the harlot
    Even here between the chaste unsmirchèd brow
    Of my true mother.

King.   What is the cause, Laertes,   120
    That thy rebellion looks so giantlike?
    Let him go, Gertrude. Do not fear° our person.
    There's such divinity doth hedge a king
    That treason can but peep to° what it would,
    Acts little of his will. Tell me, Laertes,   125
    Why thou art thus incensed. Let him go, Gertrude.
    Speak, man.

Laertes. Where is my father?

King.   Dead.

Queen.   But not by him.

King. Let him demand his fill.

Laertes. How came he dead? I'll not be juggled with.   130
    To hell allegiance, vows to the blackest devil,
    Conscience and grace to the profoundest pit!
    I dare damnation. To this point I stand,
    That both the worlds I give to negligence,°
    Let come what comes, only I'll be revenged   135
    Most throughly for my father.

King.   Who shall stay you?

Laertes. My will, not all the world's.
    And for my means, I'll husband them° so well
    They shall go far with little.

King.   Good Laertes,
    If you desire to know the certainty   140
    Of your dear father, is't writ in your revenge
    That swoopstake° you will draw both friend and foe,
    Winner and loser?

---

118 *cuckold* man whose wife is unfaithful 122 *fear* fear for
124 *peep to* i.e., look at from a distance 134 *That both . . . to
negligence* i.e., I care not what may happen (to me) in this world
or the next 138 *husband them* use them economically 142 *swoopstake* in a clean sweep

Laertes. None but his enemies.

King.   Will you know them then?

Laertes. To his good friends thus wide I'll ope my
145   arms
And like the kind life-rend'ring pelican°
Repast° them with my blood.

King.   Why, now you speak
Like a good child and a true gentleman.
That I am guiltless of your father's death,
150   And am most sensibly° in grief for it,
It shall as level to your judgment 'pear
As day does to your eye.

>   *A noise within: "Let her come in."*

Laertes. How now? What noise is that?

> *Enter Ophelia.*

O heat, dry up my brains; tears seven times salt
155   Burn out the sense and virtue° of mine eye!
By heaven, thy madness shall be paid with weight
Till our scale turn the beam.° O rose of May,
Dear maid, kind sister, sweet Ophelia!
O heavens, is't possible a young maid's wits
160   Should be as mortal as an old man's life?
Nature is fine° in love, and where 'tis fine,
It sends some precious instance° of itself
After the thing it loves.

Ophelia.   They bore him barefaced on the bier (*Song*)
165   Hey non nony, nony, hey nony
              And in his grave rained many a tear——
Fare you well, my dove!

Laertes. Hadst thou thy wits, and didst persuade re-
      venge,
It could not move thus.

170 *Ophelia.* You must sing "A-down a-down, and you call

146 *pelican* (thought to feed its young with its own blood)
147 *Repast* feed 150 *sensibly* acutely 155 *virtue* power 157 *turn
the beam* weigh down the bar (of the balance) 161 *fine* refined,
delicate 162 *instance* sample

him a-down-a." O, how the wheel° becomes it! It is
the false steward, that stole his master's daughter.

Laertes. This nothing's more than matter.°

Ophelia. There's rosemary, that's for remembrance.
Pray you, love, remember. And there is pansies, 175
that's for thoughts.

Laertes. A document° in madness, thoughts and remembrance fitted.

Ophelia. There's fennel° for you, and columbines.
There's rue for you, and here's some for me. We 180
may call it herb of grace o' Sundays. O, you must
wear your rue with a difference. There's a daisy. I
would give you some violets, but they withered all
when my father died. They say 'a made a good end.
[*Sings*]　　For bonny sweet Robin is all my joy. 185

Laertes. Thought and affliction, passion, hell itself,
She turns to favor° and to prettiness.

Ophelia. 　And will 'a not come again?　　　　(*Song*)
　　　　And will 'a not come again?
　　　　　　No, no, he is dead, 190
　　　　　　Go to thy deathbed,
　　　　He never will come again.

　　　　His beard was as white as snow,
　　　　All flaxen was his poll.°
　　　　　　He is gone, he is gone, 195
　　　　　　And we cast away moan.
　　　　God 'a' mercy on his soul!
And of all Christian souls, I pray God. God bye you.
　　　　　　　　　　　　　　　　　　[*Exit.*]

171 *wheel* (of uncertain meaning, but probably a turn or dance of
Ophelia's, rather than Fortune's wheel)　173 *This nothing's more
than matter* this nonsense has more meaning than matters of consequence　177 *document* lesson　179 *fennel* (the distribution of
flowers in the ensuing lines has symbolic meaning, but the meaning
is disputed. Perhaps *fennel*, flattery; *columbines*, cuckoldry; *rue*,
sorrow for Ophelia and repentance for the Queen; *daisy*, dissem-
bling; *violets*, faithfulness. For other interpretations, see J. W.
Lever in *Review of English Studies*, New Series 3 [1952], pp. 123–
29)　187 *favor* charm, beauty　194 *All flaxen was his poll* white
as flax was his head

Laertes. Do you see this, O God?

200 *King.* Laertes, I must commune with your grief,
    Or you deny me right. Go but apart,
    Make choice of whom your wisest friends you will,
    And they shall hear and judge 'twixt you and me.
    If by direct or by collateral° hand
205 They find us touched,° we will our kingdom give,
    Our crown, our life, and all that we call ours,
    To you in satisfaction; but if not,
    Be you content to lend your patience to us,
    And we shall jointly labor with your soul
    To give it due content.

210 *Laertes.*   Let this be so.
    His means of death, his obscure funeral—
    No trophy, sword, nor hatchment° o'er his bones,
    No noble rite nor formal ostentation°—
    Cry to be heard, as 'twere from heaven to earth,
    That I must call't in question.

215 *King.*   So you shall;
    And where th' offense is, let the great ax fall.
    I pray you go with me.   *Exeunt.*

[Scene VI. *The castle.*]

Enter Horatio and others.

Horatio. What are they that would speak with me?

Gentleman. Seafaring men, sir. They say they have
    letters for you.

Horatio. Let them come in.   [*Exit Attendant.*]
5   I do not know from what part of the world
    I should be greeted, if not from Lord Hamlet.

204 *collateral* indirect   205 *touched* implicated   212 *hatchment*
tablet bearing the coat of arms of the dead   213 *ostentation* ceremony

Enter Sailors.

Sailor. God bless you, sir.

Horatio. Let Him bless thee too.

Sailor. 'A shall, sir, an't please Him. There's a letter
for you, sir—it came from th' ambassador that was　10
bound for England—if your name be Horatio, as
I am let to know it is.

Horatio. [*Reads the letter.*] "Horatio, when thou shalt
have overlooked° this, give these fellows some
means to the King. They have letters for him. Ere　15
we were two days old at sea, a pirate of very warlike
appointment° gave us chase. Finding ourselves too
slow of sail, we put on a compelled valor, and in
the grapple I boarded them. On the instant they
got clear of our ship; so I alone became their　20
prisoner. They have dealt with me like thieves of
mercy, but they knew what they did: I am to do a
good turn for them. Let the King have the letters
I have sent, and repair thou to me with as much
speed as thou wouldest fly death. I have words to　25
speak in thine ear will make thee dumb; yet are they
much too light for the bore° of the matter. These
good fellows will bring thee where I am. Rosencrantz and Guildenstern hold their course for England. Of them I have much to tell thee. Farewell.　30

　　　　He that thou knowest thine, HAMLET."
Come, I will give you way for these your letters,
And do't the speedier that you may direct me
To him from whom you brought them.　　*Exeunt.*

IV.vi.14 *overlooked* surveyed　　17 *appointment* equipment　　27 *bore*
caliber (here, "importance")

[Scene VII. *The castle.*]

Enter King and Laertes.

King. Now must your conscience my acquittance seal,
 And you must put me in your heart for friend,
 Sith you have heard, and with a knowing ear,
 That he which hath your noble father slain
 Pursued my life.

5 *Laertes.*   It well appears. But tell me
 Why you proceeded not against these feats
 So criminal and so capital° in nature,
 As by your safety, greatness, wisdom, all things else,
 You mainly° were stirred up.

King.   O, for two special reasons,
10 Which may to you perhaps seem much unsinewed,°
 But yet to me they're strong. The Queen his mother
 Lives almost by his looks, and for myself—
 My virtue or my plague, be it either which—
 She is so conjunctive° to my life and soul,
15 That, as the star moves not but in his sphere,
 I could not but by her. The other motive
 Why to a public count° I might not go
 Is the great love the general gender° bear him,
 Who, dipping all his faults in their affection,
20 Would, like the spring that turneth wood to stone,°
 Convert his gyves° to graces; so that my arrows,
 Too slightly timbered° for so loud a wind,
 Would have reverted to my bow again,
 And not where I had aimed them.

IV.vii.7 *capital* deserving death 9 *mainly* powerfully 10 *unsinewed*
weak 14 *conjunctive* closely united 17 *count* reckoning 18 *general gender* common people 20 *spring that turneth wood to stone*
(a spring in Shakespeare's county was so charged with lime that it
would petrify wood placed in it) 21 *gyves* fetters 22 *timbered*
shafted

Laertes. And so have I a noble father lost,   25
  A sister driven into desp'rate terms,°
  Whose worth, if praises may go back again,°
  Stood challenger on mount of all the age
  For her perfections. But my revenge will come.

King. Break not your sleeps for that. You must not
    think   30
  That we are made of stuff so flat and dull
  That we can let our beard be shook with danger,
  And think it pastime. You shortly shall hear more.
  I loved your father, and we love ourself,
  And that, I hope, will teach you to imagine——   35

       Enter a Messenger with letters.

How now? What news?

Messenger.   Letters, my lord, from Hamlet:
  These to your Majesty; this to the Queen.

King. From Hamlet? Who brought them?

Messenger. Sailors, my lord, they say; I saw them not.
  They were given me by Claudio; he received them   40
  Of him that brought them.

King.   Laertes, you shall hear them.——
  Leave us.   *Exit Messenger.*
  [*Reads.*] "High and mighty, you shall know I am set
  naked° on your kingdom. Tomorrow shall I beg
  leave to see your kingly eyes; when I shall (first   45
  asking your pardon thereunto) recount the occasion
  of my sudden and more strange return.

                     HAMLET."
  What should this mean? Are all the rest come back?
  Or is it some abuse,° and no such thing?   50

Laertes. Know you the hand?

King.   'Tis Hamlet's character.° "Naked"!

26 *terms* conditions 27 *go back again* revert to what is past 44
naked destitute 50 *abuse* deception 51 *character* handwriting

And in a postscript here, he says "alone."
Can you devise° me?

Laertes. I am lost in it, my lord. But let him come.
55   It warms the very sickness in my heart
That I shall live and tell him to his teeth,
"Thus did'st thou."

King.   If it be so, Laertes
(As how should it be so? How otherwise?),
Will you be ruled by me?

Laertes.   Ay, my lord,
60   So you will not o'errule me to a peace.

King. To thine own peace. If he be now returned,
As checking at° his voyage, and that he means
No more to undertake it, I will work him
To an exploit now ripe in my device,
65   Under the which he shall not choose but fall;
And for his death no wind of blame shall breathe,
But even his mother shall uncharge the practice°
And call it accident.

Laertes.   My lord, I will be ruled;
The rather if you could devise it so
That I might be the organ.

70 *King.*   It falls right.
You have been talked of since your travel much,
And that in Hamlet's hearing, for a quality
Wherein they say you shine. Your sum of parts
Did not together pluck such envy from him
75   As did that one, and that, in my regard,
Of the unworthiest siege.°

Laertes.   What part is that, my lord?

King. A very riband in the cap of youth,
Yet needful too, for youth no less becomes
The light and careless livery that it wears
80   Than settled age his sables and his weeds,°
Importing health and graveness. Two months since

53 *devise* advise 62 *checking at* turning away from (a term in falconry) 67 *uncharge the practice* not charge the device with treachery 76 *siege* rank 80 *sables and his weeds* i.e., sober attire

Here was a gentleman of Normandy.
I have seen myself, and served against, the French,
And they can° well on horseback, but this gallant
Had witchcraft in't. He grew unto his seat,   85
And to such wondrous doing brought his horse
As had he been incorpsed and deminatured
With the brave beast. So far he topped my thought
That I, in forgery° of shapes and tricks,
Come short of what he did.

Laertes.   A Norman was't?   90

King. A Norman.

Laertes. Upon my life, Lamord.

King.   The very same.

Laertes. I know him well. He is the brooch° indeed
And gem of all the nation.

King. He made confession° of you,   95
And gave you such a masterly report,
For art and exercise in your defense,
And for your rapier most especial,
That he cried out 'twould be a sight indeed
If one could match you. The scrimers° of their
        nation   100
He swore had neither motion, guard, nor eye,
If you opposed them. Sir, this report of his
Did Hamlet so envenom with his envy
That he could nothing do but wish and beg
Your sudden coming o'er to play with you.   105
Now, out of this——

Laertes.   What out of this, my lord?

King. Laertes, was your father dear to you?
Or are you like the painting of a sorrow,
A face without a heart?

Laertes.   Why ask you this?

King. Not that I think you did not love your father,   110

84 *can* do   89 *forgery* invention   93 *brooch* ornament   95 *confession* report   100 *scrimers* fencers

But that I know love is begun by time,
And that I see, in passages of proof,°
Time qualifies° the spark and fire of it.
There lives within the very flame of love
113   A kind of wick or snuff° that will abate it,
And nothing is at a like goodness still,°
For goodness, growing to a plurisy,°
Dies in his own too-much. That we would do
We should do when we would, for this "would" changes,
120   And hath abatements and delays as many
As there are tongues, are hands, are accidents,
And then this "should" is like a spendthrift sigh,°
That hurts by easing. But to the quick° of th' ulcer—
Hamlet comes back; what would you undertake
125   To show yourself in deed your father's son
More than in words?

Laertes.   To cut his throat i' th' church!

King. No place indeed should murder sanctuarize;°
Revenge should have no bounds. But, good Laertes,
Will you do this? Keep close within your chamber.
130   Hamlet returned shall know you are come home.
We'll put on those° shall praise your excellence
And set a double varnish on the fame
The Frenchman gave you, bring you in fine° together
And wager on your heads. He, being remiss,
135   Most generous, and free from all contriving,
Will not peruse the foils, so that with ease,
Or with a little shuffling, you may choose
A sword unbated,° and, in a pass of practice,°
Requite him for your father.

Laertes.   I will do't,

112 *passages of proof* proved cases 113 *qualifies* diminishes 115 *snuff* residue of burnt wick (which dims the light) 116 *still* always 117 *plurisy* fullness, excess 122 *spendthrift sigh* (sighing provides ease, but because it was thought to thin the blood and so shorten life it was spendthrift) 123 *quick* sensitive flesh 127 *sanctuarize* protect 131 *We'll put on those* we'll incite persons who 133 *in fine* finally 138 *unbated* not blunted 138 *pass of practice* treacherous thrust

And for that purpose I'll anoint my sword.   140
I bought an unction of a mountebank,°
So mortal that, but dip a knife in it,
Where it draws blood, no cataplasm° so rare,
Collected from all simples° that have virtue°
Under the moon, can save the thing from death   145
That is but scratched withal. I'll touch my point
With this contagion, that, if I gall him slightly,
It may be death.

King.   Let's further think of this,
Weigh what convenience both of time and means
May fit us to our shape.° If this should fail,   150
And that our drift look through° our bad per-
      formance,
'Twere better not assayed. Therefore this project
Should have a back or second, that might hold
If this did blast in proof.° Soft, let me see.
We'll make a solemn wager on your cunnings—   155
I ha't!
When in your motion you are hot and dry—
As make your bouts more violent to that end—
And that he calls for drink, I'll have prepared him
A chalice for the nonce,° whereon but sipping,   160
If he by chance escape your venomed stuck,°
Our purpose may hold there.—But stay, what noise?

Enter Queen.

Queen. One woe doth tread upon another's heel.
So fast they follow. Your sister's drowned, Laertes.

Laertes. Drowned! O, where?   165

Queen. There is a willow grows askant° the brook,
That shows his hoar° leaves in the glassy stream:
Therewith° fantastic garlands did she make
Of crowflowers, nettles, daisies, and long purples,

141 *mountebank* quack   143 *cataplasm* poultice   144 *simplex* me-
dicinal herbs   144 *virtue power* (to heal)   150 *shape* role   151 *drift
look through* purpose show through   154 *blast in proof* burst (fail)
in performance   160 *nonce* occasion   161 *stuck* thrust   166 *askant*
aslant   167 *hoar* silver-gray   168 *Therewith* i.e., with willow twigs

170 That liberal° shepherds give a grosser name,
But our cold maids do dead men's fingers call them.
There on the pendent boughs her crownet° weeds
Clamb'ring to hang, an envious sliver° broke,
When down her weedy trophies and herself
175 Fell in the weeping brook. Her clothes spread wide,
And mermaidlike awhile they bore her up,
Which time she chanted snatches of old lauds,°
As one incapable° of her own distress,
Or like a creature native and indued°
180 Unto that element. But long it could not be
Till that her garments, heavy with their drink,
Pulled the poor wretch from her melodious lay
To muddy death.

Laertes.   Alas, then she is drowned?

Queen. Drowned, drowned.

185 *Laertes.* Too much of water hast thou, poor Ophelia,
And therefore I forbid my tears; but yet
It is our trick;° nature her custom holds,
Let shame say what it will: when these are gone,
The woman° will be out. Adieu, my lord.
190 I have a speech o' fire, that fain would blaze,
But that this folly drowns it.   *Exit.*

King.   Let's follow, Gertrude.
How much I had to do to calm his rage!
Now fear I this will give it start again;
Therefore let's follow.   *Exeunt.*

---

170 *liberal* free-spoken, coarse-mouthed   172 *crownet* coronet   173
envious sliver malicious branch   177 *lauds* hymns   178 *incapable*
unaware   179 *indued* in harmony with   187 *trick* trait, way   189
woman i.e., womanly part of me

[ACT V

Scene I. *A churchyard.*]

Enter two Clowns.°

Clown. Is she to be buried in Christian burial when she willfully seeks her own salvation?

Other. I tell thee she is. Therefore make her grave straight.° The crowner° hath sate on her, and finds it Christian burial. 5

Clown. How can that be, unless she drowned herself in her own defense?

Other. Why, 'tis found so.

Clown. It must be *se offendendo;*° it cannot be else. For here lies the point: if I drown myself wittingly, 10 it argues an act, and an act hath three branches— it is to act, to do, to perform. Argal,° she drowned herself wittingly.

Other. Nay, but hear you, Goodman Delver.

Clown. Give me leave. Here lies the water—good. 15 Here stands the man—good. If the man go to this water and drown himself, it is, will he nill he,° he goes; mark you that. But if the water come to him and drown him, he drowns not himself. Argal, he

V.i.s.d. *Clowns* rustics 4 *straight* straightway 4 *crowner* coroner
9 *se offendendo* (blunder for *se defendendo*, a legal term meaning "in self-defense") 12 *Argal* (blunder for Latin *ergo*, "therefore")
17 *will he nill he* will he or will he not (whether he will or will not)

20 that is not guilty of his own death, shortens not his
own life.

Other. But is this law?

Clown. Ay marry, is't—crowner's quest° law.

Other. Will you ha' the truth on't? If this had not been
25 a gentlewoman, she should have been buried out
o' Christian burial.

Clown. Why, there thou say'st. And the more pity
that great folk should have count'nance° in this
world to drown or hang themselves more than their
30 even-Christen.° Come, my spade. There is no ancient gentlemen but gard'ners, ditchers, and grave-
makers. They hold up° Adam's profession.

Other. Was he a gentleman?

Clown. 'A was the first that ever bore arms.°

35 *Other.* Why, he had none.

Clown. What, art a heathen? How dost thou understand the Scripture? The Scripture says Adam
digged. Could he dig without arms? I'll put another
question to thee. If thou answerest me not to the
40 purpose, confess thyself——

Other. Go to.

Clown. What is he that builds stronger than either the
mason, the shipwright, or the carpenter?

Other. The gallowsmaker, for that frame outlives a
45 thousand tenants.

Clown. I like thy wit well, in good faith. The gallows
does well. But how does it well? It does well to those
that do ill. Now thou dost ill to say the gallows
is built stronger than the church. Argal, the gallows
50 may do well to thee. To't again, come.

Other. Who builds stronger than a mason, a shipwright, or a carpenter?

23 *quest* inquest   28 *count'nance* privilege   30 *even-Christen* fellow
Christian   32 *hold up* keep up   34 *bore arms* had a coat of arms
(the sign of a gentleman)

Clown. Ay, tell me that, and unyoke.°

Other. Marry, now I can tell.

Clown. To't.   55

Other. Mass,° I cannot tell.

Enter Hamlet and Horatio afar off.

Clown. Cudgel thy brains no more about it, for your
dull ass will not mend his pace with beating. And
when you are asked this question next, say "a gravemaker." The houses he makes lasts till doomsday.   60
Go, get thee in, and fetch me a stoup° of liquor.

                              [Exit Other Clown.]

In youth when I did love, did love,   *(Song)*
   Methought it was very sweet
To contract—O—the time for—a—my behove,°
   O, methought there—a—was nothing—a—meet.   65

Hamlet. Has this fellow no feeling of his business? 'A
sings in gravemaking.

Horatio. Custom hath made it in him a property of
easiness.°

Hamlet. 'Tis e'en so. The hand of little employment   70
hath the daintier sense.°

Clown.   But age with his stealing steps   *(Song)*
      Hath clawed me in his clutch,
And hath shipped me into the land,
   As if I had never been such.   75

                        [Throws up a skull.]

Hamlet. That skull had a tongue in it, and could sing
once. How the knave jowls° it to the ground, as if
'twere Cain's jawbone, that did the first murder!
This might be the pate of a politician, which this

53 *unyoke* i.e., stop work for the day 56 *Mass* by the mass 61
stoup tankard 64 *behove* advantage 68–69 *in him a property of
easiness* easy for him 71 *hath the daintier sense* is more sensitive
(because it is not calloused) 77 *jowls* hurls

80   ass now o'erreaches,° one that would circumvent
      God, might it not?

Horatio. It might, my lord.

Hamlet. Or of a courtier, which could say "Good
      morrow, sweet lord! How dost thou, sweet lord?"
85   This might be my Lord Such-a-one, that praised
      my Lord Such-a-one's horse when 'a went to beg
      it, might it not?

Horatio. Ay, my lord.

Hamlet. Why, e'en so, and now my Lady Worm's,
90   chapless,° and knocked about the mazzard° with a
      sexton's spade. Here's fine revolution, an we had
      the trick to see't. Did these bones cost no more
      the breeding but to play at loggets° with them?
      Mine ache to think on't.

93 *Clown.*   A pickax and a spade, a spade,   (*Song*)
                  For and a shrouding sheet;
               O, a pit of clay for to be made
                  For such a guest is meet.
                              [*Throws up another skull.*]

Hamlet. There's another. Why may not that be the
100   skull of a lawyer? Where be his quiddities° now, his
      quillities,° his cases, his tenures,° and his tricks?
      Why does he suffer this mad knave now to knock
      him about the sconce° with a dirty shovel, and will
      not tell him of his action of battery? Hum! This
105·   fellow might be in's time a great buyer of land, with
      his statutes, his recognizances, his fines,° his double
      vouchers, his recoveries. Is this the fine° of his fines,
      and the recovery of his recoveries, to have his fine
      pate full of fine dirt? Will his vouchers vouch him

80 *o'erreaches* (1) reaches over (2) has the advantage over   90
chapless lacking the lower jaw   90 *mazzard* head   93 *loggets* (a
game in which small pieces of wood were thrown at an object)
100 *quiddities* subtle arguments (from Latin *quidditas*, "what-
ness")   101 *quillities* fine distinctions   101 *tenures* legal means of
holding land   103 *sconce* head   106 *his statutes, his recognizances,
his fines* his documents giving a creditor control of a debtor's land,
his bonds of surety, his documents changing an entailed estate into
fee simple (unrestricted ownership)   107 *fine* end

no more of his purchases, and double ones too, than *110*
the length and breadth of a pair of indentures?°
The very conveyances° of his lands will scarcely
lie in this box, and must th' inheritor himself have no
more, ha?

Horatio. Not a jot more, my lord.   *115*

Hamlet. Is not parchment made of sheepskins?

Horatio. Ay, my lord, and of calveskins too.

Hamlet. They are sheep and calves which seek out
assurance° in that. I will speak to this fellow. Whose
grave's this, sirrah?   *120*

Clown. Mine, sir.
[*Sings.*]   O, a pit of clay for to be made
               For such a guest is meet.

Hamlet. I think it be thine indeed, for thou liest in't.

Clown. You lie out on't, sir, and therefore 'tis not *125*
yours. For my part, I do not lie in't, yet it is mine.

Hamlet. Thou dost lie in't, to be in't and say it is
thine. 'Tis for the dead, not for the quick;° therefore thou liest.

Clown. 'Tis a quick lie, sir; 'twill away again from *130*
me to you.

Hamlet. What man dost thou dig it for?

Clown. For no man, sir.

Hamlet. What woman then?

Clown. For none neither.   *135*

Hamlet. Who is to be buried in't?

Clown. One that was a woman, sir; but, rest her soul,
she's dead.

Hamlet. How absolute° the knave is! We must speak by
the card,° or equivocation° will undo us. By the *140*

111 *indentures* contracts   112 *conveyances* legal documents for the
transference of land   119 *assurance* safety   128 *quick* living   139
absolute positive, decided   139–40 *by the card* by the compass card,
i.e., exactly   140 *equivocation* ambiguity

Lord, Horatio, this three years I have took note of
it, the age is grown so picked° that the toe of the
peasant comes so near the heel of the courtier he
galls his kibe.° How long hast thou been a grave-
145 maker?

Clown. Of all the days i' th' year, I came to't that day
that our last king Hamlet overcame Fortinbras.

Hamlet. How long is that since?

Clown. Cannot you tell that? Every fool can tell that. It
150 was that very day that young Hamlet was born—
he that is mad, and sent into England.

Hamlet. Ay, marry, why was he sent into England?

Clown. Why, because 'a was mad. 'A shall recover his
wits there; or, if 'a do not, 'tis no great matter there.

155 *Hamlet.* Why?

Clown. 'Twill not be seen in him there. There the men
are as mad as he.

Hamlet. How came he mad?

Clown. Very strangely, they say.

160 *Hamlet.* How strangely?

Clown. Faith, e'en with losing his wits.

Hamlet. Upon what ground?

Clown. Why, here in Denmark. I have been sexton
here, man and boy, thirty years.

165 *Hamlet.* How long will a man lie i' th' earth ere he rot?

Clown. Faith, if 'a be not rotten before 'a die (as we
have many pocky corses° nowadays that will scarce
hold the laying in), 'a will last you some eight year
or nine year. A tanner will last you nine year.

170 *Hamlet.* Why he, more than another?

Clown. Why, sir, his hide is so tanned with his trade

142 *picked* refined 144 *kibe* sore on the back of the heel 167
pocky corses bodies of persons who had been infected with the
pox (syphilis)

that 'a will keep out water a great while, and your
water is a sore decayer of your whoreson dead body.
Here's a skull now hath lien you i' th' earth three and
twenty years.   175

Hamlet. Whose was it?

Clown. A whoreson mad fellow's it was. Whose do you
think it was?

Hamlet. Nay, I know not.

Clown. A pestilence on him for a mad rogue! 'A poured 180
a flagon of Rhenish on my head once. This same
skull, sir, was, sir, Yorick's skull, the King's jester.

Hamlet. This?

Clown. E'en that.

Hamlet. Let me see. [*Takes the skull.*] Alas, poor 185
Yorick! I knew him, Horatio, a fellow of infinite
jest, of most excellent fancy. He hath borne me on
his back a thousand times. And now how abhorred
in my imagination it is! My gorge rises at it. Here
hung those lips that I have kissed I know not how 190
oft. Where be your gibes now? Your gambols, your
songs, your flashes of merriment that were wont to
set the table on a roar? Not one now to mock your
own grinning? Quite chapfall'n°? Now get you to my
lady's chamber, and tell her, let her paint an inch 195
thick, to this favor° she must come. Make her laugh
at that. Prithee, Horatio, tell me one thing.

Horatio. What's that, my lord?

Hamlet. Dost thou think Alexander looked o' this
fashion i' th' earth?   200

Horatio. E'en so.

Hamlet. And smelt so? Pah!   [*Puts down the skull.*]

Horatio. E'en so, my lord.

---

194 *chapfall'n* (1) down in the mouth (2) jawless 196 *favor*
facial appearance

Hamlet. To what base uses we may return, Horatio!
205 Why may not imagination trace the noble dust of
    Alexander till 'a find it stopping a bunghole?

Horatio. 'Twere to consider too curiously,° to consider
    so.

Hamlet. No, faith, not a jot, but to follow him thither
210 with modesty enough,° and likelihood to lead it; as
    thus: Alexander died, Alexander was buried, Alex-
    ander returneth to dust; the dust is earth; of earth
    we make loam; and why of that loam whereto he was
    converted might they not stop a beer barrel?
215 Imperious Caesar, dead and turned to clay,
    Might stop a hole to keep the wind away.
    O, that that earth which kept the world in awe
    Should patch a wall t' expel the winter's flaw!°
    But soft, but soft awhile! Here comes the King.

*Enter King, Queen, Laertes, and a coffin, with Lords
    attendant [and a Doctor of Divinity].*

220 The Queen, the courtiers. Who is this they follow?
    And with such maimèd° rites? This doth betoken
    The corse they follow did with desp'rate hand
    Fordo it° own life. 'Twas of some estate.°
    Couch° we awhile, and mark. [*Retires with Horatio.*]

Laertes. What ceremony else?

225 *Hamlet.*   That is Laertes,
    A very noble youth. Mark.

Laertes. What ceremony else?

Doctor. Her obsequies have been as far enlarged
    As we have warranty. Her death was doubtful,°
230 And, but that great command o'ersways the order,
    She should in ground unsanctified been lodged
    Till the last trumpet. For charitable prayers,

207 *curiously* minutely 210 *with modesty enough* without exag-
geration 218 *flaw* gust 221 *maimèd* incomplete 223 *Fordo it*
destroy its 223 *estate* high rank 224 *Couch* hide 229 *doubtful*
suspicious

Shards,° flints, and pebbles should be thrown on her.
Yet here she is allowed her virgin crants,°
Her maiden strewments,° and the bringing home   235
Of bell and burial.

Laertes. Must there no more be done?

Doctor.   No more be done.
We should profane the service of the dead
To sing a requiem and such rest to her
As to peace-parted souls.

Laertes.   Lay her i' th' earth,   240
And from her fair and unpolluted flesh
May violets spring! I tell thee, churlish priest,
A minist'ring angel shall my sister be
When thou liest howling!

Hamlet.   What, the fair Ophelia?

Queen. Sweets to the sweet! Farewell.   245
                              [*Scatters flowers.*]
I hoped thou shouldst have been my Hamlet's wife.
I thought thy bride bed to have decked, sweet maid,
And not have strewed thy grave.

Laertes.   O, treble woe
Fall ten times treble on that cursèd head
Whose wicked deed thy most ingenious sense°   250
Deprived thee of! Hold off the earth awhile,
Till I have caught her once more in mine arms.
                              Leaps in the grave.
Now pile your dust upon the quick and dead
Till of this flat a mountain you have made
T'o'ertop old Pelion° or the skyish head   255
Of blue Olympus.

Hamlet.   [*Coming forward*] What is he whose grief

---

233 *Shards* broken pieces of pottery 234 *crants* garlands 235
strewments i.e., of flowers 250 *most ingenious sense* finely en-
dowed mind 255 *Pelion* (according to classical legend, giants in
their fight with the gods sought to reach heaven by piling Mount
Pelion and Mount Ossa on Mount Olympus)

Bears such an emphasis, whose phrase of sorrow
Conjures the wand'ring stars,° and makes them
    stand
Like wonder-wounded hearers? This is I,
Hamlet the Dane.

260 *Laertes.*   The devil take thy soul!
                              [*Grapples with him.*]°

Hamlet. Thou pray'st not well.
    I prithee take thy fingers from my throat,
    For, though I am not splenitive° and rash,
    Yet have I in me something dangerous,
265 Which let thy wisdom fear. Hold off thy hand.

King. Pluck them asunder.

Queen.   Hamlet, Hamlet!

All. Gentlemen!

Horatio.   Good my lord, be quiet.
                        [*Attendants part them.*]

Hamlet. Why, I will fight with him upon this theme
    Until my eyelids will no longer wag.

270 *Queen.* O my son, what theme?

Hamlet. I loved Ophelia. Forty thousand brothers
    Could not with all their quantity of love
    Make up my sum. What wilt thou do for her?

King. O, he is mad, Laertes.

275 *Queen.* For love of God forbear him.

Hamlet. 'Swounds, show me what thou't do.
    Woo't weep? Woo't fight? Woo't fast? Woo't tear
        thyself?
    Woo't drink up eisel?° Eat a crocodile?

258 *wand'ring stars* planets   260 s.d.*Grapples with him* (Q1, a bad
quarto, presumably reporting a version that toured, has a previous
direction saying "Hamlet leaps in after Laertes." Possibly he does
so, somewhat hysterically. But such a direction—absent from the
two good texts, Q2 and F—makes Hamlet the aggressor, somewhat
contradicting his next speech. Perhaps Laertes leaps out of the
grave to attack Hamlet)   263 *splenitive* fiery (the spleen was
thought to be the seat of anger)   278 *eisel* vinegar

I'll do't. Dost thou come here to whine?
To outface me with leaping in her grave?   280
Be buried quick with her, and so will I.
And if thou prate of mountains, let them throw
Millions of acres on us, till our ground,
Singeing his pate against the burning zone,°
Make Ossa like a wart! Nay, an thou'lt mouth,   285
I'll rant as well as thou.

Queen.   This is mere madness;
And thus a while the fit will work on him.
Anon, as patient as the female dove
When that her golden couplets arc disclosed,°
His silence will sit drooping.

Hamlet.   Hear you, sir.   290
What is the reason that you use me thus?
I loved you ever. But it is no matter.
Let Hercules himself do what he may,
The cat will mew, and dog will have his day.

King. I pray thee, good Horatio, wait upon him.   295
                    Exit Hamlet and Horatio.
[*To Laertes*] Strengthen your patience in our last
   night's speech.
We'll put the matter to the present push.°
Good Gertrude, set some watch over your son.
This grave shall have a living° monument.
An hour of quiet shortly shall we see;   300
Till then in patience our proceeding be.   *Exeunt.*

---

284 *burning zone* sun's orbit   289 *golden couplets are disclosed*
(the dove lays two eggs, and the newly hatched [*disclosed*] young
are covered with golden down)   297 *present push* immediate test
299 *living* lasting (with perhaps also a reference to the plot against
Hamlet's life)

[Scene II. *The castle.*]

Enter Hamlet and Horatio.

Hamlet. So much for this, sir; now shall you see the other.
You do remember all the circumstance?

Horatio. Remember it, my lord!

Hamlet. Sir, in my heart there was a kind of fighting
5   That would not let me sleep. Methought I lay
Worse than the mutines in the bilboes.° Rashly
(And praised be rashness for it) let us know,
Our indiscretion sometime serves us well
When our deep plots do pall,° and that should learn us
10   There's a divinity that shapes our ends,
Rough-hew them how we will.

Horatio.   That is most certain.

Hamlet. Up from my cabin,
My sea gown scarfed about me, in the dark
Groped I to find out them, had my desire,
15   Fingered° their packet, and in fine° withdrew
To mine own room again, making so bold,
My fears forgetting manners, to unseal
Their grand commission; where I found, Horatio—
Ah, royal knavery!—an exact command,
20   Larded° with many several sorts of reasons,
Importing Denmark's health, and England's too,
With, ho, such bugs and goblins in my life,°
That on the supervise,° no leisure bated,°
No, not to stay the grinding of the ax,

V.ii.6 *mutines in the bilboes* mutineers in fetters 9 *pall* fail 15
Fingered stole 15 *in fine* finally 20 *Larded* enriched 22 *such bugs and goblins in my life* such bugbears and imagined terrors if I were allowed to live 23 *supervise* reading 23 *leisure bated* delay allowed

My head should be struck off.

Horatio.   Is't possible?   25

Hamlet. Here's the commission; read it at more leisure.
But wilt thou hear now how I did proceed?

Horatio. I beseech you.

Hamlet. Being thus benetted round with villains,
Or° I could make a prologue to my brains,   30
They had begun the play. I sat me down,
Devised a new commission, wrote it fair.
I once did hold it, as our statists° do,
A baseness to write fair,° and labored much
How to forget that learning, but, sir, now   35
It did me yeoman's service. Wilt thou know
Th' effect° of what I wrote?

Horatio.   Ay, good my lord.

Hamlet. An earnest conjuration from the King,
As England was his faithful tributary,
As love between them like the palm might flourish,   40
As peace should still her wheaten garland wear
And stand a comma° 'tween their amities,
And many suchlike as's of great charge,°
That on the view and knowing of these contents,
Without debatement further, more or less,   45
He should those bearers put to sudden death,
Not shriving° time allowed.

Horatio.   How was this sealed?

Hamlet. Why, even in that was heaven ordinant.°
I had my father's signet in my purse,
Which was the model° of that Danish seal,   50
Folded the writ up in the form of th' other,
Subscribed it, gave't th' impression, placed it safely,
The changeling never known. Now, the next day
Was our sea fight, and what to this was sequent
Thou knowest already.   55

30 *Or* ere   33 *statists* statesmen   34 *fair* clearly   37 *effect* purport
42 *comma* link   43 *great charge* (1) serious exhortation (2) heavy
burden (punning on *as's* and "asses")   47 *shriving* absolution   48
ordinant ruling   50 *model* counterpart

Horatio. So Guildenstern and Rosencrantz go to't.

Hamlet. Why, man, they did make love to this employment.
They are not near my conscience; their defeat
Does by their own insinuation° grow.
60 'Tis dangerous when the baser nature comes
Between the pass° and fell° incensèd points
Of mighty opposites.

Horatio.   Why, what a king is this!

Hamlet. Does it not, think thee, stand me now upon°—
He that hath killed my king, and whored my mother,
65 Popped in between th' election° and my hopes,
Thrown out his angle° for my proper life,°
And with such coz'nage°—is't not perfect conscience
To quit° him with this arm? And is't not to be damned
To let this canker of our nature come
70 In further evil?

Horatio. It must be shortly known to him from England
What is the issue of the business there.

Hamlet. It will be short; the interim's mine,
And a man's life's no more than to say "one."
75 But I am very sorry, good Horatio,
That to Laertes I forgot myself,
For by the image of my cause I see
The portraiture of his. I'll court his favors.
But sure the bravery° of his grief did put me
Into a tow'ring passion.

80 *Horatio.*   Peace, who comes here?

Enter young Osric, a courtier.

Osric. Your lordship is right welcome back to Denmark.

59 *insinuation* meddling 61 *pass* thrust 61 *fell* cruel 63 *stand me now upon* become incumbent upon me 65 *election* (the Danish monarchy was elective) 66 *angle* fishing line 66 *my proper life* my own life 67 *coz'nage* trickery 68 *quit* pay back 79 *bravery* bravado

Hamlet. I humbly thank you, sir. [*Aside to Horatio*]
Dost know this waterfly?

Horatio. [*Aside to Hamlet*] No, my good lord.

Hamlet. [*Aside to Horatio*] Thy state is the more gra- 85
cious, for 'tis a vice to know him. He hath much
land, and fertile. Let a beast be lord of beasts, and
his crib shall stand at the king's mess.° 'Tis a
chough,° but, as I say, spacious° in the possession
of dirt. 90

Osric. Sweet lord, if your lordship were at leisure, I
should impart a thing to you from his Majesty.

Hamlet. I will receive it, sir, with all diligence of spirit.
Put your bonnet to his right use. 'Tis for the head.

Osric. I thank your lordship, it is very hot. 95

Hamlet. No, believe me, 'tis very cold; the wind is
northerly.

Osric. It is indifferent cold, my lord, indeed.

Hamlet. But yet methinks it is very sultry and hot for
my complexion.° 100

Osric. Exceedingly, my lord; it is very sultry, as 'twere
—I cannot tell how. But, my lord, his Majesty bade
me signify to you that 'a has laid a great wager on
your head. Sir, this is the matter——

Hamlet. I beseech you remember. 105
　　　　　　　[*Hamlet moves him to put on his hat.*]

Osric. Nay, good my lord; for my ease, in good faith.
Sir, here is newly come to court Laertes—believe
me, an absolute gentleman, full of most excellent
differences,° of very soft society and great showing.
Indeed, to speak feelingly° of him, he is the card° 110
or calendar of gentry; for you shall find in him the
continent° of what part a gentleman would see.

88 *mess* table　　89 *chough* jackdaw (here, chatterer)　　89 *spacious*
well off　　100 *complexion* temperament　　109 *differences* distinguishing characteristics　　110 *feelingly* justly　　110 *card* chart　　112 *con-
tinent* summary

Hamlet. Sir, his definement° suffers no perdition° in
you, though, I know, to divide him inventorially
115   would dozy° th' arithmetic of memory, and yet but
yaw neither in respect of his quick sail.° But, in the
verity of extolment, I take him to be a soul of great
article,° and his infusion° of such dearth and rare-
ness as, to make true diction° of him, his semblable°
120   is his mirror, and who else would trace him, his umbrage,° nothing more.

Osric. Your lordship speaks most infallibly of him.

Hamlet. The concernancy,° sir? Why do we wrap the
gentleman in our more rawer breath?

125   *Osric.* Sir?

Horatio. Is't not possible to understand in another
tongue? You will to't,° sir, really.

Hamlet. What imports the nomination of this gentleman?

130   *Osric.* Of Laertes?

Horatio. [*Aside to Hamlet*] His purse is empty already.
All's golden words are spent.

Hamlet. Of him, sir.

Osric. I know you are not ignorant——

135   *Hamlet.* I would you did, sir; yet, in faith, if you did, it
would not much approve° me. Well, sir?

Osric. You are not ignorant of what excellence Laertes
is——

Hamlet. I dare not confess that, lest I should compare
140   with him in excellence; but to know a man well were
to know himself.

113 *definement* description   113 *perdition* loss   115 *dozy* dizzy
115–16 *and yet . . . quick sail* i.e., and yet only stagger despite all
(*yaw neither*) in trying to overtake his virtues   118 *article* (literally, "item," but here perhaps "traits" or "importance")   118 *in-
fusion* essential quality   119 *diction* description   119 *semblable*
likeness   120–21 *umbrage* shadow   123 *concernancy* meaning   127
will to't will get there   136 *approve* commend

Osric. I mean, sir, for his weapon; but in the imputa-
    tion° laid on him by them, in his meed° he's un-
    fellowed.

Hamlet. What's his weapon?   145

Osric. Rapier and dagger.

Hamlet. That's two of his weapons—but well.

Osric. The King, sir, hath wagered with him six Bar-
    bary horses, against the which he has impawned,° as
    I take it, six French rapiers and poniards, with their   150
    assigns,° as girdle, hangers,° and so. Three of the
    carriages,° in faith, are very dear to fancy, very re-
    sponsive° to the hilts, most delicate carriages, and
    of very liberal conceit.°

Hamlet. What call you the carriages?   155

Horatio. [*Aside to Hamlet*] I knew you must be edified
    by the margent° ere you had done.

Osric. The carriages, sir, are the hangers.

Hamlet. The phrase would be more germane to the
    matter if we could carry a cannon by our sides. I   160
    would it might be hangers till then. But on! Six Bar-
    bary horses against six French swords, their assigns,
    and three liberal-conceited carriages—that's the
    French bet against the Danish. Why is this all im-
    pawned, as you call it?   165

Osric. The King, sir, hath laid, sir, that in a dozen
    passes between yourself and him he shall not exceed
    you three hits; he hath laid on twelve for nine, and
    it would come to immediate trial if your lordship
    would vouchsafe the answer.   170

Hamlet. How if I answer no?

Osric. I mean, my lord, the opposition of your person
    in trial.

142–43 *imputation* reputation   143 *meed* merit   149 *impawned*
wagered   151 *assigns* accompaniments   151 *hangers* straps hanging the sword to the belt   152 *carriages* (an affected word for
hangers)   152–53 *responsive* corresponding   154 *liberal conceit*
elaborate design   157 *margent* i.e., marginal (explanatory) comment

Hamlet. Sir, I will walk here in the hall. If it please
175   his Majesty, it is the breathing time of day with me.°
     Let the foils be brought, the gentleman willing, and
     the King hold his purpose, I will win for him an I
     can; if not, I will gain nothing but my shame and
     the odd hits.

180 *Osric.* Shall I deliver you e'en so?

Hamlet. To this effect, sir, after what flourish your
     nature will.

Osric. I commend my duty to your lordship.

Hamlet. Yours, yours. [*Exit Osric.*] He does well to
185   commend it himself; there are no tongues else for's
     turn.

Horatio. This lapwing° runs away with the shell on his
     head.

Hamlet. 'A did comply, sir, with his dug° before 'a
190   sucked it. Thus has he, and many more of the
     same breed that I know the drossy age dotes on,
     only got the tune of the time and, out of an habit of
     encounter,° a kind of yeasty° collection, which
     carries them through and through the most fanned
195   and winnowed opinions; and do but blow them to
     their trial, the bubbles are out.°

Enter a Lord.

Lord. My lord, his Majesty commended him to you by
     young Osric, who brings back to him that you
     attend him in the hall. He sends to know if your
200   pleasure hold to play with Laertes, or that you will
     take longer time.

Hamlet. I am constant to my purposes; they follow the

---

175 *breathing time of day with me* time when I take exercise   187 *lapwing* (the new-hatched lapwing was thought to run around with half its shell on its head)   189 *'A did comply, sir, with his dug* he was ceremoniously polite to his mother's breast   192–93 *out of an habit of encounter* out of his own superficial way of meeting and conversing with people   193 *yeasty* frothy   196 *the bubbles are out* i.e., they are blown away (the reference is to the "yeasty collection")

King's pleasure. If his fitness speaks, mine is ready;
now or whensoever, provided I be so able as now.

Lord. The King and Queen and all are coming down. 205

Hamlet. In happy time.

Lord. The Queen desires you to use some gentle enter-
tainment° to Laertes before you fall to play.

Hamlet. She well instructs me.   [*Exit Lord.*]

Horatio. You will lose this wager, my lord.   210

Hamlet. I do not think so. Since he went into France
I have been in continual practice. I shall win at the
odds. But thou wouldst not think how ill all's here
about my heart. But it is no matter.

Horatio. Nay, good my lord——   215

Hamlet. It is but foolery, but it is such a kind of gain-
giving° as would perhaps trouble a woman.

Horatio. If your mind dislike anything, obey it. I will
forestall their repair hither and say you are not fit.

Hamlet. Not a whit, we defy augury. There is special 220
providence in the fall of a sparrow.° If it be now,
'tis not to come; if it be not to come, it will be now;
if it be not now, yet it will come. The readiness is
all. Since no man of aught he leaves knows, what
is't to leave betimes?° Let be.   225

A table prepared. [*Enter*] *Trumpets, Drums, and
Officers with cushions; King, Queen,* [*Osric,*] *and
all the State,* [*with*] *foils, daggers,* [*and stoups
of wine borne in*]*; and Laertes.*

King. Come, Hamlet, come, and take this hand from
me.

[*The King puts Laertes' hand into Hamlet's.*]

207–08 *to use some gentle entertainment* to be courteous 217 *gaingiving* misgiving 221 *the fall of a sparrow* (cf. Matthew 10:29
"Are not two sparrows sold for a farthing? and one of them shall
not fall on the ground without your Father") 225 *betimes* early

Hamlet. Give me your pardon, sir. I have done you
    wrong,
    But pardon't, as you are a gentleman.
    This presence° knows, and you must needs have
    heard,
230   How I am punished with a sore distraction.
    What I have done
    That might your nature, honor, and exception°
    Roughly awake, I here proclaim was madness.
    Was't Hamlet wronged Laertes? Never Hamlet.
235   If Hamlet from himself be ta'en away,
    And when he's not himself does wrong Laertes,
    Then Hamlet does it not, Hamlet denies it.
    Who does it then? His madness. If't be so,
    Hamlet is of the faction° that is wronged;
240   His madness is poor Hamlet's enemy.
    Sir, in this audience,
    Let my disclaiming from a purposed evil
    Free me so far in your most generous thoughts
    That I have shot my arrow o'er the house
    And hurt my brother.

245 *Laertes.*   I am satisfied in nature,
    Whose motive in this case should stir me most
    To my revenge. But in my terms of honor
    I stand aloof, and will no reconcilement
    Till by some elder masters of known honor
250   I have a voice and precedent° of peace
    To keep my name ungored. But till that time
    I do receive your offered love like love,
    And will not wrong it.

Hamlet.   I embrace it freely,
    And will this brother's wager frankly play.
    Give us the foils. Come on.

255 *Laertes.*   Come, one for me.

Hamlet. I'll be your foil,° Laertes. In mine ignorance

229 *presence* royal assembly   232 *exception* disapproval   239 *faction* party, side   250 *voice and precedent* authoritative opinion justified by precedent   256 *foil* (1) blunt sword (2) background (of metallic leaf) for a jewel

　Your skill shall, like a star i' th' darkest night,
　Stick fiery off° indeed.

Laertes.　　　　　　　　You mock me, sir.

Hamlet. No, by this hand.

King. Give them the foils, young Osric. Cousin Hamlet, 260
　You know the wager?

Hamlet.　　　　　　　　Very well, my lord.
　Your grace has laid the odds o' th' weaker side.

King. I do not fear it, I have seen you both;
　But since he is bettered,° we have therefore odds.

Laertes. This is too heavy; let me see another.　　　265

Hamlet. This likes me well. These foils have all a
　　length?

　　　　　　　　　　　　　　　Prepare to play.

Osric. Ay, my good lord.

King. Set me the stoups of wine upon that table.
　If Hamlet give the first or second hit,
　Or quit° in answer of the third exchange,　　　270
　Let all the battlements their ordnance fire.
　The King shall drink to Hamlet's better breath,
　And in the cup an union° shall he throw
　Richer than that which four successive kings
　In Denmark's crown have worn. Give me the cups, 275
　And let the kettle° to the trumpet speak,
　The trumpet to the cannoneer without,
　The cannons to the heavens, the heaven to earth,
　"Now the King drinks to Hamlet." Come, begin.
　　　　　　　　　　　　　Trumpets the while.
　And you, the judges, bear a wary eye.　　　280

Hamlet. Come on, sir.

Laertes.　　　　　　Come, my lord.　　　*They play.*

Hamlet.　　　　　　　　　　One.

Laertes.　　　　　　　　　　　　No.

258 *Stick fiery off* stand out brilliantly　264 *bettered* has improved
(in France)　270 *quit* repay, hit back　273 *union* pearl　276 *kettle*
kettledrum

Hamlet.   Judgment?

Osric. A hit, a very palpable hit.
    Drum, trumpets, and shot. Flourish; a piece goes off.

Laertes.   Well, again.

King. Stay, give me drink. Hamlet, this pearl is thine.
    Here's to thy health. Give him the cup.

285 *Hamlet.* I'll play this bout first; set it by awhile.
    Come. [*They play.*] Another hit. What say you?

Laertes. A touch, a touch; I do confess't.

King. Our son shall win.

Queen.   He's fat,° and scant of breath.
    Here, Hamlet, take my napkin, rub thy brows.
290   The Queen carouses to thy fortune, Hamlet.

Hamlet. Good madam!

King.   Gertrude, do not drink.

Queen. I will, my lord; I pray you pardon me. [*Drinks.*]

King. [*Aside*] It is the poisoned cup; it is too late.

Hamlet. I dare not drink yet, madam—by and by.

295 *Queen.* Come, let me wipe thy face.

Laertes. My lord, I'll hit him now.

King.   I do not think't.

Laertes. [*Aside*] And yet it is almost against my con-
    science.

Hamlet. Come for the third, Laertes. You do but dally.
    I pray you pass with your best violence;
300   I am sure you make a wanton° of me.

Laertes. Say you so? Come on.   [*They*] *play.*

Osric. Nothing neither way.

Laertes. Have at you now!
        In scuffling they change rapiers, [and both are
                       wounded].

288 *fat* (1) sweaty (2) out of training   300 *wanton* spoiled child

King.   Part them. They are incensed.

Hamlet. Nay, come—again!   [*The Queen falls.*]

Osric.   Look to the Queen there, ho!

Horatio. They bleed on both sides. How is it, my lord?   305

Osric. How is't, Laertes?

Laertes. Why, as a woodcock to mine own springe,°
   Osric.
   I am justly killed with mine own treachery.

Hamlet. How does the Queen?

King.   She sounds° to see them bleed.

Queen. No, no, the drink, the drink! O my dear
   Hamlet!   310
   The drink, the drink! I am poisoned.   [*Dies.*]

Hamlet. O villainy! Ho! Let the door be locked.
   Treachery! Seek it out.   [*Laertes falls.*]

Laertes. It is here, Hamlet. Hamlet, thou art slain;
   No med'cine in the world can do thee good.   315
   In thee there is not half an hour's life.
   The treacherous instrument is in thy hand,
   Unbated and envenomed. The foul practice°
   Hath turned itself on me. Lo, here I lie,
   Never to rise again. Thy mother's poisoned.   320
   I can no more. The King, the King's to blame.

Hamlet. The point envenomed too?
   Then, venom, to thy work.   *Hurts the King.*

All. Treason! Treason!

King. O, yet defend me, friends. I am but hurt.   325

Hamlet. Here, thou incestuous, murd'rous, damnèd
   Dane,
   Drink off this potion. Is thy union here?
   Follow my mother.   *King dies.*

Laertes.   He is justly served.

307 *springe* snare   309 *sounds* swoons   318 *practice* deception

It is a poison tempered° by himself.
330   Exchange forgiveness with me, noble Hamlet.
Mine and my father's death come not upon thee,
Nor thine on me!   *Dies.*

Hamlet. Heaven make thee free of it! I follow thee.
I am dead, Horatio. Wretched Queen, adieu!
335   You that look pale and tremble at this chance,
That are but mutes° or audience to this act,
Had I but time (as this fell sergeant,° Death,
Is strict in his arrest) O, I could tell you—
But let it be. Horatio, I am dead;
340   Thou livest; report me and my cause aright
To the unsatisfied.°

Horatio.   Never believe it.
I am more an antique Roman° than a Dane.
Here's yet some liquor left.

Hamlet.   As th' art a man,
Give me the cup. Let go. By heaven, I'll ha't!
345   O God, Horatio, what a wounded name,
Things standing thus unknown, shall live behind me!
If thou didst ever hold me in thy heart,
Absent thee from felicity° awhile,
And in this harsh world draw thy breath in pain,
To tell my story.   *A march afar off. [Exit Osric.]*
350   What warlike noise is this?

                                      Enter Osric.

Osric. Young Fortinbras, with conquest come from
       Poland,
To th' ambassadors of England gives
This warlike volley.

Hamlet.   O, I die, Horatio!
The potent poison quite o'ercrows° my spirit.
355   I cannot live to hear the news from England,

329 *tempered* mixed   336 *mutes* performers who have no words to
speak   337 *fell sergeant* dread sheriff's officer   341 *unsatisfied* un-
informed   342 *antique Roman* (with reference to the old Roman
fashion of suicide)   348 *felicity* i.e., the felicity of death   354 *o'er-
crows* overpowers (as a triumphant cock crows over its weak
opponent)

But I do prophesy th' election lights
On Fortinbras. He has my dying voice.
So tell him, with th' occurrents,° more and less,
Which have solicited°—the rest is silence.   *Dies.*

Horatio. Now cracks a noble heart. Good night, sweet
    Prince,   860
And flights of angels sing thee to thy rest.
                            [*March within.*]
Why does the drum come hither?

   *Enter Fortinbras, with the Ambassadors with
        Drum, Colors, and Attendants.*

Fortinbras. Where is this sight?

Horatio.   What is it you would see?
If aught of woe or wonder, cease your search.

Fortinbras. This quarry° cries on havoc.° O proud
    Death,   365
What feast is toward° in thine eternal cell
That thou so many princes at a shot
So bloodily hast struck?

Ambassador.   The sight is dismal;
And our affairs from England come too late.
The ears are senseless that should give us hearing   370
To tell him his commandment is fulfilled,
That Rosencrantz and Guildenstern are dead.
Where should we have our thanks?

Horatio.   Not from his° mouth,
Had it th' ability of life to thank you.
He never gave commandment for their death.   375
But since, so jump° upon this bloody question,
You from the Polack wars, and you from England,
Are here arrived, give order that these bodies
High on a stage° be placèd to the view,
And let me speak to th' yet unknowing world   380
How these things came about. So shall you hear

358 *occurrents* occurrences 359 *solicited* incited 365 *quarry* heap
of slain bodies 365 *cries on havoc* proclaims general slaughter
366 *toward* in preparation 373 *his* (Claudius') 376 *jump* precisely 379 *stage* platform

Of carnal, bloody, and unnatural acts,
Of accidental judgments, casual° slaughters,
Of deaths put on by cunning and forced cause,
385 And, in this upshot, purposes mistook
Fall'n on th' inventors' heads. All this can I
Truly deliver.

Fortinbras.   Let us haste to hear it,
And call the noblest to the audience.
For me, with sorrow I embrace my fortune.
390 I have some rights of memory° in this kingdom,
Which now to claim my vantage doth invite me.

Horatio. Of that I shall have also cause to speak,
And from his mouth whose voice will draw on°
     more.
But let this same be presently performed,
Even while men's minds are wild, lest more mis-
395   chance
On° plots and errors happen.

Fortinbras.   Let four captains
Bear Hamlet like a soldier to the stage,
For he was likely, had he been put on,°
To have proved most royal; and for his passage°
400 The soldiers' music and the rite of war
Speak loudly for him.
Take up the bodies. Such a sight as this
Becomes the field,° but here shows much amiss.
Go, bid the soldiers shoot.

*Exeunt marching; after the which a peal of ordnance
                              are shot off.*

FINIS

383 *casual* not humanly planned, chance 390 *rights of memory*
remembered claims 393 *voice will draw on* vote will influence
396 *On* on top of 398 *put on* advanced (to the throne) 399 *passage* death 403 *field* battlefield

Textual Note

Shakespeare's *Hamlet* comes to us in three versions. The first of them, known as the First Quarto, was published in 1603 by N. L. [Nicholas Ling] and John Trundell, who advertised it on the title page as having been played "by his Highness Servants in the City of London, as also in the two universities of Cambridge and Oxford, and elsewhere." This was a pirated edition, published without the consent of the owners, and Shakespeare had nothing to do with it. In the preceding year an attempt had been made to forestall just such a venture. On July 26, 1602, James Roberts, a printer friendly to Shakespeare's company, had entered in the Stationers' Register "A book called The Revenge of Hamlet Prince of Denmark as it was lately acted by the Lord Chamberlain his Servants." This was intended to serve as a kind of copyright. It should be said in passing that "his Highness Servants" were the King's Men and that the Chamberlain's Men became the King's Men on May 19, 1603, when James I took Shakespeare's company under his direct protection.

The copy which Ling and Trundell sent to the printer was an extraordinary hodgepodge, so that the First Quarto gives us a very poor notion of Shakespeare's play. How this copy came into being has been the subject of much investigation, but there is little agreement. In general there are three schools of thought: (1) the First Quarto is a badly reported version of *Hamlet* as Shakespeare wrote it once and for all; (2) it is a badly reported version of an early draft of Shakespeare's play; and (3) it was

expanded from some actor's parts of an early version of
the play. This last seems most likely, since some of the lines,
notably those of Marcellus, are accurate, other passages
are partially correct, and still others are sheer invention.
All three levels are to be found in the soliloquy beginning
"To be or not to be."

> To be or not to be, ay there's the point,
> To die, to sleep, is that all? Ay all:
> No, to sleep, to dream, ay marry there it goes,
> For in that dream of death, when we awake,
> And borne before an everlasting judge,
> From whence no passenger ever returned,
> The undiscovered country, at whose sight
> The happy smile, and the accursed damned.
> But for this, the joyful hope of this,
> Who'd bear the scorns and flattery of the world,
> Scorned by the right rich, the rich cursed of the poor?
> The widow being oppressed, the orphan wronged,
> The taste of hunger, or a tyrant's reign,
> And thousand more calamities besides,
> To grunt and sweat under this weary life,
> When that he may his full quietus make,
> With a bare bodkin, who would this endure,
> But for a hope of something after death?
> Which pulses the brain, and doth confound the sense,
> Which makes us rather bear those evils we have,
> Than fly to others that we know not of.
> Ay that, O this conscience makes cowards of us all,
> Lady in thy orisons, be all my sins rememb'red

It is clear that there is a hand other than Shakespeare's in
this. That the First Quarto is a debased version of an early
version of the play is suggested by, most notably, changes
in names. Why should Polonius, for instance, become
Corambis if the copy were based on the version Shakespeare wrote once and for all?

It was not considered good business to publish a play
while it was still popular in the theater, for it could then
be acted in the provinces by other than its owners, reduc-
ing the public for the play when Shakespeare's company

took it on tour. This being so, the publication of the First Quarto had done Shakespeare a double injury: the play was in print, and it misrepresented its author. Shakespeare had some leisure at this time, the theaters being closed because of the plague from March 1603 to April 1604. We may suppose that he decided to revise the play and have it printed. In any case, another edition of *Hamlet* appeared in 1604. The title page seems designed to tell the public that this is the genuine article: "The Tragical History of Hamlet, Prince of Denmark. By William Shakespeare. Newly imprinted and enlarged to almost as much again as it was, according to the true and perfect copy." The statement is literally true. The Second Quarto is almost twice as long as the First Quarto, and although it lacks some passages preserved in the First Folio, the Second Quarto is the fullest and best version of the play.

The third version of *Hamlet* is to be found in the First Folio, 1623, the collected edition of Shakespeare's plays made by his friends and associates in the theater, John Heminges and Henry Condell. Here the text is based on the acting version of the play. The Folio gives us some ninety lines not found in the Second Quarto. These include two passages of considerable length, II.ii.243–74 and II.ii.345–70, but the Folio does not give us some two hundred lines found in the Second Quarto. These are mostly reflective passages, including Hamlet's last soliloquy, "How all occasions do inform against me." As befits an acting version, the Folio stage directions are more numerous and frequently are fuller. Modern editions are made by collation of the Second Quarto and the First Folio and are therefore longer than either of them.

Because the Second Quarto is the longest version, giving us more of the play as Shakespeare conceived it than either of the others, it serves as the basic version for this text. Unfortunately the printers of it often worked carelessly. Words and phrases are omitted, there are plain misreadings of Shakespeare's manuscript, speeches are sometimes wrongly assigned. It was therefore necessary to turn to the First Folio for many readings. Neither the First Quarto nor the Second Quarto is divided into acts

or scenes; the Folio indicates only the following: I.i, I.ii,
I.iii, II, II.ii. The present edition, to allow for easy
reference, follows the traditional divisions of the Globe
edition, placing them (as well as indications of locale)
in brackets to indicate that they are editorial, not authorial.
Punctuation and spelling are modernized (*and* is given
as *an* when it means "if"), obvious typographical errors
are corrected, abbreviations are expanded, speech prefixes
are regularized and the positions of stage directions are
slightly altered where necessary. Other departures from the
Second Quarto are listed below. First is given the adopted
reading, in italic, and then the Second Quarto's reading, in
roman. The vast majority of these adopted readings are
from the Folio; if an adopted reading is not from the Folio,
the fact is indicated by a bracketed remark explaining, for
example, that it is drawn from the First Quarto [Q1] or
the Second Folio [F2] or an editor's conjecture [ed].

I.i.16 *soldier* souldiers   63 *Polacks* [F has "Pollax"] pollax   68 *my*
mine   73 *why* with   73 *cast* cost   88 *those* these   91 *returned*
returne   94 *designed* [F2] design   112 *mote* [ed] moth   121 *feared*
[ed] feare   138 *you* your   140 *at it* it   142 s.d. *Exit Ghost* [Q2
omits]

I.ii.1 s.d. *Councilors* [ed] Counsaile: as   41 s.d. *Exit Voltemand
and Cornelius* [Q2 omits]   58 *He hath* Hath   67 *so* so much
77 *good* coold   82 *shapes* [ed; F has "shewes"] chapes   96 *a mind* or
minde   132 *self-slaughter* seale slaughter   133 *weary* wary   137 *to
this* thus   143 *would* should   149 *even she* [Q2 omits]   175 *to
drink deep* for to drinke   178 *to see* to   209 *Where, as* [ed]
Whereas   224 *Indeed, indeed, sirs* Indeede Sirs   237 *Very like,
very like* Very like   238 *hundred* hundreth   257 *foul* fonde

I.iii.3 *convoy is* conuay in   12 *bulk* bulkes   18 *For he himself is
subject to his birth* [Q2 omits]   49 *like a* a   68 *thine* thy   74 *Are*
Or   75 *be* boy   76 *loan* loue   83 *invites* inuests   109 *Tend'ring*
[Q1] Wrong [F has "Roaming"]   115 *springes* springs   123 *parley*
parle   125 *tether* tider   131 *beguile* beguide

I.iv.1 *shrewdly* shroudly   2 *a nipping* nipping   6 s.d. *go* [ed] goes
19 *clepe* [ed] clip   27 *the* [ed] their   33 *Their* [ed] His   36 *evil*
[ed] eale   57 s.d. *Ghost beckons Hamlet* Beckins   69 *my lord* my
70 *summit* [ed] somnet [F has "sonnet"]   82 *artere* [ed] arture
[F has "artire"]   87 *imagination* imagion

I.v.47 *what a* what   55 *lust* but   56 *sate* sort   64 *leperous* leaprous
68 *posset* possesse   91 s.d. *Exit*   [Q2 omits]   95 *stiffly* swiftly
113 *Horatio and Marcellus (Within)* Enter Horatio and Marcellus
[Q2 gives the speech to Horatio]   116 *bird* and   122 *heaven, my
lord* heauen   132 *Look you, I'll* I will   170 *some'er* [ed] so mere
[F has "so ere"]

II.i. s.d. *Reynaldo* or two   28 *Faith, no* Fayth   38 *warrant* wit
39 *sullies* sallies   40 *i' th'* with   52–53 *at "friend or so," and
"gentleman"* [Q2 omits]   112 *quoted* coted

II.ii.43 *Assure you* I assure   57 *o'erhasty* hastie   58 s.d. *Enter
Polonius, Voltemand, and Cornelius* Enter Embassadors   90 *since
brevity* breuitie   108 s.d. *the letter* [Q2 omits, but has "letter" at
side of line 116]   126 *above* about   137 *winking* working   143
his her   148 *watch* wath   149 *a lightness* lightnes   151 *'tis this*
this   167 s.d. *Enter Hamlet reading on a book* Enter Hamlet
190 *far gone, far gone* far gone   205 *you yourself* your selfe   205
should be shall growe   212 *sanity* sanctity   214–15 *and suddenly
. . . between him* [Q2 omits]   217 *will* will not   227 *excellent* extent   231 *overhappy* euer happy   232 *cap* lap   240 *but that* but
the   243–74 *Let me question . . . dreadfully attended* [Q2 omits]
278 *even* euer   285 *Why anything* Any thing   312 *a piece* peece
318 *woman* women   329 *of me* on me   332–33 *the clown . . .
o' th' sere* [from F, but F has "tickled a" for "tickle o'"; Q2 omits]
334 *blank* black   345–70 *Hamlet. How comes . . . load too* [Q2
omits]   350 *berattle* [ed; F has "be-ratled"; Q2 omits]   357 *most
like* [ed; F has "like most"; Q2 omits]   381 *lest my* let me   407–08
tragical-historical, tragical-comical-historical-pastoral [Q2 omits]
434 *By'r Lady* by lady   439 *French falconers* friendly Fankners
454 *affectation* affection   457 *tale* talke   467 *heraldry* heraldy
485 *Then senseless Ilium* [Q2 omits]   492 *And like* Like   506
fellies [ed] follies   515 *Mobled queen is good* [F has "Inobled"
for "Mobled"; Q2 omits]   525 *husband's* husband   530 *whe'r* [ed]
where   550–51 *a need* neede   551 *or sixteen lines* lines, or six-
teene lines   556 *till* tell   564 *his visage* the visage   569 *to Hecuba*
to her   571 *the cue* that   590 *ha' fatted* [F has "have fatted"] a
fatted   593 *O, vengeance* [Q2 omits]   595 *father* [Q4; Q2 and F
omit]   611 *devil, and the devil* deale, and the deale

III.i.32–33 *myself (lawful espials) Will* myself Wee'le   46 *loneliness* lowliness   55 *Let's withdraw* with-draw   83 *cowards of us
all* cowards   85 *sicklied* sickled   92 *well, well, well* well   107
your honesty you   121 *to a nunnery* a Nunry   129 *knaves all*
knaues   139 *Go, farewell,* farewell   146 *lisp* list   148 *your ignorance* ignorance   155 *expectancy* expectation   160 *that* what

162 *feature* stature   164 [Q2 concludes the line with a stage direction, "Exit"]   191 *unwatched* vnmatcht

III.ii.1 *pronounced* pronound   24 *own feature* feature   28 *the which* which   31 *praise* praysd   39 *us, sir* vs   47 s.d. *Exit Players* [Q2 omits]   51 s.d. *Exit Polonius* [Q2 omits]   54 *ho* [F has "hoa"] howe   91 *detecting* detected   91 s.d. *Rosencrantz . . . Flourish* [Q2 omits]   117–18 *Hamlet. I mean . . . my lord* [Q2 omits]   140 s.d. *sound* [ed] sounds   140 s.d. *very lovingly* [Q2 omits] 140 s.d. *She kneels . . . unto him* [Q2 omits]   140 s.d. *Exeunt* [Q2 omits]   142 *is miching* munching   147 *keep counsel* keepe   161 *ground* the ground   169 *your* our   174 *In neither* Eyther none, in neither   175 *love* Lord   196 *like* the   205 *Grief joys* Greefe ioy   225 *An* [ed] And   229 *a* I be a   233 s.d. *sleeps* [Q2 omits]   234 s.d. *Exit* Exeunt   262 *Confederate* Considerat   264 *infected* inuected   266 s.d. *Pours the poison in his ears* [Q2 omits]   272 *Hamlet. What . . . fire* [Q2 omits]   282–83 *two Provincial* prouinciall   316 *start* stare   325 *my business* busines   366 *and thumb* & the vmber   375 *the top of my* my   379 *you can* you   394–95 *Polonius . . . friends* Leaue me friends. I will, say so. By and by is easily said   397 *breathes* breakes   399 *bitter business as the day* buisnes as the bitter day   404 *daggers* dagger

III.iii.19 *huge* hough   22 *ruin* raine   23 *with a* a   50 *pardoned* pardon   58 *shove* showe   73 *pat* but   79 *hire and salary* base and silly

III.iv.5–6 *with him . . . Mother, Mother, Mother* [Q2 omits]   7 *warrant* wait   21 *inmost* most   23 *ho* [F has "hoa"] how   23 *ho* [F has "hoa"] how   25 s.d. *kills Polonius* [Q2 omits]   53 *That roars . . . index* [Q2 gives to Hamlet]   60 *heaven-kissing* heaue, a kissing   89 *panders* pardons   90 *mine eyes into my very soul* my very eyes into my soule   91 *grainèd* greeued   92 *will not* will   98 *tithe* kyth   140 *Ecstasy* [Q2 omits]   144 *And I* And   159 *live* leaue   166 *Refrain tonight* to refraine night   180 *Thus* This   187 *ravel* rouell   216 *foolish* most foolish   218 s.d. *exit Hamlet, tugging in Polonius* Exit

IV.i.35 *dragged* dreg'd

IV.ii.1 s.d. *Enter Hamlet* Enter Hamlet, Rosencraus, and others   2 *Gentlemen. (Within) Hamlet! Lord Hamlet!* [Q2 omits]   4 s.d. *Enter Rosencrantz and Guildenstern* [Q2 omits]   6 *Compounded* Compound   18 *ape* apple   30–31 *Hide fox, and all after* [Q2 omits]

IV.iii.15 *Ho* [F has "Hoa"] How   43 *With fiery quickness* [Q2 omits]   52 *and so* so   68 *were ne'er begun* will nere begin

IV.v.16 *Queen* [Q2 gives line 16 as part of the previous speech]   20 s.d. *Enter Ophelia distracted* Enter Ophelia [placed after line 16]   39 *grave* ground   42 *God* good   52 *clothes* close   57 *Indeed, la* Indeede   73 s.d. *Exit* [Q2 omits]   82 *in their* in   89 *his* this   96 *Queen. Alack, what noise is this* [Q2 omits]   97 *are* is   106 *They* The   142 *swoopstake* [ed] soopstake   152 s.d. *Let her come in* [Q2 gives to Laertes]   157 *Till* Tell   160 *an old* a poore   161–63 *Nature . . . loves* [Q2 omits]   165 *Hey . . . hey* nony [Q2 omits]   181 *O, you must* you may   186 *affliction* afflictions   194 *All flaxen* Flaxen   198 *Christian souls, I pray God* Christians soules   199 *see this* this

IV.vi.9 *an't* and   23 *good turn* turne   27 *bore* bord   31 *He* So   32 *give you* you

IV.vii.6 *proceeded* proceede   14 *conjunctive* concliue   20 *Would* Worke   22 *loud a wind* loued Arm'd   24 *And* But   24 *had* haue   36 *How now . . . Hamlet* [Q2 omits]   42 s.d. *Exit Messenger* [Q2 omits]   46 *your pardon* you pardon   47 *and more strange return* returne   48 *Hamlet* [Q2 omits]   56 *shall live* liue   62 *checking* the King   88 *my* me   115 *wick* [ed] weeke   119 *changes* change   122 *spendthrift* [ed] spend thirfts   125 *in deed* [ed] indeede   134 *on* ore   138 *pass* pace   140 *for that* for   156 *ha't* hate   159 *prepared* prefard   167 *hoar* horry   171 *cold* cull-cold

V.i.9 *se offendendo* so offended   12 *Argall* or all   35–38 *Other. Why . . . without arms* [Q2 omits]   44 *that frame* that   56 s.d. *Enter Hamlet and Horatio afar off* Enter Hamlet and Horatio [Q2 places after line 65]   61 *stoup* soope   71 *daintier* dintier   90 *mazzard* massene   107–08 *Is this . . . recoveries* [Q2 omits]   109 *his vouchers* vouchers   110 *double ones* doubles   122 *O* or   123 *For such a guest is meet* [Q2 omits]   144–45 *a gravemaker* Graue-maker   146 *all the days* the dayes   167 *corses now-a-days* corses   174–75 *three and twenty* 23   185 *Let me see* [Q2 omits]   187 *borne* bore   195 *chamber* table   210–11 *as thus* [Q2 omits]   218 *winter's* waters   219 s.d. *Enter King . . . Lords attendant* Enter K. Q. Laertes and the corse   233 *Shards, flints* Flints   248 *treble* double   252 s.d. *Leaps in the grave* [Q2 omits]   263 *and rash* rash   279 *Dost thou* doost   287 *thus* this   300 *shortly* thirtie   301 *Till* Tell

V.ii.5 *Methought* my thought   6 *bilboes* bilbo   17 *unseal* vnfold   19 *Ah* [ed; F has "Oh"] A   43 *as's* [F has "assis"] as sir   52 *Sub-*

scribed Subcribe 57 *Why, man . . . employment* [Q2 omits]
68–80 *To quit . . . comes here* [Q2 omits] 78 *court* [ed; F has
"count"; Q2 omits] 80 s.d. *Young Osric* [Q2 omits] 81 *Osric*
[Q2 prints "Cour" consistently as the speech prefix] 83 *humbly*
humble 94 *Put your* your 99 *sultry* sully 99 *for* or 102 *But,
my* my 108 *gentleman* [ed] gentlemen 110 *feelingly* [ed] sell-
ingly 142 *his weapon* [ed] this weapon 151 *hangers* [ed] hanger
158 *carriages* carriage 161 *might be* be 164–65 *all impawned, as*
all 180 *e'en so so* so 184 *Yours, yours.* He Yours 189 *did comply*
did 193 *yeasty* histy 194 *fanned* [ed; F has "fond"] prophane
195 *winnowed* trennowed 208 *to Laertes* [ed] Laertes 210 *lose
this wager* loose 213 *But thou* thou 217 *gaingiving* gamgiuing
221 *If it be now* if it be 223 *will come* well come 241 *Sir, in
this audience* [Q2 omits] 251 *keep my* my 251 *till* all 254
Come on [Q2 omits] 264 *bettered* better 266 s.d. *Prepare to
play* [Q2 omits] 273 *union* Vnice 281 s.d. *They play* [Q2 omits]
287 *A touch, a touch* [Q2 omits] 301 s.d. *play* [Q2 omits] 303
s.d. *In scuffling they change rapiers* [Q2 omits] 304 *ho* [F has
"hoa"] howe 312 *Ho* [ed] how 314 *Hamlet. Hamlet* Hamlet
317 *thy* my 323 s.d. *Hurts the King* [Q2 omits] 326 *murd'rous,
damnèd* damned 327 *thy union* the Onixe 328 s.d. *King dies* [Q2
omits] 332 s.d. *Dies* [Q2 omits] 346 *live* I leaue 359 *Dies*
[Q2 omits] 362 s.d. *with Drum, Colors, and Attendants* [Q2
omits] 380 *th' yet* yet 384 *forced* for no 393 *on* no 400
rite [ed; F has "rites"] right 404 s.d. *marching . . . shot off*
[Q2 omits]

A Note on the Sources of "Hamlet"

The story of Hamlet is an ancient one. No doubt it had its origin in one of the family feuds familiar in Northern history and saga. Sailors carried it to Ireland, where it picked up accretions of Celtic folklore and legend, and later returned to Scandinavia to become part of the traditional history of Denmark. It was incorporated into written literature in the second half of the twelfth century when a learned clerk, Saxo Grammaticus, retold it in his *Historia Danica*. His narrative is a story of early and relatively barbaric times. For instance, the dismembered body of the prototype of Polonius is thrown into an open latrine to be devoured by scavenging hogs, and there is no trace of the ideals of chivalry and courtesy that we find in Shakespeare's play. Still, the basic elements of Shakespeare's plot are there: the killing of the Danish ruler by his brother, the marriage of the brother and the widowed queen, the pretended madness and real craft of the dead king's son, the son's evasion of the sanity tests, his voyage to England with letters bearing his death warrant, his alteration of the letters, his return, and the accomplishment of his revenge. Saxo also gives us, under different names, the chief characters of the story as we know it in Shakespeare: Claudius (Feng), Gertrude (Gerutha), Hamlet (Amlethus), unnamed prototypes of Ophelia, Polonius, Rosencrantz, and Guildenstern, and perhaps even of Horatio.

Saxo's narrative circulated widely in manuscript. It was printed in Paris in 1514, reprinted elsewhere, and came in time to the attention of François de Belleforest, who in 1576 told his version of the Hamlet story in the fifth volume of his *Histoires Tragiques*. He made one notable addition to the story. He states that the Queen committed adultery with her brother-in-law during her marriage to the King. This remains in Shakespeare in the ghost's epithet for his brother, "adulterate," and in Hamlet's "He that hath killed my king, and whored my mother," and it operates as part of the motivation for the revulsion which Hamlet sometimes feels for womankind. Belleforest's *Histoires* seems to have been a popular book. His version was translated very badly into English under the title *The Hystorie of Hamblet* in 1608, too late to serve as a source for Shakespeare. In all likelihood it was called into being by the popularity of Shakespeare's play.

The next version of the Hamlet story was an English play of the 1580's based on Belleforest. It was never printed, and the manuscript seems to be irretrievably lost. Since the late eighteenth century it has been attributed more or less confidently to Thomas Kyd (1557?–1595?). Kyd was a scrivener and playwright, the author of the well-known *Spanish Tragedy*. His works show some advance over that of his predecessors in the creation of character and, especially, in the manipulation of plot. He could wring from a scene all the melodrama it afforded. Kyd's play on the Hamlet story, if, indeed, it is his, served as the immediate source of Shakespeare's play and is called by scholars the *Ur-Hamlet*. The first reference to it is found in Thomas Nashe's preface to Robert Greene's *Menaphon*, 1589. In it Nashe, an established writer, indulged in an attack on certain "trivial translators" and "shifting companions" who "leave the trade of noverint [scribe, copyist] whereto they were born, and busy themselves with the endeavors of art that could scarcely Latinize their neck verse. . . . Yet English Seneca . . . yields many good sentences . . . and if you entreat him fair in a frosty morning, he will afford you whole *Hamlets*, I should say handfuls of tragical speeches. . . . Seneca, let blood, line by line and page by page, at length must needs die to our stage; which makes his famished followers to imitate the Kid in Aesop . . . and these men to inter-meddle with Italian translations." The passage has been much debated, but it seems clear that Nashe, by a pun on Kid, associated the Senecan play of *Hamlet* with Kyd. The play is next mentioned in the diary of Philip Henslowe, the theatrical producer, who records that a play called *Hamlet* was performed at the suburban theater of Newington Butts in June, 1594, by the Admiral's and the Chamberlain's Men. It was apparently Henslowe's custom to indicate a new play with the letters "ne," and since there is no such indication at this entry, we may perhaps assume that the play was old; and since the receipts for this performance were only eight shillings, it is possible that *Hamlet* was no longer popular in the playhouse. It seems likely that this is the play to which Nashe referred.

The play was next referred to by Thomas Lodge in his *Wit's Misery,* 1596. He speaks there of the "ghost which cried so miserably at The Theater, like an oyster wife, 'Hamlet, revenge.' " The scorn of Lodge's statement suggests that the play was an outmoded one, and his mention of The Theater as the playhouse at which the ghost cried out tells us that the Chamberlain's Men, the theatrical company to which Shakespeare belonged, had taken over the drama, for the playhouse at which they were then playing was called The Theater. The play, then, was the property of Shakespeare's company, and he was free to use the story for his own purposes. Scholars have been assiduous in their attempts to reconstruct the *Ur-Hamlet* from references to it and from the versions of the story which preceded and followed it. And they have yet another version of the story at hand. There is a German play on the Hamlet story called *Der bestrafte Brudermord oder Prinz Hamlet aus Daennemark.* It was first printed in 1781 from a manuscript dated 1710. The manuscript has been lost, but the printed version has survived.

We know that a *Hamlet* was played by English actors at Dresden in 1626 and that there was another performance of the play, probably in German, in 1665. The latter is probably the origin of *Der bestrafte Brudermord,* a play which, by the eighteenth century, had grossly deteriorated from its original. Still, its dependence on an English *Hamlet* is certain. We must ask if it derives from an early version by Shakespeare as misrepresented in the First Quarto or from the *Ur-Hamlet,* and the scholars give us a divided answer. The name Corambus of the German version recalls Corambis of the First Quarto and suggests that as a source. On the other hand, Corambis may well have been the name in the *Ur-Hamlet.* There are other similarities to Shakespeare's quarto, but there are great differences from it. The German play opens with a prologue in which Night calls upon the Furies to spur the revenge against the king. This is Senecan rather than Shakespearean. The ghost tells Hamlet that it was reported that he had died of an apoplexy, whereas in the First Quarto it was said that he had died of a snake bite. There is no trace of Hamlet's great soliloquies which exist in the First Quarto in mangled form. On the whole it seems more likely that *Der bestrafte Brudermord* derives from the *Ur-Hamlet* than from the First Quarto.

What, then, was the immediate source of Shakespeare's *Hamlet* like? In answering this question it must be acknowledged that we are not on firm ground, but an informed surmise is better than nothing, provided we remember that we are being tentative. It was Senecan and, in name at least, a tragedy, though in reality a melodrama. A Senecan play would be gory, with the stage cluttered with corpses in the final scene. It was by Thomas Kyd. Why else should Nashe have associated "Kid" and "noverint" with the play? Kyd had been a scrivener, and unlike Nashe, he was not a university man. He had made translations from both Italian and French, and he had turned dramatist. He was able to read Belleforest in French. He knew Seneca intimately. In the play the ghost calls for revenge, and the revengeful ghost is characteristic of Seneca. In Saxo Grammaticus there is no ghost. There is no need for one; the murderer of the king was known to be his brother, and there was, therefore, nothing for the ghost to reveal. The ghost is one of Kyd's contributions to the story. He had used a ghost effectively in his *Spanish Tragedy,* and he was here repeating one of his successful

devices. In the *Ur-Hamlet* the ghost made the revelation
and urged upon Hamlet the obligation of revenge. In
Saxo, Hamlet feigned madness in self-protection and in
order to get at the person of the king. Kyd retained the
pretended madness, but we cannot know what uses he
made of it. The play ended, of course, with Hamlet's
triumph and death in a bloody massacre.

Commentaries

SAMUEL TAYLOR COLERIDGE

from *The Lectures of 1811–1812, Lecture XII*

We will now pass to *Hamlet,* in order to obviate some of the general prejudices against the author, in reference to the character of the hero. Much has been objected to, which ought to have been praised, and many beauties of the highest kind have been neglected, because they are somewhat hidden.

The first question we should ask ourselves is—What did Shakespeare mean when he drew the character of Hamlet? He never wrote anything without design, and what was his design when he sat down to produce this tragedy? My belief is that he always regarded his story, before he began to write, much in the same light as a painter regards his canvas, before he begins to paint—as a mere vehicle for his thoughts—as the ground upon which he was to work.

From *Shakespearean Criticism* by Samuel Taylor Coleridge. 2nd ed., ed. Thomas Middleton Raysor. 2 vols. New York: E. P. Dutton and Company, Inc., 1960; London: J. M. Dent & Sons, Ltd., 1961. The exact text of Coleridge's lecture does not exist; what is given here is the transcript of a shorthand report taken by an auditor, J. P. Collier.

What then was the point to which Shakespeare directed himself in Hamlet? He intended to portray a person, in whose view the external world, and all its incidents and objects, were comparatively dim, and of no interest in themselves, and which began to interest only when they were reflected in the mirror of his mind. Hamlet beheld external things in the same way that a man of vivid imagination, who shuts his eyes, sees what has previously made an impression on his organs.

The poet places him in the most stimulating circumstances that a human being can be placed in. He is the heir apparent of a throne; his father dies suspiciously; his mother excludes her son from his throne by marrying his uncle. This is not enough; but the ghost of the murdered father is introduced, to assure the son that he was put to death by his own brother. What is the effect upon the son?—instant action and pursuit of revenge? No: endless reasoning and hesitating—constant urging and solicitation of the mind to act, and as constant an escape from action; ceaseless reproaches of himself for sloth and negligence, while the whole energy of his resolution evaporates in these reproaches. This, too, not from cowardice, for he is drawn as one of the bravest of his time—not from want of forethought or slowness of apprehension, for he sees through the very souls of all who surround him, but merely from that aversion to action, which prevails among such as have a world in themselves.

How admirable, too, is the judgment of the poet! Hamlet's own disordered fancy has not conjured up the spirit of his father; it has been seen by others: he is prepared by them to witness its reappearance, and when he does see it, Hamlet is not brought forward as having long brooded on the subject. The moment before the Ghost enters, Hamlet speaks of other matters: he mentions the coldness of the night, and observes that he has not heard the clock strike, adding, in reference to the custom of drinking, that it is

More honor'd in the breach than the observance.
Act I., Scene 4.

Owing to the tranquil state of his mind, he indulges in some moral reflections. Afterwards, the Ghost suddenly enters.

Horatio.   Look, my lord; it comes.

Hamlet. Angels and ministers of grace defend us!

The same thing occurs in *Macbeth*: in the dagger scene, the moment before the hero sees it, he has his mind applied to some indifferent matters; "Go, tell thy mistress," &c. Thus, in both cases, the preternatural appearance has all the effect of abruptness, and the reader is totally divested of the notion, that the figure is a vision of a highly wrought imagination.

Here Shakespeare adapts himself so admirably to the situation—in other words, so puts himself into it—that, though poetry, his language is the very language of nature. No terms, associated with such feelings, can occur to us so proper as those which he has employed, especially on the highest, the most august, and the most awful subjects that can interest a human being in this sentient world. That this is no mere fancy, I can undertake to establish from hundreds, I might say thousands, of passages. No character he has drawn, in the whole list of his plays, could so well and fitly express himself as in the language Shakespeare has put into his mouth.

There is no indecision about Hamlet, as far as his own sense of duty is concerned; he knows well what he ought to do, and over and over again he makes up his mind to do it. The moment the players, and the two spies set upon him, have withdrawn, of whom he takes leave with a line so expressive of his contempt,

Ay so; good bye you.—Now I am alone,

he breaks out into a delirium of rage against himself for neglecting to perform the solemn duty he had undertaken, and contrasts the factitious and artificial display of feeling by the player with his own apparent indifference;

> What's Hecuba to him, or he to Hecuba,
> That he should weep for her?

Yet the player did weep for her, and was in an agony of grief at her sufferings, while Hamlet is unable to rouse himself to action, in order that he may perform the command of his father, who had come from the grave to incite him to revenge:

>   This is most brave!
> That I, the son of a dear father murder'd,
> Prompted to my revenge by heaven and hell,
> Must, like a whore, unpack my heart with words,
> And fall a cursing like a very drab,
> A scullion.
>
>   *Act II., Scene* 2.

It is the same feeling, the same conviction of what is his duty, that makes Hamlet exclaim in a subsequent part of the tragedy:

> How all occasions do inform against me,
> And spur my dull revenge. What is a man,
> If his chief good, and market of his time,
> Be but to sleep and feed? A beast, no more. . . .
>   . . . . I do not know
> Why yet I live to say—"this thing's to do,"
> Sith I have cause and will and strength and means
> To do't.
>
>   *Act IV., Scene* 4.

Yet with all this strong conviction of duty, and with all this resolution arising out of strong conviction, nothing is done. This admirable and consistent character, deeply acquainted with his own feelings, painting them with such wonderful power and accuracy, and firmly persuaded that a moment ought not to be lost in executing the solemn charge committed to him, still yields to the same retiring from reality, which is the result of having, what we express by the terms, a world within himself.

Such a mind as Hamlet's is near akin to madness. Dryden has somewhere said,[1]

> Great wit to madness nearly is allied,

and he was right; for he means by "wit" that greatness of genius, which led Hamlet to a perfect knowledge of his own character, which, with all strength of motive, was so weak as to be unable to carry into act his own most obvious duty.

With all this he has a sense of imperfectness, which becomes apparent when he is moralizing on the skull in the churchyard. Something is wanting to his completeness—something is deficient which remains to be supplied, and he is therefore described as attached to Ophelia. His madness is assumed, when he finds that witnesses have been placed behind the arras to listen to what passes, and when the heroine has been thrown in his way as a decoy.

Another objection has been taken by Dr. Johnson, and Shakespeare has been taxed very severely. I refer to the scene where Hamlet enters and finds his uncle praying, and refuses to take his life, excepting when he is in the height of his iniquity. To assail him at such a moment of confession and repentance, Hamlet declares,

> Why, this is hire and salary, not revenge.
> *Act III., Scene 3.*

He therefore forbears, and postpones his uncle's death, until he can catch him in some act

> That has no relish of salvation in't.

This conduct, and this sentiment, Dr. Johnson has pronounced to be so atrocious and horrible as to be unfit to be put into the mouth of a human being. The fact, however, is that Dr. Johnson did not understand the character

---

[1] "Great wits are sure to madness near allied."
Absalom and Achitophel, 163.

of Hamlet, and censured accordingly: the determination
to allow the guilty King to escape at such a moment is
only part of the indecision and irresoluteness of the hero.
Hamlet seizes hold of a pretext for not acting, when he
might have acted so instantly and effectually: therefore,
he again defers the revenge he was bound to seek, and
declares his determination to accomplish it at some time,

> When he is drunk, asleep, or in his rage,
> Or in th' incestuous pleasures of his bed.

This, allow me to impress upon you most emphatically,
was merely the excuse Hamlet made to himself for not
taking advantage of this particular and favorable moment
for doing justice upon his guilty uncle, at the urgent
instance of the spirit of his father.

Dr. Johnson farther states that in the voyage to England,
Shakespeare merely follows the novel as he found it, as
if the poet had no other reason for adhering to his original;
but Shakespeare never followed a novel because he found
such and such an incident in it, but because he saw that
the story, as he read it, contributed to enforce or to explain
some great truth inherent in human nature. He never could
lack invention to alter or improve a popular narrative;
but he did not wantonly vary from it, when he knew that,
as it was related, it would so well apply to his own great
purpose. He saw at once how consistent it was with the
character of Hamlet, that after still resolving, and still
deferring, still determining to execute, and still postponing
execution, he should finally, in the infirmity of his disposition, give himself up to his destiny, and hopelessly
place himself in the power and at the mercy of his
enemies.

Even after the scene with Osrick, we see Hamlet still
indulging in reflection, and hardly thinking of the task
he has just undertaken: he is all dispatch and resolution,
as far as words and present intentions are concerned, but
all hesitation and irresolution, when called upon to carry
his words and intentions into effect; so that, resolving
to do everything, he does nothing. He is full of purpose,

but void of that quality of mind which accomplishes purpose.

Anything finer than this conception, and working out of a great character, is merely impossible. Shakespeare wished to impress upon us the truth that action is the chief end of existence—that no faculties of intellect, however brilliant, can be considered valuable, or indeed otherwise than as misfortunes, if they withdraw us from or render us repugnant to action, and lead us to think and think of doing, until the time has elapsed when we can do anything effectually. In enforcing this moral truth, Shakespeare has shown the fullness and force of his powers: all that is amiable and excellent in nature is combined in Hamlet, with the exception of one quality. He is a man living in meditation, called upon to act by every motive human and divine, but the great object of his life is defeated by continually resolving to do, yet doing nothing but resolve.

WILLIAM HAZLITT

from *The Characters of Shakespear's Plays*

This is that Hamlet the Dane, whom we read of in our youth, and whom we may be said almost to remember in our after-years; he who made that famous soliloquy on life, who gave the advice to the players, who thought "this goodly frame, the earth, a steril promontory, and this brave o'er-hanging firmament, the air, this majestical roof fretted with golden fire, a foul and pestilent congregation of vapors"; whom "man delighted not, nor woman neither"; he who talked with the gravediggers, and moralized on Yorick's skull; the schoolfellow of Rosencrantz and Guildenstern at Wittenberg; the friend of Horatio; the lover of Ophelia; he that was mad and sent to England; the slow avenger of his father's death; who lived at the court of Horwendillus five hundred years before we were born, but all whose thoughts we seem to know as well as we do our own, because we have read them in Shakespear.

Hamlet is a name; his speeches and sayings but the idle coinage of the poet's brain. What then, are they not real? They are as real as our own thoughts. Their reality is in the reader's mind. It is *we* who are Hamlet. This play has a prophetic truth, which is above that of history.

From *The Characters of Shakespear's Plays* by William Hazlitt. 2nd ed. London: Taylor & Hessey, 1818.

Whoever has become thoughtful and melancholy through his own mishaps or those of others; whoever has borne about with him the clouded brow of reflection, and thought himself "too much i' th' sun"; whoever has seen the golden lamp of day dimmed by envious mists rising in his own breast, and could find in the world before him only a dull blank with nothing left remarkable in it; whoever has known the "pangs of despised love, the insolence of office, or the spurns which patient merit of the unworthy takes"; he who has felt his mind sink within him, and sadness cling to his heart like a malady, who has had his hopes blighted and his youth staggered by the apparitions of strange things; who cannot be well at ease while he sees evil hovering near him like a specter; whose powers of action have been eaten up by thought, he to whom the universe seems infinite, and himself nothing; whose bitterness of soul makes him careless of consequences, and who goes to a play as his best resource to shove off, to a second remove, the evils of life by a mock representation of them—this is the true Hamlet.

We have been so used to this tragedy that we hardly know how to criticize it any more than we should know how to describe our own faces. But we must make such observations as we can. It is the one of Shakespear's plays that we think of the oftenest, because it abounds most in striking reflections on human life, and because the distresses of Hamlet are transferred, by the turn of his mind, to the general account of humanity. Whatever happens to him we apply to ourselves, because he applies it to himself as a means of general reasoning. He is a great moralizer; and what makes him worth attending to is that he moralizes on his own feelings and experience. He is not a commonplace pedant. If Lear is distinguished by the greatest depth of passion, Hamlet is the most remarkable for the ingenuity, originality, and unstudied development of character. Shakespear had more magnanimity than any other poet, and he has shown more of it in this play than in any other. There is no attempt to force an interest: everything is left for time and circumstances to unfold. The attention is excited without effort, the incidents succeed each other as matters of course, the characters think and speak and act just as they might do if left entirely to themselves. There is no set purpose, no straining at a point. The observations are suggested by the passing scene —the gusts of passion come and go like sounds of music borne on the wind. The whole play is an exact transcript of what might be supposed to have taken place at the court of Denmark, at the remote period of time fixed upon before the modern refinements in morals and manners were heard of. It would have been interesting enough to have been admitted as a bystander in such a scene, at such a time, to have heard and witnessed something of what was going on. But here we are more than spectators. We have not only "the outward pageants and the signs of grief," but "we have that within which passes show." We read the thoughts of the heart, we catch the passions living as they rise. Other dramatic writers give us very fine versions and paraphrases of nature; but Shakespear, together with his own comments, gives us the original text, that we may judge for ourselves. This is a very great advantage.

The character of Hamlet stands quite by itself. It is not a character marked by strength of will or even of passion, but by refinement of thought and sentiment. Hamlet is as little of the hero as a man can well be: but he is a young and princely novice, full of high enthusiasm and quick sensibility—the sport of circumstances, questioning with fortune and refining on his own feelings, and forced from the natural bias of his disposition by the strangeness of his situation. He seems incapable of deliberate action, and is only hurried into extremities on the spur of the occasion, when he has no time to reflect, as in the scene where he kills Polonius, and again, where he alters the letters which Rosencrantz and Guildenstern are taking with them to England, purporting his death. At other times, when he is most bound to act, he remains puzzled, undecided, and skeptical, dallies with his purposes, till the occasion is lost, and finds out some pretense to relapse into indolence and thoughtfulness again. For this reason he refuses to kill the King when he is at his prayers, and by a refinement in malice, which is in truth only an excuse for his own want of resolution, defers his revenge to a more fatal opportunity, when he shall be engaged in some act "that has no relish of salvation in it."

> He kneels and prays,
> And now I'll do't, and so he goes to heaven,
> And so am I reveng'd: *that would be scann'd.*
> He kill'd my father, and for that,
> I, his sole son, send him to heaven.
> Why, this is reward, not revenge.
> Up sword and know thou a more horrid time,
> When he is drunk, asleep, or in a rage.

He is the prince of philosophical speculators; and because he cannot have his revenge perfect, according to the most refined idea his wish can form, he declines it altogether. So he scruples to trust the suggestions of the ghost, contrives the scene of the play to have surer proof of his uncle's guilt, and then rests satisfied with this confirmation of his suspicions, and the success of his experiment, instead of acting upon it. Yet he is sensible of his own weakness, taxes himself with it, and tries to reason himself out of it. . . .

Still he does nothing; and this very speculation on his own infirmity only affords him another occasion for indulging it. It is not from any want of attachment to his father or of abhorrence of his murder that Hamlet is thus dilatory, but it is more to his taste to indulge his imagination in reflecting upon the enormity of the crime and refining on his schemes of vengeance, than to put them into immediate practice. His ruling passion is to think, not to act: and any vague pretext that flatters this propensity instantly diverts him from his previous purposes. . . .

A. C. BRADLEY

from *Shakespearean Tragedy*

Let us first ask ourselves what we can gather from the play, immediately or by inference, concerning Hamlet as he was just before his father's death. And I begin by observing that the text does not bear out the idea that he was one-sidedly reflective and indisposed to action. Nobody who knew him seems to have noticed this weakness. Nobody regards him as a mere scholar who has "never formed a resolution or executed a deed." In a court which certainly would not much admire such a person, he is the observed of all observers. Though he has been disappointed of the throne everyone shows him respect; and he is the favorite of the people, who are not given to worship philosophers. Fortinbras, a sufficiently practical man, considered that he was likely, had he been put on, to have proved most royally. He has Hamlet borne by four captains "like a soldier" to his grave; and Ophelia says that Hamlet *was* a soldier. If he was fond of acting, an aesthetic pursuit, he was equally fond of fencing, an athletic one: he practiced it assiduously even in his worst days.[1] So far as we can

From *Shakespearean Tragedy* by A. C. Bradley. London: Macmillan & Co., Ltd., 1904. Reprinted by permission of Macmillan & Co., Ltd. (London), St Martin's Press, Inc. (New York), and The Macmillan Company of Canada, Ltd.

[1] He says so to Horatio, whom he has no motive for deceiving (V.ii. 212). His contrary statement (II.ii. 304) is made to Rosencrantz and Guildenstern.

conjecture from what we see of him in those bad days, he must normally have been charmingly frank, courteous, and kindly to everyone, of whatever rank, whom he liked or respected, but by no means timid or deferential to others; indeed, one would gather that he was rather the reverse, and also that he was apt to be decided and even imperious if thwarted or interfered with. He must always have been fearless—in the play he appears insensible to fear of any ordinary kind. And, finally, he must have been quick and impetuous in action; for it is downright impossible that the man we see rushing after the Ghost, killing Polonius, dealing with the King's commission on the ship, boarding the pirate, leaping into the grave, executing his final vengeance, could *ever* have been shrinking or slow in an emergency. Imagine Coleridge doing any of these things!

If we consider all this, how can we accept the notion that Hamlet's was a weak and one-sided character? "Oh, but he spent ten or twelve years at a University!" Well, even if he did, it is possible to do that without becoming the victim of excessive thought. But the statement that he did rests upon a most insecure foundation.

Where then are we to look for the seeds of danger?

(1) Trying to reconstruct from the Hamlet of the play, one would not judge that his temperament was melancholy in the present sense of the word; there seems nothing to show that; but one would judge that by temperament he was inclined to nervous instability, to rapid and perhaps extreme changes of feeling and mood, and that he was disposed to be, for the time, absorbed in the feeling or mood that possessed him, whether it were joyous or depressed. This temperament the Elizabethans would have called melancholic; and Hamlet seems to be an example of it, as Lear is of a temperament mixedly choleric and sanguine. And the doctrine of temperaments was so familiar in Shakespeare's time—as Burton, and earlier prose writers, and many of the dramatists show—that Shakespeare may quite well have given this temperament to Hamlet consciously and deliberately. Of melancholy in its developed form, a habit, not a mere temperament, he often

speaks. He more than once laughs at the passing and half-fictitious melancholy of youth and love; in Don John in *Much Ado* he had sketched the sour and surly melancholy of discontent; in Jaques a whimsical self-pleasing melancholy; in Antonio in the *Merchant of Venice* a quiet but deep melancholy, for which neither the victim nor his friends can assign any cause. He gives to Hamlet a temperament which would not develop into melancholy unless under some exceptional strain, but which still involved a danger. In the play we see the danger realized, and find a melancholy quite unlike any that Shakespeare had as yet depicted, because the temperament of Hamlet is quite different.

(2) Next, we cannot be mistaken in attributing to the Hamlet of earlier days an exquisite sensibility, to which we may give the name "moral," if that word is taken in the wide meaning it ought to bear. This, though it suffers cruelly in later days, as we saw in criticizing the sentimental view of Hamlet, never deserts him; it makes all his cynicism, grossness, and hardness appear to us morbidities, and has an inexpressibly attractive and pathetic effect. He had the soul of the youthful poet as Shelley and Tennyson have described it, an unbounded delight and faith in everything good and beautiful. We know this from himself. The world for him was *herrlich wie am ersten Tag*—"this goodly frame the earth, this most excellent canopy the air, this brave o'erhanging firmament, this majestical roof fretted with golden fire." And not nature only: "What a piece of work is a man! how noble in reason! how infinite in faculty! in form and moving how express and admirable! in action how like an angel! in apprehension how like a god!" This is no commonplace to Hamlet; it is the language of a heart thrilled with wonder and swelling into ecstasy.

Doubtless it was with the same eager enthusiasm he turned to those around him. Where else in Shakespeare is there anything like Hamlet's adoration of his father? The words melt into music whenever he speaks of him. And, if there are no signs of any such feeling towards his mother, though many signs of love, it is characteristic that he evidently never entertained a suspicion of anything unworthy in her—characteristic, and significant of his tendency to see only what is good unless he is forced to see the reverse. For we find this tendency elsewhere, and find it going so far that we must call it a disposition to idealize, to see something better than what is there, or at least to ignore deficiencies. He says to Laertes, "I loved you ever," and he describes Laertes as a "very noble youth," which he was far from being. In his first greeting of Rosencrantz and Guildenstern, where his old self revives, we trace the same affectionateness and readiness to take men at their best. His love for Ophelia, too, which seems strange to some, is surely the most natural thing in the world. He saw her innocence, simplicity, and sweetness, and it was like him to ask no more; and it is noticeable that Horatio, though entirely worthy of his friendship, is, like Ophelia, intellectually not remarkable. To the very end, however clouded, this generous disposition, this "free and open nature," this unsuspiciousness survive. They cost him his life; for the King knew them, and was sure that he was too "generous and free from all contriving" to "peruse the foils." To the very end, his soul, however sick and tortured it may be, answers instantaneously when good and evil are presented to it, loving the one and hating the other. He is called a skeptic who has no firm belief in anything, but he is never skeptical about *them*.

And the negative side of his idealism, the aversion to evil, is perhaps even more developed in the hero of the tragedy than in the Hamlet of earlier days. It is intensely characteristic. Nothing, I believe, is to be found elsewhere in Shakespeare (unless in the rage of the disillusioned idealist Timon) of quite the same kind as Hamlet's disgust at his uncle's drunkenness, his loathing of his mother's sensuality, his astonishment and horror at her shallowness, his contempt for everything pretentious or false, his indifference to everything merely external. This last characteristic appears in his choice of the friend of his heart, and in a certain impatience of distinctions of rank or wealth. When Horatio calls his father "a goodly king," he answers, surely with an emphasis on "man,"

He was a man, take him for all in all,
I shall not look upon his like again.

He will not listen to talk of Horatio being his "servant."
When the others speak of their "duty" to him, he answers,
"Your love, as mine to you." He speaks to the actor precisely as he does to an honest courtier. He is not in the
least a revolutionary, but still, in effect, a king and a beggar
are all one to him. He cares for nothing but human worth,
and his pitilessness towards Polonius and Osric and his
"schoolfellows" is not wholly due to morbidity, but belongs
in part to his original character.

Now, in Hamlet's moral sensibility there undoubtedly
lay a danger. Any great shock that life might inflict on it
would be felt with extreme intensity. Such a shock might
even produce tragic results. And, in fact, Hamlet deserves
the title "tragedy of moral idealism" quite as much as the
title "tragedy of reflection."

(3) With this temperament and this sensibility we find,
lastly, in the Hamlet of earlier days, as of later, intellectual
genius. It is chiefly this that makes him so different from
all those about him, good and bad alike, and hardly less
different from most of Shakespeare's other heroes. And
this, though on the whole the most important trait in his
nature, is also so obvious and so famous that I need not
dwell on it at length. But against one prevalent misconcep-
tion I must say a word of warning. Hamlet's intellectual
power is not a specific gift, like a genius for music or
mathematics or philosophy. It shows itself, fitfully, in the
affairs of life as unusual quickness of perception, great
agility in shifting the mental attitude, a striking rapidity and
fertility in resource; so that, when his natural belief in
others does not make him unwary, Hamlet easily sees
through them and masters them, and no one can be much
less like the typical helpless dreamer. It shows itself in
conversation chiefly in the form of wit or humor; and, alike
in conversation and in soliloquy, it shows itself in the
form of imagination quite as much as in that of thought in
the stricter sense. Further, where it takes the latter shape,
as it very often does, it is not philosophic in the technical

meaning of the word. There is really nothing in the play to
show that Hamlet ever was "a student of philosophies,"
unless it be the famous lines which, comically enough, ex-
hibit this supposed victim of philosophy as its critic:

> There are more things in heaven and earth, Horatio,
> Than are dreamt of in your philosophy.

His philosophy, if the word is to be used, was, like Shakespeare's own, the immediate product of the wondering and
meditating mind; and such thoughts as that celebrated one,
"There is nothing either good or bad but thinking makes it
so," surely needed no special training to produce them. Or
does Portia's remark, "Nothing is good without respect,"
i.e., out of relation, prove that she had studied metaphysics?

Still Hamlet had speculative genius without being a
philosopher, just as he had imaginative genius without being
a poet. Doubtless in happier days he was a close and constant observer of men and manners, noting his results in
those tables which he afterwards snatched from his breast
to make in wild irony his last note of all, that one may
smile and smile and be a villain. Again and again we remark
that passion for generalization which so occupied him, for
instance, in reflections suggested by the King's drunkenness
that he quite forgot what it was he was waiting to meet
upon the battlements. Doubtless, too, he was always considering things, as Horatio thought, too curiously. There
was a necessity in his soul driving him to penetrate below
the surface and to question what others took for granted.
That fixed habitual look which the world wears for most
men did not exist for him. He was forever unmaking his
world and rebuilding it in thought, dissolving what to others
were solid facts, and discovering what to others were old
truths. There were no old truths for Hamlet. It is for
Horatio a thing of course that there's a divinity that shapes
our ends, but for Hamlet it is a discovery hardly won. And
throughout this kingdom of the mind, where he felt that
man, who in action is only like an angel, is in apprehension
like a god, he moved (we must imagine) more than content, so that even in his dark days he declares he could be

bounded in a nutshell and yet count himself a king of infinite space, were it not that he had bad dreams.

If now we ask whether any special danger lurked *here*,
how shall we answer? We must answer, it seems to me,
"Some danger, no doubt, but, granted the ordinary chances
of life, not much." For, in the first place, that idea which
so many critics quietly take for granted—the idea that the
gift and the habit of meditative and speculative thought
tend to produce irresolution in the affairs of life—would
be found by no means easy to verify. Can you verify it,
for example, in the lives of the philosophers, or again in the
lives of men whom you have personally known to be addicted to such speculation? I cannot. Of course, individual
peculiarities being set apart, absorption in *any* intellectual
interest, together with withdrawal from affairs, may make
a man slow and unskillful in affairs; and doubtless, individual peculiarities being again set apart, a mere student is
likely to be more at a loss in a sudden and great practical
emergency than a soldier or a lawyer. But in all this there
is no difference between a physicist, a historian, and a
philosopher; and again, slowness, want of skill, and even
helplessness are something totally different from the peculiar kind of irresolution that Hamlet shows. The notion
that speculative thinking specially tends to produce *this* is
really a mere illusion.

In the second place, even if this notion were true, it has
appeared that Hamlet did *not* live the life of a mere student,
much less of a mere dreamer, and that his nature was by
no means simply or even one-sidedly intellectual, but was
healthily active. Hence, granted the ordinary chances of
life, there would seem to be no great danger in his intellectual tendency and his habit of speculation; and I would go
further and say that there was nothing in them, taken alone,
to unfit him even for the extraordinary call that was made
upon him. In fact, if the message of the Ghost had come to
him within a week of his father's death, I see no reason to
doubt that he would have acted on it as decisively as
Othello himself, though probably after a longer and more
anxious deliberation. And therefore the Schlegel-Coleridge
view (apart from its descriptive value) seems to me fatally

untrue, for it implies that Hamlet's procrastination was the normal response of an overspeculative nature confronted with a difficult practical problem.

On the other hand, under conditions of a peculiar kind, Hamlet's reflectiveness certainly might prove dangerous to him, and his genius might even (to exaggerate a little) become his doom. Suppose that violent shock to his moral being of which I spoke; and suppose that under this shock, any possible action being denied to him, he began to sink into melancholy; then, no doubt, his imaginative and generalizing habit of mind might extend the effects of this shock through his whole being and mental world. And if, the state of melancholy being thus deepened and fixed, a sudden demand for difficult and decisive action in a matter connected with the melancholy arose, this state might well have for one of its symptoms an endless and futile mental dissection of the required deed. And, finally, the futility of this process, and the shame of his delay, would further weaken him and enslave him to his melancholy still more. Thus the speculative habit would be *one* indirect cause of the morbid state which hindered action; and it would also reappear in a degenerate form as one of the *symptoms* of this morbid state.

Now this is what actually happens in the play. Turn to the first words Hamlet utters when he is alone; turn, that is to say, to the place where the author is likely to indicate his meaning most plainly. What do you hear?

> O, that this too too solid flesh would melt,
> Thaw and resolve itself into a dew!
> Or that the Everlasting had not fix'd
> His canon 'gainst self-slaughter! O God! God!
> How weary, stale, flat and unprofitable,
> Seem to me all the uses of this world!
> Fie on't! ah fie! 'tis an unweeded garden,
> That grows to seed; things rank and gross in nature
> Possess it merely.

Here are a sickness of life, and even a longing for death, so intense that nothing stands between Hamlet and suicide

except religious awe. And what has caused them? The
rest of the soliloquy so thrusts the answer upon us that it
might seem impossible to miss it. It was not his father's
death; that doubtless brought deep grief, but mere grief
for some one loved and lost does not make a noble spirit
loathe the world as a place full only of things rank and
gross. It was not the vague suspicion that we know Hamlet
felt. Still less was it the loss of the crown; for though the
subserviency of the electors might well disgust him, there is
not a reference to the subject in the soliloquy, nor any sign
elsewhere that it greatly occupied his mind. It was the
moral shock of the sudden ghastly disclosure of his
mother's true nature, falling on him when his heart was
aching with love, and his body doubtless was weakened by
sorrow. And it is essential, however disagreeable, to realize
the nature of this shock. It matters little here whether
Hamlet's age was twenty or thirty: in either case his
mother was a matron of mature years. All his life he had
believed in her, we may be sure, as such a son would. He
had seen her not merely devoted to his father, but hanging
on him like a newly wedded bride, hanging on him

> As if increase of appetite had grown
> By what it fed on.

He had seen her following his body "like Niobe, all tears."
And then within a month—"O God! a beast would have
mourned longer"—she married again, and married Hamlet's uncle, a man utterly contemptible and loathsome in
his eyes; married him in what to Hamlet was incestuous
wedlock; married him not for any reason of state, nor even
out of old family affection, but in such a way that her son
was forced to see in her action not only an astounding
shallowness of feeling but an eruption of coarse sensuality,
"rank and gross," speeding posthaste to its horrible delight.
Is it possible to conceive an experience more desolating to
a man such as we have seen Hamlet to be; and is its result
anything but perfectly natural? It brings bewildered horror,
then loathing, then despair of human nature. His whole
mind is poisoned. He can never see Ophelia in the same

light again: she is a woman, and his mother is a woman: if she mentions the word "brief" to him, the answer drops from his lips like venom, "as woman's love." The last words of the soliloquy, which is *wholly* concerned with this subject, are,

But break, my heart, for I must hold my tongue!

He can do nothing. He must lock in his heart, not any suspicion of his uncle that moves obscurely there, but that horror and loathing; and if his heart ever found relief, it was when those feelings, mingled with the love that never died out in him, poured themselves forth in a flood as he stood in his mother's chamber beside his father's marriage bed.

If we still wonder, and ask why the effect of this shock should be so tremendous, let us observe that *now* the conditions have arisen under which Hamlet's highest endowments, his moral sensibility and his genius, become his enemies. A nature morally blunter would have felt even so dreadful a revelation less keenly. A slower and more limited and positive mind might not have extended so widely through its world the disgust and disbelief that have entered it. But Hamlet has the imagination which, for evil as well as good, feels and sees all things in one. Thought is the element of his life, and his thought is infected. He cannot prevent himself from probing and lacerating the wound in his soul. One idea, full of peril, holds him fast, and he cries out in agony at it, but is impotent to free himself ("Must I remember?" "Let me not think on't"). And when, with the fading of his passion, the vividness of this idea abates, it does so only to leave behind a boundless weariness and a sick longing for death.

And this is the time which his fate chooses. In this hour of uttermost weakness, this sinking of his whole being towards annihilation, there comes on him, bursting the bounds of the natural world with a shock of astonishment and terror, the revelation of his mother's adultery and his father's murder, and, with this, the demand on him, in the name of everything dearest and most sacred, to arise and act. And for a moment, though his brain reels and totters, his soul leaps up in passion to answer this demand. But it comes too late. It does but strike home the last rivet in the melancholy which holds him bound.

> The time is out of joint! O cursed spite
> That ever I was born to set it right—

so he mutters within an hour of the moment when he vowed to give his life to the duty of revenge; and the rest of the story exhibits his vain efforts to fulfill this duty, his unconscious self-excuses and unavailing self-reproaches, and the tragic results of his delay.

"Melancholy," I said, not dejection, nor yet insanity. That Hamlet was not far from insanity is very probable. His adoption of the pretense of madness may well have been due in part to fear of the reality; to an instinct of self-preservation, a forefeeling that the pretense would enable him to give some utterance to the load that pressed on his heart and brain, and a fear that he would be unable altogether to repress such utterance. And if the pathologist calls his state melancholia, and even proceeds to determine its species, I see nothing to object to in that; I am grateful to him for emphasizing the fact that Hamlet's melancholy was no mere common depression of spirits; and I have no doubt that many readers of the play would understand it better if they read an account of melancholia in a work on mental diseases. If we like to use the word "disease" loosely, Hamlet's condition may truly be called diseased. No exertion of will could have dispelled it. Even if he had been able at once to do the bidding of the Ghost he would doubtless have still remained for some time under the cloud. It would be absurdly unjust to call *Hamlet* a study of melancholy, but it contains such a study.

But this melancholy is something very different from insanity, in anything like the usual meaning of that word. No doubt it might develop into insanity. The longing for death might become an irresistible impulse to self-destruction; the disorder of feeling and will might extend to sense and intellect; delusions might arise; and the man might become, as we say, incapable and irresponsible. But Hamlet's melancholy is some way from this condition. It is a totally different thing from the madness which he feigns; and he never, when alone or in company with Horatio alone, exhibits the signs of that madness. Nor is the dramatic use of this melancholy, again, open to the objections which would justly be made to the portrayal of an insanity which brought the hero to a tragic end. The man who suffers as Hamlet suffers—and thousands go about their business suffering thus in greater or less degree —is considered irresponsible neither by other people nor by himself: he is only too keenly conscious of his responsibility. He is therefore, so far, quite capable of being a tragic agent, which an insane person, at any rate according to Shakespeare's practice, is not. And, finally, Hamlet's state is not one which a healthy mind is unable sufficiently to imagine. It is probably not further from average experience, nor more difficult to realize, than the great tragic passions of Othello, Antony, or Macbeth.

HARLEY GRANVILLE-BARKER

from *Prefaces to Shakespeare*

PLACE STRUCTURE AND TIME STRUCTURE

There is both a place structure and a time structure in *Hamlet*. The place structure depends upon no exact localization of scenes. The time structure answers to no scheme of act division. But each has its dramatic import.

The action of *Hamlet* is concentrated at Elsinore; and this though there is much external interest, and the story abounds in journeys. As a rule in such a case, unless they are mere messengers, we travel with the travelers. But we do not see Laertes in Paris, nor, more surprisingly, Hamlet among the pirates; and the Norwegian affair is dealt with by hearsay till the play is two-thirds over. This is not done to economize time, or to leave space for more capital events. Scenes in Norway or Paris or aboard ship need be no longer than the talk of them, and Hamlet's discovery of the King's plot against him is a capital event. Shakespeare is deliberately concentrating his action at Elsinore. When he does at last introduce Fortinbras he stretches probability to bring him and his army seemingly to its very suburbs; and, sooner than that Hamlet should carry the action

From *Prefaces to Shakespeare*, I, by Harley Granville-Barker. Princeton, N. J.: Princeton University Press, 1946. Copyright 1946 by Princeton University Press. Reprinted by permission of the publishers. Some deletions have been made in the footnotes.

abroad with him, Horatio is left behind there to keep him in our minds. On the other hand he still, by allusion, makes the most of this movement abroad which he does not represent; he even adds to our sense of it by such seemingly superfluous touches as tell us that Horatio has journeyed from Wittenberg, that Rosencrantz and Guildenstern have been "sent for"—and even the Players are traveling.

The double dramatic purpose is plain. Here is a tragedy of inaction; the center of it is Hamlet, who is physically inactive too, has "foregone all custom of exercises," will not "walk out of the air," but only, book in hand, for "four hours together, here in the lobby." The concentration at Elsinore of all that happens enhances the impression of this inactivity, which is enhanced again by the sense also given us of the constant coming and going around Hamlet of the busier world without. The place itself, moreover, thus acquires a personality, and even develops a sort of sinister power; so that when at last Hamlet does depart from it (his duty still unfulfilled) and we are left with the conscience-sick Gertrude and the guilty King, the mad Ophelia, a Laertes set on his own revenge, among a

> people muddied,
> Thick and unwholesome in their thoughts and whispers . . .

we almost seem to feel it, and the unpurged sin of it, summoning him back to his duty and his doom. Shakespeare has, in fact, here adopted something very like unity of place; upon no principle, but to gain a specific dramatic end.

He turns time to dramatic use also, ignores or remarks its passing, and uses clock or calendar or falsifies or neglects them just as it suits him.

The play opens upon the stroke of midnight, an ominous and "dramatic" hour. The first scene is measured out to dawn and gains importance by that. In the second Hamlet's "not two months dead" and "within a month . . ." give past events convincing definition, and his "tonight . . . tonight . . . upon the platform 'twixt eleven and twelve" a specific imminence to what is to come. The second scene upon the platform is also definitely measured out from midnight to near dawn. This framing of the exordium to the tragedy within a precise two nights and a day gives a convincing lifelikeness to the action, and sets its pulse beating rhythmically and arrestingly.[1]

But now the conduct of the action changes, and with this the treatment of time. Hamlet's resolution—we shall soon gather—has paled, his purpose has slackened. He passes hour upon hour pacing the lobbies, reading or lost in thought, oblivious apparently to time's passing, lapsed— he himself supplies the phrase later—"lapsed in time." So Shakespeare also for a while tacitly ignores the calendar. When Polonius dispatches Reynaldo we are not told whether Laertes has already reached Paris. Presumably he has, but the point is left vague. The Ambassadors return from their mission to Norway. They must, one would suppose, have been absent for some weeks; but again, we are not told. Why not insist at once that Hamlet has let a solid two months pass and made no move, instead of letting us learn it quite incidentally later? There is more than one reason for not doing so. If the fact is explicitly stated that two months separate this scene from the last, that breaks our sense of a continuity in the action; a thing not to be done if it can be avoided, for this sense of continuity helps to sustain illusion, and so to hold us attentive. An alternative would be to insert a scene or more dealing with occurrences during these two months, and thus bridge the gap in time. But a surplusage of incidental matter is also and

---

[1] It is perhaps worth remarking that, while the first scene upon the platform closes with Horatio's cheerfully beautiful

> But look, the morn, in russet mantle clad,
> Walks o'er the dew of yon high eastern hill. . . .

in the second, when the Ghost scents the morning air, we have:

> The glowworm shows the matin to be near,
> And 'gins to pale his uneffectual fire. . . .

—and then no more, nothing of hopeful dawn or cheerful day at all. An audience may not consciously observe the difference. Shakespeare evidently did not attach much importance to it, and he had, of course, no means of giving it scenic effect. But the producer of today, with light at his command, may do well to indicate it.

always to be avoided. Polonius' talk to Reynaldo, Shakespeare feels, is relaxation and distraction enough; for with that scene only halfway through he returns to his main theme.

He could, however, circumvent such difficulties if he would. His capital reason for ignoring time hereabouts is that Hamlet is ignoring it, and he wants to attune the whole action—and us—to Hamlet's mood. He takes advantage of this passivity; we learn to know our man, as it were, at leisure. Facet after facet of him is turned to us. Polonius and Rosencrantz and Guildenstern are mirrors surrounding and reflecting him. His silence as he sits listening to the Players—and we, as we listen, watch him—admits us to closer touch with him. And when, lest the tension of the action slacken too much in this atmosphere of timelessness, the clock must be restarted, a simple, incidental, phrase or two is made to serve.

It is not until later that Shakespeare, by a cunning little stroke, puts himself right—so to speak—with the past. *The Murder of Gonzago* is about to begin when Hamlet says to Ophelia:

look you, how cheerfully my mother looks, and my father died within's two hours.

—to be answered

Nay, 'tis twice two months, my lord.

There is the calendar re-established; unostentatiously, and therefore with no forfeiting of illusion. Yet at that moment we are expectantly attentive, so every word will tell. And it is a stroke of character too. For here is Hamlet, himself so lately roused from his obliviousness, gibing at his mother for hers.

But the use of time for current effect has begun again, and very appropriately, with Hamlet's fresh impulse to action, and his decision, reached while he listens abstractedly to the Player's speech, to test the King's guilt:

we'll hear a play to-morrow. Dost thou hear me, old friend;
can you play the Murder of Gonzago? . . . We'll ha't to-morrow night.

We do not yet know what is in his mind. But from this
moment the pressure and pace of the play's action are to
increase; and the brisk "tomorrow" and "tomorrow night"
help give the initial impulse. The increase is progressive. In
the next scene the play is no longer to be "tomorrow" but
"tonight." The King, a little later, adds to the pressure.
When he has overheard Hamlet with Ophelia:

> I have in quick determination
> Thus set it down; he shall with speed to England. . . .

And this—still progressively—becomes, after the play
scene and the killing of Polonius:

> The sun no sooner shall the mountains touch
> But we will ship him hence. . . .

After the spell of timelessness, then, we have an exciting
stretch of the action carried through in a demonstrated day
and a night. But the time measure is not in itself the important thing. It is only used to validate the dramatic speed,
even as was timelessness to help slow the action down.

After this comes more ignoring of the calendar, though
the dramatic purpose in doing so is somewhat different. The
scene which follows Hamlet's departure opens with the
news of Ophelia's madness. We are not told how much
time has elapsed. For the moment the incidental signs are
against any pronounced gap. Polonius has already been
buried, but "in huggermugger"; and Ophelia, whom we last
saw smiling and suffering under Hamlet's torture, might
well have lost her wits at the very news that her father had
been killed, and that the man she loved had killed him.
But suddenly Laertes appears in full-blown rebellion. With
this it is clear why the calendar has been ignored. Shakespeare has had to face the same sort of difficulty as before.
Let him admit a definite gap in time, realistically required

for the return of Laertes and the raising of the rebellion,
and he must either break the seeming continuity of the
action, or build a bridge of superfluous matter and slacken
a tension already sufficiently slackened by the passing of
the Fortinbras army and Hamlet's "How all occasions . . ."
soliloquy. So he takes a similar way out, ignoring incon-
gruities, merely putting in the King's mouth the passing
excuse that Laertes

> is *in secret* come from France . . .
> And wants not buzzers to infect his ear
> With pestilent speeches of his father's death . . .

—an excuse which would hardly bear consideration if we
were allowed to consider it; but it is at this very instant that
the tumult begins. And once again the technical maneuver-
ing is turned to dramatic account. The surprise of Laertes'
appearance, the very inadequacy and confusion of its explanation, and his prompt success, are in pertinent contrast
to Hamlet's elaborate preparations—and his failure.

Only with news of Hamlet do we revert to the calendar,
and then with good reason. By setting a certain time for
his return, the tension of the action is automatically increased. First, in the letter to Horatio, the past is built up:

> Ere we were *two days* old at sea, a pirate of very warlike
> appointment gave us chase.

Then, in a letter to the King:

> *Tomorrow* shall I beg leave to see your kingly eyes. . . .

—the resumption of the war between them is made imminent. The scene in the graveyard thus takes place on the
morrow; and this is verified for us as it ends, by the King's
whisper to Laertes:

> Strengthen your patience in our *last night's* speech. . . .

The general effect produced—not, and it need not be, a very
marked one—is of events moving steadily now, unhurriedly,

according to plan; the deliberation of Hamlet's returning talk to the Gravediggers suggests this, and it accords with the King's cold-blooded plot and Laertes' resolution.

The calendar must again be ignored after the angry parting of Hamlet and Laertes over Ophelia's grave. If it were not, Shakespeare would either have to bring in super-fluous matter and most probably slacken tension (which he will certainly not want to do so near the end of his play) or explain and excuse an indecently swift passing from a funeral to a fencing match. He inserts instead a solid wedge of the history of the King's treachery and the trick played on the wretched Rosencrantz and Guildenstern. This suffi-ciently absorbs our attention, and dramatically separates the two incongruous events. It incidentally builds up the past still more solidly; and there is again a falsifying hint of time elapsed in Horatio's comment that

It must be shortly known to him [Claudius] from England
What is the issue of the business there.

—which is to be justified when all is over by the actual arrival of the English ambassadors to announce that the

commandment is fulfilled,
That Rosencrantz and Guildenstern are dead.

But this will simply be to give a sense of completeness to the action. Nothing is said or done to check its steady prog-ress from the graveyard scene to the end; for that is the capital consideration involved.

It comes to this, I think. Shakespeare's true concern is with *tempo,* not time. He uses time as an auxiliary, and makes free with it, and with the calendar to make his use of it convincing.[2]

When he came to playwriting, time, it is true enough to say, was commonly being put to no dramatic use at all. A few passing references to "tonight," "tomorrow" or "the

[2] Exceptionally the story itself (as with *The Merchant of Venice*) or a part of it (as in *Romeo and Juliet*) may depend upon a question of time. He must then give it attention for its own sake; but he will manage to keep it fairly malleable, and to make something of his habitual use of it, even so.

other day" there might be; for the rest, a play's end would leave a vague impression that so many events must have asked a fair amount of time for their enacting. This was not freedom—though it might seem to be—but anarchy; and he soon saw that some scheme of time would strengthen a play's action and add to the illusion. For the unlikeliest story can be made more convincing by supplying it with a date or so.

An accurately realistic time scheme, with the clock of the action going tick by tick with the watches in our pockets— that the theater can hardly be brought to accommodate. Few good stories can be made to pass in the two or three hours allowed for the acting of a play, still fewer if they must include striking and varied events. There are three main ways of dealing with the matter. Each belongs to a different sort of theater and a different type of drama. There is the so-called "classic" way. This may involve rather the ignoring than any plain falsifying of time. The drama accommodating it is apt to concentrate upon one capital event, the approaches to it elaborately prepared; and—with a master dramatist at work—motive after motive, trait after trait of character, will be unfolded like petals, till the heart of the matter is disclosed and the inevitable conclusion reached. There is the normal modern method of a suggested realism in "time," appropriate to a scenic theater's realism of place. This commonly goes with a selecting of various events to be presented, one (or it may be more) to an act, the gaps in time between them accounted for by the act divisions, the rest of the story relegated to hearsay and a sort of no man's land between the acts. Each act then becomes something of a play in itself as well as a part of one, the resulting whole a solid multiple structure, the economy of its technique akin to that of sound building, as thrifty and precise.

Lastly there is Shakespeare's freedom in time, which is the natural product of his stage's freedom in space, and which—coupled with this—permits him a panoramic display of his entire story if need be, and uninterrupted action. And, having brought time out of anarchy, he is not concerned to regulate his use of it very strictly. He adds it to

his other freedoms. Moreover he may take the greater
liberties with it, because, for his audience, in their own
actual world, the sense of time is so uncertain.

In nothing are we more open to illusion and suggestion
than in our sense of time. We live imaginative lives of our
own to quite another measure than the calendar's; a year
ago might be yesterday; tomorrow will be days in coming,
and gone in an hour. The Elizabethan convention of freedom in space, which depended upon the planning of the
theater, shrank with each restrictive change in this and at
last disappeared; but the dramatist may still exercise—in
the most realistic surroundings—a discreet freedom in
time. We readily welcome that fiction.[3]

Study of Shakespeare's stagecraft has shown us how we
wrong it by depriving the plays when we present them of
their freedom in space, by obstructing those swift, friction-
less passages from here to there, or by defining whereabouts
when he knew better than to define it. This freedom in time
is also a part of his imaginative privilege. He makes his
play a thing of movement, even as music is, and obedient to
much the same laws; and the clock and the calendar are
merely among the means by which this movement is made
expressive.

For our convenience in performing the play, one or two
stopping places can be found; there are two, at least, where
the check and the pause will do little harm. For the purpose of this study, then, and as a hint to producers, I divide
the play into three parts. But, as a reminder, "movements"
will perhaps be the better word to use for them. The first
will carry us from the beginning to Hamlet's acceptance of
his mission (it coincides with the first act of the editors);
the second from Reynaldo's dispatch to Hamlet's departure
for England; the third from the news of Ophelia's madness
to the end.

[3] Shakespeare's treatment of time is most notable in *Othello*. There is
the undisguised freedom of the scene of the landing at Cyprus, when
three separate vessels come into sight, ride out the storm, make harbor,
and disembark their passengers within the undivided speaking space of
180 lines. There is the complex latent use of time throughout the rest of
the play.

WOLFGANG H. CLEMEN

from *The Development of Shakespeare's Imagery*

The surprisingly new possibilities of language which make this play appear a turning point in the development of Shakespeare's style[1] seem to have their origin in the personality of Hamlet. The new language comes from him, in him it attains to perfection. The language of the King and the Queen, of Laertes and Polonius, although subtly adapted to their character, still treads the well-worn paths; it is less novel, because the people by whom it is spoken are not in need of a new form of expression—on the contrary, they may be more aptly characterized by a conventional mode of speech. But Hamlet's nature can only find expression in a wholly new language. This also applies to the imagery in the play. It is Hamlet who creates the most significant images, images marking the atmosphere and theme of the play, which are paler and less pregnant in the speech of the other characters. Hamlet's way of employing images is unique in Shakespeare's drama. When he begins to speak, the images fairly stream to him without the slightest effort—not as similes or conscious para-

From *The Development of Shakespeare's Imagery* by Wolfgang H. Clemen. Cambridge, Mass.: Harvard University Press; London: Methuen & Co., Ltd., 1951. Reprinted by permission of the publishers. Some deletions have been made in the footnotes.

[1] On the style in *Hamlet* see L. L. Schücking, *The Meaning of Hamlet*, London, 1937, I. i. and I. iv.

phrases, but as immediate and spontaneous visions.[2] Hamlet's imagery shows us that whenever he thinks and speaks, he is at the same time a visionary, a seer, for whom the living things of the world about him embody and symbolize thought. His first monologue may show this; the short space of time which lies between his father's death and his mother's remarriage is to him a series of pictures taken from real life:

> A little month, or ere those shoes were old
> With which she follow'd my poor father's body,
> Like Niobe, all tears: (I.ii.147–49)

> Ere yet the salt of most unrighteous tears
> Had left the flushing in her galled eyes,   (I.ii.154–55)

or a little later, addressed to Horatio:

> the funeral baked meats
> Did coldly furnish forth the marriage tables. (I.ii.180–81)

These are no poetic similes, but keen observations of reality. Hamlet does not translate the general thought into an image paraphrasing it; on the contrary, he uses the opposite method: he refers the generalization to the events and objects of the reality underlying the thought. This sense of reality finds expression in all the images Hamlet employs. Peculiar to them all is that closeness to reality which is often carried to the point of an unsparing poignancy. They

[2] The spontaneous and unpremeditated character of Hamlet's imagery will become obvious through a comparison with Claudius' language. Claudius' speeches are studied and give the impression of having been previously prepared. His images often are consciously inserted. Dr. Schmetz notes that while Claudius often uses comparisons, linking object and image by "as" or "like," Hamlet's imagination fuses both into a metaphor (cf. IV.i. 40–44, IV.v. 94–96 with III.i. 83–84, III.ii. 404). Further examples for Claudius' comparisons: III.iii. 41; IV.vii. 15; IV.iv. 87. This is, of course, only one aspect of the manifold differences between Claudius' and Hamlet's language. The whole problem has been exhaustively dealt with in Dr. Schmetz's study. For the difference between the imagery of Claudius' public and that of his private language, and for further distinguishing features in Claudius' imagery see Una Ellis-Fermor, *The Frontiers of Drama*, London, 1945, p. 88.

are mostly very concrete and precise, simple and, as to their subject matter, easy to understand; common and ordinary things, things familiar to the man in the street dominate, rather than lofty, strange or rare objects. Illuminating in this connection is the absence of hyperbole, of great dimensions in his imagery. In contrast to Othello or Lear, for example, who awaken heaven and the elements in their imagery [3] and who lend expression to their mighty passions in images of soaring magnificence, Hamlet prefers to keep his language within the scope of reality, indeed, within the everyday world. It is not spacious scenery and nature which dominate in Hamlet's imagery, but rather trades and callings, objects of daily use, popular games and technical terms; his images are not beautiful, poetic, magnificent, but they always hit their mark, the matter in question, with surprisingly unerring sureness. They do not waft the things of reality into a dream world of the imagination; on the contrary, they make them truly *real*, they reveal their inmost, naked being. All this, the wealth of realistic observation, of real objects, of associations taken from everyday life, is enough to prove that Hamlet is no abstract thinker and dreamer. As his imagery betrays to us, he is rather a man gifted with greater powers of observation than the others. He is capable of scanning reality with a keener eye and of penetrating the veil of semblance even to the very core of things. "I know not seems."

At the same time, Hamlet's imagery reveals the hero's wide educational background, his many-sidedness and the extraordinary range of his experience. That metaphors taken from natural sciences are specially frequent in Hamlet's language again emphasizes his power of observation, his critical objective way of looking at things. But Hamlet is also at home in classical antiquity or Greek mythology, in the terminology of law, he is not only familiar with the theater and with acting—as everyone knows—but also with the fine arts, with falconry and hunting, with the soldier's

---

[3] Hamlet, too, invokes God and the heavenly powers, but these invocations never take the form of grandiose images, they are mostly brief and often restricted to mere references (cf. I.ii. 132, 150, 195; I.v. 92; I.iv. 85; V. ii. 333, 345).

trade and strategy, with the courtier's way of life. All these spheres disclosing Hamlet's personality as that of a "courtier, soldier, and scholar" (in Ophelia's words, III.i.154) are evoked by the imagery which, however, turns them to living account by a fit application to situations, persons, and moods. Hamlet commands so many levels of expression that he can attune his diction as well as his imagery to the situation and to the person to whom he is speaking. This adaptability and versatility is another feature in Hamlet's use of language which can also be traced in his imagery.

At the same time, this wide range of imagery can, in certain passages, serve to give relief to his conflicting moods, to his being torn between extremes and to the abruptness of his changes of mood. This characteristic which has been particularly emphasized and partly attributed to "melancholy" by L. L. Schücking and John Dover Wilson, also expresses itself in the sudden change of language and in the juxtaposition of passages which are sharply contrasted in their diction. With no other character in Shakespeare do we find this sharp contrast between images marked by a pensive mood and those which unsparingly use vulgar words and display a frivolous and sarcastic disgust for the world.

Let us consider further how Hamlet's use of imagery reflects his ability to penetrate to the real nature of men and things and his relentless breaking down of the barriers raised by hypocrisy. Many of his images seem in fact designed to unmask men; they are meant to strip them of their fine appearances and to show them up in their true nature. Thus, by means of the simile of fortune's pipe, Hamlet shows Rosencrantz and Guildenstern that he has seen through their intent, and thus he unmasks Rosencrantz when he calls him a "sponge," "that soaks up the king's countenance" (IV.ii.15). He splits his mother's heart "in twain," because he tells her the truth from which she shrinks and which she conceals from herself. And again it is by means of images that he seeks to lead her to a recognition of the truth. He renews the memory of his father in her by means of that forceful description of his

outward appearance which could be compared with
Hyperion, Mars, and Mercury. On the other hand, another
series of comparisons seeks to bring home to his mother
the real nature of Claudius:

> a mildew'd ear,
> Blasting his wholesome brother.   (III.iv.65–66)

> a vice of kings;
> A cutpurse of the empire and the rule,
> That from a shelf the precious diadem stole,
> And put it in his pocket!

> A king of shreds and patches,   (III.iv.99–102, 103)

So Hamlet sees through men and things. He perceives
what is false, visualizing his recognition through imagery.

Hamlet's imagery, which thus calls things by their
right names, acquires a peculiar freedom from his feigned
madness. Hamlet needs images for his "antic disposition."
He would betray himself if he used open, direct language.
Hence he must speak ambiguously and cloak his real
meaning under quibbles and puns,[4] images, and parables.
The other characters do not understand him and continue
to think he is mad, but the audience can gain an insight
into the true situation. Under the protection of that mask
of "antic disposition," Hamlet says more shrewd things
than all the rest of the courtiers together. So we find the
images here in an entirely new rôle, unique in Shakespeare's
drama. Only the images of the fool in *King Lear* have a
similar function.

Hamlet suffers an injustice when he is accused of merely
theoretical and abstract speculation which would lead him
away from reality. His thoughts carry further than those of
others, because he sees more and deeper than they, not
because he would leave reality unheeded. It is true that his
is a nature more prone to thought than to action; but that

[4] Through John Dover Wilson's edition of *Hamlet* (Cambridge, 1934)
many of these puns and quibbles which so far had remained unintelligible (or were falsely understood) have been cleared up. On the importance of quibbles in *Hamlet* see John Dover Wilson's Introduction, p.
xxxiii. sqq.

signifies by no means, as the Hamlet critics would often have us believe, that he is a philosopher and dreamer and no man of the world. When, in the graveyard scene, he holds Yorick's skull in his hand, he sees *more* in it than the others, for whom the skull is merely a lifeless object. And precisely because he is more deeply moved by the reality and significance of these earthly remains, his fantasy is able to follow the "noble dust of Alexander" through all its metamorphoses. The comparisons which spring from this faculty of thinking a thing to the end, as it were, derive in fact from a more intense experience of reality.

It is a fundamental tenet of Hamlet criticism that Hamlet's overdeveloped intellect makes it impossible for him to act. In this connection the following famous passage is generally quoted:

> And thus the native hue of resolution
> Is sicklied o'er with the pale cast of thought,
> And enterprises of great pith and moment
> With this regard their currents turn awry,
> And lose the name of action.   (III.i.84–88)

The customary interpretation of this passage, "reflection hinders action," does it an injustice. For Hamlet does not says "reflection hinders action," he simply utters this image. The fact that he does not utter that general maxim, but this image, makes all the difference. For this image is the unique and specific form of expression of the thought underlying it, it cannot be separated from it. If we say "reflection hinders action," we make a false generalization; we replace a specific formulation by an apothegm. And thereby we eradicate in this passage that quality which is peculiarly Shakespeare's or, what is more, peculiarly Hamlet's. Here the image does not serve the purpose of merely casting a decorative cloak about the thought; it is much rather an intrinsic part of the thought.

"Reflection hinders action"—this phrase carries in it something absolute, something damning. We sense a moralizing undertone. Action and reflection are thus conceived of as two mutually inimical abstract principles.

But not so in Shakespeare's metaphorical language. "Native hue of resolution" suggests that Shakespeare viewed resolution as an innate human quality, not as a moral virtue to be consciously striven after. But the Hamlet criticism of the nineteenth century saw the problem in this light of a moral virtue. We see, then, that a careful consideration of Shakespeare's imagery may sometimes correct false interpretations.

"Reflection hinders action." Polonius, the sententious lover of maxims, could have said this, for a general saying carries no sense of personal obligation; it places a distance between the speaker and what he would say. But just as it is characteristic of Polonius to utter banalities and sententious effusions, so, too, it is characteristic of Hamlet, to express even those things which would have permitted of a generalizing formulation, in a language which bears the stamp of a unique and personal experience.

Hamlet sees this problem under the aspect of a process of the human organism. The original bright coloring of the skin is concealed by an ailment. Thus the relation between thought and action appears not as an opposition between two abstract principles between which a free choice is possible, but as an unavoidable condition of human nature. The image of the leprous ailment emphasizes the malignant, disabling, slowly disintegrating nature of the process. It is by no mere chance that Hamlet employs just this image. Perusing the description which the ghost of Hamlet's father gives of his poisoning by Claudius (I.v.63) one cannot help being struck by the vividness with which the process of poisoning, the malicious spreading of the disease, is portrayed:.

> And in the porches of my ears did pour
> The leperous distillment; whose effect
> Holds such an enmity with blood of man
> That swift as quicksilver it courses through
> The natural gates and alleys of the body,
> And with a sudden vigor it doth posset
> And curd, like eager droppings into milk,
> The thin and wholesome blood: so did it mine;

> And a most instant tetter bark'd about,
> Most lazarlike, with vile and loathsome crust,
> All my smooth body.   (I.v.63–73)

A real event described at the beginning of the drama
has exercised a profound influence upon the whole imagery
of the play. What is later metaphor, is here still reality. The
picture of the leprous skin disease, which is here—in the
first act—described by Hamlet's father, has buried itself
deep in Hamlet's imagination and continues to lead its
subterranean existence, as it were, until it reappears in
metaphorical form.

As Miss Spurgeon has shown, the idea of an ulcer
dominates the imagery, infecting and fatally eating away
the whole body; on every occasion repulsive images of
sickness make their appearance.[5] It is certain that this
imagery is derived from that one real event. Hamlet's
father describes in that passage how the poison invades the
body during sleep and how the healthy organism is de-
stroyed from within, not having a chance to defend itself
against attack. But this now becomes the leitmotiv of the
imagery: the individual occurrence is expanded into a
symbol for the central problem of the play. The corruption
of land and people throughout Denmark is understood as
an imperceptible and irresistible process of poisoning. And,
furthermore, this poisoning reappears as a leitmotiv in the
action as well—as a poisoning in the "dumb show," and
finally, as the poisoning of all the major characters in the
last act. Thus imagery and action continually play into
each other's hands and we see how the term "dramatic
imagery" gains a new significance.

The imagery appears to be influenced by yet another
event in the action underlying the play: Hamlet feels
himself to be sullied by his mother's incest which, according
to the conception of the time, she committed in marrying
Claudius. For him this is a poisoning idea which finds
expression in his language. Professor Dover Wilson has
defended the reading of the Second Quarto with convincing arguments:

[5] Spurgeon, *Shakespeare's Imagery*, p. 316 sqq.

> O, that this too too sullied flesh would melt,
> Thaw and resolve itself into a dew!   (I.ii.129–30)

It is therefore probable that this idea is present in Hamlet's mind at many moments when images of decay and rot appear in his language.

The leitmotiv occasionally appears in a disguised form at a point where it seems to have no real connection with the main issue of the play, for instance, in the following passage:

> So, oft it chances in particular men,
> That for some vicious mole of nature in them,
> As, in their birth—wherein they are not guilty
> Since nature cannot choose his origin—
> By the o'ergrowth of some complexion,
> Oft breaking down the pales and forts of reason,
> Or by some habit, that too much o'erleavens
> The form of plausive manners, that these men,
> Carrying, I say, the stamp of one defect,
> Being nature's livery, or fortune's star,
> Their virtues else—be they as pure as grace,
> As infinite as man may undergo—
> Shall in the general censure take corruption
> From that particular fault: the dram of eale
> Doth all the noble substance of a doubt
> To his own scandal.
>   (I.iv.23–38)

Hamlet has spoken of the excessive revels and drinking bouts among his people and has said that this was disparaging to the Danes in the eyes of the other peoples. Then follows this general reflection. The question arises: Why does Hamlet speak in such detail of these matters here? For at this point in the play he has as yet heard nothing of his uncle's murderous deed. And still he touches in this speech upon that leitmotiv of the whole play; he describes how human nature may be brought to decay through a tiny birthmark, just as from one "dram of evil" [6] a destructive

---

[6] The emendation *evil* has been accepted by several editors, e.g., by John Dover Wilson in the *New Shakespeare* edition.

eflect may spread over the whole organism. *O'erleavens*
already points to *sicklied o'er,* and, as in the passage discussed, the notion of the human body is in the background.
As in later passages, the balance of the powers in man is
the theme here, and "corruption," a basic motif in the
whole play, already makes its appearance. This general
reflection on gradual and irresistible infection is made in
passing, as it were. Thus Shakespeare makes use of every
opportunity to suggest the fundamental theme of the play.
When the King says to Laertes in the fourth act:

> There lives within the very flame of love
> A kind of wick or snuff that will abate it;

the same motif occurs again: corruption through a "dram
of evil."

The following passage, too, from Laertes' words of
warning to his sister, has never been examined for its value
as "dramatic presaging."

> The canker galls the infants of the spring,
> Too oft before their buttons be disclosed,
> And in the morn and liquid dew of youth
> Contagious blastments are most imminent.   (I.iii.39–42)

It is no mere chance that this sententious little image,
which is so neatly woven in and so conventional, touches
upon a motif later to be worked out more clearly. The
worm in the bud, like ulcer and eruption, is also an irresistible force destroying the organism from within. Light
is cast upon this early passage when, in the last act, it is
said of Claudius: "this canker of our nature" (V.ii.69). But
here we still know nothing of the coming developments.
The image is a faint warning, preparing the way, together
with other hints, for the future.

The Pyrrhus episode which the first Player recites
before Hamlet contains features which are also of importance for the theme of the play. For here it is related of
Pyrrhus with vigorous emphasis how "Aroused vengeance
sets him new a-work" (II.ii.499). For Hamlet it must be

a gentle warning that vengeance calls forth so bloody a deed
in another without delay. On the other hand, the previous
lines described Pyrrhus as being in suspense, unable to act,
"neutral to his will" as Hamlet still is:

> So, as a painted tyrant, Pyrrhus stood,
> And like a neutral to his will and matter,
> Did nothing.   (II.ii.491)

The mention of "strumpet Fortune" and the picture of her
broken wheel rolled "down the hill of heaven" at the end
of this passage, is likewise a hint; in the third act this
image of the wheel plunging down from the height, reappears in the conversation between Rosencrantz and the
King:

> The cease of majesty
> Dies not alone; but, like a gulf, doth draw
> What's near it with it: it is a massy wheel,
> Fix'd on the summit of the highest mount,
> To whose huge spokes ten thousand lesser things
> Are mortised and adjoin'd; which, when it falls,
> Each small annexment, petty consequence,
> Attends the boisterous ruin.   (III.iii.15–22)

Through these images, which are also spun out from a
more general reflection, the coming catastrophe is already
significantly foreshadowed.

The imagery in Shakespeare's tragedies often shows
how a number of other images are grouped around the
central symbol which express the same idea, but in quite
other terms. Several degrees, as it were, of the metaphorical
expression of a fundamental idea may be distinguished.
Besides images which express a motif with the greatest
clarity and emphasis, we find others which utter the
thought in a veiled and indirect manner. An examination
of the way in which the images are spread over the play,
can reveal how subtly Shakespeare modifies and varies
according to character and situation.

The most striking images of sickness, which Miss

Spurgeon has already listed, make their first appearance,
significantly enough, in the second half of the play, and
most notably in the scene in which Hamlet seeks to bring
his mother to a change of heart. Here the plainness and
clarity of the images is meant to awaken the conscience of
the Queen; they can scarcely be forceful enough; "let me
wring your heart," Hamlet has said at the beginning of the
meeting. In the first part of the play the atmosphere of corruption and decay is spread in a more indirect and general
way. Hamlet declares in the first and second acts how
the world appears to him:

> . . . Ah fie! 'tis an unweeded garden,
> That grows to seed; things rank and gross in nature
> Possess it merely.   (I.ii.135–37)

. . . and indeed it goes so heavily with my disposition that
this goodly frame, the earth, seems to me a sterile promontory,
this most excellent canopy, the air, look you, this brave
o'erhanging firmament, this majestical roof fretted with golden
fire, why, it appears no other thing to me than a foul and
pestilent congregation of vapors.   (II.ii.305)

The image of weeds, touched upon in the word "unweeded," is related to the imagery of sickness in Shakespeare's work. It appears three times in *Hamlet*. The
ghost says to Hamlet:

> And duller shouldst thou be than the fat weed
> That roots itself in ease on Lethe wharf,   (I.v.32–33)

In the dialogue with his mother, this image immediately
follows upon the image of the ulcer:

> And do not spread the compost on the weeds,
> To make them ranker,   (III.iv.152–53)

Images of rot, decay and corruption are especially numerous in the long second scene of the second act. There are,
for example, Hamlet's remarks on the maggots which the
sun breeds in a dead dog (II.ii.181), on the deep dungeons

in the prison Denmark (II.ii.250), on the strumpet Fortune (II.ii.239), who reappears in the speech of the first Player (II.ii.504), his comparison of himself with a whore, a drab, and a scullion (II.ii.599).

Seen individually, such images do not seem to be very important. But in their totality they contribute considerably to the tone of the play.

MAYNARD MACK

The World of "Hamlet"

My subject is the world of *Hamlet*. I do not of course
mean Denmark, except as Denmark is given a body by the
play; and I do not mean Elizabethan England, though this
is necessarily close behind the scenes. I mean simply the
imaginative environment that the play asks us to enter when
we read it or go to see it.

Great plays, as we know, do present us with something
that can be called a world, a microcosm—a world like our
own in being made of people, actions, situations, thoughts,
feelings, and much more, but unlike our own in being
perfectly, or almost perfectly, significant and coherent. In
a play's world, each part implies the other parts, and each
lives, each means, with the life and meaning of the rest.

This is the reason, as we also know, that the worlds of
great plays greatly differ. Othello in Hamlet's position, we
sometimes say, would have no problem; but what we are
really saying is that Othello in Hamlet's position would
not exist. The conception we have of Othello is a function
of the characters who help define him, Desdemona, honest
Iago, Cassio, and the rest; of his history of travel and war;
of a great storm that divides his ship from Cassio's, and a
handkerchief; of a quiet night in Venice broken by cries

From *The Yale Review*, XLI (1952), 502–23. Copyright 1952 by
the Yale University Press. Reprinted by permission of the author.

about an old black ram; of a quiet night in Cyprus broken
by swordplay; of a quiet bedroom where a woman goes
to bed in her wedding sheets and a man comes in with a
light to put out the light; and above all, of a language, a
language with many voices in it, gentle, rasping, queru-
lous, or foul, but all counterpointing the one great voice:

> Put up your bright swords, for the dew will rust them.

> O thou weed
> Who art so lovely fair and smell'st so sweet
> That the sense aches at thee. . . .

> Yet I'll not shed her blood
> Nor scar that whiter skin of hers than snow,
> And smooth as monumental alabaster.

> I pray you in your letters,
> When you shall these unlucky deeds relate,
> Speak of me as I am; nothing extenuate,
> Nor set down aught in malice; then must you speak
> Of one that loved not wisely but too well;
> Of one not easily jealous, but being wrought,
> Perplex'd in th' extreme; of one whose hand,
> Like the base Indian, threw a pearl away
> Richer than all his tribe. . . .

Without his particular world of voices, persons, events,
the world that both expresses and contains him, Othello is
unimaginable. And so, I think, are Antony, King Lear,
Macbeth—and Hamlet. We come back then to Hamlet's
world, of all the tragic worlds that Shakespeare made, easily
the most various and brilliant, the most elusive. It is with
no thought of doing justice to it that I have singled out
three of its attributes for comment. I know too well, if I
may echo a sentiment of Mr. E. M. W. Tillyard's, that no
one is likely to accept another man's reading of *Hamlet*,
that anyone who tries to throw light on one part of the
play usually throws the rest into deeper shadow, and that

what I have to say leaves out many problems—to mention only one, the knotty problem of the text. All I would say in defense of the materials I have chosen is that they seem to me interesting, close to the root of the matter even if we continue to differ about what the root of the matter is, and explanatory, in a modest way, of this play's peculiar hold on everyone's imagination, its almost mythic status, one might say, as a paradigm of the life of man.

The first attribute that impresses us, I think, is mysteriousness. We often hear it said, perhaps with truth, that every great work of art has a mystery at the heart; but the mystery of *Hamlet* is something else. We feel its presence in the numberless explanations that have been brought forward for Hamlet's delay, his madness, his ghost, his treatment of Polonius, or Ophelia, or his mother; and in the controversies that still go on about whether the play is "undoubtedly a failure" (Eliot's phrase) or one of the greatest artistic triumphs; whether, if it is a triumph, it belongs to the highest order of tragedy; whether, if it is such a tragedy, its hero is to be taken as a man of exquisite moral sensibility (Bradley's view) or an egomaniac (Madariaga's view).

Doubtless there have been more of these controversies and explanations than the play requires; for in Hamlet, to paraphrase a remark of Falstaff's, we have a character who is not only mad in himself but a cause that madness is in the rest of us. Still, the very existence of so many theories and countertheories, many of them formulated by sober heads, gives food for thought. *Hamlet* seems to lie closer to the illogical logic of life than Shakespeare's other tragedies. And while the causes of this situation may be sought by saying that Shakespeare revised the play so often that eventually the motivations were smudged over, or that the original old play has been here or there imperfectly digested, or that the problems of Hamlet lay so close to Shakespeare's heart that he could not quite distance them in the formal terms of art, we have still as critics to deal with effects, not causes. If I may quote again from Mr. Tillyard, the play's very lack of a rigorous type of causal logic seems to be a part of its point.

Moreover, the matter goes deeper than this. Hamlet's world is pre-eminently in the interrogative mood. It reverberates with questions, anguished, meditative, alarmed. There are questions that in this play, to an extent I think unparalleled in any other, mark the phases and even the nuances of the action, helping to establish its peculiar baffled tone. There are other questions whose interrogations, innocent at first glance, are subsequently seen to have reached beyond their contexts and to point towards some pervasive inscrutability in Hamlet's world as a whole. Such is that tense series of challenges with which the tragedy begins: Bernardo's of Francisco, "Who's there?" Francisco's of Horatio and Marcellus, "Who is there?" Horatio's of the ghost, "What art thou . . . ?" And then there are the famous questions. In them the interrogations seem to point not only beyond the context but beyond the play, out of Hamlet's predicaments into everyone's: "What a piece of work is a man! . . . And yet to me what is this quintessence of dust?" "To be, or not to be, that is the question." "Get thee to a nunnery. Why wouldst thou be a breeder of sinners?" "I am very proud, revengeful, ambitious, with more offenses at my beck than I have thoughts to put them in, imagination to give them shape, or time to act them in. What should such fellows as I do crawling between earth and heaven?" "Dost thou think Alexander look'd o' this fashion i' th' earth? . . . And smelt so?"

Further, Hamlet's world is a world of riddles. The hero's own language is often riddling, as the critics have pointed out. When he puns, his puns have receding depths in them, like the one which constitutes his first speech: "A little more than kin, and less than kind." His utterances in madness, even if wild and whirling, are simultaneously, as Polonius discovers, pregnant: "Do you know me, my lord?" "Excellent well. You are a fishmonger." Even the madness itself is riddling: How much is real? How much is feigned? What does it mean? Sane or mad, Hamlet's mind plays restlessly about his world, turning up one riddle upon another. The riddle of character, for example, and how it is that in a man whose virtues else are "pure as grace," some vicious mole of nature, some "dram of eale," can

"all the noble substance oft adulter." Or the riddle of the
player's art, and how a man can so project himself into a
fiction, a dream of passion, that he can weep for Hecuba.
Or the riddle of action: how we may think too little—
"What to ourselves in passion we propose," says the player-
king, "The passion ending, doth the purpose lose"; and
again, how we may think too much: "Thus conscience does
make cowards of us all, And thus the native hue of resolution Is sicklied o'er with the pale cast of thought."

There are also more immediate riddles. His mother—
how could she "on this fair mountain leave to feed, And
batten on this moor?" The ghost—which may be a devil,
for "the de'il hath power T' assume a pleasing shape."
Ophelia—what does her behavior to him mean? Surprising
her in her closet, he falls to such perusal of her face as
he would draw it. Even the king at his prayers is a riddle.
Will a revenge that takes him in the purging of his soul
be vengeance, or hire and salary? As for himself, Hamlet
realizes, he is the greatest riddle of all—a mystery, he
warns Rosencrantz and Guildenstern, from which he will
not have the heart plucked out. He cannot tell why he has
of late lost all his mirth, forgone all custom of exercises.
Still less can he tell why he delays: "I do not know Why
yet I live to say, 'This thing's to do,' Sith I have cause and
will and strength and means To do't."

Thus the mysteriousness of Hamlet's world is of a piece.
It is not simply a matter of missing motivations, to be
expunged if only we could find the perfect clue. It is built
in. It is evidently an important part of what the play wishes
to say to us. And it is certainly an element that the play
thrusts upon us from the opening word. Everyone, I think,
recalls the mysteriousness of that first scene. The cold
middle of the night on the castle platform, the muffled
sentries, the uneasy atmosphere of apprehension, the
challenges leaping out of the dark, the questions that follow the challenges, feeling out the darkness, searching for
identities, for relations, for assurance. "Bernardo?" "Have
you had quiet guard?" "Who hath reliev'd you?" "What,
is Horatio there?" "What, has this thing appear'd again
tonight?" "Looks 'a not like the king?" "How now, Horatio!

. . . Is not this something more than fantasy? What think you on 't?" "Is it not like the king?" "Why this same strict and most observant watch . . . ?" "Shall I strike at it with my partisan?" "Do you consent we shall acquaint [young Hamlet] with it?"

We need not be surprised that critics and playgoers alike have been tempted to see in this an evocation not simply of Hamlet's world but of their own. Man in his aspect of bafflement, moving in darkness on a rampart between two worlds, unable to reject, or quite accept, the one that, when he faces it, "to-shakes" his disposition with thoughts beyond the reaches of his soul—comforting himself with hints and guesses. We hear these hints and guesses whispering through the darkness as the several watchers speak. "At least, the whisper goes so," says one. "I think it be no other but e'en so," says another. "I have heard" that on the crowing of the cock "Th' extravagant and erring spirit hies To his confine," says a third. "Some say" at Christmas time "this bird of dawning" sings all night, "And then, they say, no spirit dare stir abroad." "So have I heard," says the first, "and do in part believe it." However we choose to take the scene, it is clear that it creates a world where uncertainties are of the essence.

Meantime, such is Shakespeare's economy, a second attribute of Hamlet's world has been put before us. This is the problematic nature of reality and the relation of reality to appearance. The play begins with an appearance, an "apparition," to use Marcellus's term—the ghost. And the ghost is somehow real, indeed the vehicle of realities. Through its revelation, the glittering surface of Claudius's court is pierced, and Hamlet comes to know, and we do, that the king is not only hateful to him but the murderer of his father, that his mother is guilty of adultery as well as incest. Yet there is a dilemma in the revelation. For possibly the apparition *is* an apparition, a devil who has assumed his father's shape.

This dilemma, once established, recurs on every hand. From the court's point of view, there is Hamlet's madness. Polonius investigates and gets some strange advice about his daughter: "Conception is a blessing, but as your

daughter may conceive, friend, look to 't." Rosencrantz
and Guildenstern investigate and get the strange confidence
that "Man delights not me; no, nor woman neither."
Ophelia is "loosed" to Hamlet (Polonius's vulgar word),
while Polonius and the king hide behind the arras; and
what they hear is a strange indictment of human nature,
and a riddling threat: "Those that are married already, all
but one, shall live."

On the other hand, from Hamlet's point of view, there
is Ophelia. Kneeling here at her prayers, she seems the
image of innocence and devotion. Yet she is of the sex
for whom he has already found the name Frailty, and she
is also, as he seems either madly or sanely to divine, a
decoy in a trick. The famous cry—"Get thee to a nunnery"
—shows the anguish of his uncertainty. If Ophelia is what
she seems, this dirty-minded world of murder, incest, lust,
adultery, is no place for her. Were she "as chaste as ice,
as pure as snow," she could not escape its calumny. And
if she is not what she seems, then a nunnery in its other
sense of brothel is relevant to her. In the scene that follows he treats her as if she were indeed an inmate of a
brothel.

Likewise, from Hamlet's point of view, there is the
enigma of the king. If the ghost is *only* an appearance,
then possibly the king's appearance is reality. He must try
it further. By means of a second and different kind of
"apparition," the play within the play, he does so. But
then, immediately after, he stumbles on the king at prayer.
This appearance has a relish of salvation in it. If the king
dies now, his soul may yet be saved. Yet actually, as we
know, the king's efforts to come to terms with heaven have
been unavailing; his words fly up, his thoughts remain
below. If Hamlet means the conventional revenger's reasons that he gives for sparing Claudius, it was the perfect
moment not to spare him—when the sinner was acknowl-
edging his guilt, yet unrepentant. The perfect moment, but
it was hidden, like so much else in the play, behind an
arras.

There are two arrases in his mother's room. Hamlet
thrusts his sword through one of them. Now at last he has

got to the heart of the evil, or so he thinks. But now it is
the wrong man; now he himself is a murderer. The other
arras he stabs through with his words—like daggers, says
the queen. He makes her shrink under the contrast he
points between her present husband and his father. But
as the play now stands (matters are somewhat clearer in
the bad Quarto), it is hard to be sure how far the queen
grasps the fact that her second husband is the murderer of
her first. And it is hard to say what may be signified by
her inability to see the ghost, who now for the last time
appears. In one sense at least, the ghost is the supreme
reality, representative of the hidden ultimate power, in
Bradley's terms—witnessing from beyond the grave against
this hollow world. Yet the man who is capable of seeing
through to this reality, the queen thinks is mad. "To
whom do you speak this?" she cries to her son. "Do you
see nothing there?" he asks, incredulous. And she replies:
"Nothing at all; yet all that is I see." Here certainly we have
the imperturbable self-confidence of the worldly world,
its layers on layers of habituation, so that when the reality
is before its very eyes it cannot detect its presence.

Like mystery, this problem of reality is central to the
play and written deep into its idiom. Shakespeare's favorite
terms in *Hamlet* are words of ordinary usage that pose
the question of appearances in a fundamental form.
"Apparition" I have already mentioned. Another term
is "seems." When we say, as Ophelia says of Hamlet
leaving her closet, "He seem'd to find his way without his
eyes," we mean one thing. When we say, as Hamlet says
to his mother in the first court scene, "Seems, Madam!
. . . I know not 'seems,'" we mean another. And when
we say, as Hamlet says to Horatio before the play within
the play, "And after, we will both our judgments join
In censure of his seeming," we mean both at once. The
ambiguities of "seem" coil and uncoil throughout this
play, and over against them is set the idea of "seeing."
So Hamlet challenges the king in his triumphant letter
announcing his return to Denmark: "Tomorrow shall I
beg leave to see your kingly eyes." Yet "seeing" itself can
be ambiguous, as we recognize from Hamlet's uncertainty

about the ghost; or from that statement of his mother's already quoted: "Nothing at all; yet all that is I see."

Another term of like importance is "assume." What we assume may be what we are not: "The de'il hath power T' assume a pleasing shape." But it may be what we are: "If it assume my noble father's person, I'll speak to it." And it may be what we are not yet, but would become; thus Hamlet advises his mother, "Assume a virtue, if you have it not." The perplexity in the word points to a real perplexity in Hamlet's and our own experience. We assume our habits—and habits are like costumes, as the word implies: "My father in his habit as he liv'd!" Yet these habits become ourselves in time: "That monster, custom, who all sense doth eat Of habits evil, is angel yet in this, That to the use of actions fair and good He likewise gives a frock or livery That aptly is put on."

Two other terms I wish to instance are "put on" and "shape." The shape of something is the form under which we are accustomed to apprehend it: "Do you see yonder cloud that's almost in shape of a camel?" But a shape may also be a disguise—even, in Shakespeare's time, an actor's costume or an actor's role. This is the meaning when the king says to Laertes as they lay the plot against Hamlet's life: "Weigh what convenience both of time and means May fit us to our shape." "Put on" supplies an analogous ambiguity. Shakespeare's mind seems to worry this phrase in the play much as Hamlet's mind worries the problem of acting in a world of surfaces, or the king's mind worries the meaning of Hamlet's transformation. Hamlet has put an antic disposition on, that the king knows. But what does "put on" mean? A mask, or a frock or livery—our "habit"? The king is left guessing, and so are we.

What is found in the play's key terms is also found in its imagery. Miss Spurgeon has called attention to a pattern of disease images in *Hamlet,* to which I shall return. But the play has other patterns equally striking. One of these, as my earlier quotations hint, is based on clothes. In the world of surfaces to which Shakespeare exposes us in Hamlet, clothes are naturally a factor of importance. "The apparel oft proclaims the man," Polonius assures

Laertes, cataloguing maxims in the young man's ear as he is about to leave for Paris. Oft, but not always. And so he sends his man Reynaldo to look into Laertes' life there—even, if need be, to put a false dress of accusation upon his son ("What forgeries you please"), the better by indirections to find directions out. On the same grounds, he takes Hamlet's vows to Ophelia as false apparel. They are bawds, he tells her—or if we do not like Theobald's emendation, they are bonds—in masquerade, "Not of that dye which their investments show, But mere implorators of unholy suits."

This breach between the outer and the inner stirs no special emotion in Polonius, because he is always either behind an arras or prying into one, but it shakes Hamlet to the core. Here so recently was his mother in her widow's weeds, the tears still flushing in her galled eyes; yet now within a month, a little month, before even her funeral shoes are old, she has married with his uncle. Her mourning was all clothes. Not so his own, he bitterly replies, when she asks him to cast his "nighted color off." "Tis not alone my inky cloak, good mother"—and not alone, he adds, the sighs, the tears, the dejected havior of the visage —"that can denote me truly."

> These indeed seem,
> For they are actions that a man might play;
> But I have that within which passes show;
> These but the trappings and the suits of woe.

What we must not overlook here is Hamlet's visible attire, giving the verbal imagery a theatrical extension. Hamlet's apparel now is his inky cloak, mark of his grief for his father, mark also of his character as a man of melancholy, mark possibly too of his being one in whom appearance and reality are attuned. Later, in his madness, with his mind disordered, he will wear his costume in a corresponding disarray, the disarray that Ophelia describes so vividly to Polonius and that producers of the play rarely give sufficient heed to: "Lord Hamlet with his doublet all unbrac'd, No hat upon his head; his stockings foul'd, Ungarter'd, and down-gyved to his ankle." Here the only question will be, as with the madness itself, how much is studied, how much is real. Still later, by a third costume, the simple traveler's garb in which we find him new come from shipboard, Shakespeare will show us that we have a third aspect of the man.

A second pattern of imagery springs from terms of painting: the paints, the colorings, the varnishes that may either conceal, or, as in the painter's art, reveal. Art in Claudius conceals. "The harlot's cheek," he tells us in his one aside, "beautied with plastering art, Is not more ugly to the thing that helps it Than is my deed to my most painted word." Art in Ophelia, loosed to Hamlet in the episode already noticed to which this speech of the king's is prelude, is more complex. She looks so beautiful— "the celestial, and my soul's idol, the most beautified Ophelia," Hamlet has called her in his love letter. But now, what does beautified mean? Perfected with all the innocent beauties of a lovely woman? Or "beautied" like the harlot's cheek? "I have heard of your paintings too, well enough. God hath given you one face, and you make yourselves another."

Yet art, differently used, may serve the truth. By using an "image" (his own word) of a murder done in Vienna, Hamlet cuts through to the king's guilt; holds "as 'twere, the mirror up to nature," shows "virtue her own feature, scorn her own image, and the very age and body of the time"—which is out of joint—"his form and pressure." Something similar he does again in his mother's bedroom, painting for her in words "the rank sweat of an enseamed bed," making her recoil in horror from his "counterfeit presentment of two brothers," and holding, if we may trust a stage tradition, his father's picture beside his uncle's. Here again the verbal imagery is realized visually on the stage.

The most pervasive of Shakespeare's image patterns in this play, however, is the pattern evolved around the three words, "show," "act," "play." "Show" seems to be Shakespeare's unifying image in *Hamlet*. Through it he pulls together and exhibits in a single focus much of the diverse material in his play. The ideas of seeming, assuming, and putting on; the images of clothing, painting, mirroring; the episode of the dumb show and the play within the play; the characters of Polonius, Laertes, Ophelia, Claudius, Gertrude, Rosencrantz and Guildenstern, Hamlet himself —all these at one time or another, and usually more than once, are drawn into the range of implications flung round the play by "show."

"Act," on the other hand, I take to be the play's radical metaphor. It distills the various perplexities about the character of reality into a residual perplexity about the character of an act. What, this play asks again and again, is an act? What is its relation to the inner act, the intent? "If I drown myself wittingly," says the clown in the grave-yard, "it argues an act, and an act hath three branches; it is to act, to do, to perform." Or again, the play asks, how does action relate to passion, that "laps'd in time and passion" I can let "go by Th' important acting of your dread command"; and to thought, which can so sickly o'er the native hue of resolution that "enterprises of great pitch and moment With this regard their currents turn awry, And lose the name of action"; and to words, which are not acts, and so we dare not be content to unpack our hearts with them, and yet are acts of a sort, for we may speak daggers though we use none. Or still again, how does an act (a deed) relate to an act (a pretense)? For an action may be nothing but pretense. So Polonius readying Ophelia for the interview with Hamlet, with "pious action," as he phrases it, "sugar[s] o'er The devil himself." Or it may not be a pretense, yet not what it appears. So Hamlet spares the king, finding him in an act that has some "relish of salvation in 't." Or it may be a pretense that is also the first foothold of a new reality, as when we assume a virtue though we have it not. Or it may be a pretense that is actually a mirroring of reality, like the play within the play, or the tragedy of *Hamlet*.

To this network of implications, the third term, "play," adds an additional dimension. "Play" is a more precise word, in Elizabethan parlance at least, for all the elements in *Hamlet* that pertain to the art of the theater; and it extends their field of reference till we see that every major personage in the tragedy is a player in some sense, and every major episode a play. The court plays, Hamlet plays, the players play, Rosencrantz and Guildenstern try to play on Hamlet, though they cannot play on his recorders —here we have an extension to a musical sense. And the final duel, by a further extension, becomes itself a play, in which everyone but Claudius and Laertes plays his role in ignorance: "The queen desires you to show some gentle entertainment to Laertes before you fall to play." "I . . . will this brother's wager frankly play." "Give him the cup."—"I'll play this bout first."

The full extension of this theme is best evidenced in the play within the play itself. Here, in the bodily presence of these traveling players, bringing with them the latest playhouse gossip out of London, we have suddenly a situation that tends to dissolve the normal barriers between the fictive and the real. For here on the stage before us is a play of false appearances in which an actor called the player-king is playing. But there is also on the stage, Claudius, another player-king, who is a spectator of this player. And there is on the stage, besides, a prince who is a spectator of both these player-kings and who plays with great intensity a player's role himself. And around these kings and that prince is a group of courtly spectators— Gertrude, Rosencrantz, Guildenstern, Polonius, and the rest—and they, as we have come to know, are players too. And lastly there are ourselves, an audience watching all these audiences who are also players. Where, it may suddenly occur to us to ask, does the playing end? Which *are* the guilty creatures sitting at a play? When is an act not an "act"?

The mysteriousness of Hamlet's world, while it pervades the tragedy, finds its point of greatest dramatic concentration in the first act, and its symbol in the first scene. The problems of appearance and reality also pervade the play as a whole, but come to a climax in Acts II and III, and possibly their best symbol is the play within the play. Our third attribute, though again it is one that crops out everywhere, reaches its full development in Acts IV and V. It is not easy to find an appropriate name for this attribute, but perhaps "mortality" will serve, if we remember to mean by mortality the heartache and the thousand natural shocks that flesh is heir to, not simply death.

The powerful sense of mortality in *Hamlet* is conveyed to us, I think, in three ways. First, there is the play's emphasis on human weakness, the instability of human purpose, the subjection of humanity to fortune—all that we might call the aspect of failure in man. Hamlet opens this theme in Act I, when he describes how from that single blemish, perhaps not even the victim's fault, a man's whole character may take corruption. Claudius dwells on it again, to an extent that goes far beyond the needs of the occasion, while engaged in seducing Laertes to step behind the arras of a seemer's world and dispose of Hamlet by a trick. Time qualifies everything, Claudius says, including love, including purpose. As for love—it has a "plurisy" in it and dies of its own too much. As for purpose—"That we would do, We should do when we would, for this 'would' changes, And hath abatements and delays as many As there are tongues, are hands, are accidents; And then this 'should' is like a spendthrift's sigh, That hurts by easing." The player-king, in his long speeches to his queen in the play within the play, sets the matter in a still darker light. She means these protestations of undying love, he know, but our purposes depend on our memory, and our memory fades fast. Or else, he suggests, we propose something to ourselves in a condition of strong feeling, but then the feeling goes, and with it the resolve. Or else our fortunes change, he adds, and with these our loves: "The great man down, you mark his favorite flies." The subjection of human aims to fortune is a reiterated theme in *Hamlet*, as subsequently in *Lear*. Fortune is the harlot goddess in whose secret parts men like Rosencrantz and Guildenstern live and thrive: the strumpet who threw down Troy and Hecuba and Priam; the outrageous foe whose slings and arrows a man of principle must suffer or seek release in suicide. Horatio suffers them with composure: he is one of the blessed few "Whose blood and

judgment are so well co-mingled That they are not a pipe
for fortune's finger To sound what stop she please." For
Hamlet the task is of a greater difficulty.

Next, and intimately related to this matter of infirmity,
is the emphasis on infection—the ulcer, the hidden abscess,
"th' imposthume of much wealth and peace That inward
breaks and shows no cause without Why the man dies."
Miss Spurgeon, who was the first to call attention to this
aspect of the play, has well remarked that so far as Shakespeare's pictorial imagination is concerned, the problem in
Hamlet is not a problem of the will and reason, "of a
mind too philosophical or a nature temperamentally un-
fitted to act quickly," nor even a problem of an individual
at all. Rather, it is a condition—"a condition for which
the individual himself is apparently not responsible, any
more than the sick man is to blame for the infection which
strikes and devours him, but which, nevertheless, in its
course and development, impartially and relentlessly, an-
nihilates him and others, innocent and guilty alike."
"That," she adds, "is the tragedy of *Hamlet,* as it is perhaps the chief tragic mystery of life." This is a perceptive
comment, for it reminds us that Hamlet's situation is
mainly not of his own manufacture, as are the situations
of Shakespeare's other tragic heroes. He has inherited it; he
is "born to set it right."

We must not, however, neglect to add to this what
another student of Shakespeare's imagery has noticed—
that the infection in Denmark is presented alternatively
as poison. Here, of course, responsibility is implied, for
the poisoner of the play is Claudius. The juice he pours
into the ear of the elder Hamlet is a combined poison and
disease, a "leperous distillment" that curds "the thin and
wholesome blood." From this fatal center, unwholesome-
ness spreads out till there is something rotten in all Denmark. Hamlet tells us that his "wit's diseased," the queen
speaks of her "sick soul," the king is troubled by "the
hectic" in his blood, Laertes meditates revenge to warm
"the sickness in my heart," the people of the kingdom
grow "muddied, Thick and unwholesome in their
thoughts"; and even Ophelia's madness is said to be "the

poison of deep grief." In the end, all save Ophelia die of that poison in a literal as well as figurative sense.

But the chief form in which the theme of mortality reaches us, it seems to me, is as a profound consciousness of loss. Hamlet's father expresses something of the kind when he tells Hamlet how his "[most] seeming-virtuous queen," betraying a love which "was of that dignity That it went hand in hand even with the vow I made to her in marriage," had chosen to "decline Upon a wretch whose natural gifts were poor To those of mine." "O Hamlet, what a falling off was there!" Ophelia expresses it again, on hearing Hamlet's denunciation of love and woman in the nunnery scene, which she takes to be the product of a disordered brain:

> O what a noble mind is here o'erthrown!
> The courtier's, soldier's, scholar's, eye, tongue, sword;
> Th' expectancy and rose of the fair state,
> The glass of fashion and the mold of form,
> Th' observ'd of all observers, quite, quite down!

The passage invites us to remember that we have never actually seen such a Hamlet—that his mother's marriage has brought a falling off in him before we meet him. And then there is that further falling off, if I may call it so, when Ophelia too goes mad—"Divided from herself and her fair judgment, Without the which we are pictures, or mere beasts."

Time was, the play keeps reminding us, when Denmark was a different place. That was before Hamlet's mother took off "the rose From the fair forehead of an innocent love" and set a blister there. Hamlet then was still "Th' expectancy and rose of the fair state"; Ophelia, the "rose of May." For Denmark was a garden then, when his father ruled. There had been something heroic about his father—a king who met the threats to Denmark in open battle, fought with Norway, smote the sledded Polacks on the ice, slew the elder Fortinbras in an honorable trial of strength. There had been something godlike about his father too: "Hyperion's curls, the front of Jove himself,

An eye like Mars . . , A station like the herald
Mercury." But, the ghost reveals, a serpent was in the
garden, and "the serpent that did sting thy father's life
Now wears his crown." The martial virtues are put by
now. The threats to Denmark are attended to by policy,
by agents working deviously for and through an uncle.
The moral virtues are put by too. Hyperion's throne is
occupied by "a vice of kings," "a king of shreds and
patches"; Hyperion's bed, by a satyr, a paddock, a bat,
a gib, a bloat king with reechy kisses. The garden is
unweeded now, and "grows to seed; things rank and gross
in nature Possess it merely." Even in himself he feels the
taint, the taint of being his mother's son; and that other
taint, from an earlier garden, of which he admonishes
Ophelia: "Our virtue cannot so inoculate our old stock but
we shall relish of it." "Why wouldst thou be a breeder of
sinners?" "What should such fellows as I do crawling
between earth and heaven?"

"Hamlet is painfully aware," says Professor Tillyard, "of
the baffling human predicament between the angels and
the beasts, between the glory of having been made in God's
image and the incrimination of being descended from
fallen Adam." To this we may add, I think, that Hamlet
is more than aware of it; he exemplifies it; and it is for
this reason that his problem appeals to us so powerfully
as an image of our own.

Hamlet's problem, in its crudest form, is simply the
problem of the avenger: he must carry out the injunction of
the ghost and kill the king. But this problem, as I ventured
to suggest at the outset, is presented in terms of a certain
kind of world. The ghost's injunction to act becomes so
inextricably bound up for Hamlet with the character of
the world in which the action must be taken—its mysteriousness, its baffling appearances, its deep consciousness of
infection, frailty, and loss—that he cannot come to terms
with either without coming to terms with both.

When we first see him in the play, he is clearly a very
young man, sensitive and idealistic, suffering the first
shock of growing up. He has taken the garden at face
value, we might say, supposing mankind to be only a little

lower than the angels. Now in his mother's hasty and
incestuous marriage, he discovers evidence of something
else, something bestial—though even a beast, he thinks,
would have mourned longer. Then comes the revelation of
the ghost, bringing a second shock. Not so much because
he now knows that his serpent-uncle killed his father;
his prophetic soul had almost suspected this. Not entirely,
even, because he knows now how far below the angels
humanity has fallen in his mother, and how lust—these
were the ghost's words—"though to a radiant angel link'd
Will sate itself in a celestial bed, And prey on garbage."
Rather, because he now sees everywhere, but especially
in his own nature, the general taint, taking from life its
meaning, from woman her integrity, from the will its
strength, turning reason into madness. "Why wouldst
thou be a breeder of sinners?" "What should such fellows
as I do crawling between earth and heaven?" Hamlet is
not the first young man to have felt the heavy and the
weary weight of all this unintelligible world; and, like the
others, he must come to terms with it.

The ghost's injunction to revenge unfolds a different
facet of his problem. The young man growing up is not
to be allowed simply to endure a rotten world, he must
also act in it. Yet how to begin, among so many enigmatic
surfaces? Even Claudius, whom he now knows to be the
core of the ulcer, has a plausible exterior. And around
Claudius, swathing the evil out of sight, he encounters all
those other exteriors, as we have seen. Some of them
already deeply infected beneath, like his mother. Some
noble, but marked for infection, like Laertes. Some not
particularly corrupt but infinitely corruptible, like Rosencrantz and Guildenstern; some mostly weak and foolish
like Polonius and Osric. Some, like Ophelia, innocent, yet
in their innocence still serving to "skin and film the
ulcerous place."

And this is not all. The act required of him, though
retributive justice, is one that necessarily involves the doer
in the general guilt. Not only because it involves a killing;
but because to get at the world of seeming one sometimes
has to use its weapons. He himself, before he finishes, has

become a player, has put an antic disposition on, has killed a man—the wrong man—has helped drive Ophelia mad, and has sent two friends of his youth to death, mining below their mines, and hoisting the engineer with his own petard. He had never meant to dirty himself with these things, but from the moment of the ghost's challenge to act, this dirtying was inevitable. It is the condition of living at all in such a world. To quote Polonius, who knew that world so well, men become "a little soil'd i' th' working." Here is another matter with which Hamlet has to come to terms.

Human infirmity—all that I have discussed with reference to instability, infection, loss—supplies the problem with its third phase. Hamlet has not only to accept the mystery of man's condition between the angels and the brutes, and not only to act in a perplexing and soiling world. He has also to act within the human limits—"with shabby equipment always deteriorating," if I may adapt some phrases from Eliot's *East Coker*, "In the general mess of imprecision of feeling, Undisciplined squads of emotion." Hamlet is aware of that fine poise of body and mind, feeling and thought, that suits the action to the word, the word to the action; that acquires and begets a temperance in the very torrent, tempest, and whirlwind of passion; but he cannot at first achieve it in himself. He vacillates between undisciplined squads of emotion and thinking too precisely on the event. He learns to his cost how easily action can be lost in "acting," and loses it there for a time himself. But these again are only the terms of every man's life. As Anatole France reminds us in a now famous apostrophe to Hamlet: "What one of us thinks without contradiction and acts without incoherence? What one of us is not mad? What one of us does not say with a mixture of pity, comradeship, admiration, and horror, Goodnight, sweet Prince!"

In the last act of the play (or so it seems to me, for I know there can be differences on this point), Hamlet accepts his world and we discover a different man. Shakespeare does not outline for us the process of acceptance any more than he had done with Romeo or was to do with Othello. But he leads us strongly to expect an altered

Hamlet, and then, in my opinion, provides him. We must recall that at this point Hamlet has been absent from the stage during several scenes, and that such absences in Shakespearean tragedy usually warn us to be on the watch for a new phase in the development of the character. It is so when we leave King Lear in Gloucester's farmhouse and find him again in Dover fields. It is so when we leave Macbeth at the witches' cave and rejoin him at Dunsinane, hearing of the armies that beset it. Furthermore, and this is an important matter in the theater—especially important in a play in which the symbolism of clothing has figured largely—Hamlet now looks different. He is wearing a different dress—probably, as Granville-Barker thinks, his "seagown scarf'd" about him, but in any case no longer the disordered costume of his antic disposition. The effect is not entirely dissimilar to that in *Lear,* when the old king wakes out of his madness to find fresh garments on him.

Still more important, Hamlet displays a considerable change of mood. This is not a matter of the way we take the passage about defying augury, as Mr. Tillyard among others seems to think. It is a matter of Hamlet's whole deportment, in which I feel we may legitimately see the deportment of a man who has been "illuminated" in the tragic sense. Bradley's term for it is fatalism, but if this is what we wish to call it, we must at least acknowledge that it is fatalism of a very distinctive kind—a kind that Shakespeare has been willing to touch with the associations of the saying in St. Matthew about the fall of a sparrow, and with Hamlet's recognition that a divinity shapes our ends. The point is not that Hamlet has suddenly become religious; he has been religious all through the play. The point is that he has now learned, and accepted, the boundaries in which human action, human judgment, are enclosed.

Till his return from the voyage he had been trying to act beyond these, had been encroaching on the role of providence, if I may exaggerate to make a vital point. He had been too quick to take the burden of the whole world and its condition upon his limited and finite self. Faced with a task of sufficient difficulty in its own right, he had dilated it into a cosmic problem—as indeed every task is, but if we think about this too precisely we cannot act at all. The whole time is out of joint, he feels, and in his young man's egocentricity, he will set it right. Hence he misjudges Ophelia, seeing in her only a breeder of sinners. Hence he misjudges himself, seeing himself a vermin crawling between earth and heaven. Hence he takes it upon himself to be his mother's conscience, though the ghost has warned that this is no fit task for him, and returns to repeat the warning: "Leave her to heaven, And to those thorns that in her bosom lodge." Even with the king, Hamlet has sought to play at God. *He* it must be who decides the issue of Claudius's salvation, saving him for a more damnable occasion. Now, he has learned that there are limits to the before and after that human reason can comprehend. Rashness, even, is sometimes good. Through rashness he has saved his life from the commission for his death, "and prais'd be rashness for it." This happy circumstance and the unexpected arrival of the pirate ship make it plain that the roles of life are not entirely self-assigned. "There is a divinity that shapes our ends, Rough-hew them how we will." Hamlet is ready now for what may happen, seeking neither to foreknow it nor avoid it. "If it be now, 'tis not to come; if it be not to come, it will be now; if it be not now, yet it will come: the readiness is all."

The crucial evidence of Hamlet's new frame of mind, as I understand it, is the graveyard scene. Here, in its ultimate symbol, he confronts, recognizes, and accepts the condition of being man. It is not simply that he now accepts death, though Shakespeare shows him accepting it in ever more poignant forms: first, in the imagined persons of the politician, the courtier, and the lawyer, who laid their little schemes "to circumvent God," as Hamlet puts it, but now lie here; then in Yorick, whom he knew and played with as a child; and then in Ophelia. This last death tears from him a final cry of passion, but the striking contrast between his behavior and Laertes's reveals how deeply he has changed.

Still, it is not the fact of death that invests this scene with its peculiar power. It is instead the haunting mystery of life itself that Hamlet's speeches point to, holding in its inscrutable folds those other mysteries that he has wrestled with so long. These he now knows for what they are, and lays them by. The mystery of evil is present here—for this is after all the universal graveyard, where, as the clown says humorously, he holds up Adam's profession; where the scheming politician, the hollow courtier, the tricky lawyer, the emperor and the clown and the beautiful young maiden, all come together in an emblem of the world; where even, Hamlet murmurs, one might expect to stumble on "Cain's jawbone, that did the first murther." The mystery of reality is here too—for death puts the question, "What is real?" in its irreducible form, and in the end uncovers all appearances: "Is this the fine of his fines and the recovery of his recoveries, to have his fine pate full of fine dirt?" "Now get you to my lady's chamber, and tell her, let her paint an inch thick, to this favor she must come." Or if we need more evidence of this mystery, there is the anger of Laertes at the lack of ceremonial trappings, and the ambiguous character of Ophelia's own death. "Is she to be buried in Christian burial when she willfully seeks her own salvation?" asks the gravedigger. And last of all, but most pervasive of all, there is the mystery of human limitation. The grotesque nature of man's little joys, his big ambitions. The fact that the man who used to bear us on his back is now a skull that smells; that the noble dust of Alexander somewhere plugs a bunghole; that "Imperious Caesar, dead and turn'd to clay, Might stop a hole to keep the wind away." Above all, the fact that a pit of clay is "meet" for such a guest as man, as the gravedigger tells us in his song, and yet that, despite all frailties and limitations, "That skull had a tongue in it and could sing once."

After the graveyard and what it indicates has come to pass in him, we know that Hamlet is ready for the final contest of mighty opposites. He accepts the world as it is, the world as a duel, in which, whether we know it or not, evil holds the poisoned rapier and the poisoned chalice waits; and in which, if we win at all, it costs not less than everything. I think we understand by the close of Shakespeare's *Hamlet* why it is that unlike the other tragic heroes he is given a soldier's rites upon the stage. For as William Butler Yeats once said, "Why should we honor those who die on the field of battle? A man may show as reckless a courage in entering into the abyss of himself."

. . . . .

ROBERT ORNSTEIN

from *The Moral Vision of Jacobean Tragedy*

The impression of vastness in *Macbeth* is created almost
entirely by poetic suggestion. The play lacks the intellectual
dimension and richness of thought which makes *Hamlet*
seem to the critics the most philosophical of Shakespeare's
plays. Honor, revenge, justice, political order, Stoicism,
friendship, familial piety—how many Renaissance ideas
and ideals come under scrutiny in the halls of Elsinore. And
yet how little is there in the lines of *Hamlet* which testi-
fies to Shakespeare's intellectual or philosophical powers.
Subjected to philosophical analysis the great speeches in
Hamlet yield commonplaces. We treasure them for their
incomparable poetry, not for their depth and originality of
thought—for their revelation of Hamlet's soul, not for
their discovery of the human condition. Many questions
are raised in the play but few are answered. The question
of action in an evil society, one might say, is resolved by
an expedient dear to Victorian novelists: a change of air,
a sea voyage from which the hero returns calm if not
resolute, buoyed by a vaguely optimistic fatalism that is
half-Christian, half-Stoic.

My point is not that Shakespeare tricks us into accepting a sham or meretricious resolution in *Hamlet*, but that

From *The Moral Vision of Jacobean Tragedy* by Robert Ornstein.
Madison, Wisconsin: The University of Wisconsin Press, 1960. Reprinted
by permission of the copyright owners, the Regents of The University of
Wisconsin.

we do not find in Shakespearean drama the intellectual
schemes of Chapman's tragedies. Even when Shakespeare
seems to dramatize a thesis, he does not debate philosophical positions. He is not interested in abstract thought but
in characters who think, who have intellectual as well as
emotional needs, and who, like Pirandello's characters,
cry aloud the reason of their suffering. The "problem" of
Hamlet is not an intellectual puzzle. It arises because the
play creates so marvelous a sense of the actual improvisa-
tion of life that we can find no simple logic in its sprawling
action. Unable to comprehend or accept the totality of
Shakespeare's many-sided hero, we search for a more
logical, more consistent, or more pleasant Hamlet than
the play affords. We try to arrive at Shakespeare's moral
ideas by reading Elizabethan treatises of psychology and
moral philosophy, when it is only by studying the total artifice of *Hamlet* that we can understand why its hero seems
to us the most noble, pure-minded, and blameless of Shakespeare's tragic protagonists. What is not near Hamlet's
conscience is not near our own because he is our moral
interpreter. He is the voice of ethical sensibility in a
sophisticated, courtly milieu; his bitter asides, which penetrate Claudius' façade of kingly virtue and propriety,
initiate, so to speak, the moral action of the play. And
throughout the play our identification with Hamlet's moral
vision is such that we hate what he hates, admire what he
admires. As centuries of Shakespeare criticism reveal, we
accuse Hamlet primarily of what he accuses himself:
namely, his slowness to revenge.

Our moral impression of Hamlet's character derives
primarily from what he says rather than what he does.
It is an almost intuitive awareness of the beauty, depth,
and refinement of his moral nature, upon which is thrust
a savage burden of revenge and of disillusion. If Shakespeare's characters are illusions created by dramatic artifice,
then what we love in Hamlet is an illusion within an
illusion: i.e., the suggestion of Hamlet's former self, the
Hamlet whom Ophelia remembers and who poignantly
reappears in the conversations with Horatio, particularly
before the catastrophe. Through his consummate artistry

Shakespeare creates within us a sympathy with Hamlet which becomes almost an act of faith—a confidence in the untouched and untouchable core of his spiritual nature. This act of faith, renewed by the great speeches throughout the play, allows us to accept Hamlet's brutality towards Ophelia, his reaction to Polonius' death, his savage refusal to kill Claudius at prayer, and his Machiavellian delight in disposing of Rosencrantz and Guildenstern. Without the memory of the great soliloquies which preceded it, our impression of the closet scene would be vastly different. And, in fact, to attempt to define Hamlet's character by weighing his motives and actions against any system of Renaissance thought is to stage *Hamlet* morally without the Prince of Denmark, i.e., without the felt impression of Hamlet's moral nature which is created by poetic nuance.

Life is mysterious and unpredictable in *Hamlet*. Appearances are deceptive, little is what it seems to be, and no man can foresee the consequence of his acts. Yet we are not left with the sense that Shakespeare's characters move through the mist which envelops Webster's tragic universe. We see with a perfect clarity that the pattern of catastrophe emerges inexorably as the consequence of Claudius' hidden guilt and from his need for deviousness and secrecy. If the ambiguities and the mysteries of *Hamlet* irritate us, it is because we expect an omniscient view of character in drama; we are not used to seeing a play almost entirely from the point of view of a single character. We do not realize that our identification with Hamlet is as complete as with a first-person narrator of a novel. We see little more than he sees; we know little more about the other characters—about Gertrude's crimes or Rosencrantz and Guildenstern's treachery—than he finally knows. If we had to examine objectively the facts of the play to decide whether Hamlet should have had Rosencrantz and Guildenstern executed, then their innocence or guilt would be a crucial matter; but since like Hamlet we identify Rosencrantz and Guildenstern with Claudius' cause, what they knew or did not know of Claudius' plans "does not matter."

It is Hamlet (not the Romantic critics) who creates

the problem of his delay in revenge. Were it not for the self-lacerating soliloquies in which he accuses himself of the grossness and insensitivity which he despises in his mother, the thought that he delays would not occur to us. During a performance of the play we do not feel that Hamlet procrastinates or puts off action. From his first appearance, he is engaged in a secret struggle with the shrewd and suspicious Claudius; there is scarcely a moment when he is not fending off one of the King's spies or dupes. In the study a critic can be quite bloodthirsty about Hamlet's failure to dispatch Claudius. In the theater, however, one does not feel that Hamlet should have skewered Claudius at prayer or should have been more interested in Claudius' damnation than his mother's salvation. Nor does one feel that the Hamlet who says, "The interim is mine" is "delaying."

This is not to say that Shakespeare posed an artificial problem in Hamlet's soliloquies in order to make mad the critics and appall the scholars. The problem of action in an evil world is as real in *Hamlet* as in many of the revenge plays of the period. True to his father's command, Hamlet engages in fierce struggle against the world without tainting his mind. False to himself and to his father's advice, Laertes is corrupted and debased by the hunger for vengeance. Although Hamlet commits rash and bloody deeds and comes to take a sardonic delight in flanking policy with policy, he does not, like Vindice, become unfit for life. On the contrary, we feel that he dies just when he is ready to embrace life, when his cloud of melancholy has lifted and he stands before us the very quintessence of dust—beautiful in mind and spirit, noble in thought and feeling, alert, high-spirited, superior to the accidents and passions which corrupt lesser men. We do not feel that Hamlet must die because he has sinned. The inevitability of his death is an aesthetic, not moral, expectation created by the insistent imagery of death, by the mood of the graveyard scene, by Hamlet's premonitions, and by the finality of Claudius' triple-stopped treachery. The calm of the graveyard scene, coming after the feverish action that preceded Hamlet's departure for England, seems a false recovery before death, that brief moment of detachment and lucidity which is often granted dying men. Enhancing this poignant impression are the very simple, quiet responses of Horatio, who attends the final hours of his Prince.

The problem of action in *Hamlet* is posed immediately and ultimately by Death, the philosophical tutor who forces man to consider the value of existence. Because the death of his father has made life meaningless, Hamlet wishes for the release of suicide, which is by traditional standards a cowardly evasion and negation of life. Yet, paradoxically, the willingness and eagerness of Fortinbras' army to die seems to give meaning to a cause that would be otherwise contemptible and valueless. And whether one takes arms against a sea of troubles (an apparently hopeless undertaking) or suffers the arrows and slings of outrageous fortune, there is only one possible conclusion to the action of life, the stillness of the grave. *Hamlet* begins with terrified sentries awaiting the return of the dead. It closes with the solemn march of soldiers bearing Hamlet's body "to the stage." Throughout the play Hamlet faces the most ancient and abiding philosophical problem: he must "learn how to die," i.e., how to live with the fact and thought of death. When he first appears, he seems overwhelmed by his first intimate experience of mortality—the sudden, unexpected loss of his father. Claudius may first address the court on affairs of state and then grant Laertes his "fair hour," but eventually he must deal with the gross insult of Hamlet's ostentatious mourning. In his most suave manner he offers his stepson the consolation of philosophy; he refers to the immemorial fact of mortality and grief, to the commonness and naturalness of death, to the need for the living to dedicate themselves to life. For Hamlet these platitudes have no meaning. He does not mourn because *man* dies; nor is he tormented only by the loss of a father. When he exposes his inner feelings in the first soliloquy we realize that Claudius has completely missed the point. Hamlet's problem is not to accept his father's death but to accept a world in which death has lost its meaning and its message for the living—

a world in which only the visitation of a Ghost restores
some sense of the mystery and awe of the grave. In his
disgust for Gertrude's frailty, Hamlet broods over the
debt that the living owe to the dead, the wife to the husband and the son to the father. Gertrude advises her son
not to seek his father in the dust, but the Ghost brings
the shattering command that the living owe the dead the
obligation of vengeance, of taking arms against a world
which destroys virtue. Though anguished that the time
is out of joint, Hamlet embraces revenge as a dedication
which is to give meaning to an otherwise empty existence.
And justly or not he accuses himself again and again
of failure to carry out his obligation to the dead.

When he returns to Denmark from his sea voyage,
however, he is no longer tormented by guilt; his self-
laceration and disgust with life have given way to a stoic
calm that obliterates the need for immediate action. He
has not formulated a new philosophy or come to intellectual terms with life. He has the fatalistic composure
possible only to those who have achieved an intimate
communion with death—who have killed and have nar-
rowly escaped a mortal stroke. Having passed through a
lifetime of experience in a brief span, he seems to share
Montaigne's knowledge that men do not require philosophy
to know how to die, because life provides all the requisite
information and no man has yet failed to pass the test of
his mortality. Our life, the action of *Hamlet* reveals, is a
process of dying and all roads end where the gravedigger's
work begins.

A mind that can trace Alexander's dust to a bunghole
can no longer envy the heroic dedication of a Fortinbras.
Although still intending to call Claudius to account,
Hamlet is no longer obsessed by an obligation to the dead;
he speaks mainly now of punitive justice and of his personal conflict with the King. Ironically enough, experience
has taught him the sageness of Claudius' platitudes. The
young mourner who cried out against the commonness of
death now finds solace in its vast equality and anonymity.
Counseled before not to seek his father in the dust, he now
recoils from the skull of Yorick, who played with him as

a father with a child. Compared to the stink of putrefaction, the sins of the flesh seem now more amusing than revolting to Hamlet. Once he hugged death as an escape from the burden of living; now the too too solid flesh melting from the bone no longer seems a consummation devoutly to be wished for. We see in his detached meditations on death a new dedication to life, for he is amused not by the vanity of existence but by the absurd ways in which men waste their precious hours of sentience. What do the living owe to the dead? The coarse familiarity of the gravediggers with the remains of the departed suggests a final answer.

Like all men Hamlet can triumph only over the impersonal fact of death. When he learns that the grave is for Ophelia, his jesting detachment vanishes. As the funeral procession enters the stage, the wheel comes full circle; the play begins again with another mourner in Hamlet's role. Now it is the youthful Laertes who protests with hyperbolic and theatrical gestures of grief the dishonor of his family that is symbolized by the "maimed rites" of death. His emotional extravagance elicits Hamlet's last moment of theatricality: the struggle in the grave that again strips dignity from the ceremony of death.

In the breathing space before the fencing scene there is a haunting moment of repose, of youthful communion, of laughter at Osric's absurdity; there is a poignant sense of recovery and stability. Is there also a more positive religious note? Are we to assume from Hamlet's references to heaven, divinity, and providence that he is now convinced of the great moral design of creation? Or do we see a Hamlet bowing before a universe which defies man's intellectual attempts at comprehension? The sequence of accidents that saved his life appears in retrospect providential, but it provides no guide to future action, no counsel, no direction. Although his restlessness at sea seemed a touch of grace, he shrugs off his misgivings about the fencing match. For to ascribe every premonition to heavenly guidance is to reduce belief to superstition. And Hamlet defies "augury." How much more deeply religious is his surrender to the mystery of his fate than Laertes' concern with the niceties of ceremony. Whether Ophelia deserves Christian burial is a question fit for the mocking and subtle casuistry of the gravediggers. Indeed, if the form of her burial is to determine her ultimate destiny, then she must be eternally grateful to Claudius, who forced the Church to inter her in hallowed ground. Although some modern critics argue like Laertes over the fine theological issues of the play, the perceptive reader understands that the form of Ophelia's burial matters more to the living than to the dead.

More clearly in *Hamlet* than in *The Spanish Tragedy* or *Tamburlaine* one can see the inner direction which great tragedy takes at the close of the Elizabethan age. For Shakespeare as for Kyd and Marlowe the fact of man's mortality is not the essential pathos of tragedy. That pathos lies in their heroes' anguished discovery of a universe more vast, more terrible, and more inscrutable than is dreamt of in philosophy. In *Hamlet* and Jacobean tragedy man suffers to be wise, and, indeed, his knowledge of reality is a more intense form of suffering than the illustrators of *De casibus* tales could imagine.

CAROLYN HEILBRUN

The Character of Hamlet's Mother

The character of Hamlet's mother has not received the specific critical attention it deserves. Moreover, the traditional account of her personality as rendered by the critics will not stand up under close scrutiny of Shakespeare's play.

None of the critics of course has failed to see Gertrude as vital to the action of the play; not only is she the mother of the hero, the widow of the Ghost, and the wife of the current King of Denmark, but the fact of her hasty and, to the Elizabethans, incestuous marriage, the whole question of her "falling off", occupies a position of barely secondary importance in the mind of her son, and of the Ghost. Indeed, Freud and Jones see her, the object of Hamlet's Oedipus complex, as central to the motivation of the play.[1] But the critics, with no exception that I have been able to find, have accepted Hamlet's word "frailty" as applying to her whole personality, and have seen in her not one weakness, or passion in the Elizabethan sense, but a character of which weakness and lack of depth and vigorous intelligence are the entire explanation. Of her can it truly be said that carrying the "stamp of one defect," she did "in the general censure take corruption/From that particular fault," (I. iv. 35–36).

The critics are agreed that Gertrude was not a party to

Shakespeare Quarterly 8 (1957), 201–06.
[1] Shakespeare, William: *Hamlet*, with a psycho-analytical study by Ernest Jones, M.D. London: Vision Press, 1947, pp. 7–42.

the late King's murder and indeed knew nothing of it, a point which on the clear evidence of the play, is indisputable. They have also discussed whether or not Gertrude, guilty of more than an "o'er-hasty marriage", had committed adultery with Claudius before her husband's death. I will return to this point later on. Beyond discussing these two points, those critics who have dealt specifically with the Queen have traditionally seen her as well-meaning but shallow and feminine, in the pejorative sense of the word: incapable of any sustained rational process, superficial and flighty. It is this tradition which a closer reading of the play will show to be erroneous.

Professor Bradley describes the traditional Gertrude thus:

> The Queen was not a bad-hearted woman, not at all the woman to think little of murder. But she had a soft animal nature and was very dull and very shallow. She loved to be happy, like a sheep in the sun, and to do her justice, it pleased her to see others happy, like more sheep in the sun. . . . It was pleasant to sit upon her throne and see smiling faces around her, and foolish and unkind in Hamlet to persist in grieving for his father instead of marrying Ophelia and making everything comfortable. . . . The belief at the bottom of her heart was that the world is a place constructed simply that people may be happy in it in a good-humored sensual fashion.[2]

Later on, Bradley says of her that when affliction comes to her "the good in her nature struggles to the surface through the heavy mass of sloth."

Granville-Barker is not quite so extreme. Shakespeare, he says,

> gives us in Gertrude the woman who does not mature, who clings to her youth and all that belongs to it, whose charm will not change but at last fade and wither; a pretty creature, as we see her, desperately refusing to grow old. . . . She is drawn for us with unemphatic

[2] Bradley, A. C., *Shakespearean Tragedy* (New York: Macmillan, 1949), p. 167.

strokes, and she has but a passive part in the play's action. She moves throughout in Claudius' shadow; he holds her as he won her, by the witchcraft of his wit.[3]

Elsewhere Granville-Barker says "Gertrude who will certainly never see forty-five again, might better be 'old.' [That is, portrayed by an older, mature actress.] But that would make her relations with Claudius—and *their* likelihood is vital to the play—quite incredible" (p. 226). Granville-Barker is saying here that a woman about forty-five years of age cannot feel any sexual passion or arouse it. This is one of the mistakes which lie at the heart of the misunderstanding about Gertrude.

Professor Dover Wilson sees Gertrude as more forceful than either of these two critics will admit, but even he finds the Ghost's unwillingness to shock her with knowledge of his murder to be one of the basic motivations of the play, and he says of her "Gertrude is always hoping for the best."[4]

Now whether Claudius won Gertrude before or after her husband's death, it was certainly not, as Granville-Barker implies, with "the witchcraft of his wit" alone. Granville-Barker would have us believe that Claudius won her simply by the force of his persuasive tongue. "It is plain," he writes, that the Queen "does little except echo his [Claudius'] wishes; sometimes—as in the welcome to Rosencrantz and Guildenstern—she repeats his very words" (p. 227), though Wilson must admit later that Gertrude does not tell Claudius everything. Without dwelling here on the psychology of the Ghost, or the greater burden borne by the Elizabethan words "witchcraft" and "wit," we can plainly see, for the Ghost tells us, how Claudius won the Queen: the Ghost considers his brother to be garbage, and "lust," the Ghost says, "will sate itself in a celestial bed and prey on garbage" (I.v.56–57). "Lust"—in a woman of forty-five or more—is the

[3] Granville-Barker, Harley, *Prefaces to Shakespeare* (Princeton University Press, 1946), I, 227.
[4] Wilson, J. Dover, *What Happens in Hamlet* (Cambridge University Press, 1951), p. 125.

key word here. Bradley, Granville-Barker, and to a lesser extent Professor Dover Wilson, misunderstand Gertrude largely because they are unable to see lust, the desire for sexual relations, as the passion, in the Elizabethan sense of the word, the flaw, the weakness which drives Gertrude to an incestuous marriage, appalls her son, and keeps him from the throne. Unable to explain her marriage to Claudius as the act of any but a weak-minded vacillating woman, they fail to see Gertrude for the strong-minded, intelligent, succinct, and, apart from this passion, sensible woman that she is.

To understand Gertrude properly, it is only necessary to examine the lines Shakespeare has chosen for her to say. She is, except for her description of Ophelia's death, concise and pithy in speech, with a talent for seeing the essence of every situation presented before her eyes. If she is not profound, she is certainly never silly. We first hear her asking Hamlet to stop wearing black, to stop walking about with his eyes downcast, and to realize that death is an inevitable part of life. She is, in short, asking him not to give way to the passion of grief, a passion of whose force and dangers the Elizabethans were aware, as Miss Campbell has shown.[5] Claudius echoes her with a well-reasoned argument against grief which was, in its philosophy if not in its language, a piece of commonplace Elizabethan lore. After Claudius' speech, Gertrude asks Hamlet to remain in Denmark, where he is rightly loved. Her speeches have been short, however warm and loving, and conciseness of statement is not the mark of a dull and shallow woman.

We next hear her, as Queen and gracious hostess, welcoming Rosencrantz and Guildenstern to the court, hoping, with the King, that they may cheer Hamlet and discover what is depressing him. Claudius then tells Gertrude, when they are alone, that Polonius believes he knows what is upsetting Hamlet. The Queen answers:

[5] Campbell, Lily B., *Shakespeare's Tragic Heroes* (New York: Barnes & Noble, 1952), pp. 112–113.

I doubt it is no other than the main,
His father's death and our o'er-hasty marriage.

(II. ii. 56–57)

This statement is concise, remarkably to the point, and not a little courageous. It is not the statement of a dull, slothful woman who can only echo her husband's words. Next, Polonius enters with his most unbrief apotheosis to brevity. The Queen interrupts him with five words: "More matter, with less art" (II. ii. 95). It would be difficult to find a phrase more applicable to Polonius. When this gentleman, is no way deterred from his loquacity, after purveying the startling news that he has a daughter, begins to read a letter, the Queen asks pointedly "Came this from Hamlet to her?" (II. ii. 114).

We see Gertrude next in Act III, asking Rosencrantz and Guildenstern, with her usual directness, if Hamlet received them well, and if they were able to tempt him to any pastime. But before leaving the room, she stops for a word of kindness to Ophelia. It is a humane gesture, for she is unwilling to leave Ophelia, the unhappy tool of the King and Polonius, without some kindly and intelligent appreciation of her help:

And for your part, Ophelia, I do wish
That your good beauties be the happy cause
Of Hamlet's wildness. So shall I hope your virtues
Will bring him to his wonted way again,
To both your honors.   (III. i. 38–42)

It is difficult to see in this speech, as Bradley apparently does, the gushing shallow wish of a sentimental woman that class distinctions shall not stand in the way of true love.

At the play, the Queen asks Hamlet to sit near her. She is clearly trying to make him feel he has a place in the court of Denmark. She does not speak again until Hamlet asks her how she likes the play. "The lady doth protest too much, methinks" (III. ii. 236) is her immortal comment on the player queen. The scene gives her four more words:

when Claudius leaps to his feet, she asks "How fares my Lord?" (III. ii. 273).

I will for the moment pass over the scene in the Queen's closet, to follow her quickly through the remainder of the play. After the closet scene, the Queen comes to speak to Claudius. She tells him, as Hamlet has asked her to, that he, Hamlet, is mad, and has killed Polonius. She adds, however, that he now weeps for what he has done. She does not wish Claudius to know what she now knows, how wild and fearsome Hamlet has become. Later, she does not wish to see Ophelia, but hearing how distracted she is, consents. When Laertes bursts in ready to attack Claudius, she immediately steps between Claudius and Laertes to protect the King, and tells Laertes it is not Claudius who has killed his father. Laertes will of course soon learn this, but it is Gertrude who manages to tell him before he can do any meaningless damage. She leaves Laertes and the King together, and then returns to tell Laertes that his sister is drowned. She gives her news directly, realizing that suspense will increase the pain of it, but this is the one time in the play when her usual pointed conciseness would be the mark neither of intelligence nor of kindness, and so, gently, and at some length, she tells Laertes of his sister's death, giving him time to recover from the shock of grief, and to absorb the meaning of her words. At Ophelia's funeral the Queen scatters flowers over the grave:

> Sweets to the sweet! Farewell!
> I hoped thou shouldst have been my Hamlet's wife.
> I thought thy bride-bed to have decked, sweet maid,
> And not have strewed thy grave.   (V. i. 245–248)

She is the only one present decently mourning the death of someone young, and not heated in the fire of some personal passion.

At the match between Hamlet and Laertes, the Queen believes that Hamlet is out of training, but glad to see him at some sport, she gives him her handkerchief to wipe his brow, and drinks to his success. The drink is poisoned and she dies. But before she dies she does not waste time on vituperation; she warns Hamlet that the drink is poisoned to prevent his drinking it. They are her last words. Those critics who have thought her stupid admire her death; they call it uncharacteristic.

In Act III, when Hamlet goes to his mother in her closet his nerves are pitched at the very height of tension; he is on the edge of hysteria. The possibility of murdering his mother has in fact entered his mind, and he has just met and refused an opportunity to kill Claudius. His mother, meanwhile, waiting for him, has told Polonius not to fear for her, but she knows when she sees Hamlet that he may be violently mad. Hamlet quips with her, insults her, tells her he wishes she were not his mother, and when she, still retaining dignity, attempts to end the interview, Hamlet seizes her and she cries for help. The important thing to note is that the Queen's cry "Thou wilt not murder me?" (III. iv. 22) is not foolish. She has seen from Hamlet's demeanor that he is capable of murder, as indeed in the next instant he proves himself to be.

We next learn from the Queen's startled "As kill a king?" (III. iv. 31) that she has no knowledge of the murder, though of course this is only confirmation here of what we already know. Then the Queen asks Hamlet why he is so hysterical:

> What have I done, that thou dar'st wag thy tongue
> In noise so rude against me?   (III. iv. 39–40)

Hamlet tells her: it is her lust, the need of sexual passion, which has driven her from the arms and memory of her husband to the incomparably cruder charms of his brother. He cries out that she has not even the excuse of youth for her lust:

> O shame where is thy blush? Rebellious hell,
> If thou canst mutine in a matron's bones,
> To flaming youth let virtue be as wax
> And melt in her own fire. Proclaim no shame
> When the compulsive ardor gives the charge,

Since frost itself as actively doth burn,
And reason panders will.   (III. iv. 83–89)

This is not only a lust, but a lust which throws out of joint
all the structure of human morality and relationships. And
the Queen admits it. If there is one quality that has characterized, and will characterize, every speech of Gertrude's
in the play, it is the ability to see reality clearly, and to
express it. This talent is not lost when turned upon herself:

O Hamlet, speak no more!
Thou turn'st mine eyes into my very soul,
And there I see such black and grained spots
As will not leave their tinct.   (III. iv. 89–92)

She knows that lust has driven her, that this is her sin, and
she admits it. Not that she wishes to linger in the contem-
plation of her sin. "No more," she cries, "no more." And
then the Ghost appears to Hamlet. The Queen thinks him
mad again—as well she might—but she promises Hamlet
that she will not betray him—and she does not.

Where, in all that we have seen of Gertrude, is there the
picture of "a soft animal nature, very dull and very shallow?" She may indeed be "animal" in the sense of "lustful." But it does not follow that because she wishes to
continue a life of sexual experience, her brain is soft or
her wit unperceptive.

Some critics, having accepted Gertrude as a weak and
vacillating woman, see no reason to suppose that she did
not fall victim to Claudius' charms before the death of her
husband and commit adultery with him. These critics,
Professor Bradley among them (p. 166), claim that the
elder Hamlet clearly tells his son that Gertrude has committed adultery with Claudius in the speech beginning "Ay
that incestuous, that adulterate beast" (I. v. 42ff.). Professor Dover Wilson presents the argument:

Is the Ghost speaking here of the o'er-hasty marriage of
Claudius and Gertrude? Assuredly not. His "certain
term" is drawing rapidly to an end, and he is already

beginning to "scent the morning air." Hamlet knew of the marriage, and his whole soul was filled with nausea at the thought of the speedy hasting to "incestuous sheets." Why then should the Ghost waste precious moments in telling Hamlet what he was fully cognisant of before? . . . Moreover, though the word "incestuous" was applicable to the marriage, the rest of the passage is entirely inapplicable to it. Expressions like "witchcraft", "traitorous gifts", "seduce", "shameful lust", and "seeming virtuous" may be noted in passing. But the rest of the quotation leaves no doubt upon the matter. . . . (P. 293)

Professor Dover Wilson and other critics have accepted the Ghost's word "adulterate" in its modern meaning. The Elizabethan word "adultery," however, was not restricted to its modern meaning, but was used to define any sexual relationship which could be called unchaste, including of course an incestuous one.[6] Certainly the elder Hamlet considered the marriage of Claudius and Gertrude to be unchaste and unseemly, and while his use of the word "adulterate" indicates his very strong feelings about the marriage, it would not to an Elizabethan audience necessarily mean that he believed Gertrude to have been false to him before his death. It is important to notice, too, that the Ghost does not apply the term "adulterate" to Gertrude, and he may well have considered the term a just description of Claudius' entire sexual life.

But even if the Ghost used the word "adulterate" in full awareness of its modern restricted meaning, it is not necessary to assume on the basis of this single speech (and it is the only shadow of evidence we have for such a conclusion) that Gertrude was unfaithful to him while he lived. It is quite probable that the elder Hamlet still considered himself married to Gertrude, and he is moreover revolted that her lust for him ("why she would hang on him as if increase of appetite had grown by what it fed on") should have so easily transferred itself to another.

6 See Joseph, Bertram, Conscience and the King (London: Chatto and Windus, 1953), pp. 16–19.

This is why he uses the expressions "seduce," "shameful lust," and others. Professor Dover Wilson has himself said "Hamlet knew of the marriage, and his whole soul was filled with nausea at the thought of the speedy hasting to incestuous sheets"; the soul of the elder Hamlet was undoubtedly filled with nausea too, and this could well explain his using such strong language, as well as his taking the time to mention the matter at all. It is not necessary to consider Gertrude an adulteress to account for the speech of the Ghost.

Gertrude's lust was, of course, more important to the plot than we may at first perceive. Charlton Lewis, among others, has shown how Shakespeare kept many of the facts of the plots from which he borrowed without maintaining the structures which explained them. In the original Belleforest story, Gertrude (substituting Shakespeare's more familiar names) was daughter of the king; to become king, it was necessary to marry her. The elder Hamlet, in marrying Gertrude, ousted Claudius from the throne.[7] Shakespeare retained the shell of this in his play. When she no longer has a husband, the form of election would be followed to declare the next king, in this case undoubtedly her son Hamlet. By marrying Gertrude, Claudius "Popp'd in between th' election and my hopes" (V. ii. 65), that is, kept young Hamlet from the throne. Gertrude's flaw of lust made Claudius' ambition possible, for without taking advantage of the Queen's desire still to be married, he could not have been king.

But Gertrude, if she is lustful, is also intelligent, penetrating, and gifted, with a remarkable talent for concise and pithy speech. In all the play, the person whose language hers most closely resembles is Horatio. "Sweets to the sweet," she has said at Ophelia's grave. "Good night sweet prince," Horatio says at the end. They are neither of them dull, or shallow, or slothful, though one of them is passion's slave.

7 Lewis, Charlton M., *The Genesis of Hamlet* (New York: Henry Holt & Co., 1907), p. 36.

SYLVAN BARNET

Hamlet on Stage and Screen

Hamlet advises the players, in III.ii. 1–4, to "Speak the speech . . . trippingly on the tongue"—but exactly what are the speeches that add up to *Hamlet*? This question will not seem absurd to anyone who has glanced at the Textual Note on page 175. Briefly, the note explains that *Hamlet* exists in three versions: Q1 (published in 1603), 2,154 lines; Q2 (1604), 3,723 lines; and F (1623), 3,604 lines. (Much depends on how one counts the lines, but that's not important now.) Most scholars agree that F (that is, the version printed in the Folio of 1623) is an *acting* version, i.e., a text somewhat abridged for the stage. They also agree that Q1 is a much more drastic abridgment, apparently prepared from memory by an actor or actors without access to a copy of the manuscript. The text of Q1 is often very poor (sometimes it is gibberish), but occasionally it gives insights into the performance of the play—our topic here—that are not found in either of the fuller and more coherent versions. For instance, only Q1 gives us a stage direction telling us that in v.i.259 Hamlet leaps into Ophelia's grave.

When people speak of an "uncut *Hamlet*," or of a "full text *Hamlet*," they are speaking of a version that probably never was performed in Shakespeare's time, a version that begins with Q2 (the longest of the three texts) and adds to it the passages in F that are not found in Q2. This

composite text, running to about 3,900 lines, takes four or
even four and a quarter hours to perform. Most performances of an abridged text run to about three hours, which
usually means that about a fourth of the text is cut. For
instance, Garrick (1763) used 2,684 lines; Kean (1818)
2,467, Irving (undated promptbook) 2,752, Gielgud
(1934) 2,865. There are, roughly speaking, two ways of
cutting: one is to leave out some characters (for example,
Fortinbras and everything connected with him, including
the talk in I.i about the quarrel between Hamlet Senior
and Fortinbras's father); the other is to keep a little of
everything, trimming down longer speeches, especially reflective or descriptive ones. Laertes's advice to Ophelia,
Polonius's advice to Laertes, Hamlet's disquisition on
drunkenness, his musings on Alexander, and his advice to
the players may be reduced to tokens. If one follows the
first method, omitting, say, material concerning Fortinbras,
one eliminates four speaking characters (Fortinbras, Cornelius, Voltemand, the Captain), and one thus focuses
more sharply on Hamlet's problem in a corrupt court. The
play becomes more domestic, more personal, and in some
ways more manageable, but it necessarily loses its political
dimension, for instance in the contrast between the thinking man (Hamlet) and the active man (Fortinbras). It
also loses, of course, Shakespeare's ending, which shows
order being restored after violence. If one follows the
second method of cutting, thinning down the speeches, no
single theme may be utterly neglected, but the play loses
so much of its complexity or texture or depth that it may
seem to be not much more than a melodrama.

The role of Hamlet is long and complex, and *Hamlet* is
the most frequently staged of Shakespeare's plays; this
short essay can look at only a very few productions, and
can comment on only some of their most distinctive
features. We must begin by mentioning Richard Burbage
(c.1567–1619), a member of Shakespeare's theatrical
company, who is known to have played the role—but
nothing is really known about how he played it. The
next actor of note who performed the role was Thomas
Betterton (c.1635–1710), who played his first Hamlet in

1661, when he was about twenty-six, and played his last Hamlet in 1709, when he was in his seventies. Betterton's text was a relatively slight abridgment of the folio text—it deletes about 816 lines, but, as we have seen, the Elizabethans themselves probably abridged the play. It is not known for certain who made this late seventeenth-century abridgment, but William Davenant is a strong candidate. Among the cuts are the roles of Voltemand and Cornelius, all of the Fortinbras material except the entry of Fortinbras at the end of the play, Polonius's advice to Laertes, Polonius's scene with Reynaldo, Hamlet's advice to the Players, and Hamlet's soliloquy beginning "How all occasions do inform against me." Among the speeches that are thinned out rather than entirely cut are Horatio's explanation of the preparation for war, the king's reproof of Hamlet's excessive grief, Laertes's advice to Ophelia, the Mouse Trap, and the closet scene with Gertrude. Minor changes include some elevation of the diction, in accordance with new ideas of decorum. Thus, instead of "The kettledrum and trumpet thus *bray out* / The triumph of his pledge" (I.iv.11–12), we get "The kettledrum and trumpet thus *proclaim* / The triumph of his health."

People who saw Betterton speak of his "vivacity" and "enterprize," and they describe his performance as "manly." Putting together such scraps of evidence as we have, we can say that Betterton's Hamlet (played in the dress of a courtier of Charles II, and later with a cocked hat and powdered wig) was not a neurotic or a weakling but "the glass of fashion," and a vigorous young man—even when Betterton was seventy.

In the middle of the eighteenth century, viewers used pretty much the same words that had described Betterton to describe the performance of David Garrick (1717–79), who first played the role in 1742. In the next thirty years, like his predecessors and his successors, Garrick used a somewhat abridged text, from time to time slightly altering it both by additions and deletions, but in 1772 he made a drastic revision. Although he restored 629 lines that had not been heard for a century (these included such passages as the king at prayer, and the soliloquy beginning "How all occasions do inform against me"), Garrick also in effect rewrote the fifth act, more or less in line with neo-classical ideals of decorum. (As early as 1661 John Evelyn wrote, "I saw *Hamlet, Prince of Denmark* played, but now the old plays begin to disgust this refined age.") Garrick's aim, he said, was to rescue "that whole play from all the rubbish of the fifth act." The rubbish included the gravediggers and (as it must have seemed to eighteenth-century taste) the boorish struggle between Hamlet and Laertes at Ophelia's grave. Clowns did not, in the strict neoclassical view, belong in tragedies, and courtly gentle-men did not engage in fisticuffs at a funeral. Briefly, in Garrick's revision of the fifth act, the king commands Hamlet to go to England, and Hamlet replies by stabbing him. Laertes, seeking vengeance for the deaths of Polonius and Ophelia, mortally wounds Hamlet. Horatio is about to kill Laertes when Hamlet commands him to desist, saying that Laertes has been guided by heaven to give Hamlet the "precious balm" for all his wounds. Hamlet, before he dies, lectures his mother, and commands Laertes and Horatio "to calm the troubled land." But what is most relevant to our purpose here is this: Garrick's Hamlet, though perhaps touched with melancholy, was a man of action. For the rest of the century, Garrick's interpretation remained the touchstone by which other performances of the role were judged.

After Garrick, so many notable actors played Hamlet that this essay can do little more than make what must seem to be arbitrary choices. Our first choice, John Philip Kemble (1757–1823), is summed up in a brief description by the essayist William Hazlitt:

> Mr. Kemble plays [Hamlet] like a man in armor, with a determined inveteracy of purpose, on one undeviating straight line, which is as remote from the natural grace and refined susceptibility of the characters as the sharp angles and abrupt starts which Mr. Kean introduces into the part. Mr. Kean's Hamlet is as much too splenetic and rash as Mr. Kemble's is too strong and pointed.

Kemble was able to play "one undeviating straight line" partly because he cut from the text many of Hamlet's "wild and whirling words"; but what is especially interesting here is that Kemble, who acted the role from 1783 until his retirement in 1817, continued the tradition of a "manly" Hamlet, someone without the signs of weakness, even neurosis, that in the next decades came to characterize the role. True, as early as the late eighteenth century an occasional reader suggested that Hamlet was "irresolute," vainly striving toward manly boldness, but not until Kean did the stage see an active yet angst-ridden Hamlet.

Edmund Kean (1787–1833) first played Hamlet in 1814. We have already heard Hazlitt's opinion that Kean was "too splenetic and rash"; one additional quotation from Hazlitt, describing Kean's first Hamlet, will have to suffice:

> Both the closet scene with his mother, and his remonstrances to Ophelia, were highly impressive. If there had been less vehemence of effort in the latter, it would not have lost any of its effect. But whatever nice faults might be found in this scene, they were amply redeemed by the manner of his coming back after he has gone to the extremity of the stage, from a pang of parting tenderness to press his lips to Ophelia's hand. It had an electrical effect on the house. It was the finest commentary that was ever made on Shakespeare. It explained the character at once (as he meant it), as one of disappointed hope, of bitter regret, of affection suspended, not obliterated by the distractions of the scene around him.

Clearly we still do not have the melancholy, indecisive prince of the armchair critics such as Goethe or Coleridge.

The American actor Edwin Booth (1833–93) performed the role from 1853 to 1891. His interpretation was, broadly speaking, in what can be called the romantic tradition, but it is difficult to write coherently about Booth's Hamlet, not because (as with Burbage and Betterton) we possess too little evidence, but because we possess too much; the forest is obscured by the trees. In 1870, the year of

Booth's "definitive" Hamlet, a young man named Charles Clarke wrote a sixty-thousand-word description of the performance (Clarke saw Booth perform the role eight times), detailing gestures for almost every line Booth spoke. Charles H. Shattuck has studied this account, as well as other sources, and presented his findings in a book of 321 pages.

Clarke describes Booth's Hamlet as "a man of first-class intellect and second-class will," but it is difficult to reconcile this neat formula with all of the pieces of the evidence, especially with some of Booth's own statements. Still, a few generalizations can be offered, even though, as Shattuck points out, Booth modified his Hamlet over the years, making him somewhat less active, less agonized, and more stoical. Broadly speaking, Booth's Hamlet was somewhat "feminine," yet in some scenes "savage." Booth insisted that Hamlet is always sane, and he played many scenes in a highly courteous fashion (even when aware of the treachery of Rosencrantz and Guildenstern he treated them politely if with irony), yet he played some scenes "wildly," even hysterically. The overall impression on viewers was of a man haunted by devotion to his father and anguished by the sin of his mother. When he finally killed the king, he displayed not a look of triumph but of doubt, even remorse.

Henry Irving (1838–1905), who played Hamlet from 1864 to 1885, somewhat varied his conception over the years, but essentially his Hamlet was a man overpowered by his love of Ophelia. (For a thorough discussion of Irving's interpretations of Hamlet, see Alan Hughes, *Henry Irving*.) In his first version, Irving followed tradition in cutting all references to Fortinbras, but he also cut everything that seemed to him to diminish Hamlet, for instance Hamlet's bawdy remarks (and of course Ophelia's bawdy songs, too), Hamlet's callous description of the deaths of Rosencrantz and Guildenstern, his soliloquy about murdering Claudius under particularly reprehensible conditions (III.iii.73–96), and his claim in his apology to Laertes that he was mad (Irving at first believed that Hamlet's madness always was feigned). Irving later restored the soliloquy, and he also (by 1884) allowed that Hamlet was hysterical in four scenes—after the visitation of the Ghost, with Ophelia in the nunnery scene, in the queen's closet, and at Ophelia's grave. And of course he altered some of his stage business over the years. In the nunnery scene, for instance, in 1885 he added Edmund Kean's business of returning to Ophelia, after "To a nunnery, go," and kissing her hand. One of Irving's invented pieces of business was severely criticized. In the closet scene, when Hamlet tells his mother to "Look here upon this picture, and on this" (III.iv.54), the usual business was for Hamlet to call attention to miniature portraits: Hamlet wore a miniature of his father, Gertrude a miniature of Claudius. (An alternate tradition used two framed portraits in the queen's room.) Irving, however, used no real pictures. He gesticulated his hand downstage, as though the portraits hung on the missing fourth wall between the audience and the actors—or existed in Hamlet's mind.

One other point should be made about Irving's *Hamlet*. Staging in the nineteenth century was noted for its spectacle and its illusionism, and Irving's productions were especially known for these qualities. Thus, reviewers comment admiringly on a scene in which the Ghost stands among huge rocks in moonlight, as dawn steals across a great expanse of water. Another especially memorable scene was the procession to Ophelia's grave: all available members of the cast served as priests, monks, and miscellaneous mourners, while a bell tolled and a hymn was played on a harmonium. All of this, of course, took time, which means that the text had to be fairly heavily cut.

Reacting against such productions, in 1881 William Poel, amateur actor and Elizabethan enthusiast, staged *Hamlet* in Elizabethan costumes on a stage with only a few chairs and a platform for the play-within-the-play. This was, he believed, the Elizabethan manner. Moreover, the text he chose for his production was Q1, the so-called "Bad Quarto" of 1603, "bad" because it represents an actor's corrupt abridgment of a performance of *Hamlet*. But the fact that Q1 is based on a performance made it especially attractive to Poel. He recognized that some passages of Q1 were so corrupt that they were gibberish, but, as he explained in a letter, he also believed that this text "represents more truly [Shakespeare's] dramatic conception than either Quarto 2 or our stage version."

Poel's production, which took only two hours, was reviewed most unfavorably, partly because it offended contemporary taste, and partly because it was indeed a thoroughly amateur affair. (Poel himself played Hamlet; unfortunately, his skill as an actor did not equal his enthusiasm for Elizabethan drama.) In this production, he was more concerned with the text than with the staging—that is, more concerned with showing that Q1 is good theater than with showing how an Elizabethan play ought to be staged—but critics seized on inconsistencies in his method of production. Why not, they asked, use boys to play Ophelia and Gertrude? (Poel had in fact used a boy for the Player Queen.) Why not do the play by daylight? Why not do it in contemporary—i.e., late nineteenth-century—garb, since in Shakespeare's time the actors wore the clothing of their own age? The production indeed was inconsistent, and weak, and it added little to the interpretation of Hamlet—though Poel did insist that Hamlet is not a sentimental moper but an Elizabethan gallant; but the production nevertheless marked a milestone in the recovery of Shakespeare's stage, a neutral space that allows one scene to follow another rapidly.

When reviewers teased Poel by asking why he didn't stage the play in modern dress, they touched on an important issue. In a sense, up to the late eighteenth century, *Hamlet* had regularly been done in modern dress. That is, the early performers, such as Burbage, Betterton, Garrick, and Kemble wore the clothes of their own period—Kemble, for example, at first played in modern court dress and powdered hair. But in the late eighteenth century, Kemble began to wear what has been called a Vandyck costume, with a lace collar open at the neck, thus invoking a somewhat romantic past. Edmund Kean, perhaps from the late 1820s, wore a sort of stage Elizabethan costume, thus again evoking a romantic past, and actors later in the century experimented with what were thought to be historically accurate medieval Danish costumes, though Elizabethan costume remained popular.

In short, if one goes back to the seventeenth and eighteenth centuries, one finds plenty of productions of *Hamlet* in "modern dress," though apparently after the late eighteenth century there were none until 1925, when Barry Jackson's Birmingham Repertory opened a production in London, directed by H. K. Ayliff, with Colin Keith-Johnston as Hamlet. Reviewers recognized that Jackson was not offering merely a gimmick; rather, he was trying to see the play freshly, to think about it not as a period piece to be declaimed but as something to be spoken naturally. *Hamlet* was not only dressed as a modern play, but was also acted as a modern play. (The negative side is that this conception encouraged an antipoetic reading of the lines.) Modern dress did not (for the most part) seem incongruous, partly because much of the play is set at court, allowing or even requiring formal dress and military costumes—themselves kinds of theatrical costumes. Thus, in the court scenes, the ambassadors and Polonius wore tailcoats and white ties, and Hamlet wore a tuxedo. In other scenes, however, Ophelia wore a short skirt characteristic of the twenties, the young men wore tweeds, and, in the graveyard scene, Hamlet wore loose sports knickers known as plus fours.

Modern-dress productions today are so commonplace that it is hard to realize how novel Jackson's production was. Since 1925 there has been a fashion for setting *Hamlet* in some sort of post-Elizabethan period. For instance, in 1948 Michael Benthall directed Paul Scofield in a Victorian *Hamlet* at Stratford-upon-Avon. Benthall, having already done an Elizabethan *Hamlet* in doublet and hose, concluded that the Elizabethan costume robbed the play of its "essential modern realism." Why Victorian? Because, Benthall said, the Victorian period was

near enough to our own to heighten the play's realism, and yet far enough distant to give scope for that picturesque romanticism modern life has largely betrayed. . . . And I set the play in a mid-European court where the

juxtaposition of crinolines, uniforms, and evening and
levee clothes would create the atmosphere of color and
romance associated with royalty of the period. I hoped
in this way to retain the grandeur of the tragedy without
destroying the play's vital contemporary relevance.

Still, a free adaptation of Elizabethan dress seems to
remain the favorite costume for productions of *Hamlet*—
partly because of the influence of William Poel and partly
because of the decrease in interest in trying to recreate
medieval Denmark. Readers wanting to know more about
the topic should see John Gielgud's essay on costumes for
Hamlet, printed in Rosamond Gilder's *John Gielgud's
Hamlet: A Record of Performance.* (Gielgud is not, of
course, an academic specialist on costumes. For more
strictly historical discussions of Hamlet's costumes, see an
article by D. A. Russell in *Shakespeare Survey 9,* and
corrections to this article, by R. Mander and R. Mitchenson, in *Shakespeare Survey 11.*) And it is to Gielgud's
Hamlets that we now turn. He played the role in five
productions: 1929, 1934, 1936, 1939 (at the royal castle
at Elsinore), and 1944, and, as we shall see, he directed
Richard Burton in a production in 1964. In the first of
these productions, directed by Harcourt Williams in 1929–
30, Gielgud was only a little over twenty-five. His evident
youth contributed to a sense of Hamlet's isolation in a
world of older people, but he was not an especially sympathetic figure, though it is said that in later performances
the role gained in dignity and sympathy.

In his next *Hamlet,* in 1934, Gielgud was the director as
well as the protagonist. He decided on opulent costumes
(rich furs, plumed helmets, decorated armor for the men,
and sweeping skirts and tightly laced bodices for the
women), basing them on early sixteenth-century German
art. These costumes, in Gielgud's opinion, "suggested admirably the atmosphere of sensuality and crime." Claudius
and Gertrude, he said, "looked like a pair of cruel, monstrous cats." The set consisted of various levels, linked by
slopes and steps, backed by a bluish-white cyclorama
which could be masked with richly decorated curtains for

interior scenes. Though not a set Poel would have fully approved of, it allowed for the swift changes of scene that Poel valued. Judging from reviews, this Hamlet was a sympathetic figure: "The glass of fashion and the mold of form." One piece of business that Gielgud invented for this production has become especially famous: the king, praying, puts his sword aside. Hamlet, unseen by the king, picks up the sword and contemplates killing the kneeling king, but does not. Instead, he goes off with the sword. When the king rises from prayer, he finds the sword missing—and the scene fades out with a look of alarm on Claudius's face. Among the actors who have appropriated this business are Paul Scofield (Stratford, 1948), Michael Redgrave (London, 1949), and Richard Burton (New York, 1964).

Guthrie McClintic saw Gielgud's *Hamlet* in London, and invited him to do yet another *Hamlet*, directed by McClintic, in New York. The production materialized in 1936, with decor by Jo Mielziner, and it is this production that is the basis for Rosamond Gilder's fascinating *John Gielgud's Hamlet*. Of his last *Hamlet*, the 1944 production, Gielgud said that he felt he was giving something of a "hotch-potch" of his earlier performances, but the reviews were good, and it was widely remarked that in this performance Gielgud gave Hamlet more dignity than in his earlier versions. There was very little madness in the interpretation, and a good deal of princely sophistication.

For Richard Burton's *Hamlet*, directed by John Gielgud in 1964, we have a highly detailed record, Richard L. Sterne's *John Gielgud Directs Richard Burton in Hamlet: A Journal of Rehearsals*. This remarkable book summarizes and sometimes quotes at length from tape recordings made during rehearsals. It also includes the prompt-script of the production, an interview with Gielgud, and an interview with Burton. (Also useful is a book by the actor who played Guildenstern, William Redfield's *Letters from an Actor*.) The idea behind the production was unusual: struck by the observation that actors sometimes perform better in a rehearsal run-through, with improvised props and without fancy costumes and sets, than in a public per-

formance, Gielgud conceived of this production as a
rehearsal of *Hamlet*. Thus, the play began with some
actors (who later played courtiers) bringing a few chairs
onto the stage (one of the chairs, an upholstered armchair,
served for Claudius's throne); the set was the brick rear
wall of the theater (not a real brick wall, but a set looking
like a brick wall). The actors wore ordinary clothes—but
in fact the clothes were faintly symbolic; Burton wore a
black sweater or turtleneck, Hume Cronyn (Polonius)
wore a business suit, and Alfred Drake (Claudius) wore a
shirt and tie, and a sport jacket. As the play progressed,
and pressures on Claudius increased, he loosened his neck-
tie. The lighting, too, pretended to be rehearsal lighting.
There were, for instance, no sudden blackouts, but the
lights faded or gradually rose where dramatically appropriate. Sterne's transcription of the tapes indicates that
much of Gielgud's effort was directed toward restraining
Burton's abundant energy—Burton tended to shout—but,
even so, the performance was intense rather than sensitive.
The production was extremely successful financially, but
this success may have been due partly to the publicity
attending Burton's recent marriage to Elizabeth Taylor
(they had married during the tryouts in Toronto); reviews
were mixed.

The last *Hamlet* we will look at, except for Laurence
Olivier's film, is Peter Hall's production for the Royal
Shakespeare Company, staged in 1965 with David Warner
(only twenty-four years old) as Hamlet. (The fullest account of it is a chapter in Stanley Wells, *Royal Shakespeare*, but there are also useful observations in Peter
Davison, *Hamlet: Text and Performance*.) Staged in the
turbulent sixties, when university students were vigorously
protesting against the Establishment, this Hamlet—with
his long, rust-red scarf—was very much a working-class,
alienated young man, a sometimes rebellious and sometimes apathetic student, a young man far removed from
the princely Hamlets of John Gielgud in the 1930s. Peter
Hall could hardly have been more explicit about the relation of the play to the age:

For our decade I think the play will be about the disillusionment which produces an apathy of the will so
deep that commitment to politics, to religion or to life
is impossible.

Speaking of politics, it is worth mentioning that in this
production Claudius was cool and efficient, and Polonius
was no fool (some of his most obviously foolish lines were
cut, in order to fit this characterization); that is, the
Establishment confronting Hamlet was formidable. To
some observers, it seemed inconceivable that this Hamlet,
had he lived to rule, would, in Fortinbras's words, have
"proved most royal." He seemed chiefly a neurotic young
man, not a hero seeking to avenge his father's death, and
certainly not a man who at last overcomes great obstacles
and succeeds in ridding Denmark of its foul king. The
final scene, however, had heroic elements: the duel, accompanied by drums, trumpets, and cannon, was vigorous.
Further, Hamlet's attack on Claudius was forceful: first he
nicked Claudius in the neck; then stabbed him; then, as
Claudius fell, kneed him; and finally poured the poison
drink into Claudius's ear. Still, Hamlet's dying words were
spoken with no sense of urgency or of accomplishment;
here was the "apathy" that Hall said characterized the
period. Charles Shattuck, whose monumental work on
Booth's *Hamlet* we noted earlier, in *Shakespeare Studies 3*
characterized Warner's prince as "a limp-wristed anti-hero
who dies snickering." Clearly, Shattuck saw what Hall and
Warner were striving for, but didn't like it at all.

Like several of the productions already discussed,
Laurence Olivier's film, made in 1948, has been much
written about. (The basic sources are Alan Dent, ed.,
Hamlet: The Film and the Play, and Brenda Cross, ed.,
The Film Hamlet.) Olivier had played Hamlet at Elsinore
in 1937, but when he first thought of directing a film of
the play he did not intend to take the title role. "I feel
that my style of acting," he said, "is more suited to
stronger character roles, such as Hotspur and Henry V,
rather than to the lyrical, poetical role of Hamlet." (This
quotation tells us a good deal about Olivier's conception

of the role of Hamlet. It is hard to imagine Burbage, Betterton, or Garrick talking about Hamlet this way.) At the beginning of the film we are told: "This is the tragedy of a man who could not make up his mind," a simplistic view that, fortunately, does not come anywhere near to summarizing the interpretation offered in the film. In fact, the underlying theme really seems to be the Freudian interpretation that Hamlet cannot easily avenge his father's death because he (like everyone) has an Oedipus complex, i.e., he wishes (or wished) to kill his father and to sleep with his mother. Hamlet thus cannot bring himself to act against the man who has done what he himself wanted to do. (Although Freud initiated this explanation of Hamlet's alleged irresolution at least as early as 1900, he did not discuss the play at length. The classic psychoanalytic discussion of the play is by Ernest Jones, in *Hamlet and Oedipus.*) When Tyrone Guthrie directed Olivier in the 1937 *Hamlet* at Elsinore, he drew on Freud's remarks, and Olivier even discussed the idea with Jones. Not surprisingly, then, Olivier returned to this interpretation when he made his film. The most obvious signs of Freud are in the passionate kisses (some of the scenes between Hamlet and Gertrude are virtually love scenes) and in the emphasis on the queen's bedroom, indeed on the bed itself. The text of the play tells us that Hamlet encounters Gertrude in "his mother's closet" (III.iii.27), i.e., in a private room. There is no need to think of this as a bedroom—it might well be furnished only with a small writing desk and a couple of chairs—but a bed now seems to have become indispensable. The sexual focus in Olivier's film is sharpened by Olivier's deletion of the entire Fortinbras story; that is, Olivier reduces the political elements in order to concentrate on Hamlet's relationship with his family.

The emphasis on Hamlet's psyche is partly conveyed by the set. Responding to Olivier's desire for a dreamlike cavernous area, the designer provided a castle with vast columns, long (often empty) corridors, and winding staircases, presumably symbolizing the puzzled mind. Exteriors tend to be misty. The camera does lots of panning and

tracking, slowing down the action by dwelling on the set.
Olivier seems to be trying to make scenes last as long as
possible, ending them with dreamlike dissolves—a notable
contrast, by the way, to the straight cuts used in the 1964
Russian film version by Grigori Kozintsev. Olivier ex-
ploits the camera as fully as possible. For example, the
camera moves down from a great height, approaching the
seated Hamlet, who then delivers his first soliloquy. Similarly, when the Ghost leaves at I.v.91, the camera soars
into the air (as though with the Ghost), moving above
Hamlet, and showing him fainting on the battlement.
Olivier also uses the cinematic device of voice-over for
parts of some of the soliloquies; that is, we hear Hamlet's
thoughts, but his lips do not move. Olivier took advantage
also, perhaps needlessly, of the camera's ability to show
us scenes that could not be staged, for instance Ophelia's
drowning and Hamlet's encounter with the pirates. Olivier's *Hamlet*, in short, is a film, not a filmed version of a
stage presentation.

A word about the end of Olivier's film: Laertes unfairly
thrusts at Hamlet and wounds him, drawing blood. Having
perceived that Laertes's foil is unbated, in the next round
Hamlet knocks Laertes's foil out of his hand, retrieves it
for his own use, and gives Laertes the bated foil. After
wounding Laertes, Hamlet assumes the throne (the courtiers kneel before him), asks Horatio to tell his story, and
dies. The film ends with a procession, cannon are fired, the
camera goes through the castle, passing the now-empty
throne and Gertrude's bedroom, and up to a tower, where
Hamlet's bearers are silhouetted against the sky.

There are dozens—even hundreds—of other productions that one could talk about, but beyond the few that
we have have discussed, the rest (for our purposes) is
silence.

Suggested References

The number of possible references is vast and grows alarmingly (The *Shakespeare Quarterly* devotes one issue each year to a list of the previous year's work, and *Shakespeare Survey*—an annual publication—includes a substantial review of recent scholarship, as well as an occasional essay surveying a few decades of scholarship on a chosen topic.) Though no works are indispensable, those listed below have been found especially helpful.

1. Shakespeare's Times

Byrne, M. St. Clare. *Elizabethan Life in Town and Country*. Rev. ed. New York: Barnes & Noble, 1961. Chapters on manners, beliefs, education, etc., with illustrations.

Joseph, B. L. *Shakespeare's Eden: The Commonwealth of England, 1558–1629*. New York: Barnes & Noble, 1971. An account of the social, political, economic, and cultural life of England.

Schoenbaum, S. *Shakespeare: The Globe and the World*. New York: Oxford University Press, 1979. A readable, handsomely illustrated book on the world of the Elizabethans.

Shakespeare's England. 2 vols. Oxford: Oxford University Press, 1916. A large collection of scholarly essays on a wide variety of topics (e.g. astrology, costume, gardening, horsemanship), with special attention to Shakespeare's references to these topics.

Stone, Lawrence. *The Crisis of the Aristocracy, 1558–1641*, abridged edition. London: Oxford University Press, 1967.

2. Shakespeare

Barnet, Sylvan. *A Short Guide to Shakespeare*. New York: Harcourt Brace Jovanovich, 1974. An introduction to all of the works and to the dramatic traditions behind them.

Bentley, Gerald E. *Shakespeare: A Biographical Handbook.* New Haven, Conn.: Yale University Press, 1961. The facts about Shakespeare, with virtually no conjecture intermingled.

Bush, Geoffrey. *Shakespeare and the Natural Condition.* Cambridge, Mass.: Harvard University Press, 1956. A short, sensitive account of Shakespeare's view of "Nature," touching most of the works.

Chambers, E. K. *William Shakespeare: A Study of Facts and Problems.* 2 vols. London: Oxford University Press, 1930. An invaluable, detailed reference work; not for the casual reader.

Chute, Marchette. *Shakespeare of London.* New York: Dutton, 1949. A readable biography fused with portraits of Stratford and London life.

Clemen, Wolfgang H. *The Development of Shakespeare's Imagery.* Cambridge, Mass.: Harvard University Press, 1951. (Originally published in German, 1936.) A temperate account of a subject often abused.

Granville-Barker, Harley. *Prefaces to Shakespeare.* 2 vols. Princeton, N. J.: Princeton University Press, 1946–47. Essays on ten plays by a scholarly man of the theater.

Harbage, Alfred. *As They Liked It.* New York: Macmillan, 1947. A long, sensitive essay on Shakespeare, morality, and the audience's expectations.

Kernan, Alvin B., ed. *Modern Shakespearean Criticism: Essays on Style, Dramaturgy, and the Major Plays.* New York: Harcourt Brace Jovanovich, 1970. A collection of major formalist criticism.

————. "The Plays and the Playwrights." In *The Revels History of Drama in English,* general editors Clifford Leech and T. W. Craik. Vol. III. London: Methuen, 1975. A book-length essay surveying Elizabethan drama with substantial discussions of Shakespeare's plays.

Schoenbaum, S. *Shakespeare's Lives.* Oxford: Clarendon Press, 1970. A review of the evidence, and an examination of many biographies, including those by Baconians and other heretics.

————. *William Shakespeare: A Compact Documentary Life.* New York: Oxford University Press, 1977. A readable presentation of all that the documents tell us about Shakespeare.

Traversi, D. A. *An Approach to Shakespeare*. 3rd rev. ed. 2 vols. New York: Doubleday, 1968–69. An analysis of the plays beginning with words, images, and themes, rather than with characters.

Van Doren, Mark. *Shakespeare*. New York: Holt, 1939. Brief, perceptive readings of all of the plays.

3. Shakespeare's Theater

Beckerman, Bernard. *Shakespeare at the Globe, 1599–1609.* New York: Macmillan, 1962. On the playhouse and on Elizabethan dramaturgy, acting, and staging.

Chambers, E. K. *The Elizabethan Stage*. 4 vols. New York: Oxford University Press, 1945. A major reference work on theaters, theatrical companies, and staging at court.

Cook, Ann Jennalie. *The Privileged Playgoers of Shakespeare's London, 1576–1642*. Princeton, N. J.: Princeton University Press, 1981. Sees Shakespeare's audience as more middle-class and more intellectual than Harbage (below) does.

Gurr, Andrew. *The Shakespearean Stage: 1574–1642.* 2d edition. Cambridge: Cambridge University Press, 1981. On the acting companies, the actors, the playhouses, the stages, and the audiences.

Harbage, Alfred. *Shakespeare's Audience*. New York: Columbia University Press, 1941. A study of the size and nature of the theatrical public, emphasizing its representativeness.

Hodges, C. Walter. *The Globe Restored*. London: Ernest Benn, 1953. A well-illustrated and readable attempt to reconstruct the Globe Theatre.

Hosley, Richard. "The Playhouses." In *The Revels History of Drama in English*, general editors Clifford Leech and T. W. Craik. Vol. III. London: Methuen, 1975. An essay of one hundred pages on the physical aspects of the playhouses.

Kernodle, George R. *From Art to Theatre: Form and Convention in the Renaissance*. Chicago: University of Chicago Press, 1944. Pioneering and stimulating work on the symbolic and cultural meanings of theater construction.

Nagler, A. M. *Shakespeare's Stage*. Trans. Ralph Manheim. New Haven, Conn.: Yale University Press, 1958. A very brief introduction to the physical aspects of the playhouse.

Slater, Ann Pasternak. *Shakespeare the Director*. Totowa,

N. J.: Barnes and Noble, 1982. An analysis of theatrical effects (e.g., kissing, kneeling) in stage directions and dialogue.

Thomson, Peter. *Shakespeare's Theatre*. London: Routledge and Kegan Paul, 1983. A discussion of how plays were staged in Shakespeare's time.

4. Miscellaneous Reference Works

Abbott, E. A. *A Shakespearean Grammar*. New Edition. New York: Macmillan, 1877. An examination of differences between Elizabethan and modern grammar.

Bevington, David. *Shakespeare*. Arlington Heights, Ill.: A. H. M. Publishing, 1978. A short guide to hundreds of important writings on the works.

Bullough, Geoffrey. *Narrative and Dramatic Sources of Shakespeare*. 8 vols. New York: Columbia University Press, 1957–75. A collection of many of the books Shakespeare drew upon, with judicious comments.

Campbell, Oscar James, and Edward G. Quinn. *The Reader's Encyclopedia of Shakespeare*. New York: Crowell, 1966. More than 2,600 entries, from a few sentences to a few pages, on everything related to Shakespeare.

Greg, W. W. *The Shakespeare First Folio*. New York: Oxford University Press, 1955. A detailed yet readable history of the first collection (1623) of Shakespeare's plays.

Kökeritz, Helge. *Shakespeare's Names*. New Haven, Conn.: Yale University Press, 1959. A guide to the pronunciation of some 1,800 names appearing in Shakespeare.

————. *Shakespeare's Pronunciation*. New Haven, Conn.: Yale University Press, 1953. Contains much information about puns and rhymes.

Muir, Kenneth. *The Sources of Shakespeare's Plays*. New Haven, Conn.: Yale University Press, 1978. An account of Shakespeare's use of his reading.

The Norton Facsimile: The First Folio of Shakespeare. Prepared by Charles Hinman. New York: Norton, 1968. A handsome and accurate facsimile of the first collection (1623) of Shakespeare's plays.

Onions, C. T. *A Shakespeare Glossary*. 2d ed., rev., with enlarged addenda. London: Oxford University Press, 1953. Definitions of words (or senses of words) now obsolete.

Partridge, Eric. *Shakespeare's Bawdy*. Rev. ed. New York: Dutton, 1955. A glossary of bawdy words and phrases.

Shakespeare Quarterly. See headnote to Suggested References.

Shakespeare Survey. See headnote to Suggested References.

Shakespeare's Plays in Quarto. A Facsimile Edition. Ed. Michael J. B. Allen and Kenneth Muir. Berkeley, Calif.: University of California Press, 1981. A book of nine hundred pages, containing facsimiles of twenty-two of the quarto editions of Shakespeare's plays. An invaluable complement to *The Norton Facsimile: The First Folio of Shakespeare* (see above).

Smith, Gordon Ross. *A Classified Shakespeare Bibliography 1936–1958.* University Park, Pa.: Pennsylvania State University Press, 1963. A list of some twenty thousand items on Shakespeare.

Spevack, Marvin. *The Harvard Concordance to Shakespeare.* Cambridge, Mass.: Harvard University Press, 1973. An index to Shakespeare's words.

Wells, Stanley, ed. *Shakespeare: Select Bibliographies.* London: Oxford University Press, 1973. Seventeen essays surveying scholarship and criticism of Shakespeare's life, work, and theater.

5. Hamlet

Alexander, Nigel. *Poison, Play and Duel: A Study of "Hamlet."* Lincoln, Nebraska: University of Nebraska, 1971.

Alexander, Peter. *Hamlet: Father and Son.* London: Oxford University Press, 1955.

Bamber, Linda. *Comic Women, Tragic Men.* Stanford, Cal.: Stanford University Press, 1982.

Bevington, David, ed. *Twentieth Century Interpretations of "Hamlet."* Englewood Cliffs, N. J.: Prentice-Hall, 1968.

Booth, Stephen. "On the Value of *Hamlet.*" In *Reinterpretations of Elizabethan Drama.* Ed. Norman Rabkin. New York: Columbia University Press, 1969. 137–76.

Berry, Ralph. *Changing Styles in Shakespeare.* London: Allen and Unwin, 1981.

Bradley, A. C. *Shakespearean Tragedy.* London: Macmillan, 1904. Part of the material on *Hamlet* is reprinted above.

Brown, John Russell, and Bernard Harris, eds. *Stratford-upon-Avon Studies 5: "Hamlet."* London: Edward Arnold, 1963.

Charney, Maurice. *Style in Hamlet.* Princeton, N. J.: Princeton University Press, 1969.

Edwards, Philip. "Tragic Balance in *Hamlet,*" *Shakespeare Survey,* 36 (1983), 43–52.

SUGGESTED REFERENCES

Ewbank, Inga-Stina. "*Hamlet* and the Power of Words," *Shakespeare Survey*, 30 (1977), 85–102.

Frye, Roland Mushat. *The Renaissance Hamlet*. Princeton, N. J.: Princeton University Press, 1984.

Granville-Barker, Harley. *Prefaces to Shakespeare*. 2 vols. Princeton, N. J.: Princeton University Press, 1946–47. Part of the material on *Hamlet* is reprinted above.

Honigman, E. A. J. *Shakespeare: Seven Tragedies*. London: Macmillan, 1976.

Hunter, G. K. *Dramatic Identities and Cultural Tradition: Studies in Shakespeare and His Contemporaries*. Liverpool: Liverpool University Press, 1978.

Jenkins, Harold, ed. *The Arden Edition of the Works of William Shakespeare: Hamlet*. London: Methuen, 1982.

Jones, Ernest. *Hamlet and Oedipus*. New York: Doubleday (Anchor), 1954.

Kernan, Alvin B. *The Playwright as Magician*. New Haven, Conn.: Yale University Press, 1979.

Levin, Harry. *The Question of Hamlet*. New York and London: Oxford University Press, 1959.

Mander, Raymond, and Joe Mitchenson. *Hamlet Through the Ages: A Pictorial Record from 1709*. London: Rocklift, 1952.

Muir, Kenneth. *Shakespeare: "Hamlet."* London: Edward Arnold, 1963.

Nicoll, Allardyce, ed. *Shakespeare Survey 9*.

Slights, Camille Wells. *The Casuistical Tradition*. Princeton, N. J.: Princeton University Press, 1981.

Walker, Roy. *The Time Is Out of Joint: A Study of Hamlet*. New York: Macmillan, 1948.

Webber, Joan. "*Hamlet* and the Freeing of the Mind." In *English Renaissance Drama: Essays in Honor of Madeleine Doran and Mark Eccles*. Ed. Standish Henning et al. Carbondale, Ill.: Southern Illinois University Press, 1976. 76–99.

Wilson, J. Dover. *What Happens in "Hamlet."* 3rd ed. New York: Cambridge University Press, 1951.

Wright, George T. "Hendiadys and *Hamlet*," *PMLA*, 96 (1981), 168–93.

The Signet Classic Shakespeare

- [ ] **MEASURE FOR MEASURE, S. Nagarajan**, ed., University of Poona, India.
  (524098—$3.50)
- [ ] **MACBETH, Sylvan Barnet**, ed., Tufts University.   (524446—$2.95)
- [ ] **THE MERCHANT OF VENICE, Kenneth Myrick**, ed., Tufts University.
  (521331—$2.25)
- [ ] **A MIDSUMMER NIGHT'S DREAM, Wolfgang Clemen**, ed., University of Munich.
  (524942—$2.95)
- [ ] **MUCH ADO ABOUT NOTHING, David Stevenson**, ed., Hunter College.
  (522982—$2.95)
- [ ] **OTHELLO, Alvan Kernan**, ed., Yale University.   (521323—$3.50)*
- [ ] **RICHARD II, Kenneth Muir**, ed., University of Liverpool.   (522680—$2.75)
- [ ] **RICHARD III, Mark Eccles**, ed., University of Wisconsin.   (522664—$2.75)*
- [ ] **ROMEO AND JULIET, Joseph Bryant**, ed., University of North Carolina.
  (524381—$2.95)
- [ ] **THE TAMING OF THE SHREW, Robert Heilman**, ed., University of Washington.
  (521269—$2.50)*
- [ ] **THE TEMPEST, Robert Langbaum**, ed., University of Virginia.   (521250—$2.25)*
- [ ] **TROILUS AND CRESSIDA, Daniel Seltzer**, ed., Harvard.   (522974—$3.50)
- [ ] **TWELFTH NIGHT, Herschel Clay Baker**, ed., Harvard.   (521293—$2.75)*
- [ ] **THE WINTER'S TALE, Frank Kermode**, ed., University of Bristol. (522605—$2.95)
- [ ] **THE SONNETS, William Burto**, ed., Introduction by W. H. Auden. (522621—$2.95)
- [ ] **JULIUS CAESAR, Barbara and Willian Rosen**, ed., University of Connecticut.
  (521242—$1.95)*
- [ ] **KING LEAR, Russel Fraser**, ed., Princeton University.   (524101—$2.95)
- [ ] **HAMLET, Edward Hubler**, ed., Princeton University.   (521285—$2.75)*
- [ ] **HENRY IV, Part I, Maynard Mack**, ed., Yale University.   (524055—$2.75)
- [ ] **HENRY IV, Part II, Norman Holland**, ed., Massachusetts Institute of Technology.
  (522532—$2.95)
- [ ] **FOUR GREAT TRAGEDIES, Sylvan Barnet**, ed., and introduction, Signet Classics
  Shakespeare, series, general editor.   (523180—$4.95)

  Prices slightly higher in Canada
